Stitch

STITCH & THE SAMURAI

1

ART BY HIROTO WADA

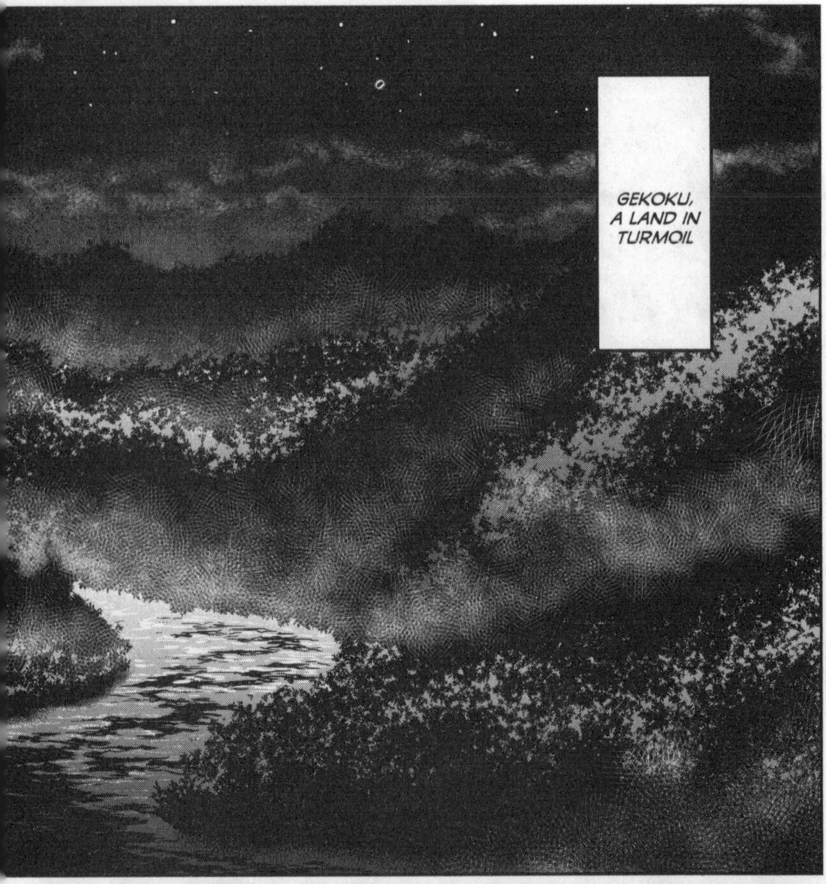
GEKOKU, A LAND IN TURMOIL

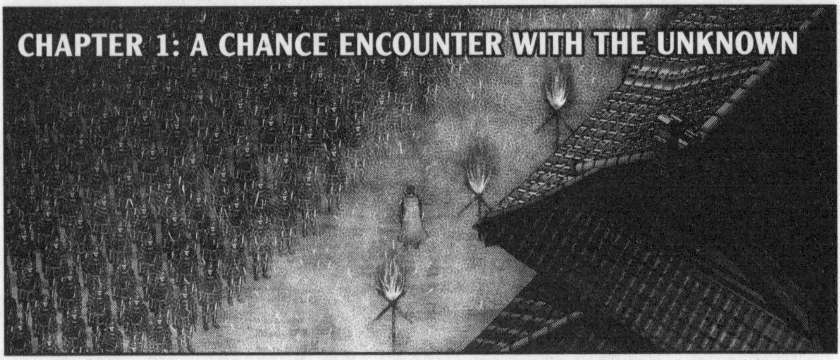
CHAPTER 1: A CHANCE ENCOUNTER WITH THE UNKNOWN

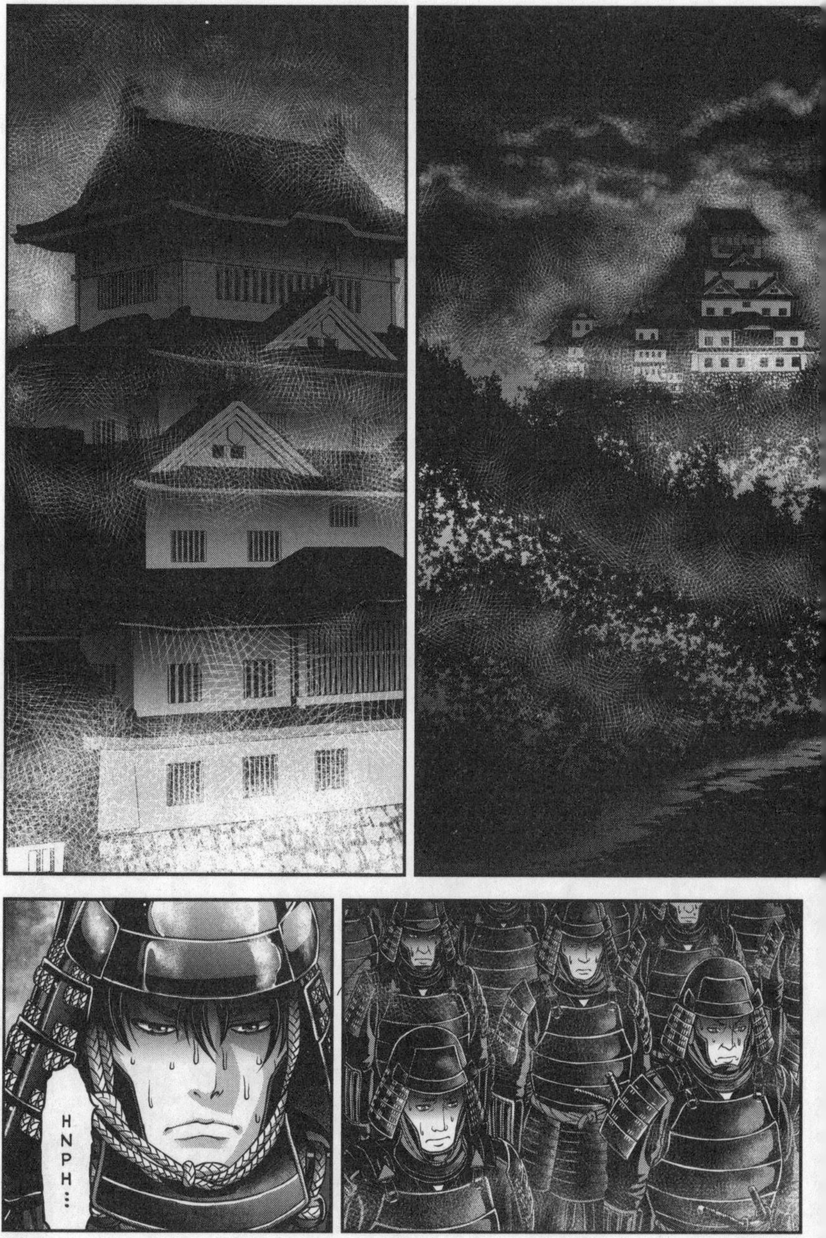
HNPH...

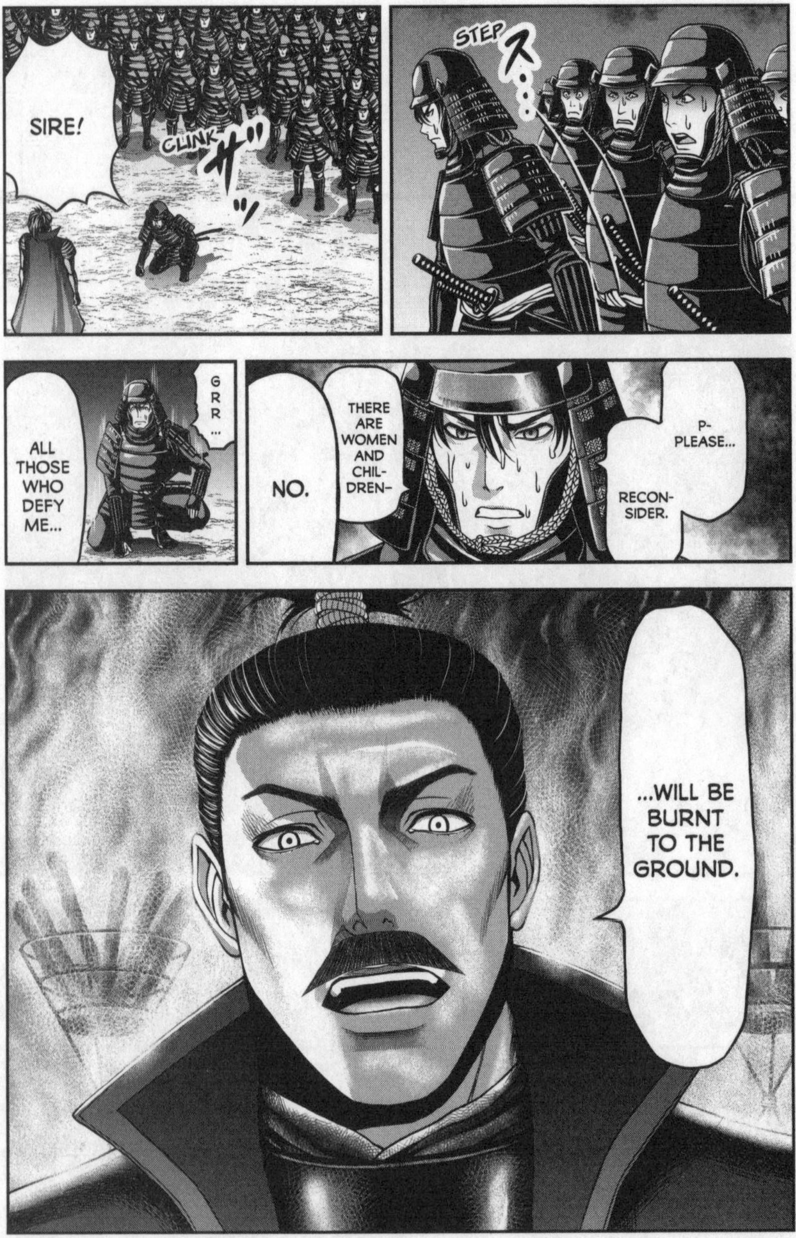
STEP
SIRE!
CLINK
P-PLEASE... RECONSIDER.
THERE ARE WOMEN AND CHIL-DREN-
NO.
GRR...
ALL THOSE WHO DEFY ME...
...WILL BE BURNT TO THE GROUND.

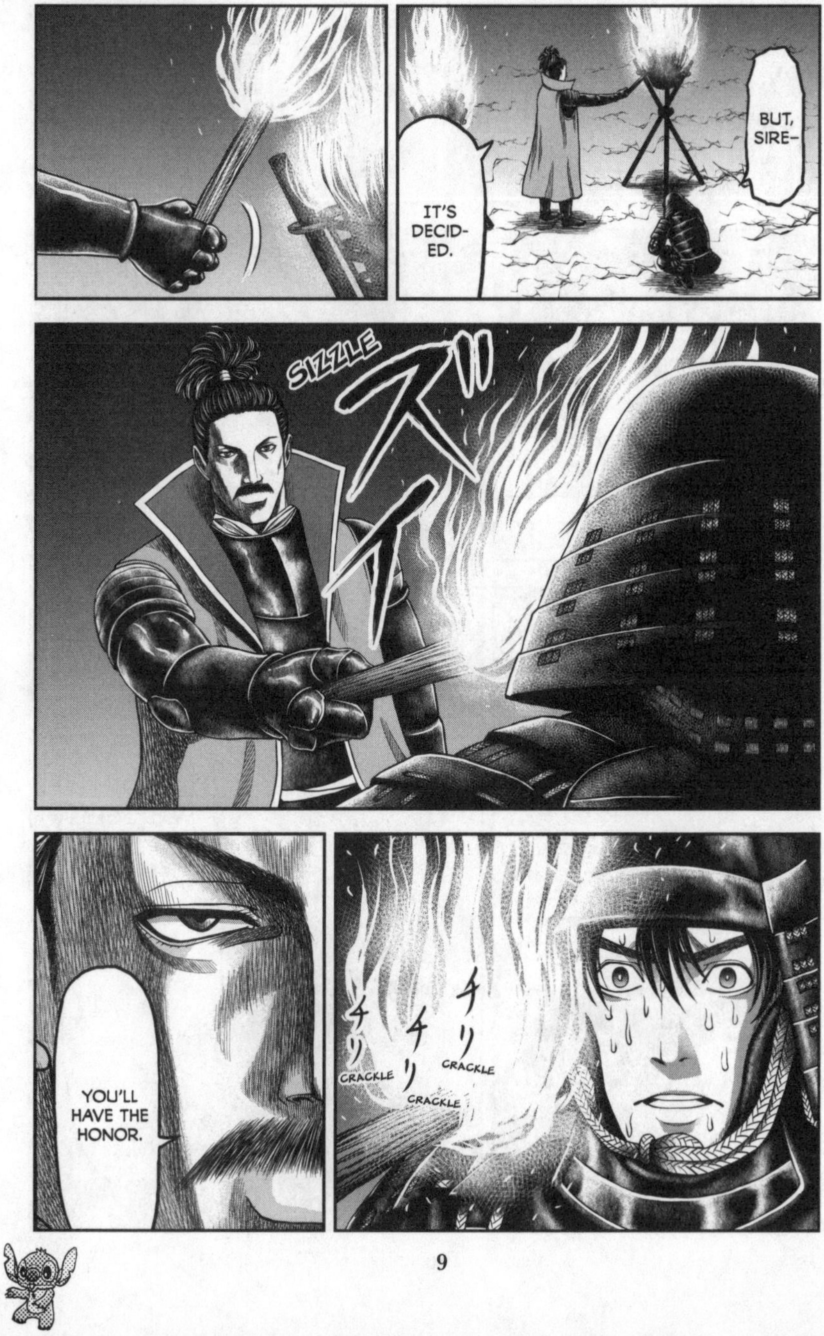
BUT, SIRE–
IT'S DECID-ED.
ズイ
SIZZLE
チリ
CRACKLE
チリ
CRACKLE
チリ
CRACKLE
YOU'LL HAVE THE HONOR.

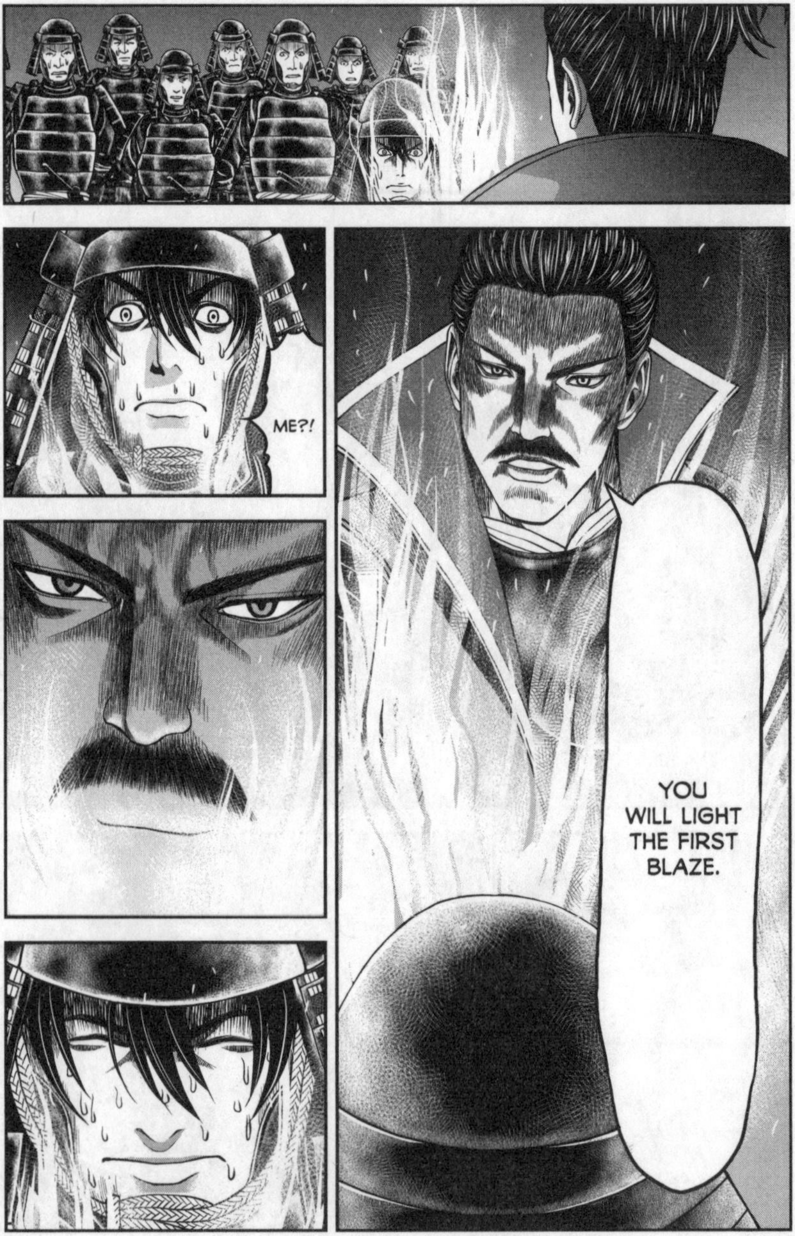
YOU WILL LIGHT THE FIRST BLAZE.
ME?!

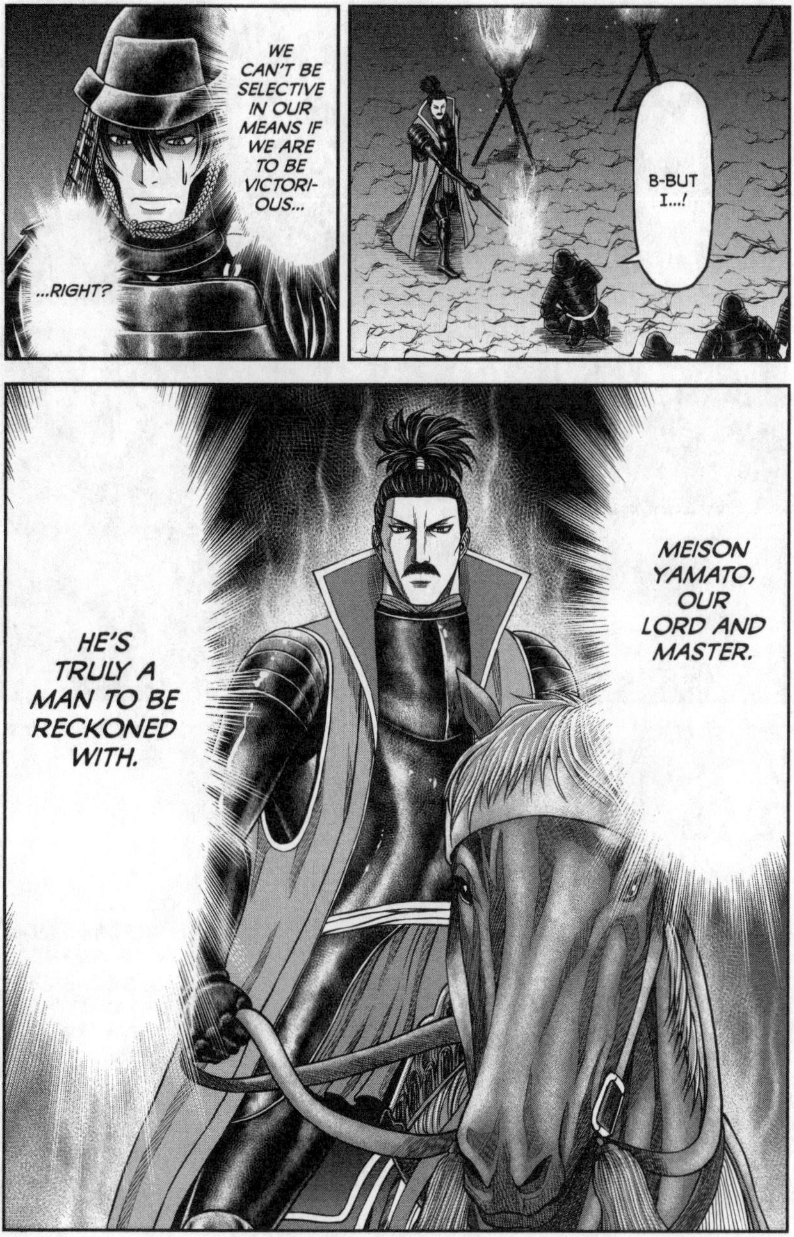
B-BUT I...!
WE CAN'T BE SELECTIVE IN OUR MEANS IF WE ARE TO BE VICTORIOUS...
...RIGHT?
MEISON YAMATO, OUR LORD AND MASTER.
HE'S TRULY A MAN TO BE RECKONED WITH.

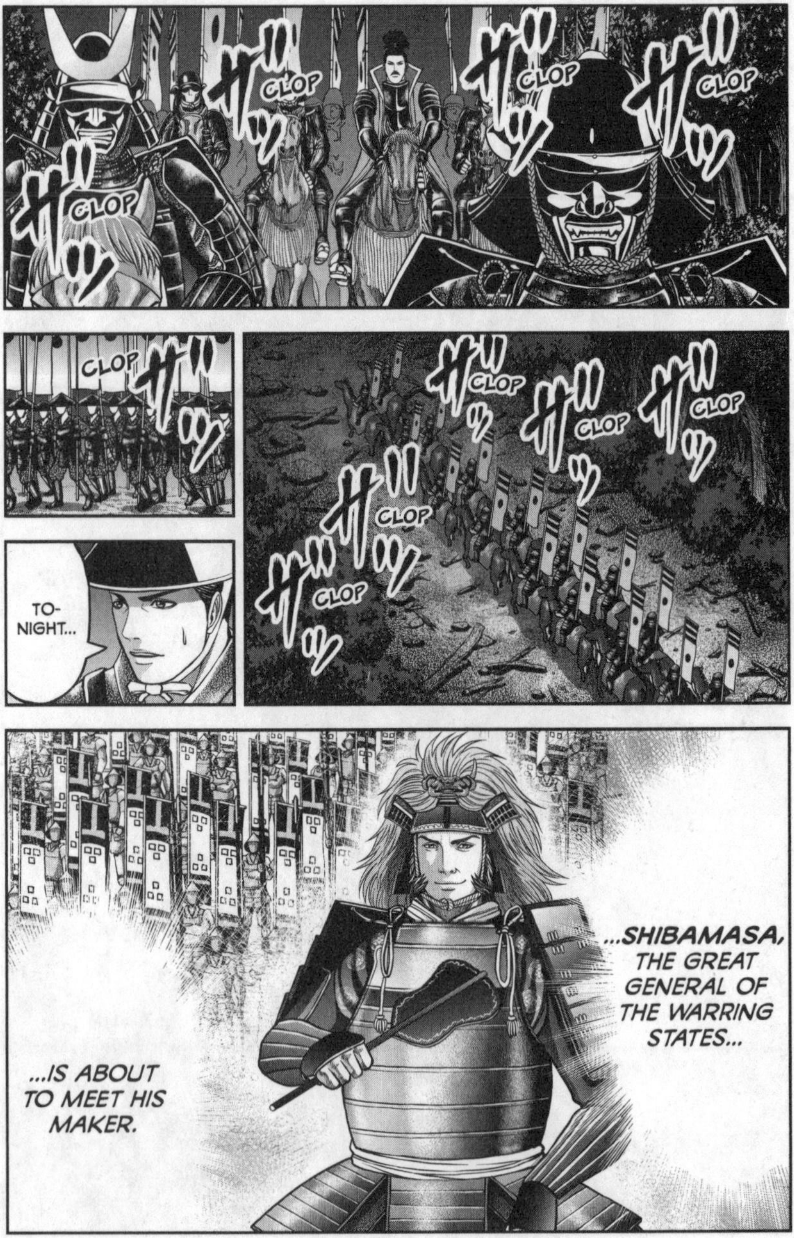
CLOP
CLOP
CLOP
CLOP
CLOP
CLOP
CLOP
CLOP
CLOP
CLOP
TO-NIGHT...
...SHIBAMASA, THE GREAT GENERAL OF THE WARRING STATES...
...IS ABOUT TO MEET HIS MAKER.

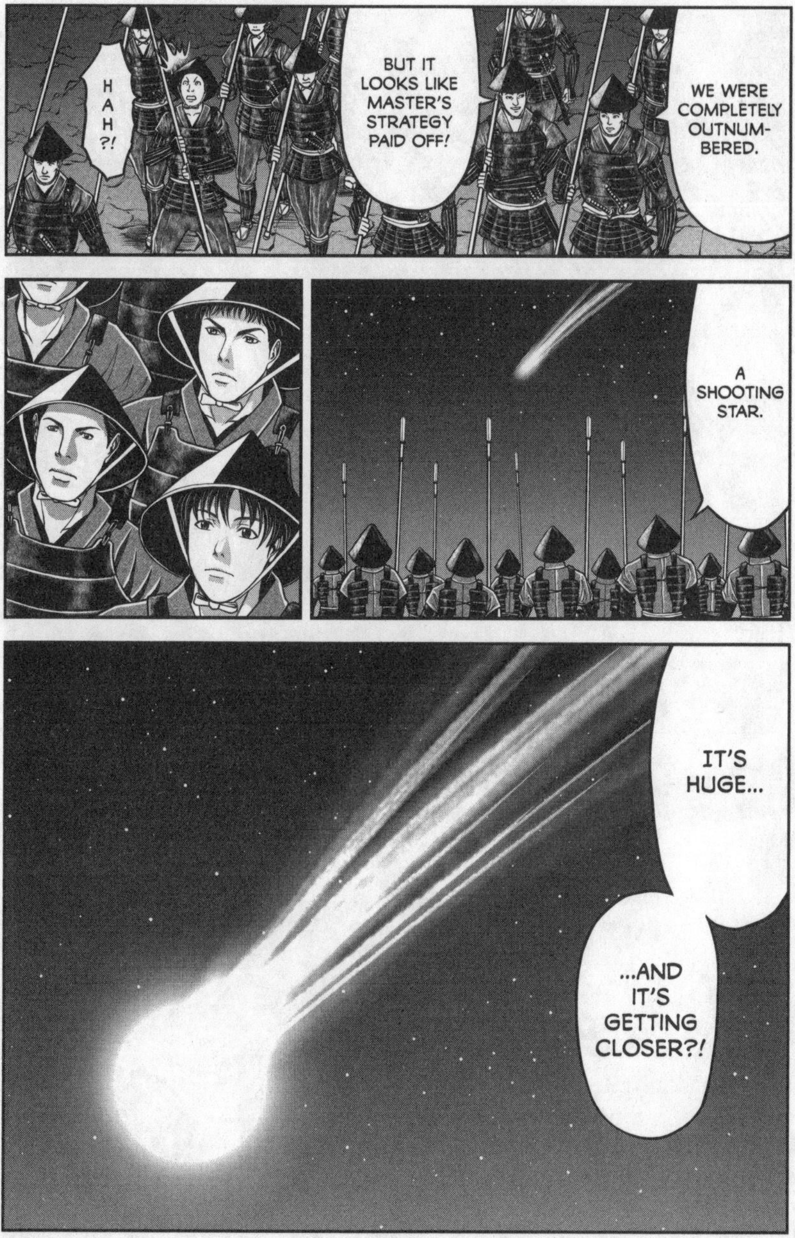
WE WERE COMPLETELY OUTNUM-BERED.
BUT IT LOOKS LIKE MASTER'S STRATEGY PAID OFF!
HAH?!
A SHOOTING STAR.
IT'S HUGE...
...AND IT'S GETTING CLOSER?!

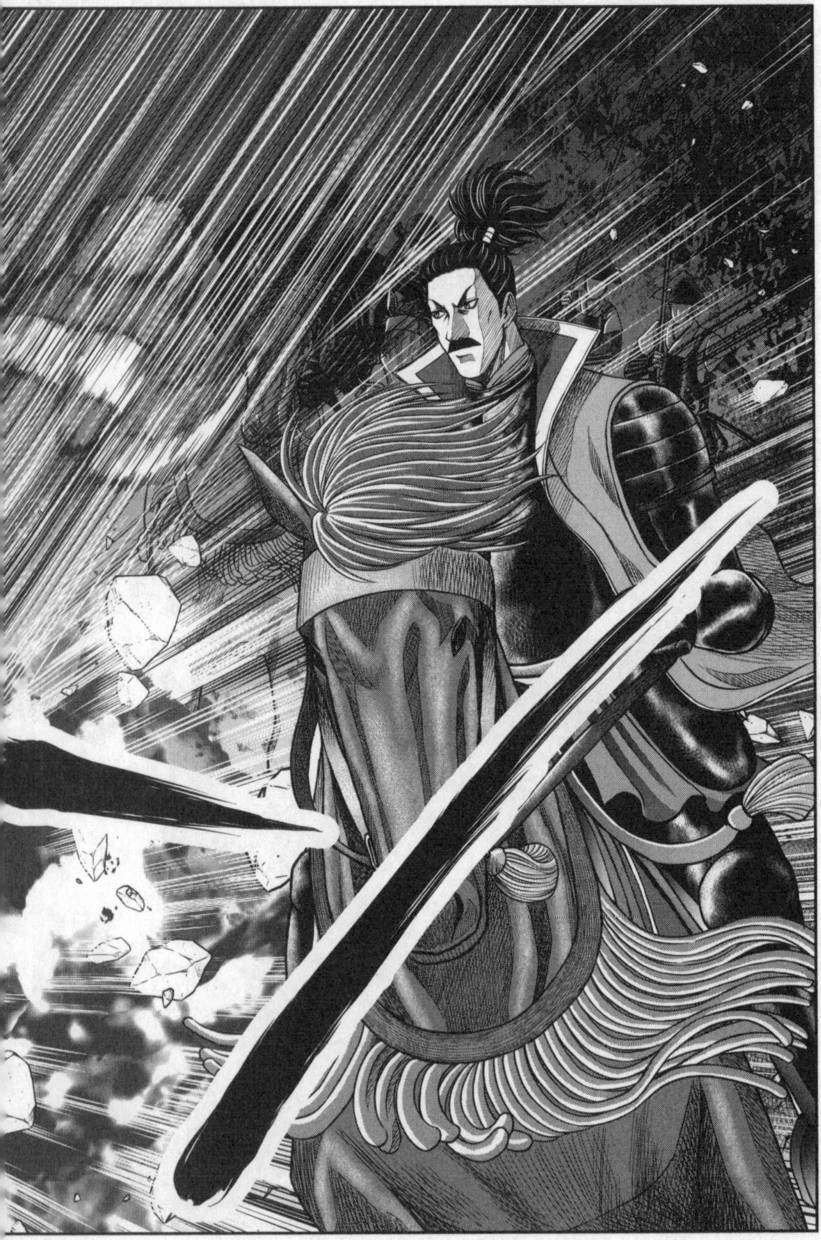

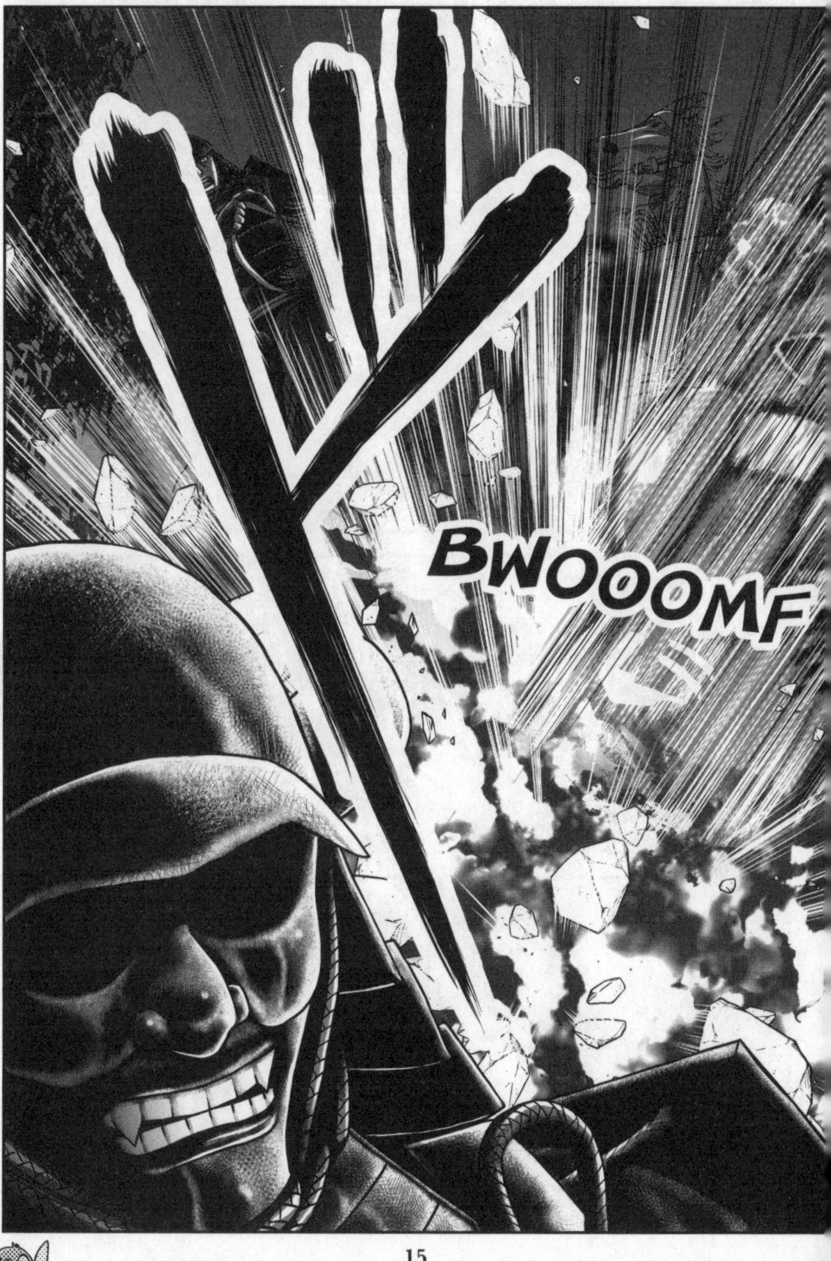
BWOOOMF

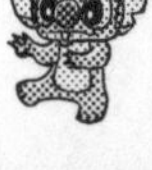

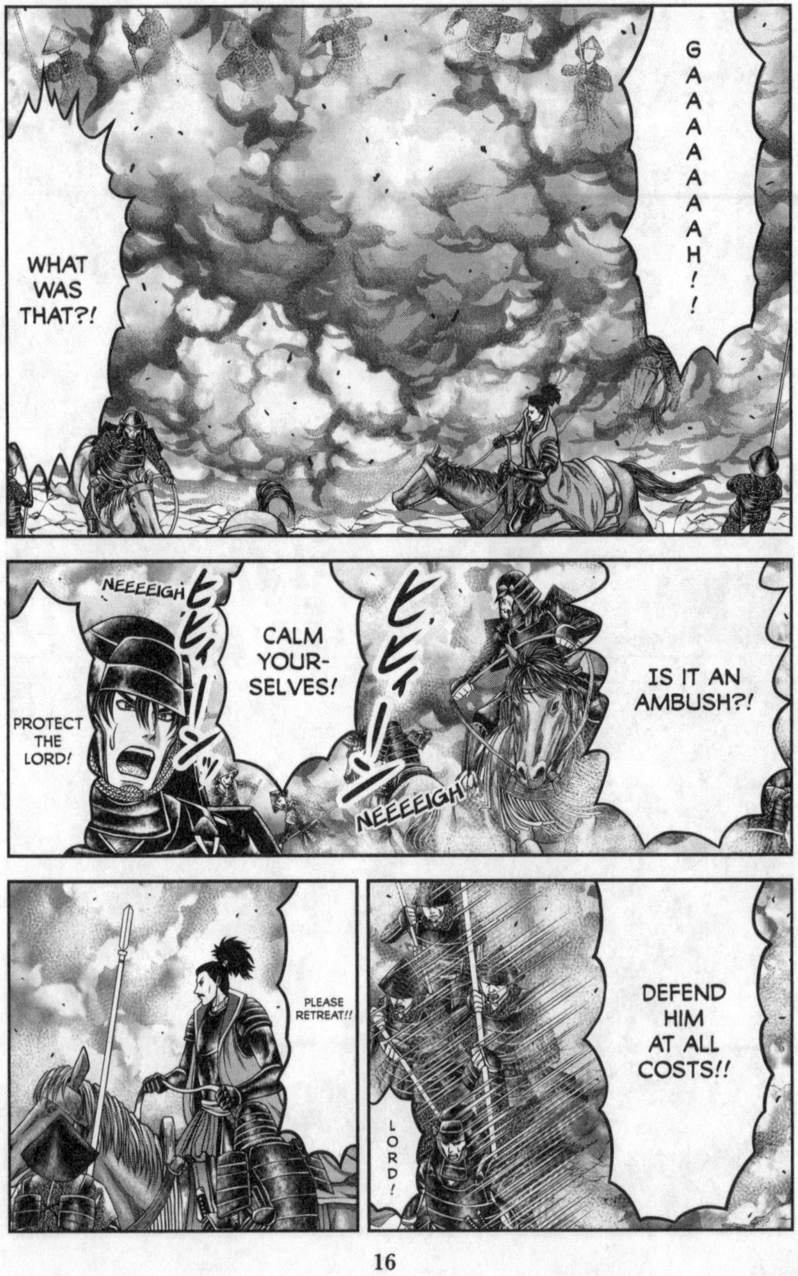
GAAAAAAAAH!!
WHAT WAS THAT?!
IS IT AN AMBUSH?!
NEEEEIGH
CALM YOURSELVES!
NEEEEIGH
PROTECT THE LORD!
DEFEND HIM AT ALL COSTS!!
LORD!
PLEASE RETREAT!!

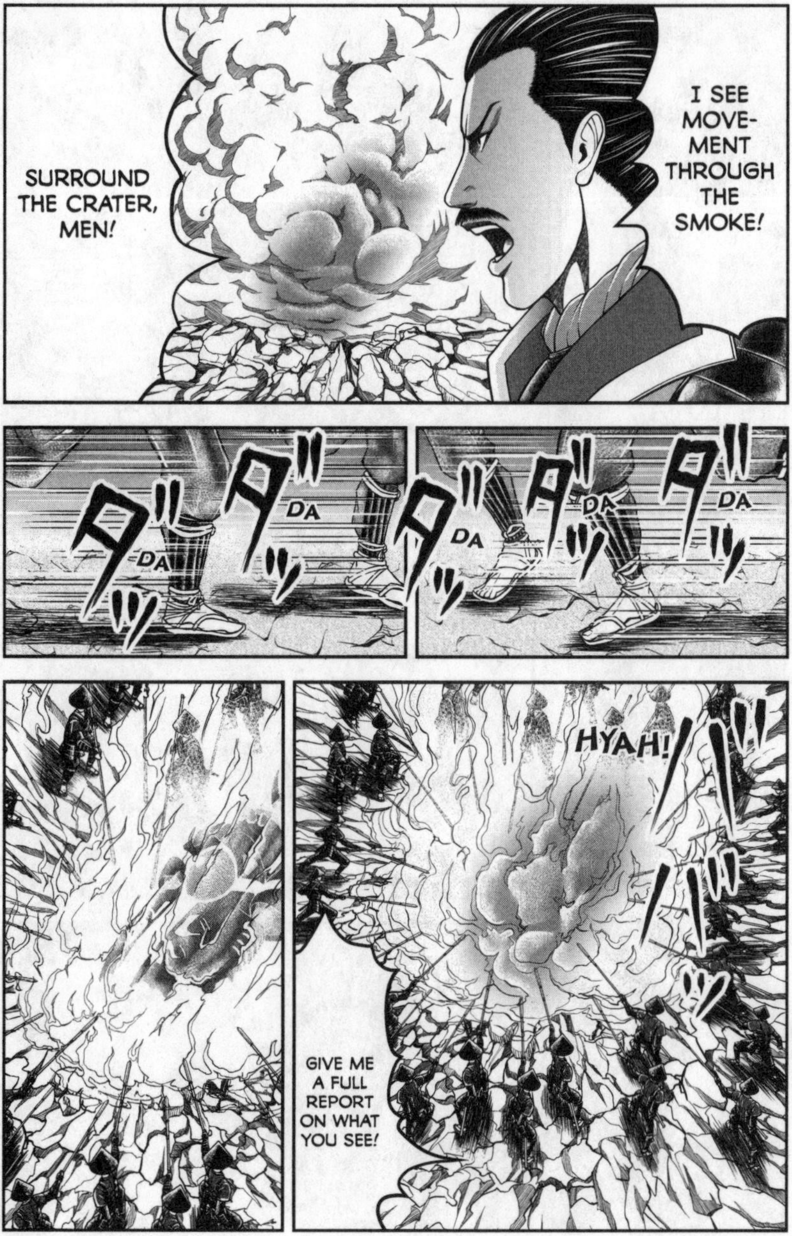
I SEE MOVE-MENT THROUGH THE SMOKE!
SURROUND THE CRATER, MEN!
DA
DA
DA
DA
DA
HYAH!
GIVE ME A FULL REPORT ON WHAT YOU SEE!

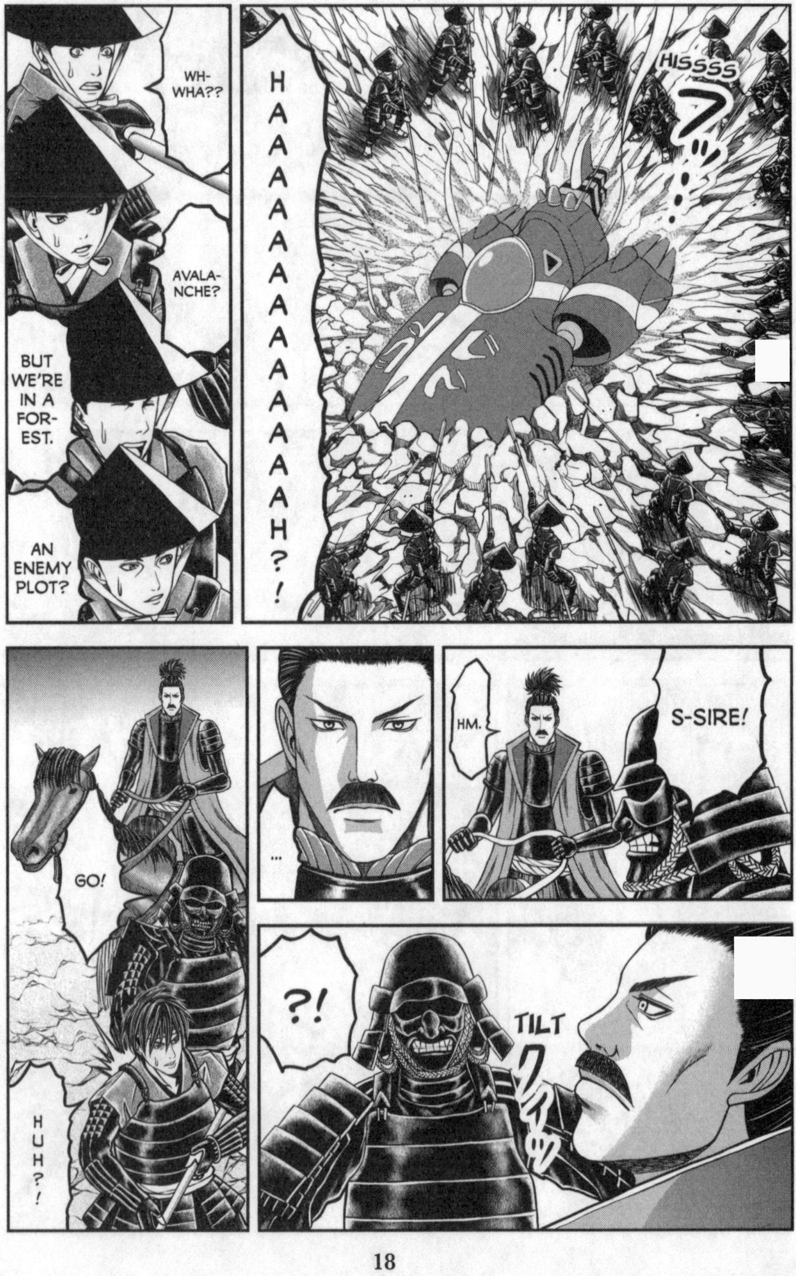
HISSSS
HAAAAAAAAAAAAAAH?!
WH-WHA??
AVALA-NCHE?
BUT WE'RE IN A FOR-EST.
AN ENEMY PLOT?
S-SIRE!
HM.
...
?!
TILT
GO!
HUH?!

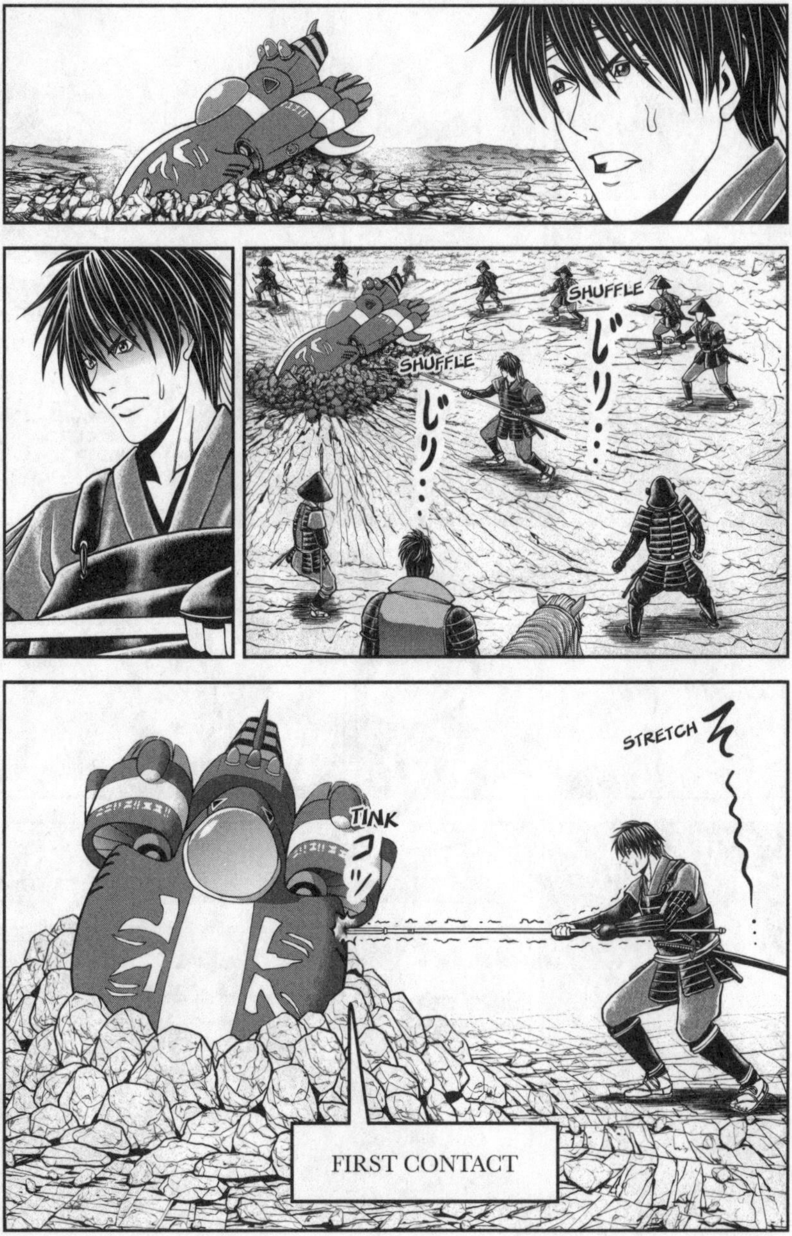
SHUFFLE
じり…
SHUFFLE
じり…
STRETCH
そ
TINK
コッ
FIRST CONTACT

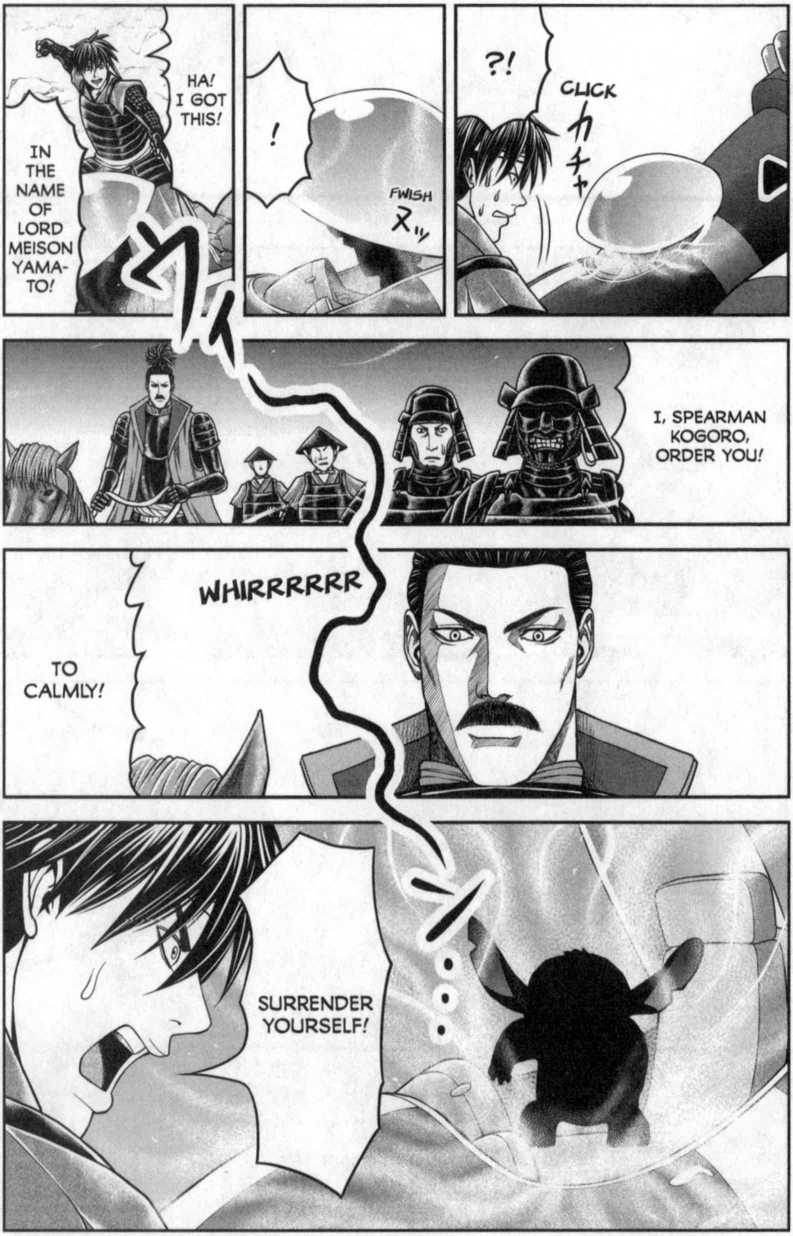
?!
CLICK
カチャ
!
FWISH
ヌッ
HA! I GOT THIS!
IN THE NAME OF LORD MEISON YAMA-TO!
I, SPEARMAN KOGORO, ORDER YOU!
WHIRRRRRR
TO CALMLY!
SURRENDER YOURSELF!
...

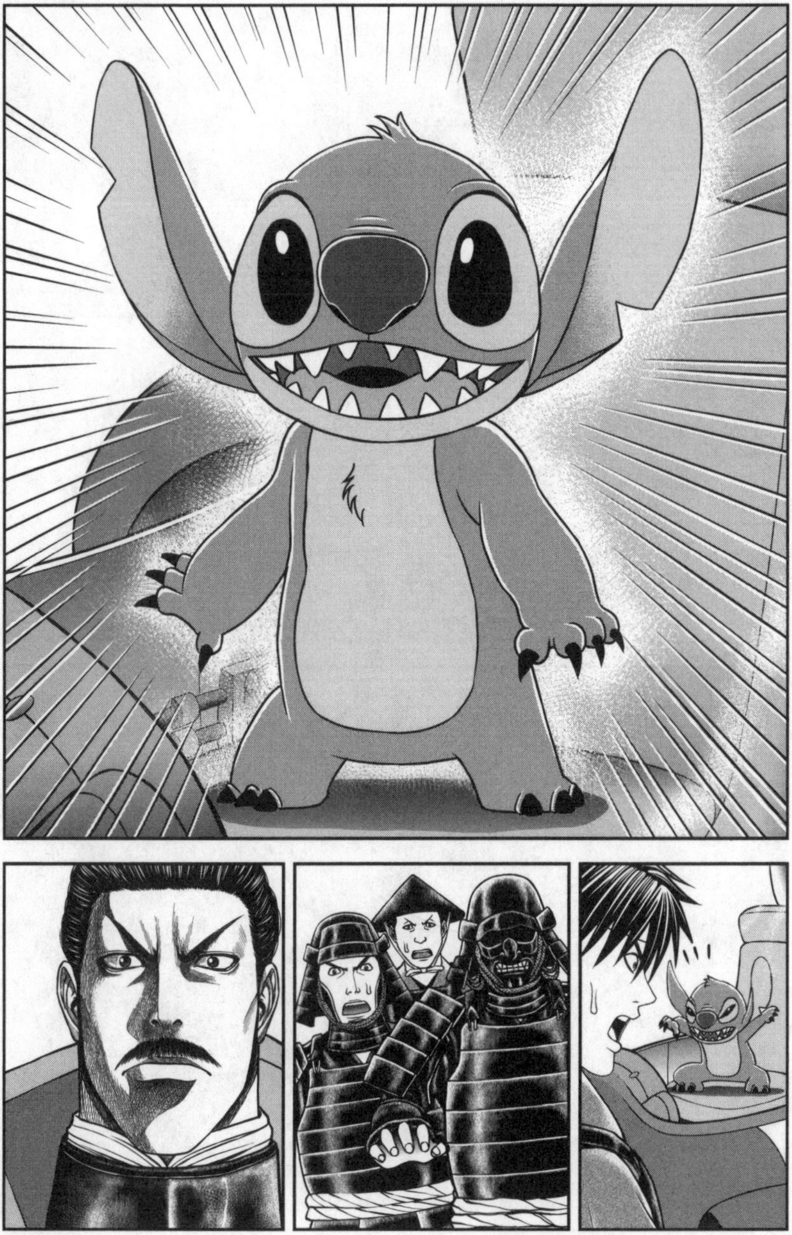

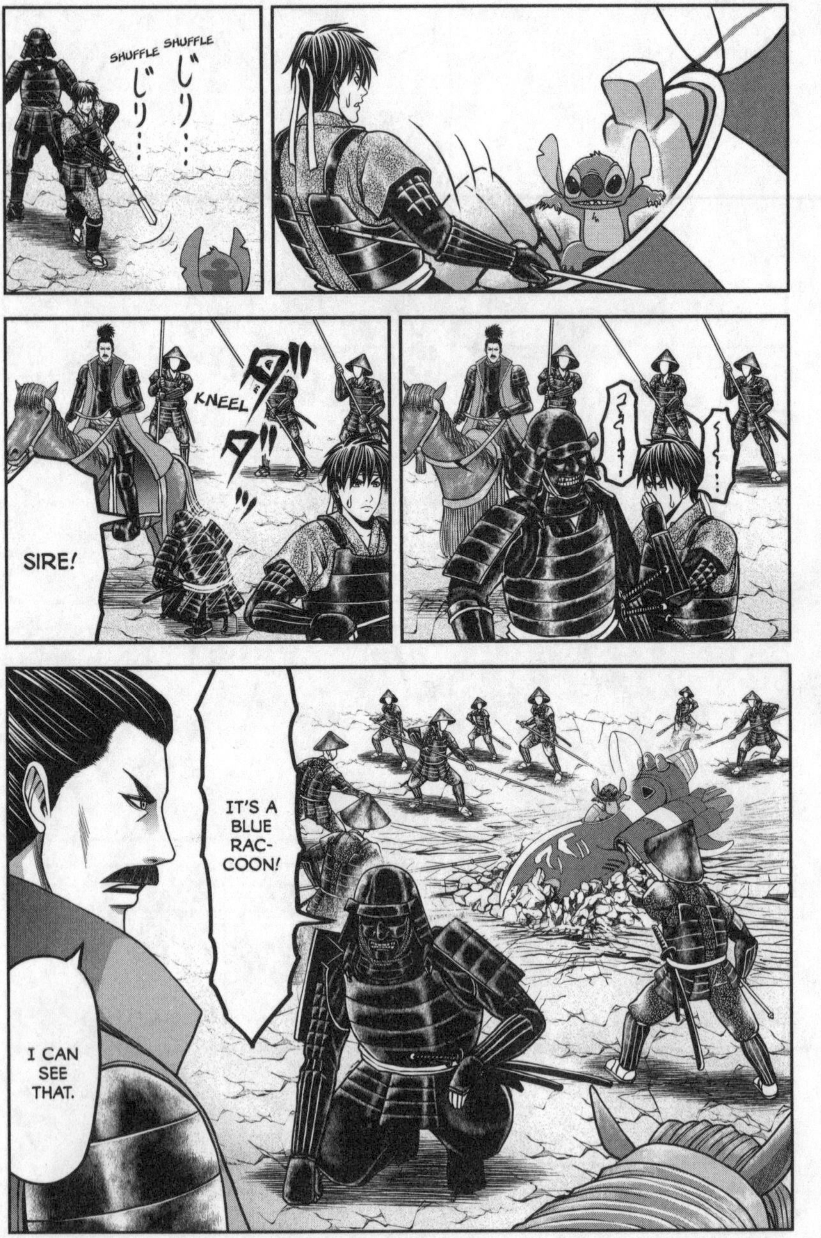
SHUFFLE SHUFFLE
じり…
じり…
KNEEL
SIRE!
IT'S A BLUE RAC-COON!
I CAN SEE THAT.

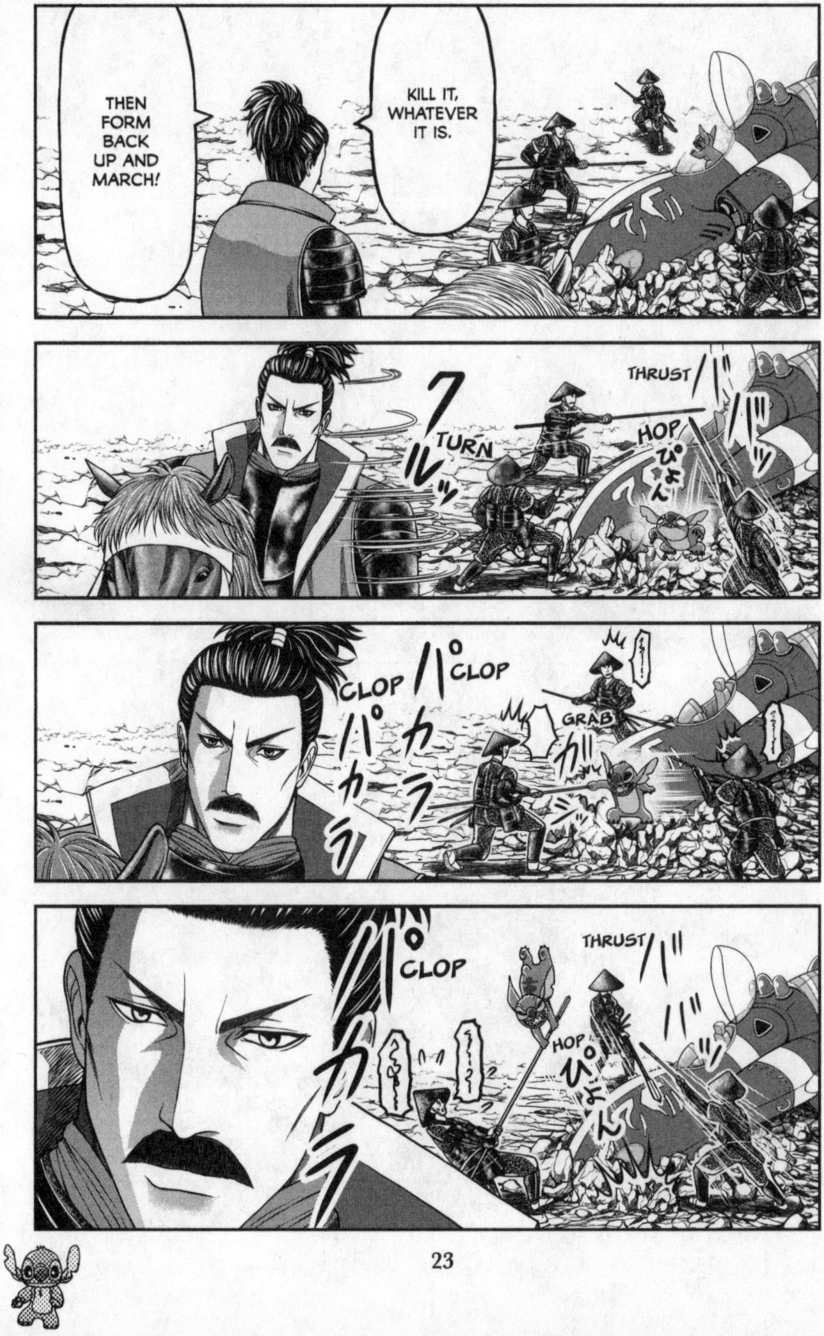
KILL IT, WHATEVER IT IS.
THEN FORM BACK UP AND MARCH!
THRUST バッ
HOP ぴょん
TURN クルッ
GRAB ガッ
CLOP パカラ
CLOP パカラ
THRUST バッ
HOP ぴょん
CLOP パカラ

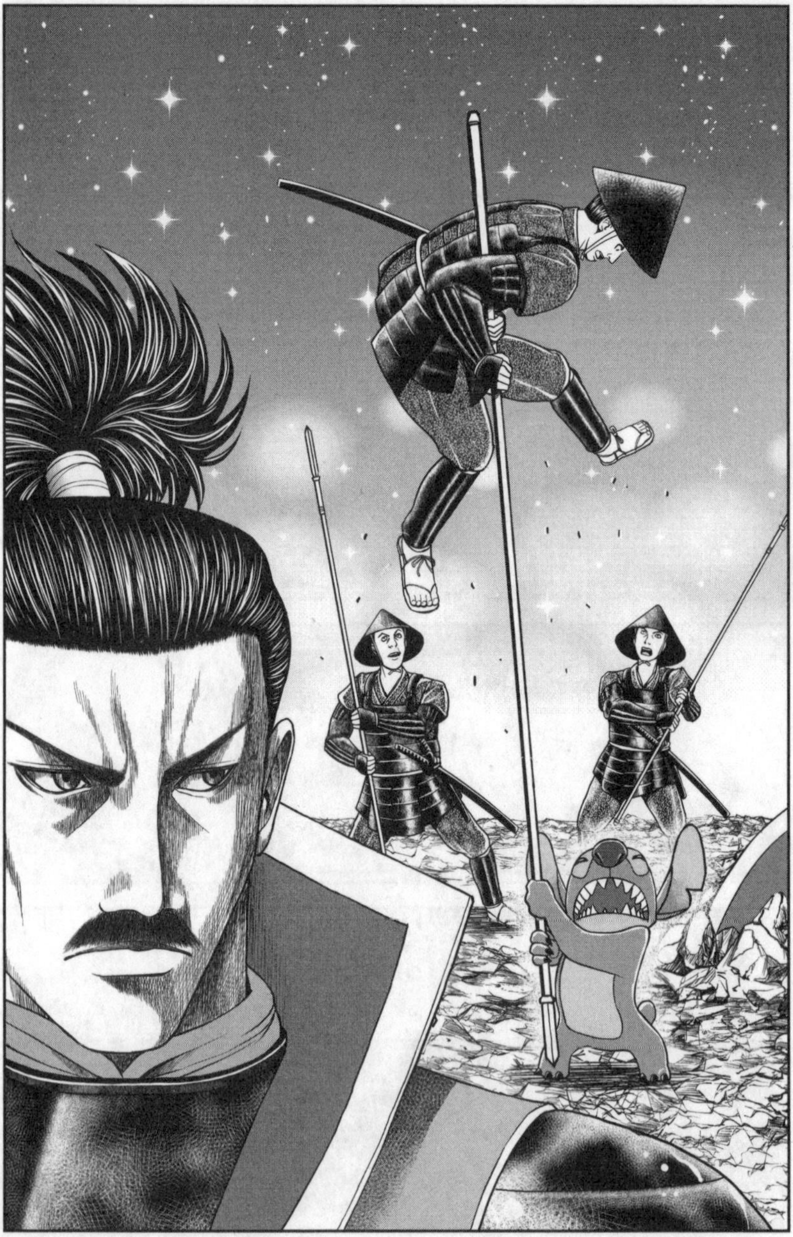

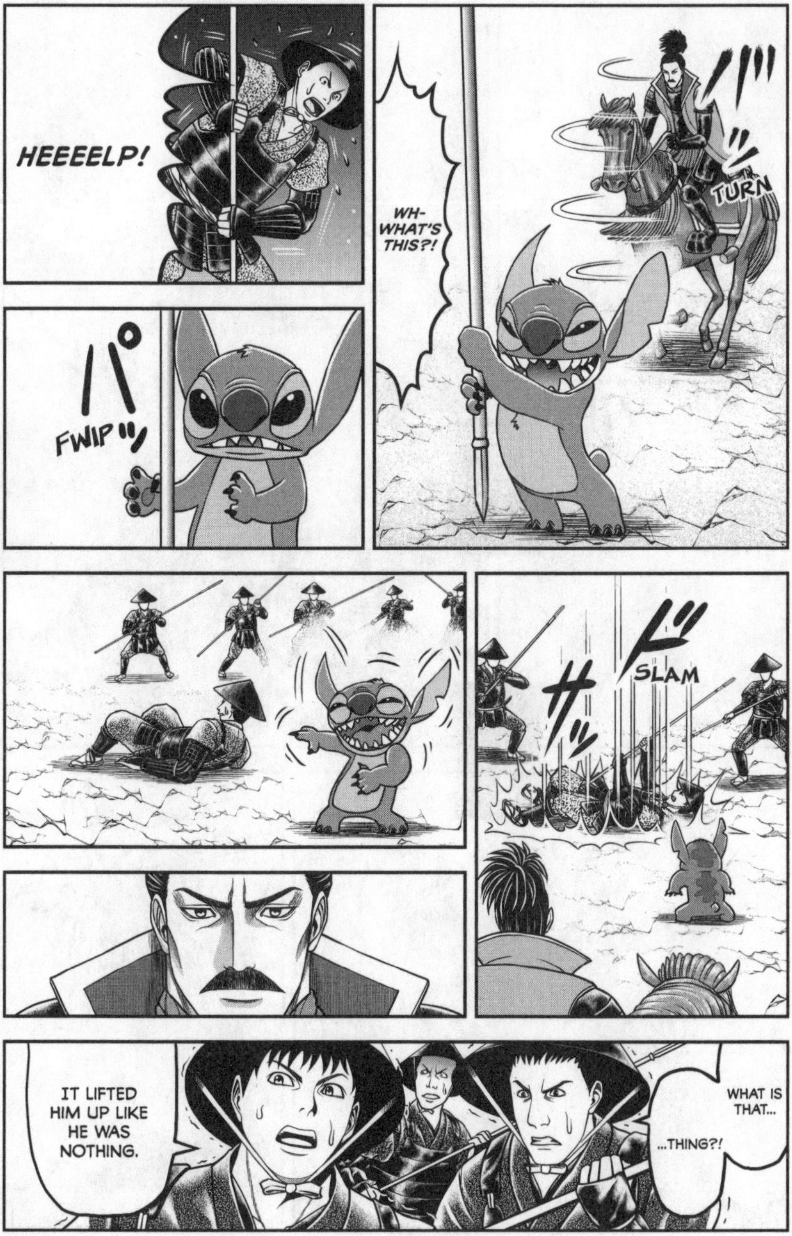
WH-WHAT'S THIS?!
TURN
HEEEELP!
FWIP
SLAM
WHAT IS THAT...
...THING?!
IT LIFTED HIM UP LIKE HE WAS NOTHING.

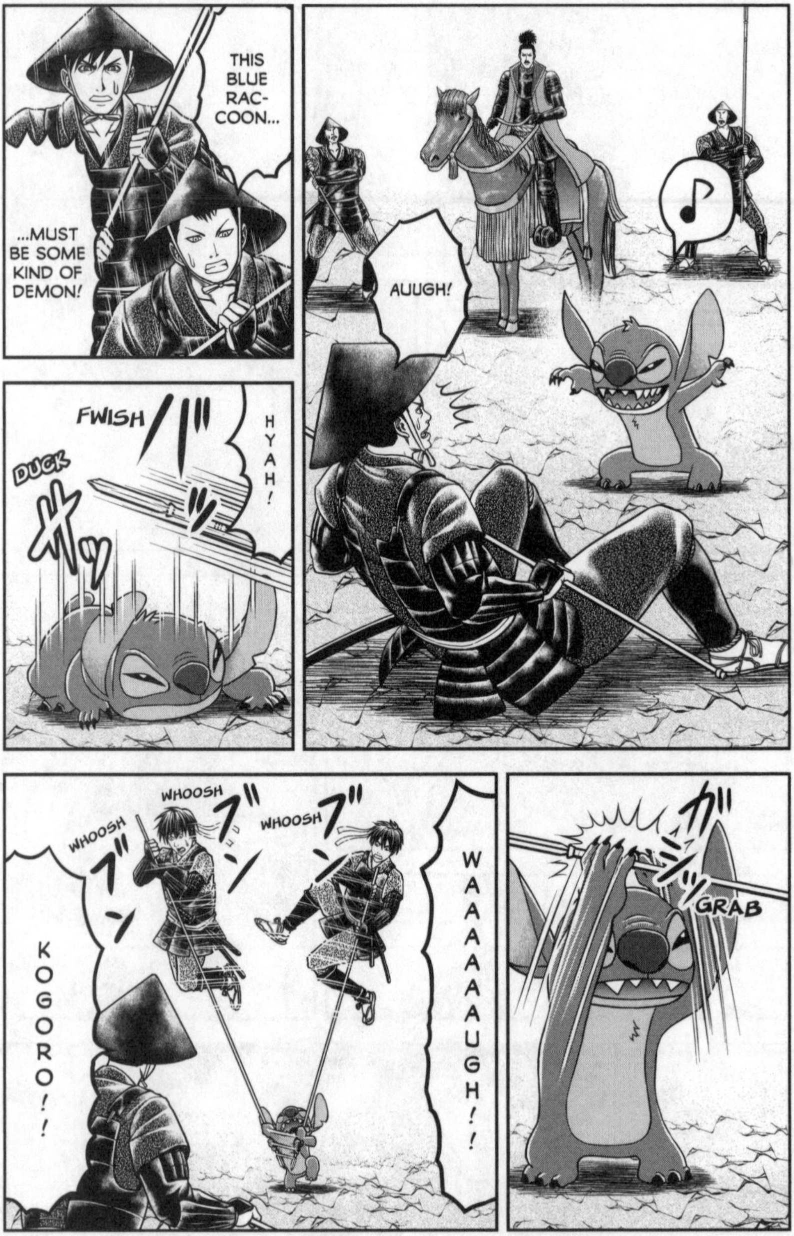
♪
AUUGH!
THIS BLUE RACCOON...
...MUST BE SOME KIND OF DEMON!
HYAH!
FWISH
DUCK
GRAB
WAAAAAAAUGH!!
WHOOSH
WHOOSH
WHOOSH
KOGORO!!

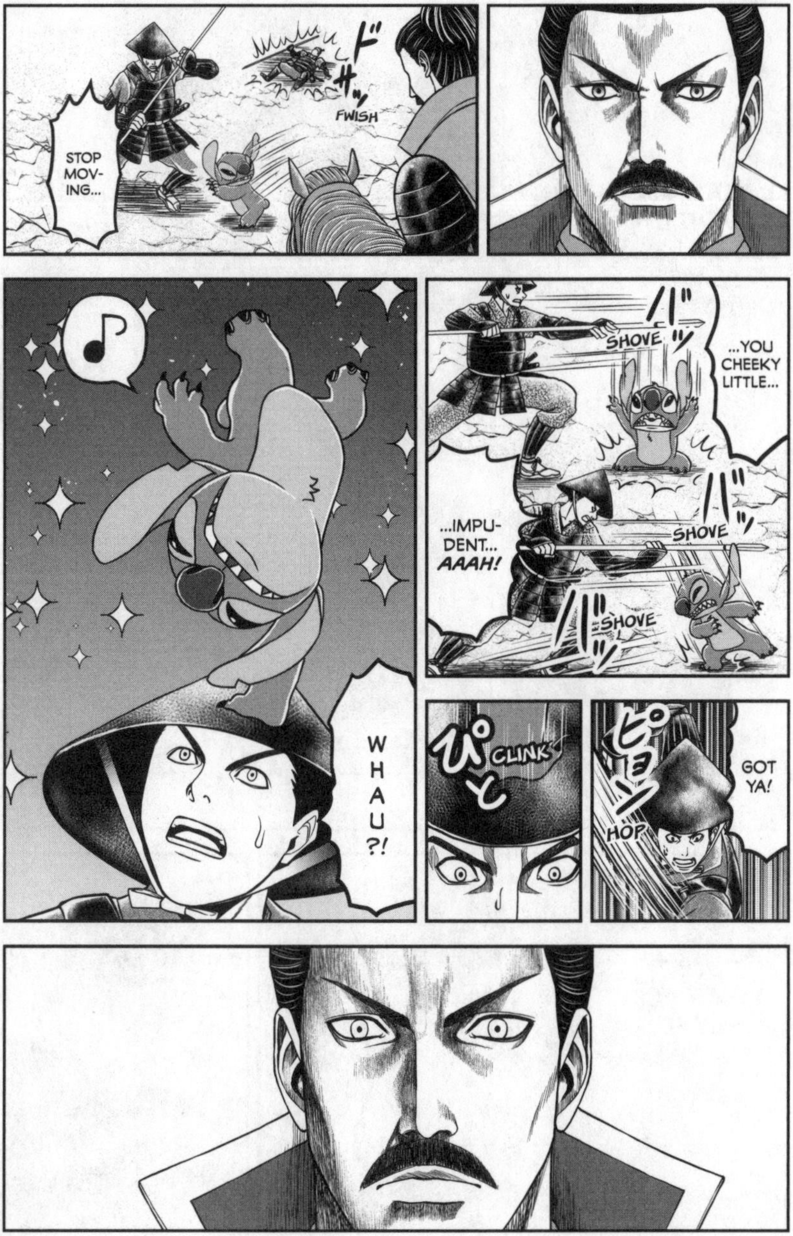
ド
ザッ
FWISH
STOP MOV-ING...
バッ
SHOVE
...YOU CHEEKY LITTLE...
...IMPU-DENT... AAAH!
バッ
SHOVE
バッ
SHOVE
ピョン
HOP
GOT YA!
ぴと
CLINK
♪
WHAU?!

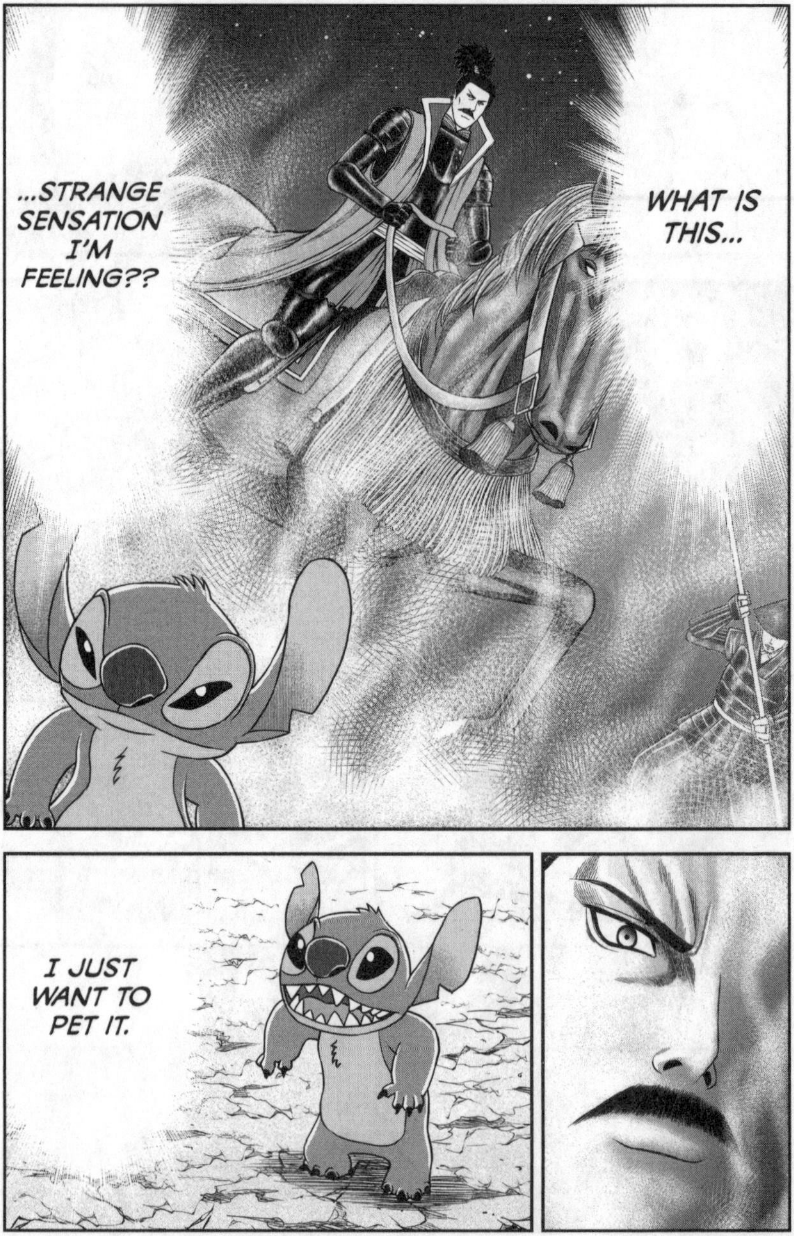
WHAT IS THIS...
...STRANGE SENSATION I'M FEELING??
I JUST WANT TO PET IT.

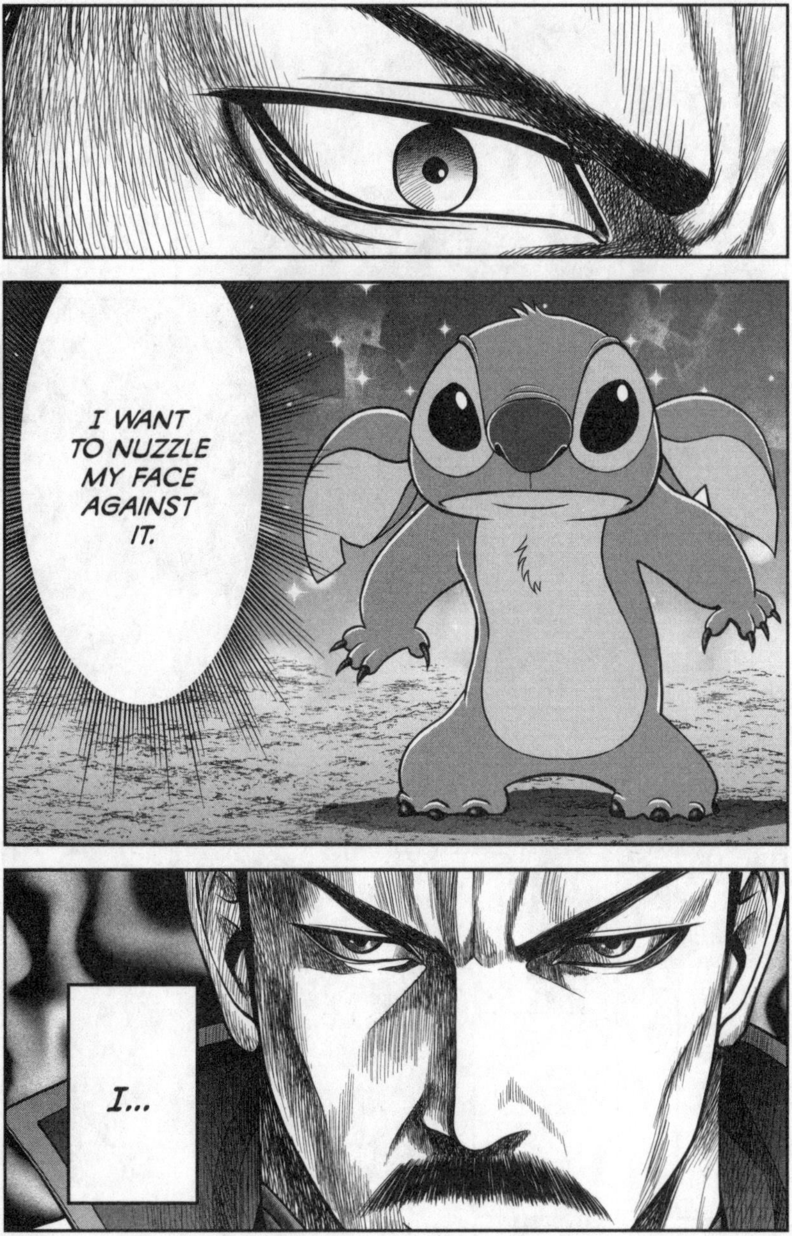
I WANT TO NUZZLE MY FACE AGAINST IT.
I...

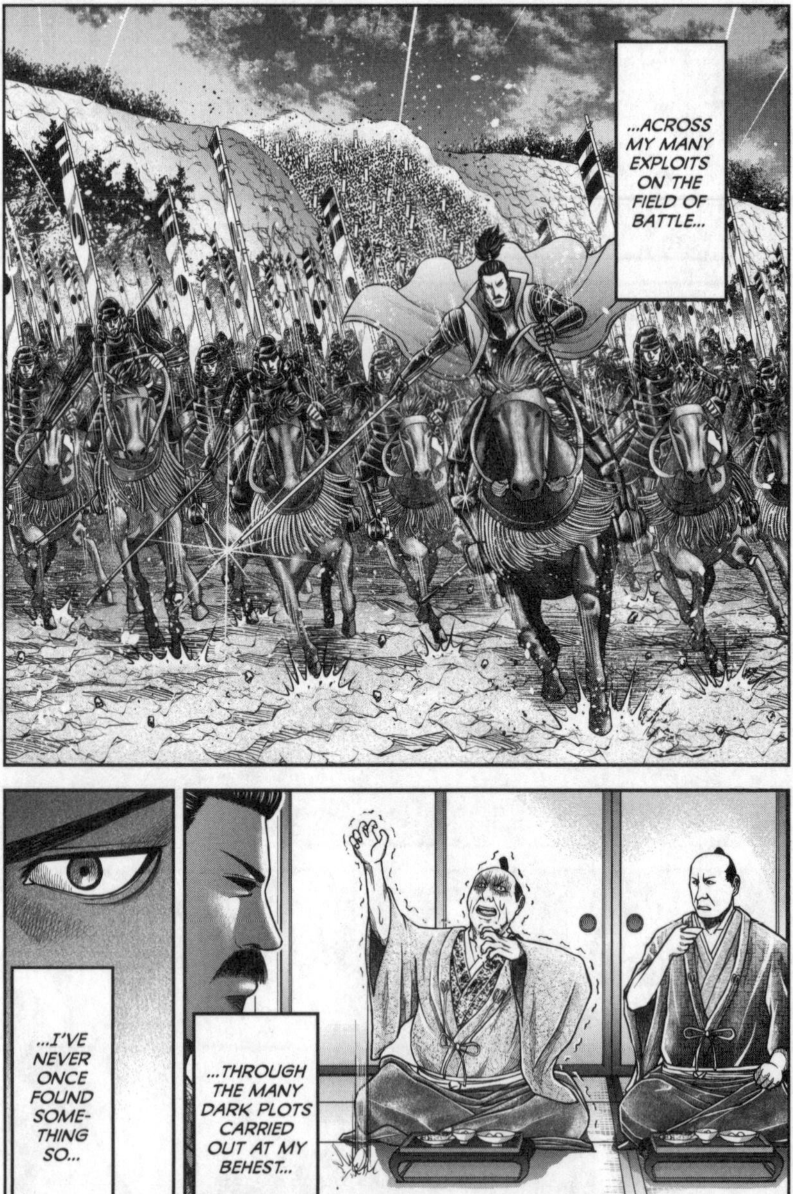
...ACROSS MY MANY EXPLOITS ON THE FIELD OF BATTLE...
...THROUGH THE MANY DARK PLOTS CARRIED OUT AT MY BEHEST...
...I'VE NEVER ONCE FOUND SOME-THING SO...

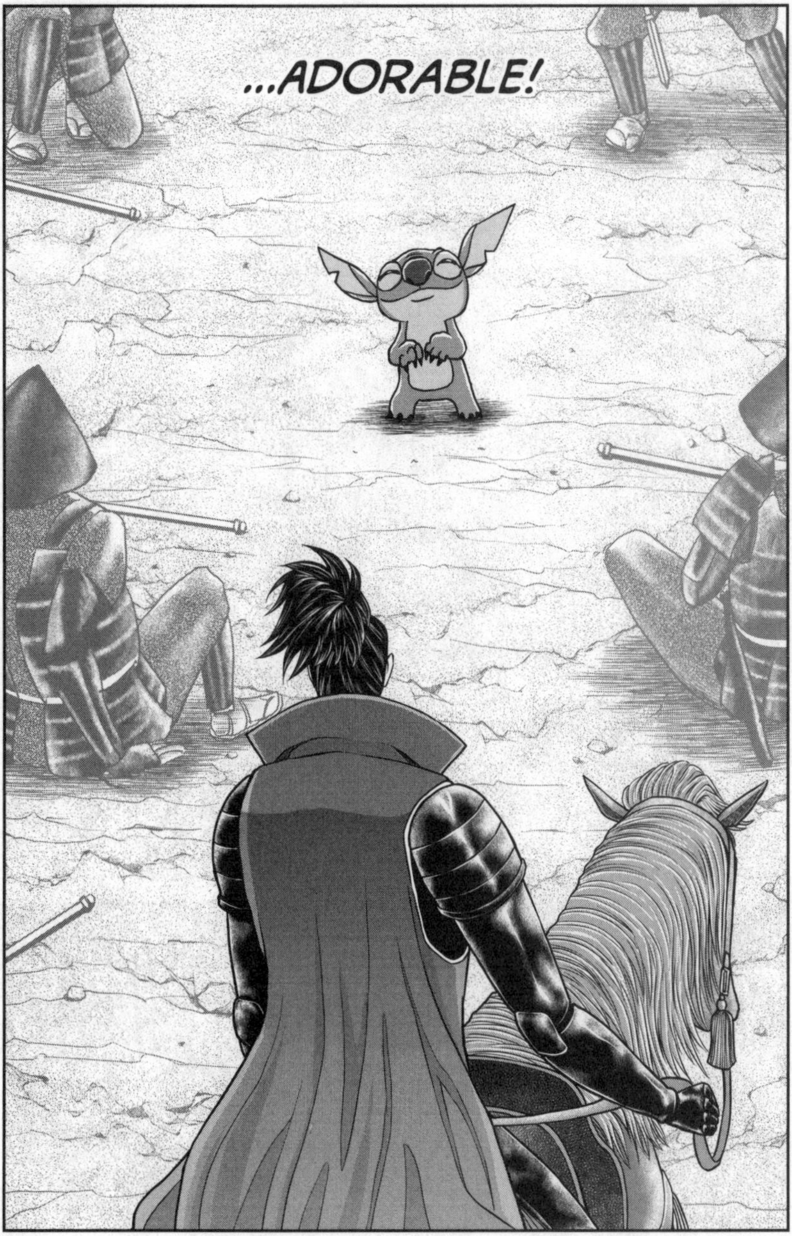
...ADORABLE!

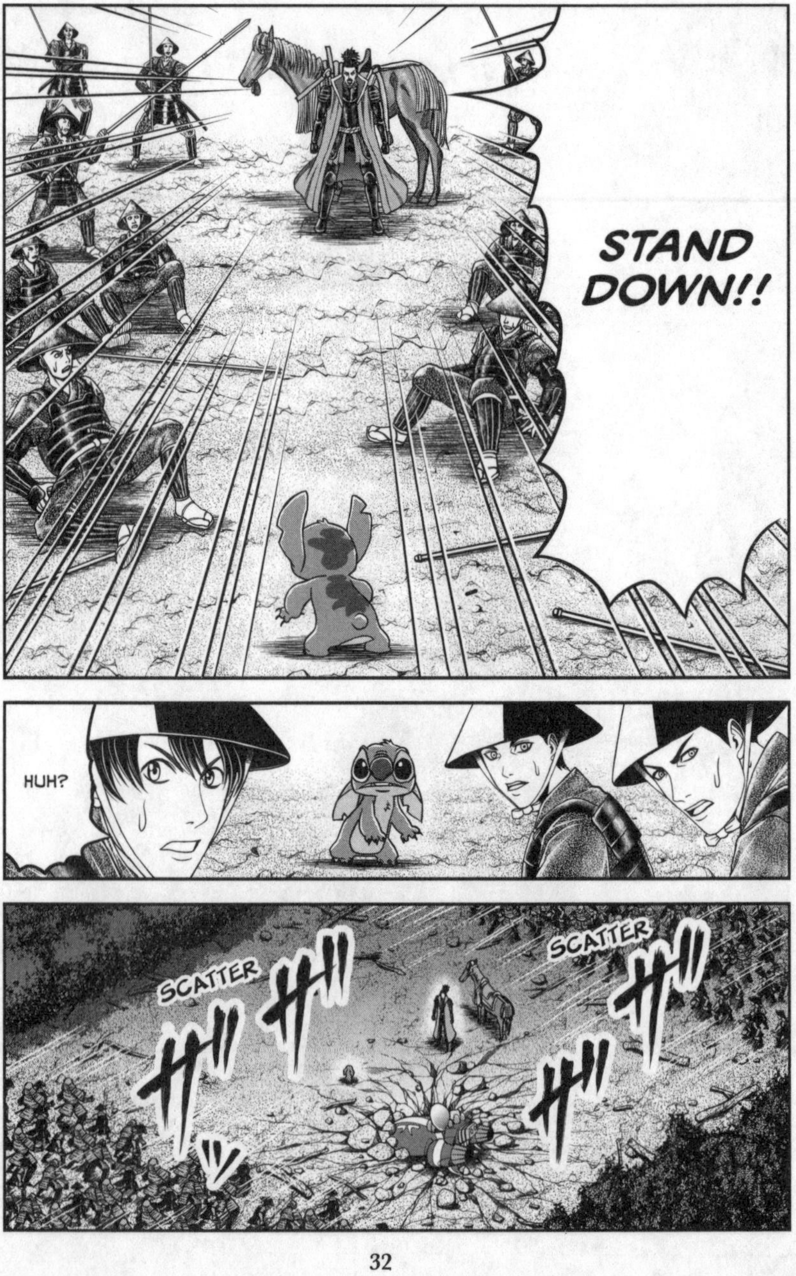
STAND DOWN!!
HUH?
SCATTER
SCATTER

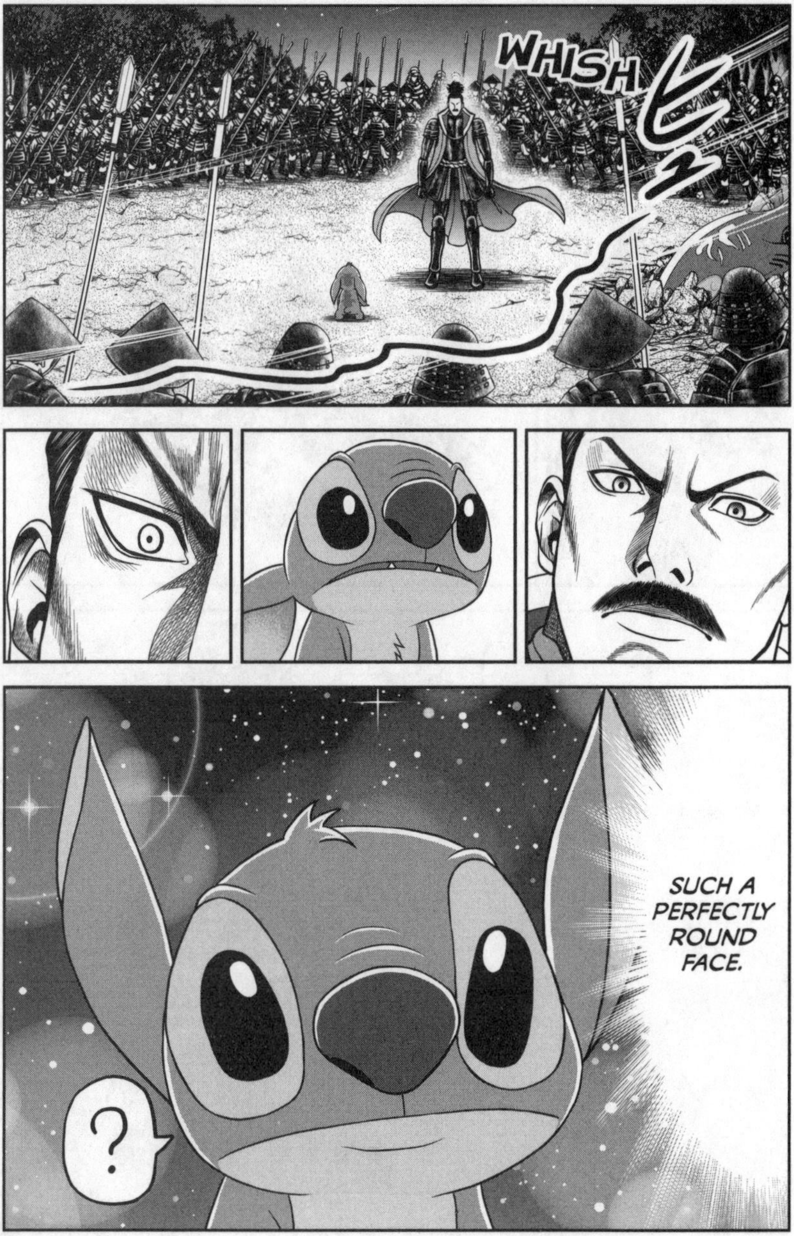
WHISH
SUCH A PERFECTLY ROUND FACE.
?

WHAT'S HE DOING?

SIRE?!

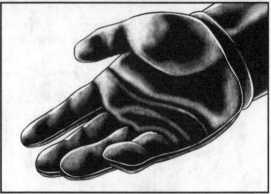

COOCHY-COO!

34

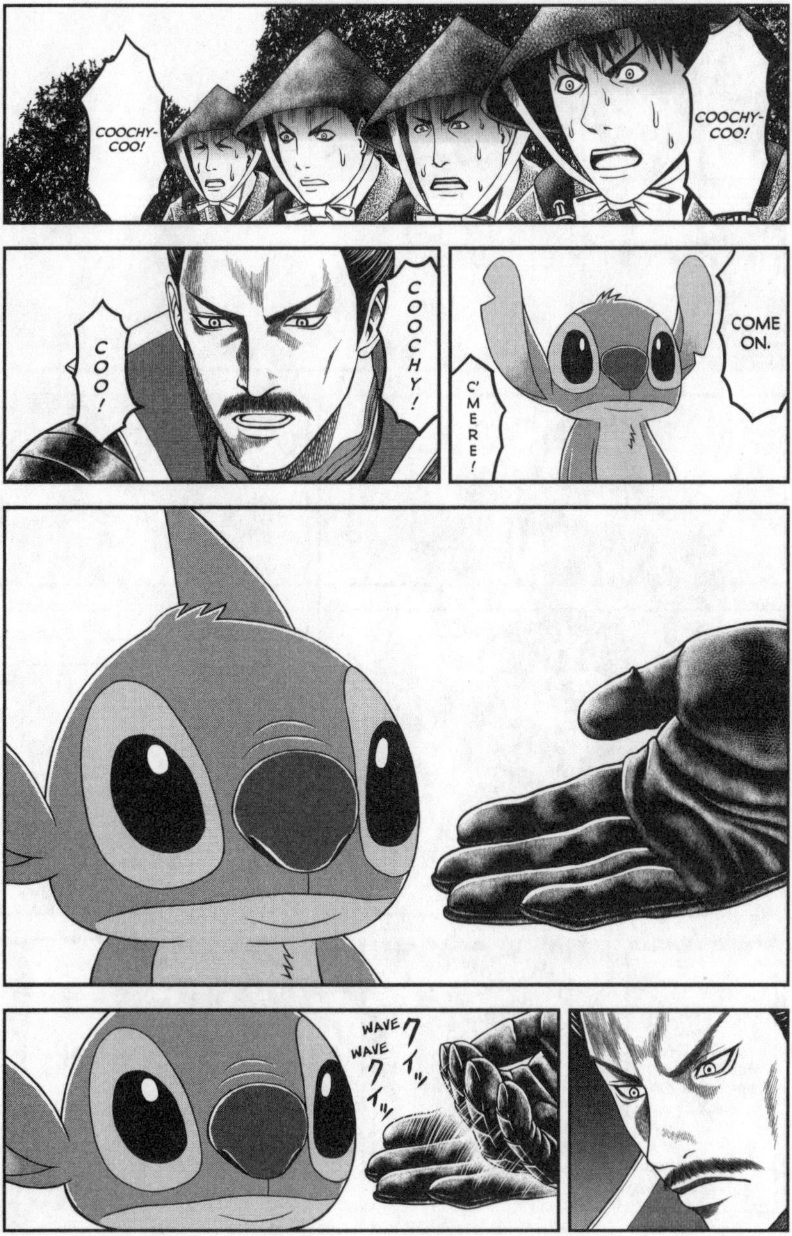
COOCHY-COO!
COOCHY-COO!
COME ON.
C'MERE!
COOCHY!
COO!
WAVE
クイッ
WAVE
クイッ

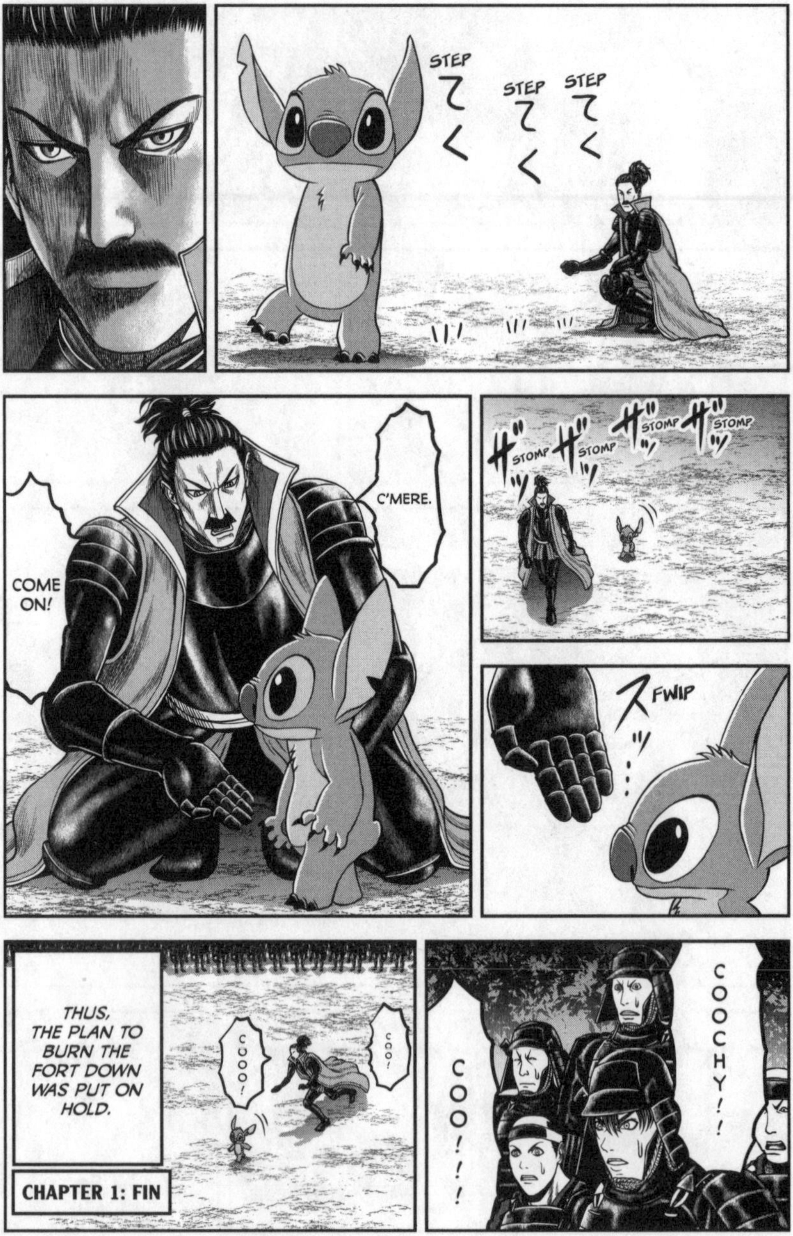
STEP てく
STEP てく
STEP てく
ザッ STOMP
ザッ STOMP
ザッ STOMP
ザッ STOMP
スッ FWIP
…
C'MERE.
COME ON!
COOCHY!!
COO!!!
COO!
COOO!
THUS, THE PLAN TO BURN THE FORT DOWN WAS PUT ON HOLD.
CHAPTER 1: FIN

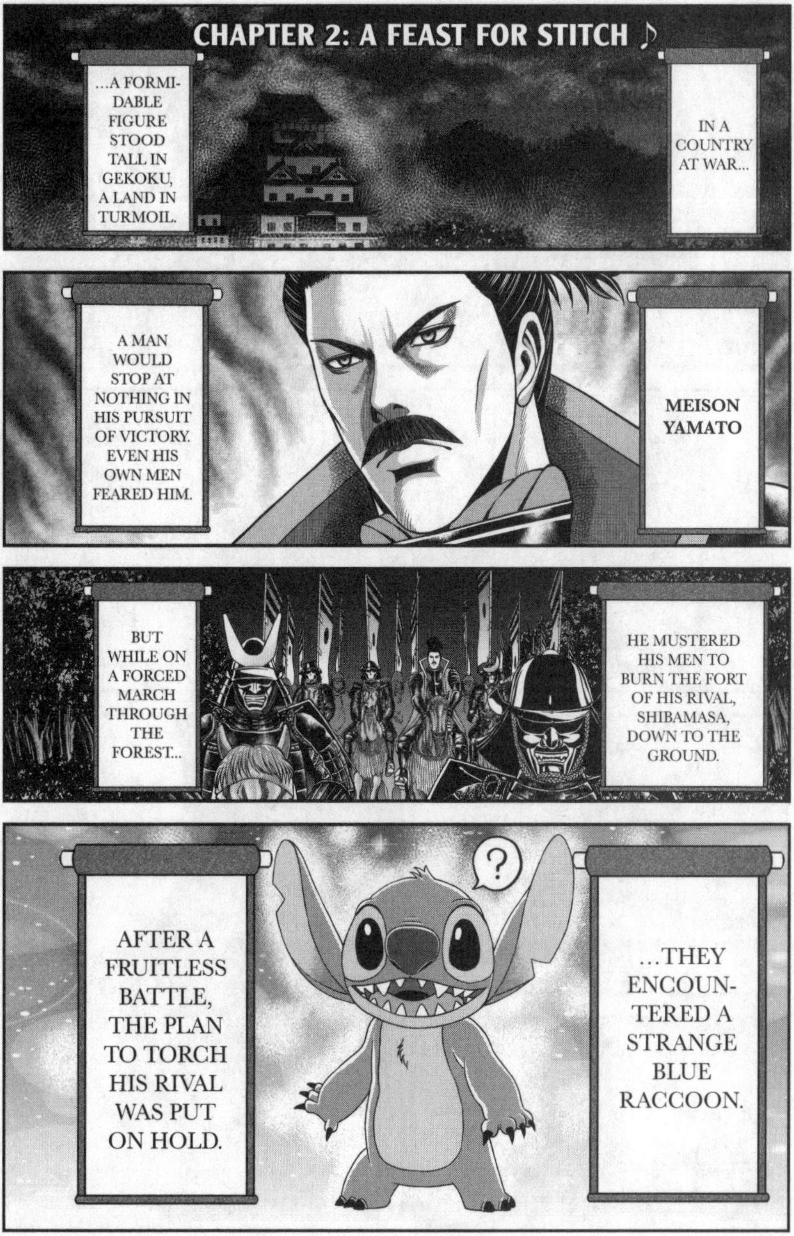
CHAPTER 2: A FEAST FOR STITCH ♪
IN A COUNTRY AT WAR...
...A FORMIDABLE FIGURE STOOD TALL IN GEKOKU, A LAND IN TURMOIL.
MEISON YAMATO
A MAN WOULD STOP AT NOTHING IN HIS PURSUIT OF VICTORY. EVEN HIS OWN MEN FEARED HIM.
HE MUSTERED HIS MEN TO BURN THE FORT OF HIS RIVAL, SHIBAMASA, DOWN TO THE GROUND.
BUT WHILE ON A FORCED MARCH THROUGH THE FOREST...
...THEY ENCOUNTERED A STRANGE BLUE RACCOON.
?
AFTER A FRUITLESS BATTLE, THE PLAN TO TORCH HIS RIVAL WAS PUT ON HOLD.

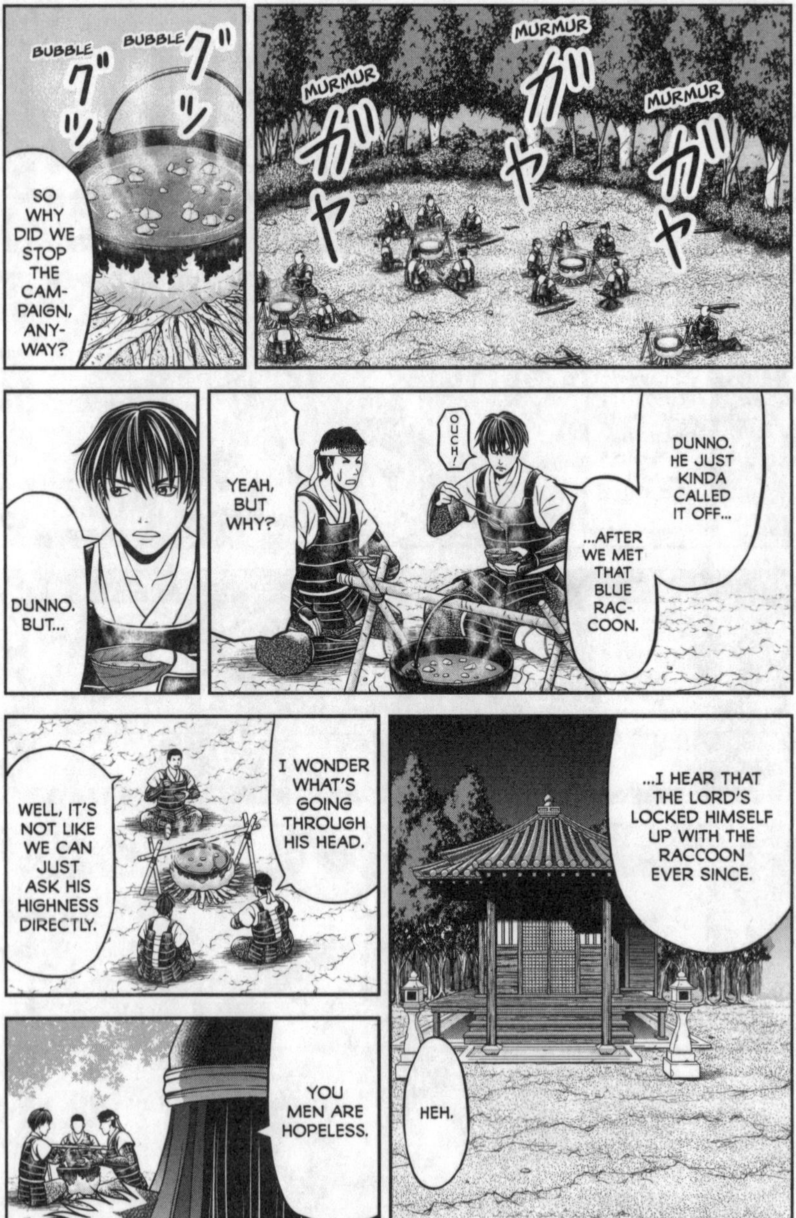
MURMUR
ガヤ
MURMUR
ガヤ
MURMUR
ガヤ
BUBBLE
グツ
BUBBLE
グツ
SO WHY DID WE STOP THE CAM-PAIGN, ANY-WAY?
DUNNO. HE JUST KINDA CALLED IT OFF...
OUCH!
YEAH, BUT WHY?
...AFTER WE MET THAT BLUE RAC-COON.
DUNNO. BUT...
...I HEAR THAT THE LORD'S LOCKED HIMSELF UP WITH THE RACCOON EVER SINCE.
HEH.
I WONDER WHAT'S GOING THROUGH HIS HEAD.
WELL, IT'S NOT LIKE WE CAN JUST ASK HIS HIGHNESS DIRECTLY.
YOU MEN ARE HOPELESS.

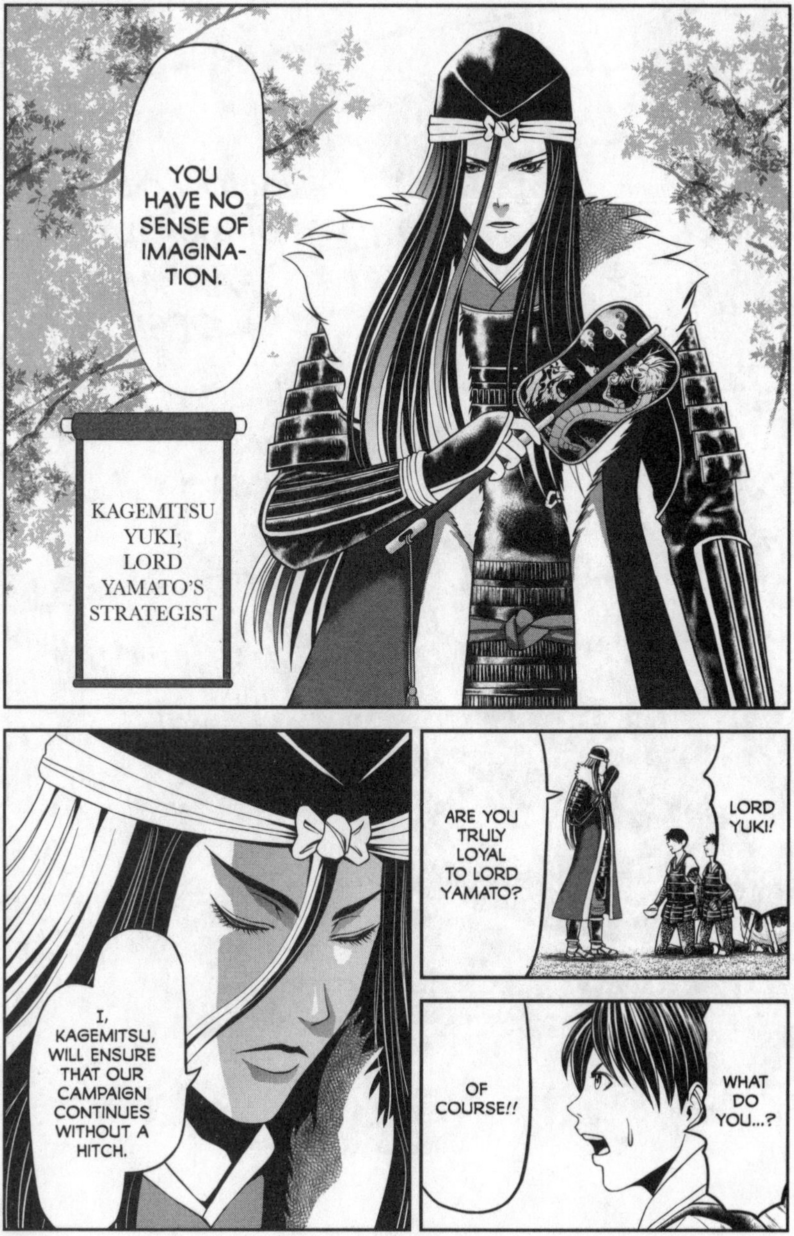
YOU HAVE NO SENSE OF IMAGINATION.
KAGEMITSU YUKI, LORD YAMATO'S STRATEGIST
LORD YUKI!
ARE YOU TRULY LOYAL TO LORD YAMATO?
WHAT DO YOU...?
OF COURSE!!
I, KAGEMITSU, WILL ENSURE THAT OUR CAMPAIGN CONTINUES WITHOUT A HITCH.

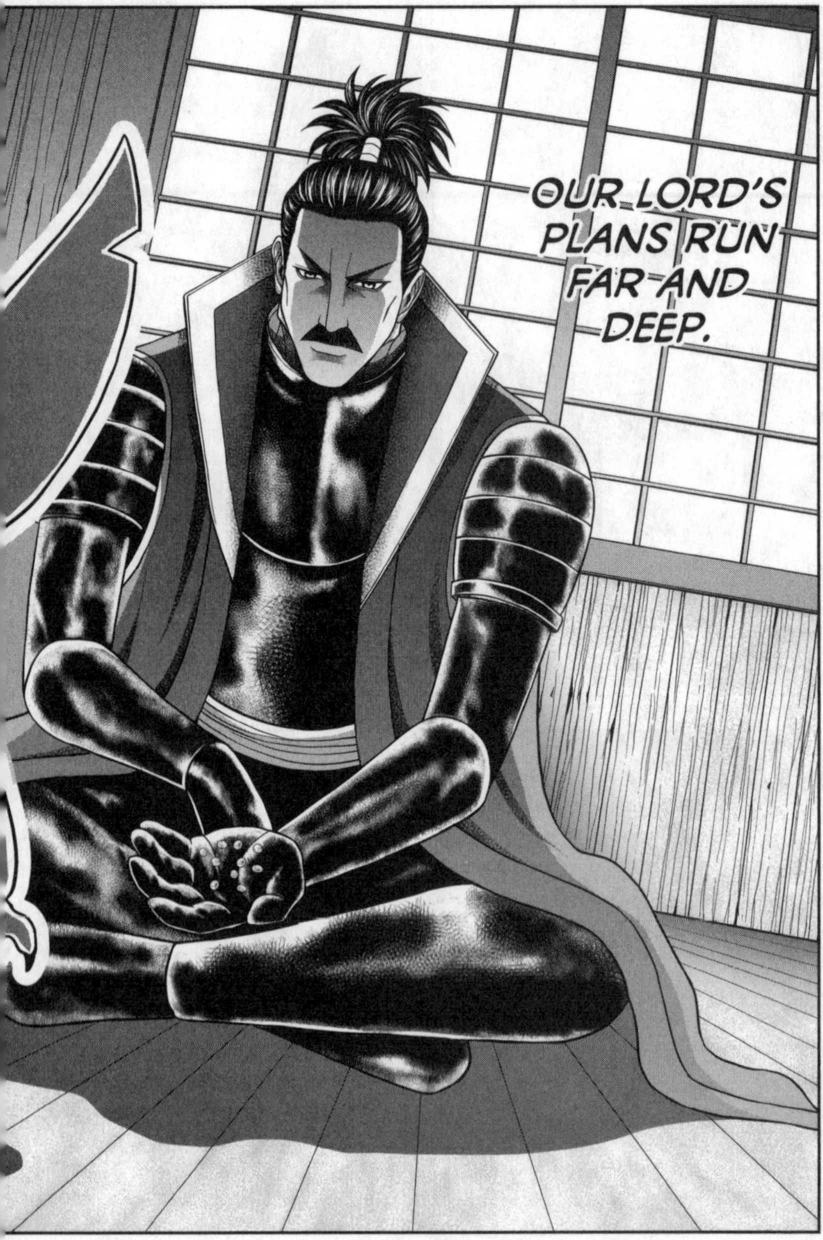
OUR LORD'S PLANS RUN FAR AND DEEP.

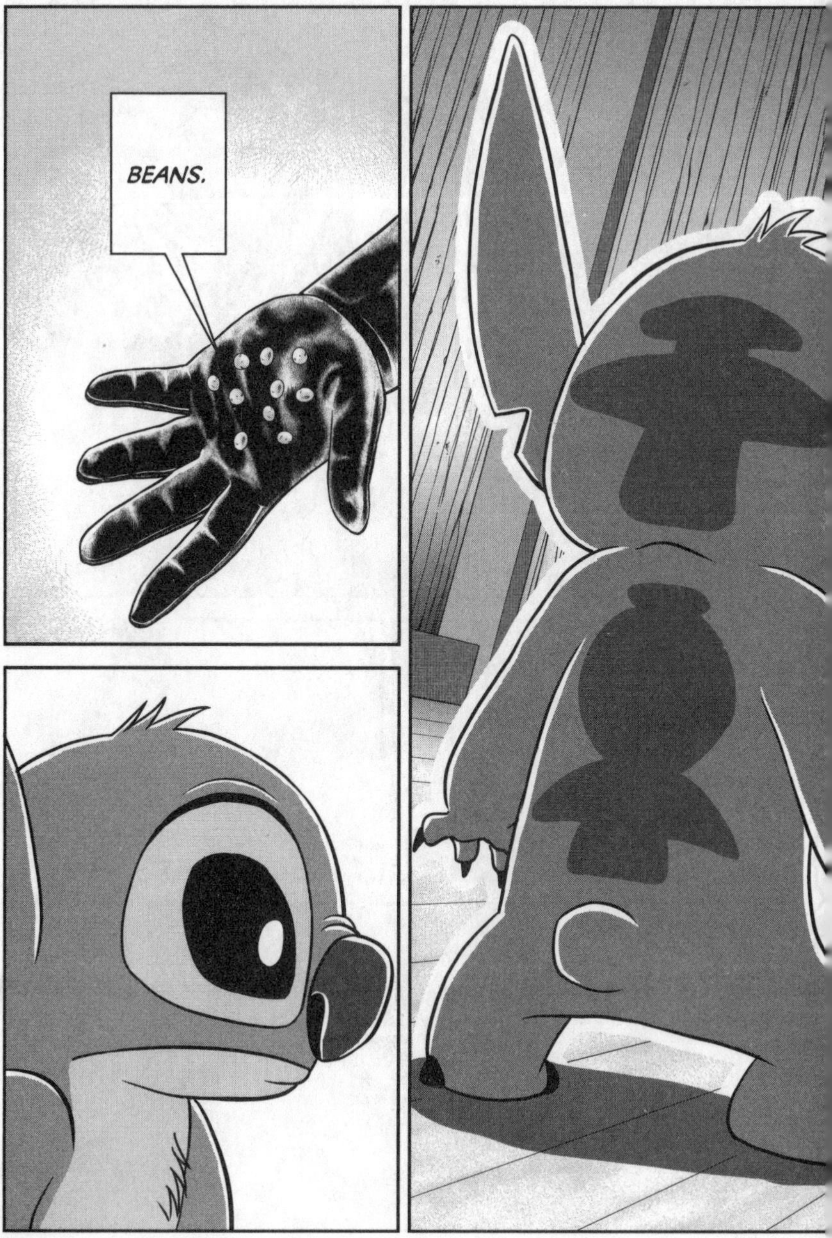
BEANS.

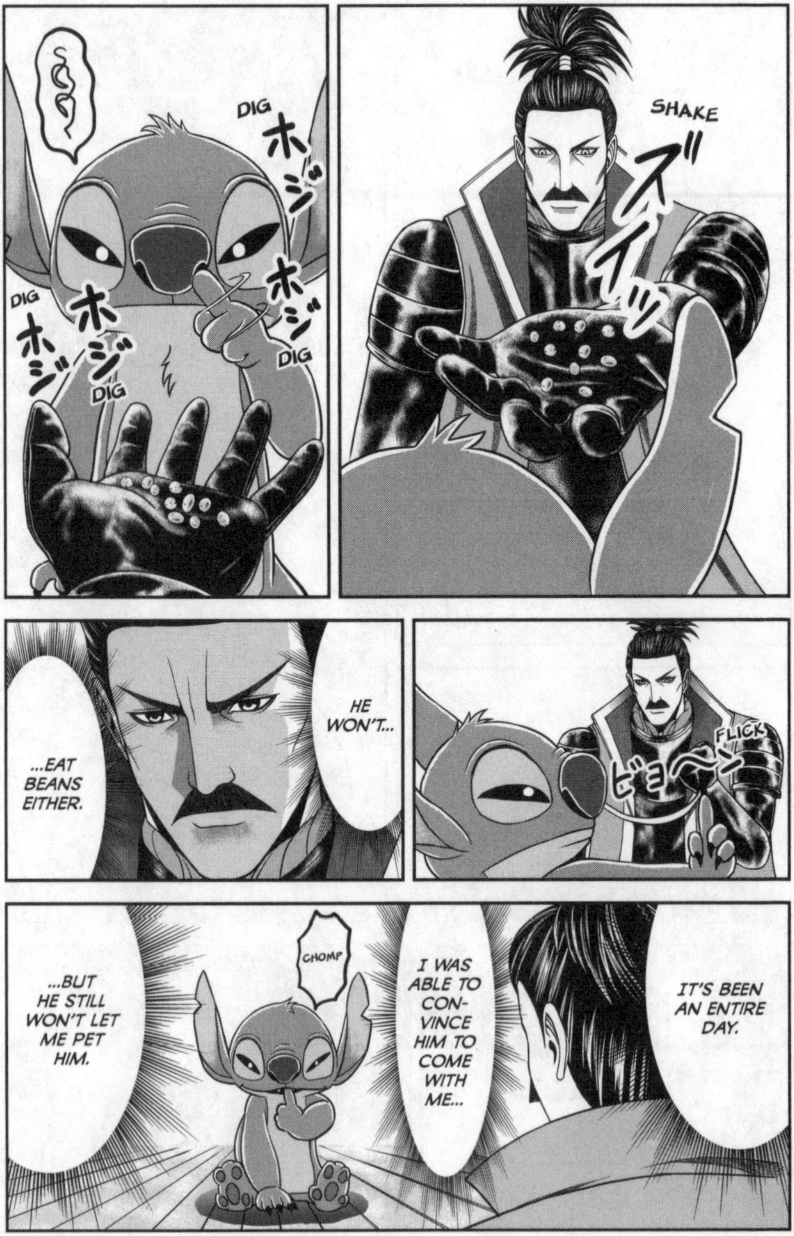
SHAKE
ズイッ
DIG
ホジ
ホジ
DIG
ホジ
ホジ
DIG
DIG
FLICK
ビョ～ン
HE WON'T...
...EAT BEANS EITHER.
IT'S BEEN AN ENTIRE DAY.
I WAS ABLE TO CON-VINCE HIM TO COME WITH ME...
CHOMP
...BUT HE STILL WON'T LET ME PET HIM.

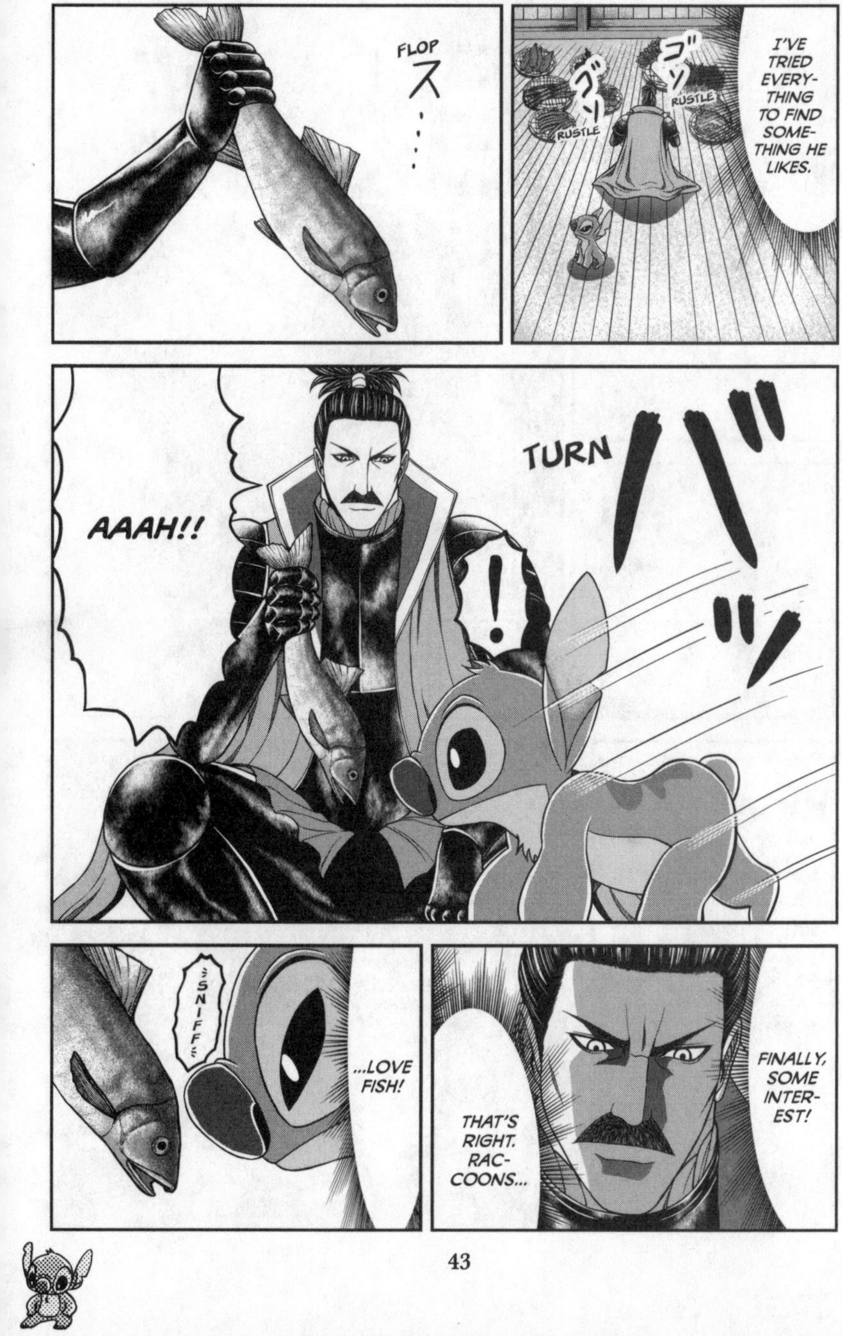

I'VE TRIED EVERYTHING TO FIND SOMETHING HE LIKES.
ゴソ
RUSTLE
ゴソ
RUSTLE
FLOP
ス・・・
TURN
バッ
!
AAAH!!
FINALLY, SOME INTEREST!
THAT'S RIGHT. RACCOONS...
...LOVE FISH!
SNIFF

MAYBE BECAUSE IT'S RAW?

≒SIGH≒

タ
RUN

IN THAT CASE...

バ
4
SIZZLE

バ
4
POP

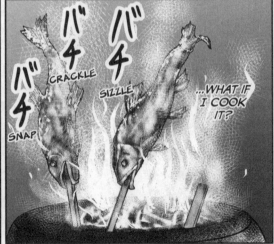

バ
4
CRACKLE

バ
4
SIZZLE

バ
4
SNAP

...WHAT IF I COOK IT?

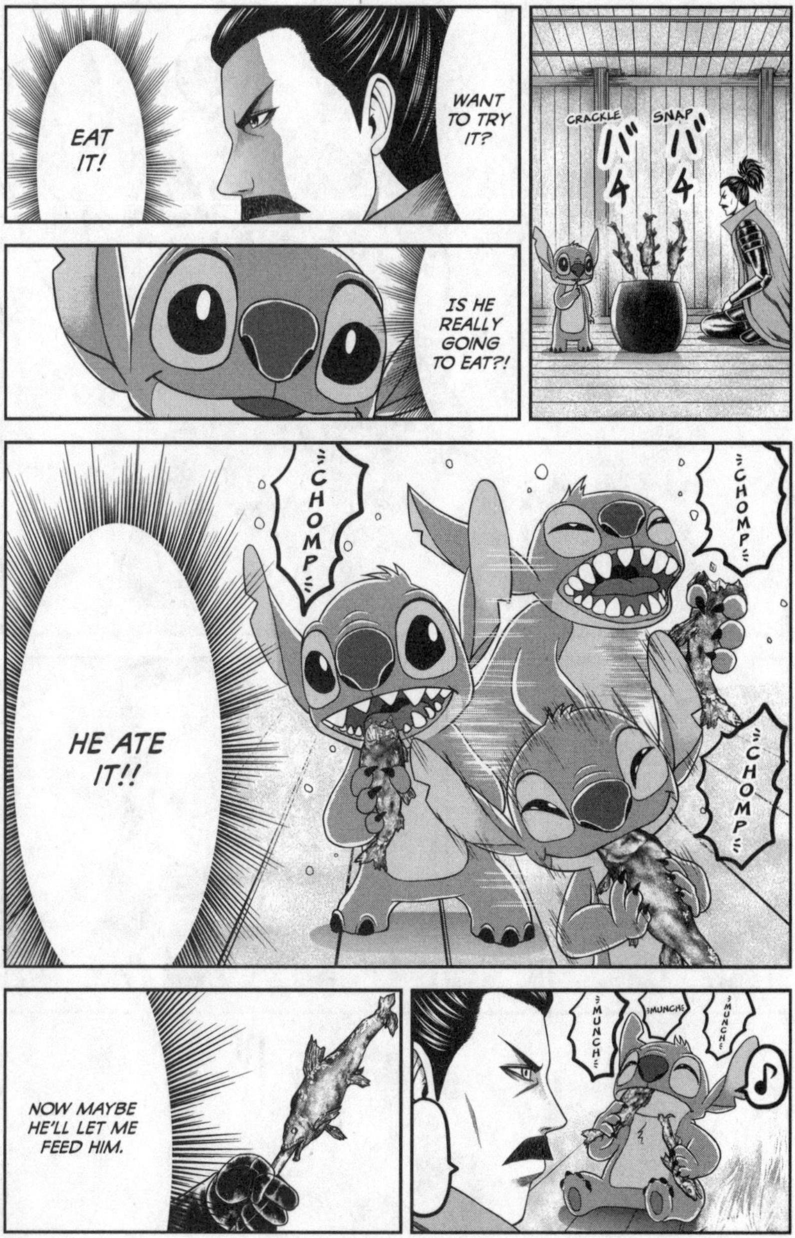
CRACKLE
SNAP
WANT TO TRY IT?
EAT IT!
IS HE REALLY GOING TO EAT?!
CHOMP
CHOMP
CHOMP
HE ATE IT!!
MUNCH
MUNCH
MUNCH
♪
NOW MAYBE HE'LL LET ME FEED HIM.

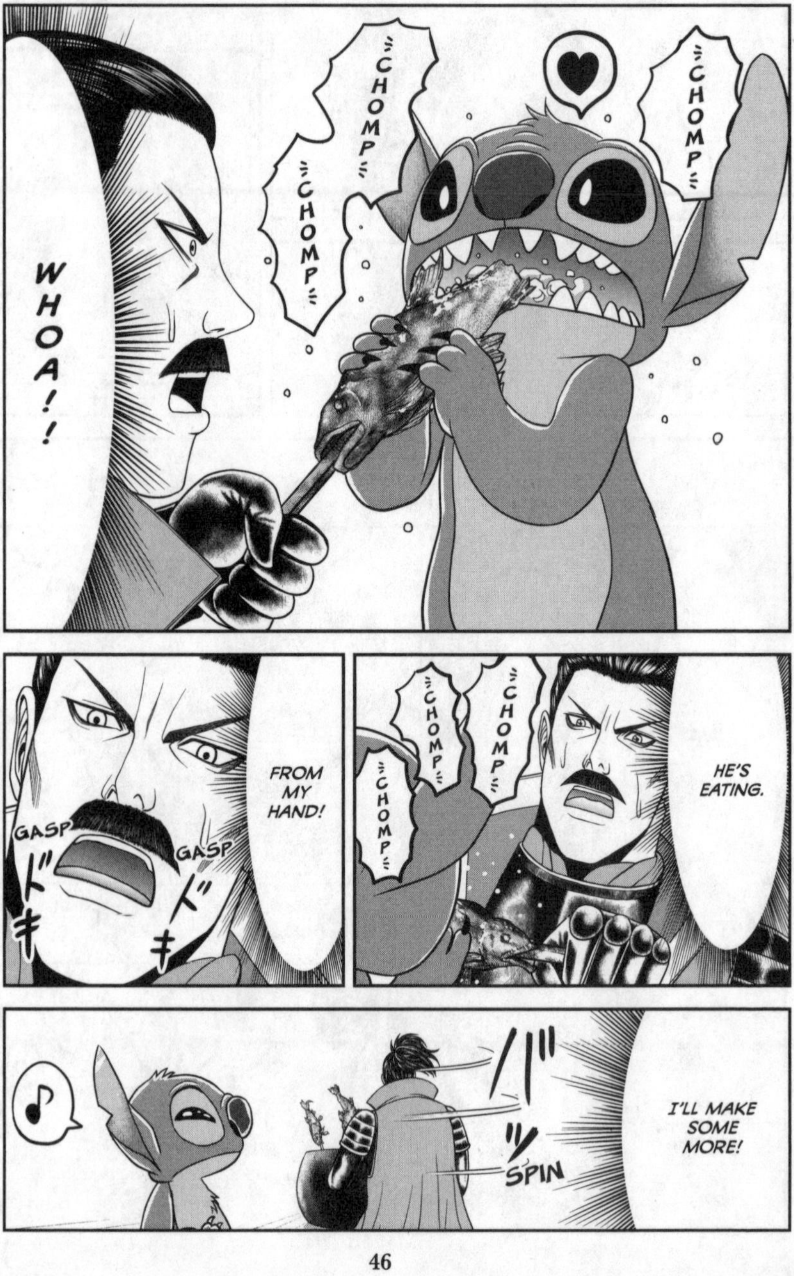
CHOMP
CHOMP
CHOMP
WHOA!!
HE'S EATING.
CHOMP
CHOMP
CHOMP
FROM MY HAND!
GASP
ドキ
GASP
ドキ
I'LL MAKE SOME MORE!
バッ
SPIN

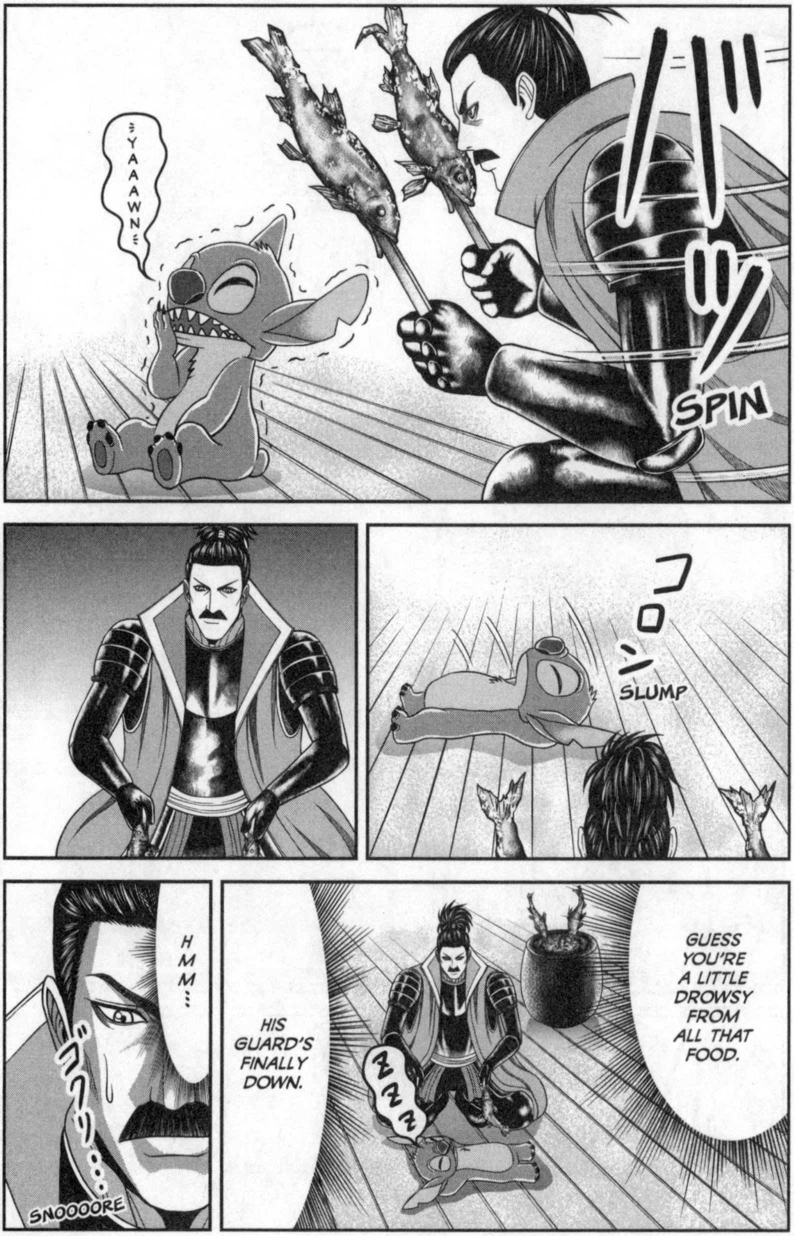
バッ
SPIN
YAAAAWN
コロン
SLUMP
GUESS YOU'RE A LITTLE DROWSY FROM ALL THAT FOOD.
HIS GUARD'S FINALLY DOWN.
ZZZ
HMM...
ゴクリ...
SNOOOORE

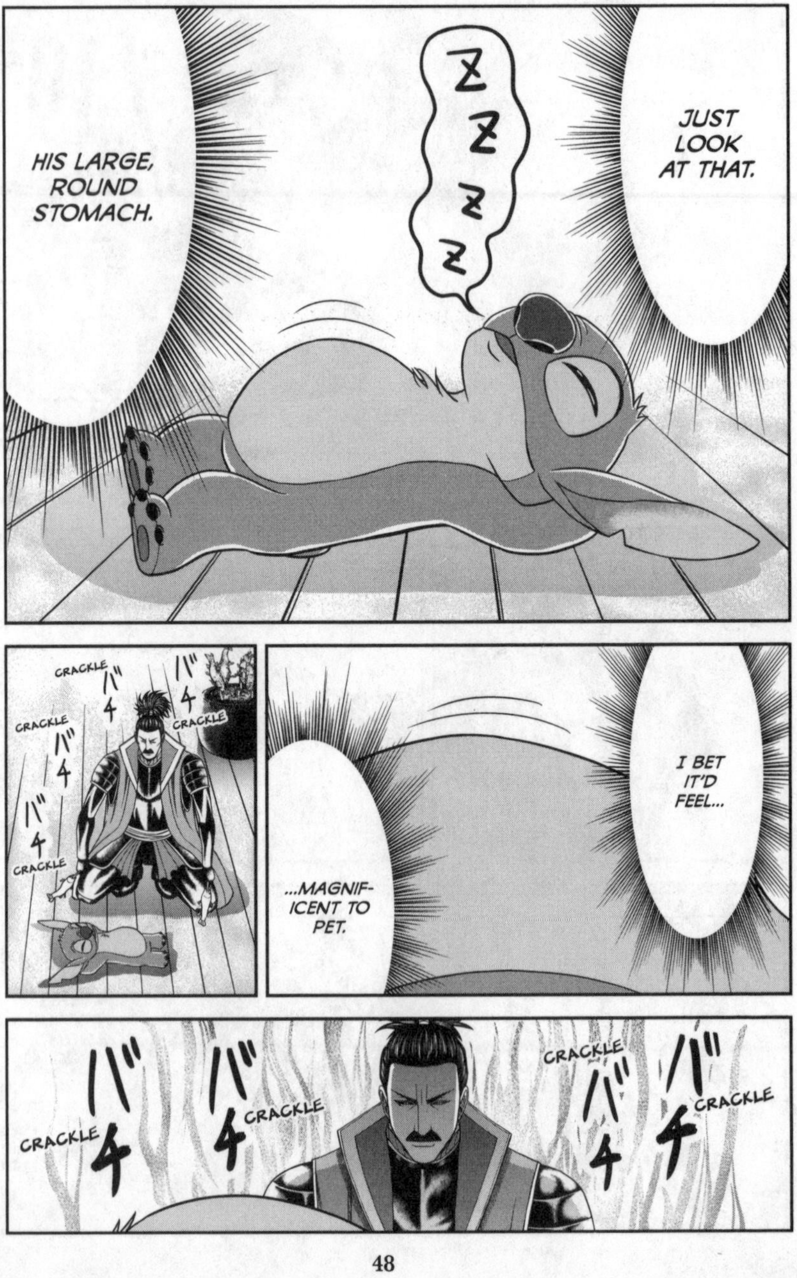
JUST LOOK AT THAT.
Z Z Z Z Z
HIS LARGE, ROUND STOMACH.
I BET IT'D FEEL...
...MAGNIF-ICENT TO PET.
バチ CRACKLE
バチ CRACKLE
バチ CRACKLE
バチ CRACKLE
バチ CRACKLE
バチ CRACKLE
バチ CRACKLE
バチ CRACKLE

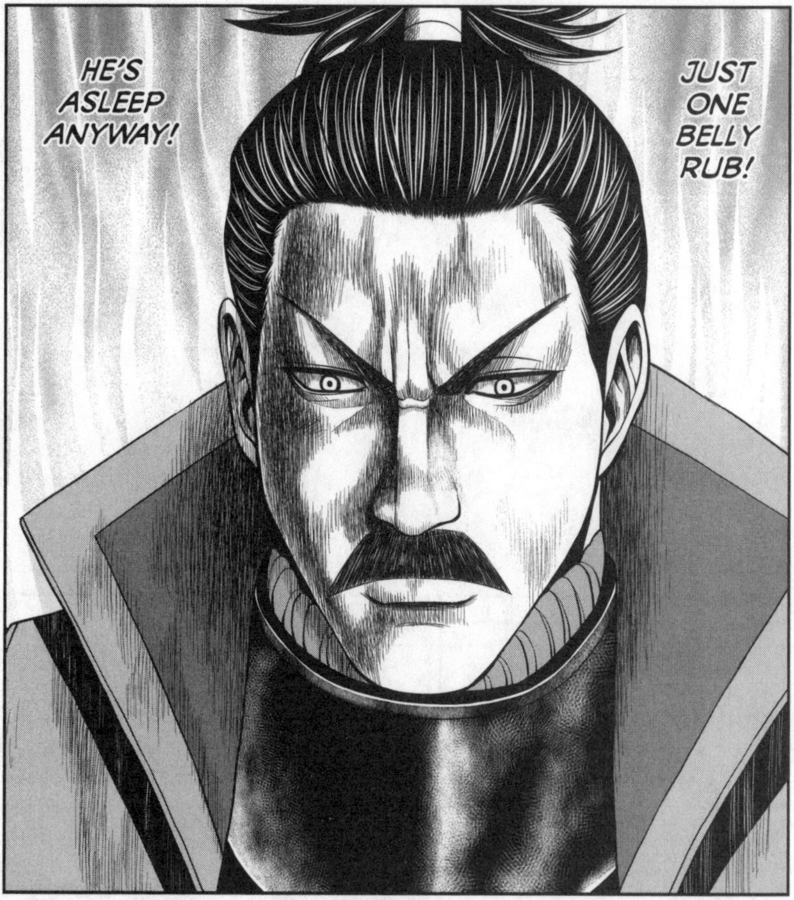
JUST ONE BELLY RUB!
HE'S ASLEEP ANYWAY!

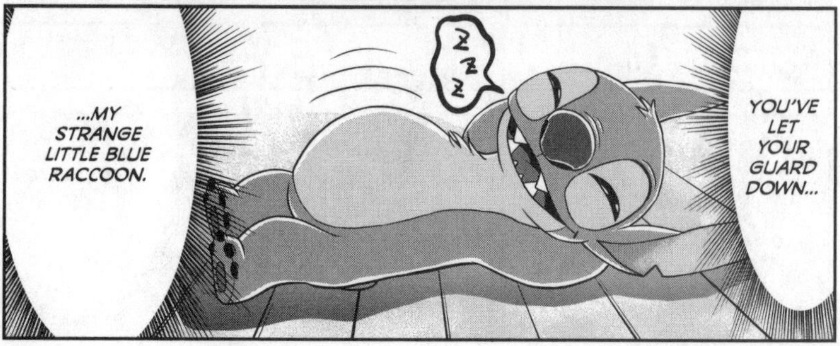
YOU'VE LET YOUR GUARD DOWN...
Z Z Z
...MY STRANGE LITTLE BLUE RACCOON.

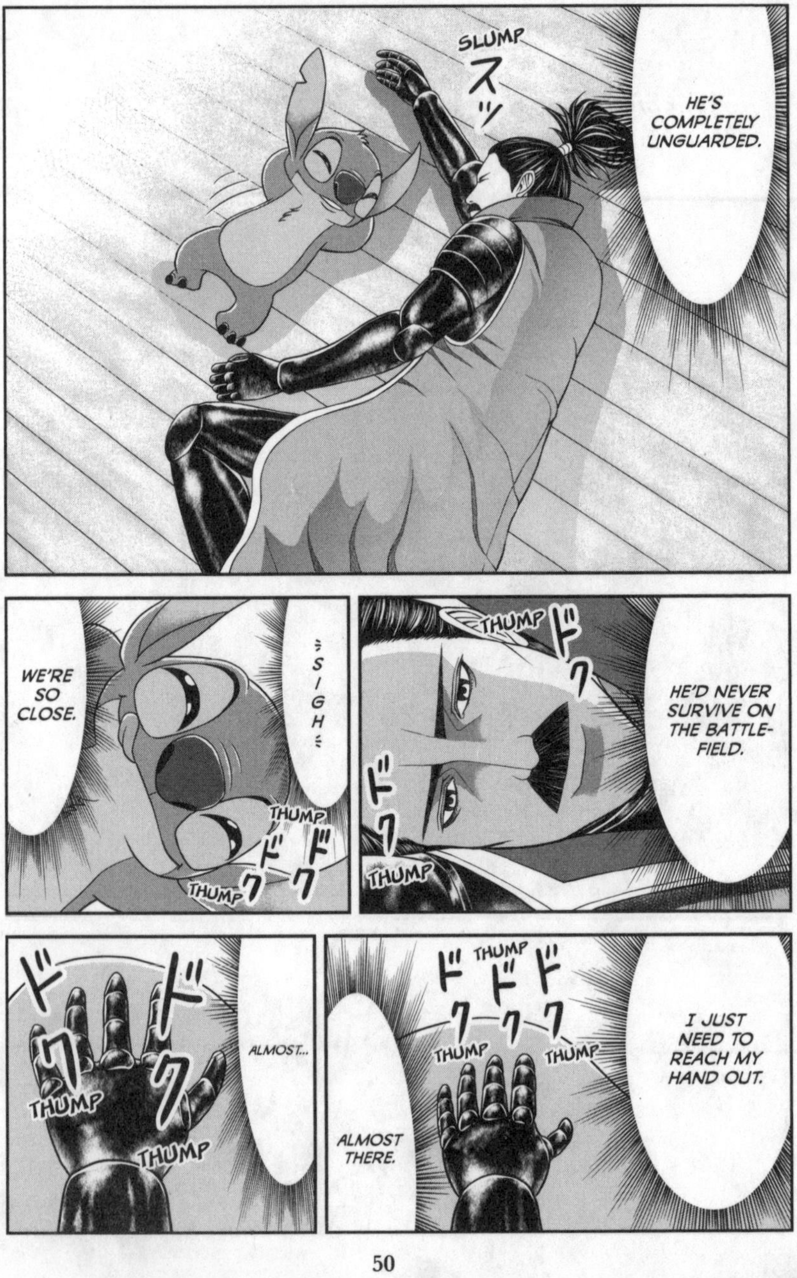
HE'S COMPLETELY UNGUARDED.
SLUMP
スッ
HE'D NEVER SURVIVE ON THE BATTLE-FIELD.
THUMP
ドク
ドク
THUMP
SIGH
WE'RE SO CLOSE.
THUMP
ドク
ドク
THUMP
I JUST NEED TO REACH MY HAND OUT.
THUMP
ドク ドク ドク
THUMP
THUMP
ALMOST THERE.
ALMOST...
ドク
ドク
THUMP
THUMP

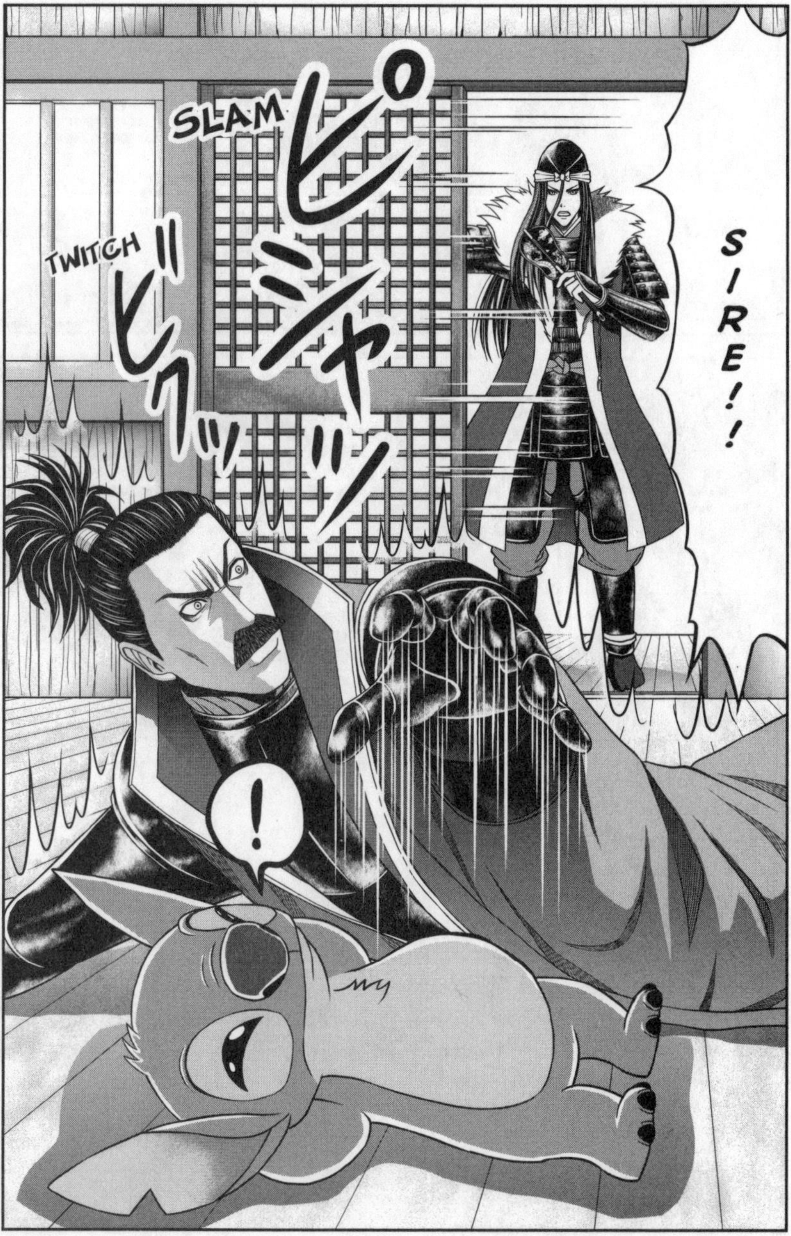
SIRE!!
SLAM
ピシャッ
TWITCH
ビクッ
!

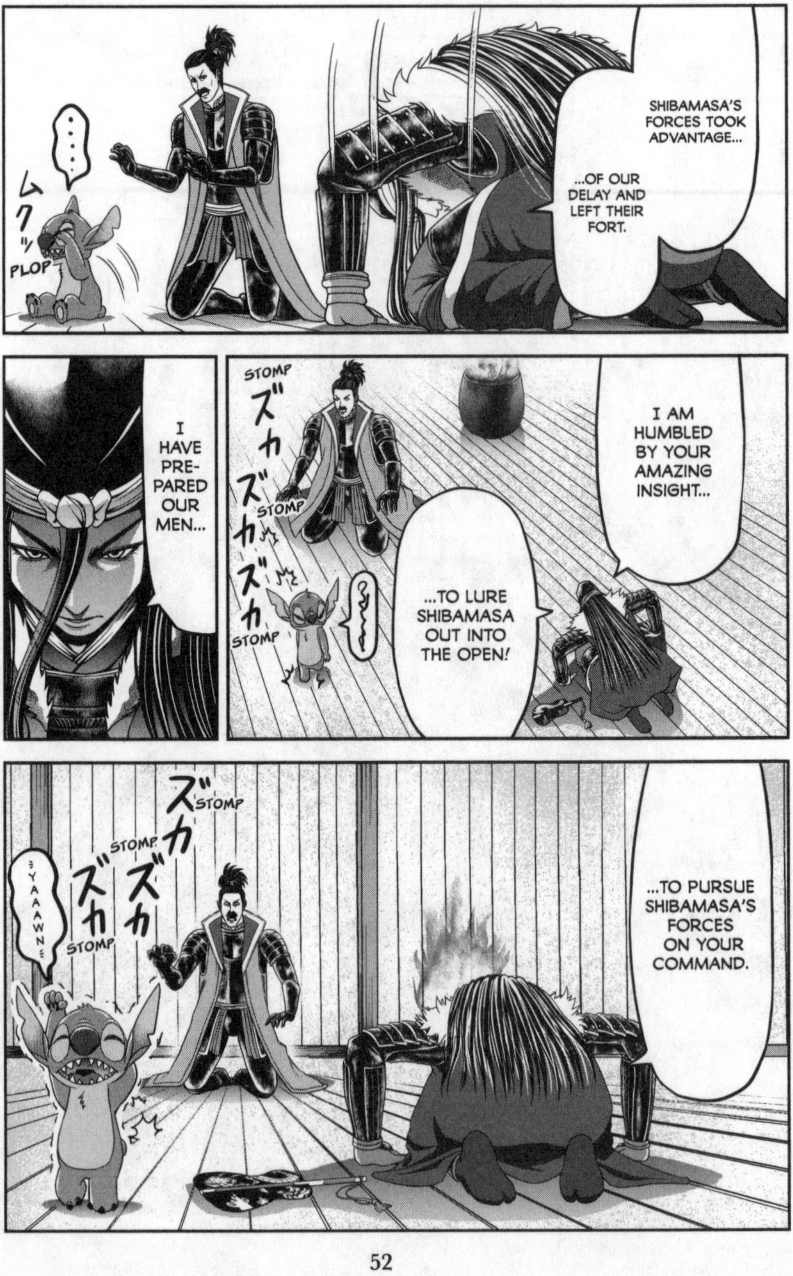
SHIBAMASA'S FORCES TOOK ADVANTAGE...
...OF OUR DELAY AND LEFT THEIR FORT.
....
ムクッ
PLOP
I AM HUMBLED BY YOUR AMAZING INSIGHT...
...TO LURE SHIBAMASA OUT INTO THE OPEN!
STOMP
ズカ
STOMP
ズカ
STOMP
ズカ
STOMP
I HAVE PRE-PARED OUR MEN...
...TO PURSUE SHIBAMASA'S FORCES ON YOUR COMMAND.
ズカ STOMP
STOMP
ズカ
ズカ
STOMP
YAAAWN

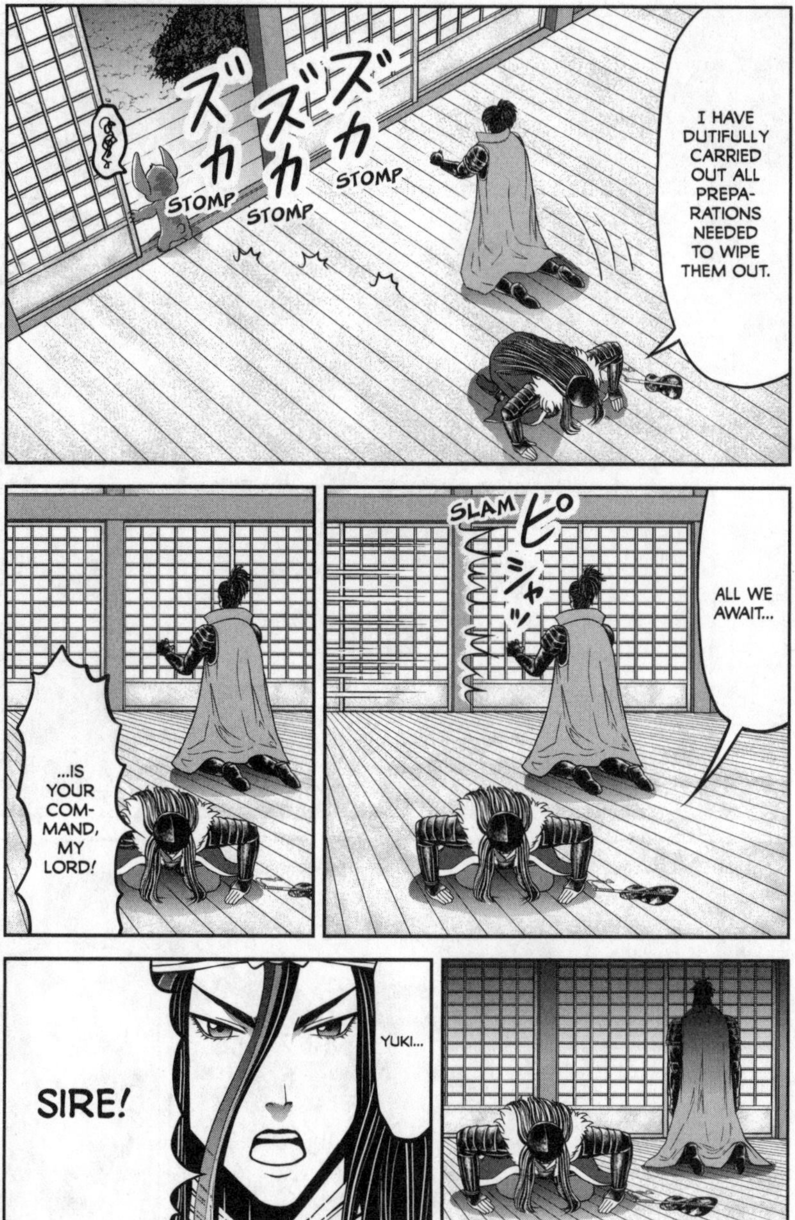
I HAVE DUTIFULLY CARRIED OUT ALL PREPA-RATIONS NEEDED TO WIPE THEM OUT.
ズカ
STOMP
ズカ
STOMP
ズカ
STOMP
SLAM
ピシャッ
ALL WE AWAIT...
...IS YOUR COM-MAND, MY LORD!
YUKI...
SIRE!

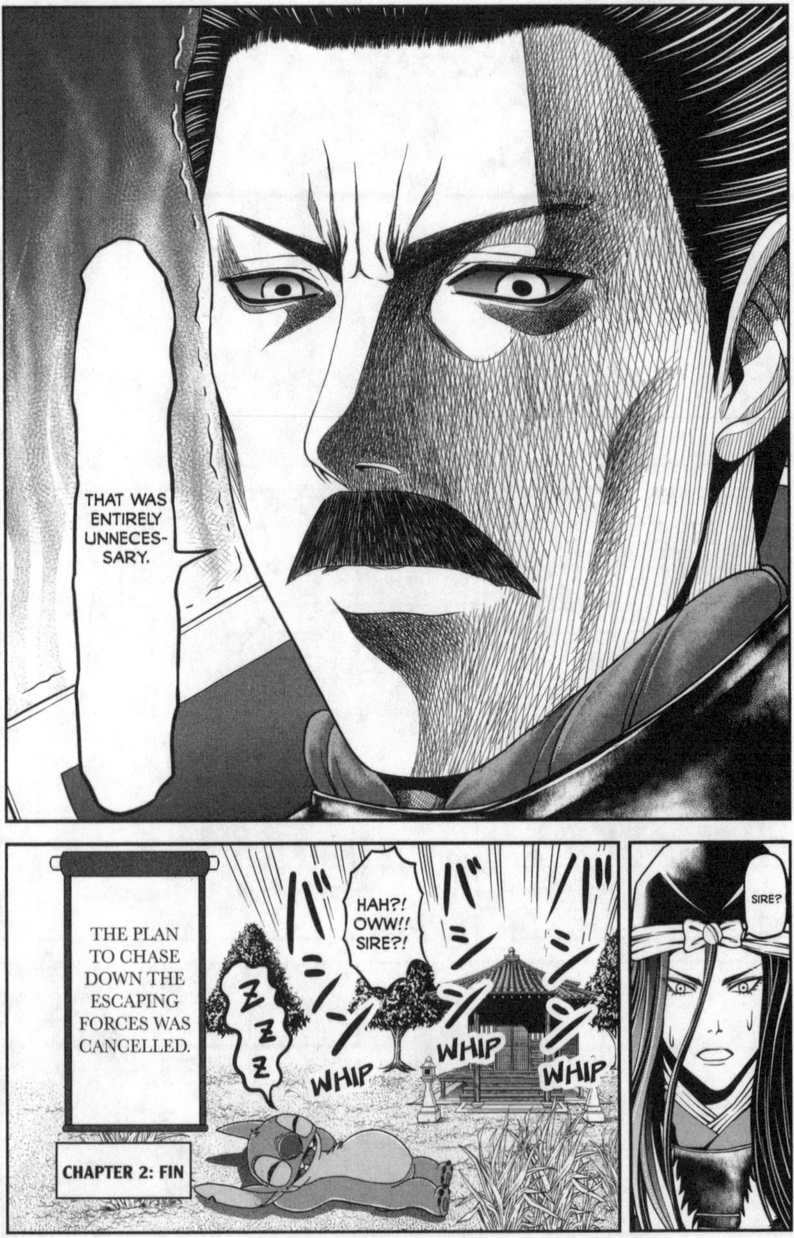
THAT WAS ENTIRELY UNNECES-SARY.
SIRE?
HAH?! OWW!! SIRE?!
WHIP
WHIP
WHIP
Z Z Z
THE PLAN TO CHASE DOWN THE ESCAPING FORCES WAS CANCELLED.
CHAPTER 2: FIN

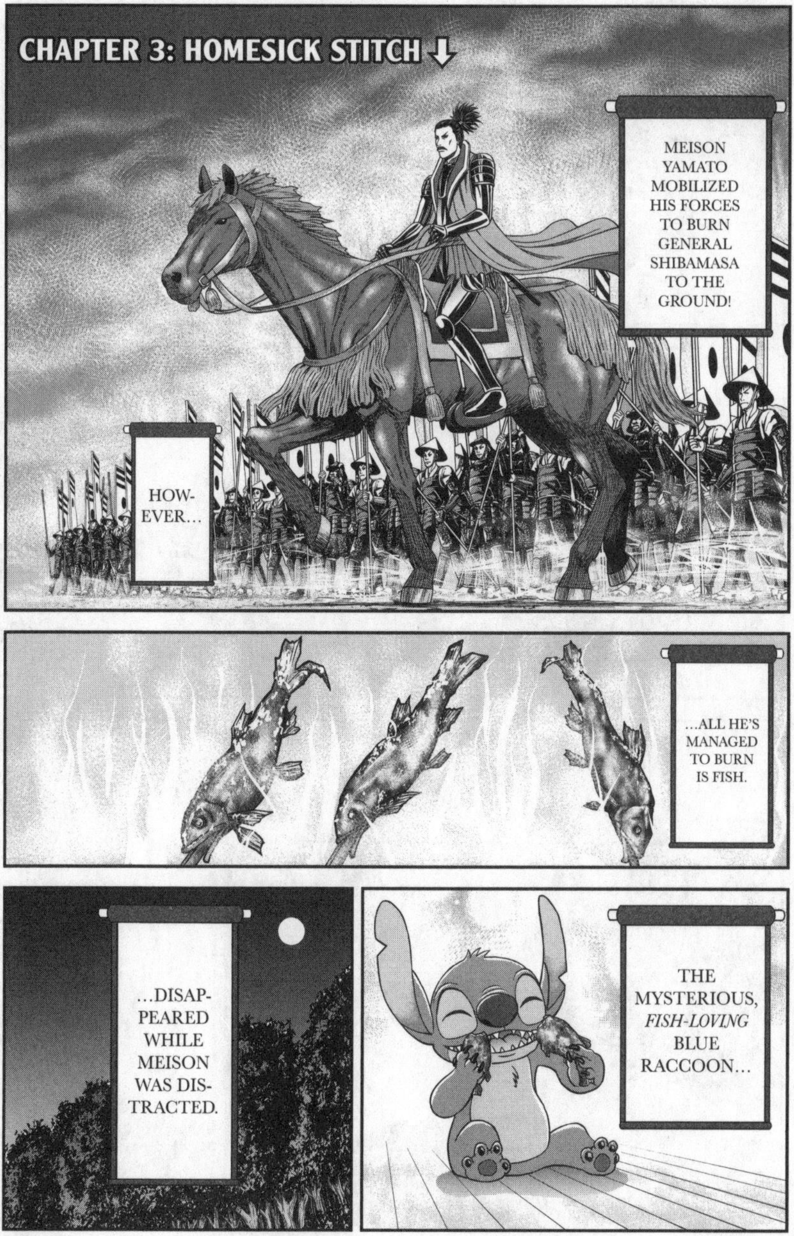
CHAPTER 3: HOMESICK STITCH
MEISON YAMATO MOBILIZED HIS FORCES TO BURN GENERAL SHIBAMASA TO THE GROUND!
HOW-EVER…
…ALL HE'S MANAGED TO BURN IS FISH.
THE MYSTERIOUS, *FISH-LOVING* BLUE RACCOON…
…DISAP-PEARED WHILE MEISON WAS DIS-TRACTED.

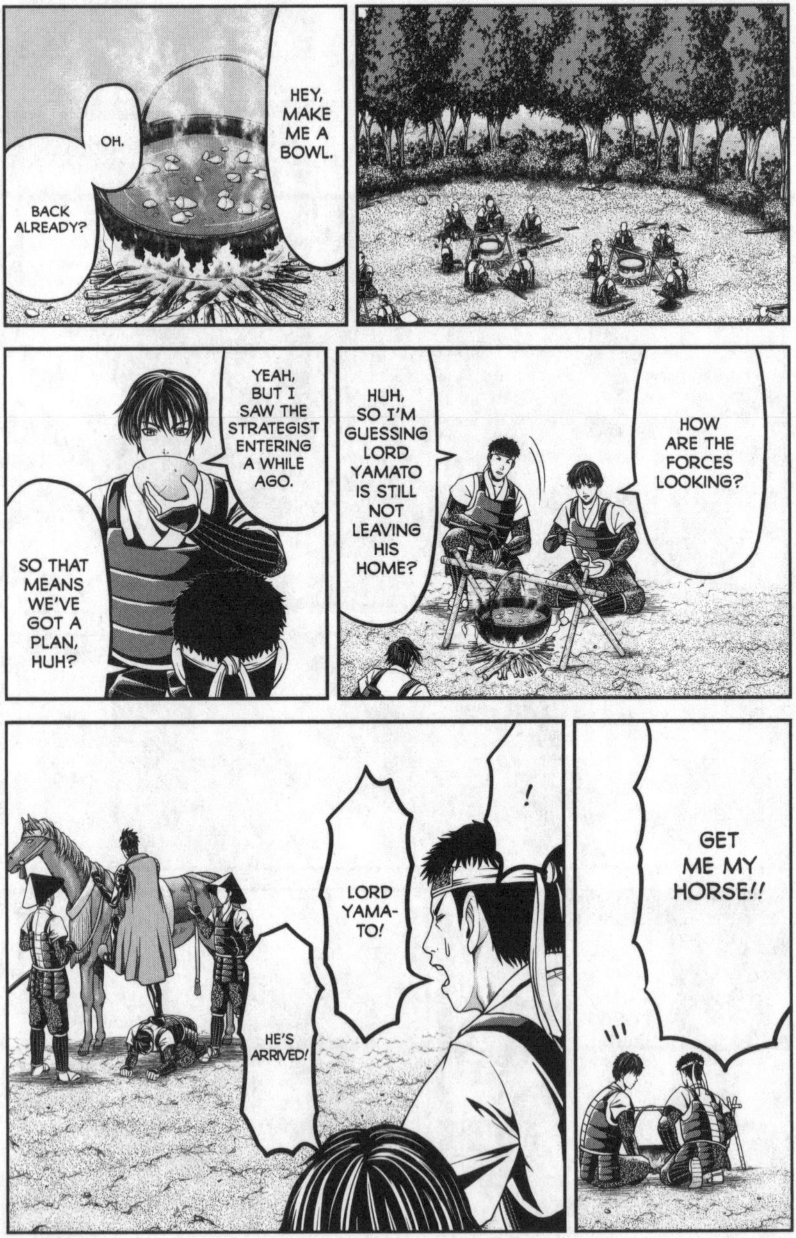
HEY, MAKE ME A BOWL.
OH.
BACK ALREADY?
HOW ARE THE FORCES LOOKING?
HUH, SO I'M GUESSING LORD YAMATO IS STILL NOT LEAVING HIS HOME?
YEAH, BUT I SAW THE STRATEGIST ENTERING A WHILE AGO.
SO THAT MEANS WE'VE GOT A PLAN, HUH?
GET ME MY HORSE!!
!
LORD YAMA-TO!
HE'S ARRIVED!

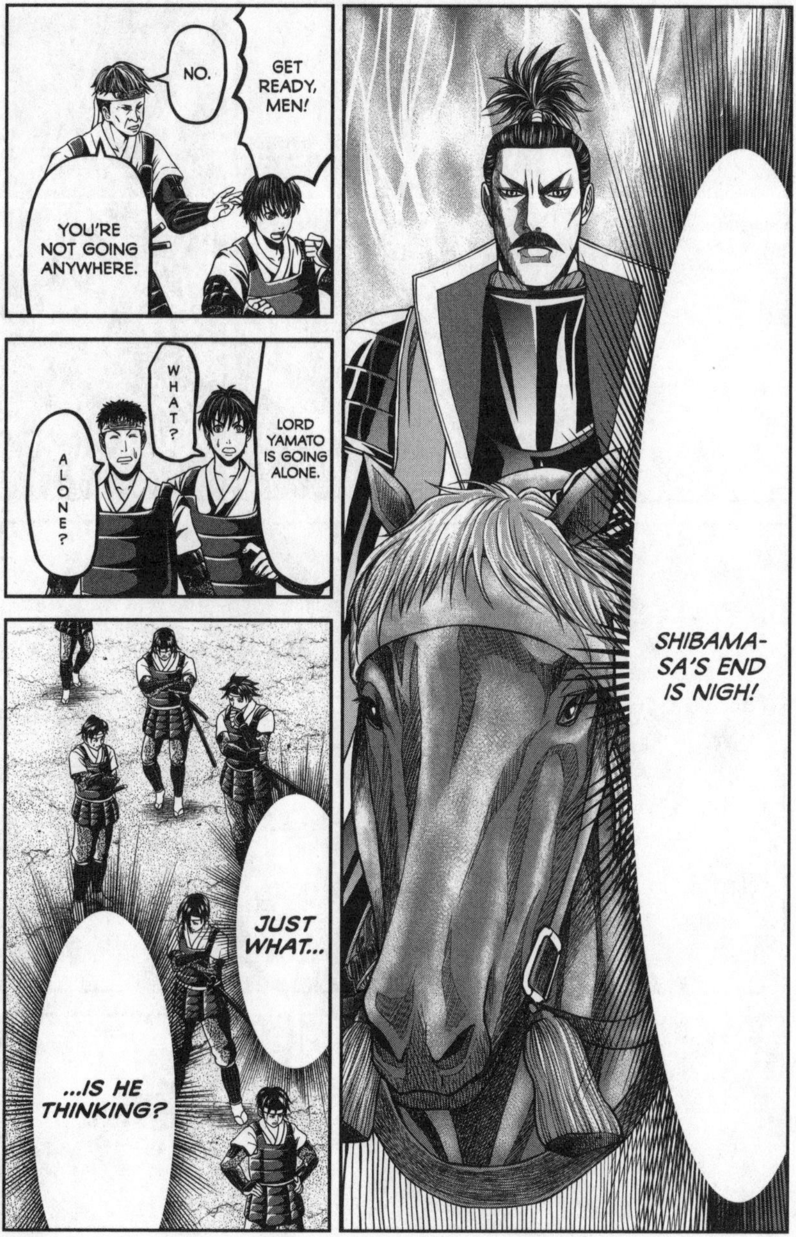
SHIBAMA-SA'S END IS NIGH!
GET READY, MEN!
NO.
YOU'RE NOT GOING ANYWHERE.
LORD YAMATO IS GOING ALONE.
WHAT?
ALONE?
JUST WHAT...
...IS HE THINKING?

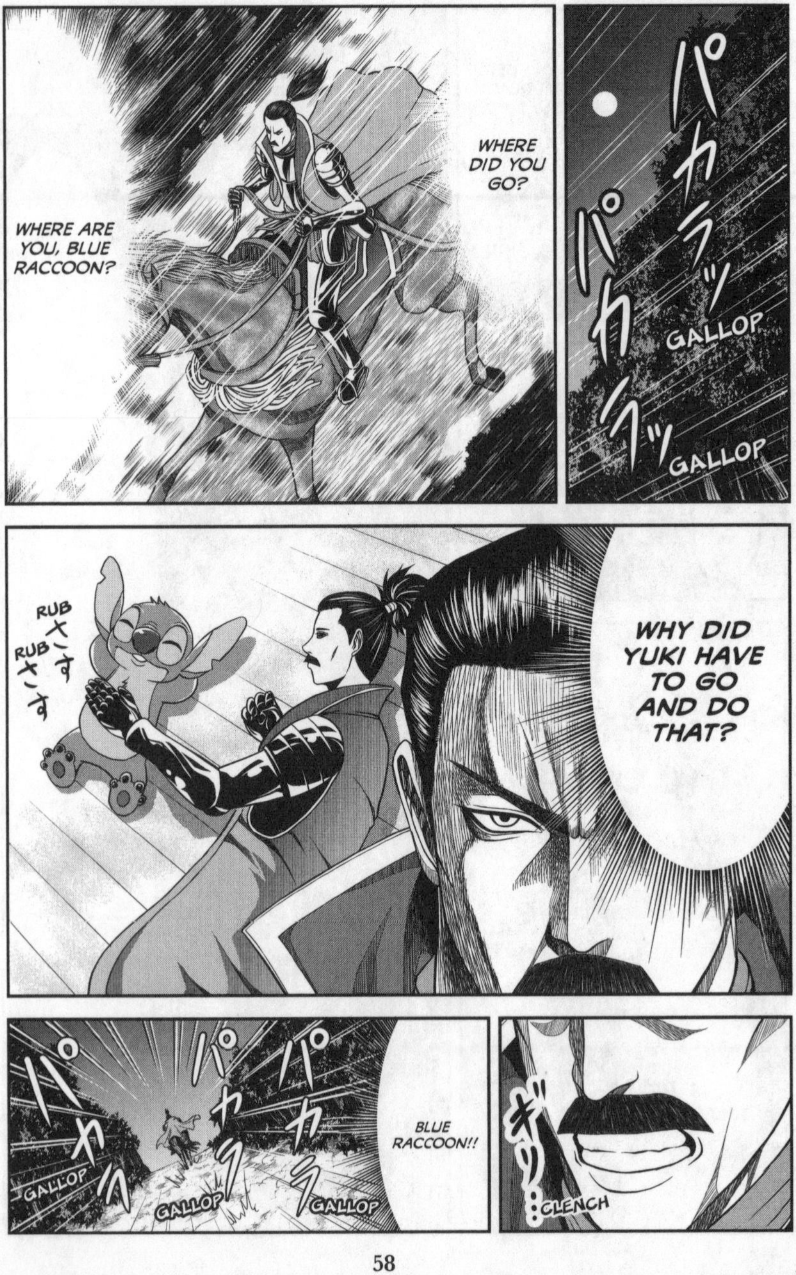

パカラッ
パカラッ
GALLOP
GALLOP
WHERE DID YOU GO?
WHERE ARE YOU, BLUE RACCOON?
WHY DID YUKI HAVE TO GO AND DO THAT?
RUB さす
RUB さす
ぎり…
CLENCH
BLUE RACCOON!!
パカラ
GALLOP
パカラ
GALLOP
GALLOP

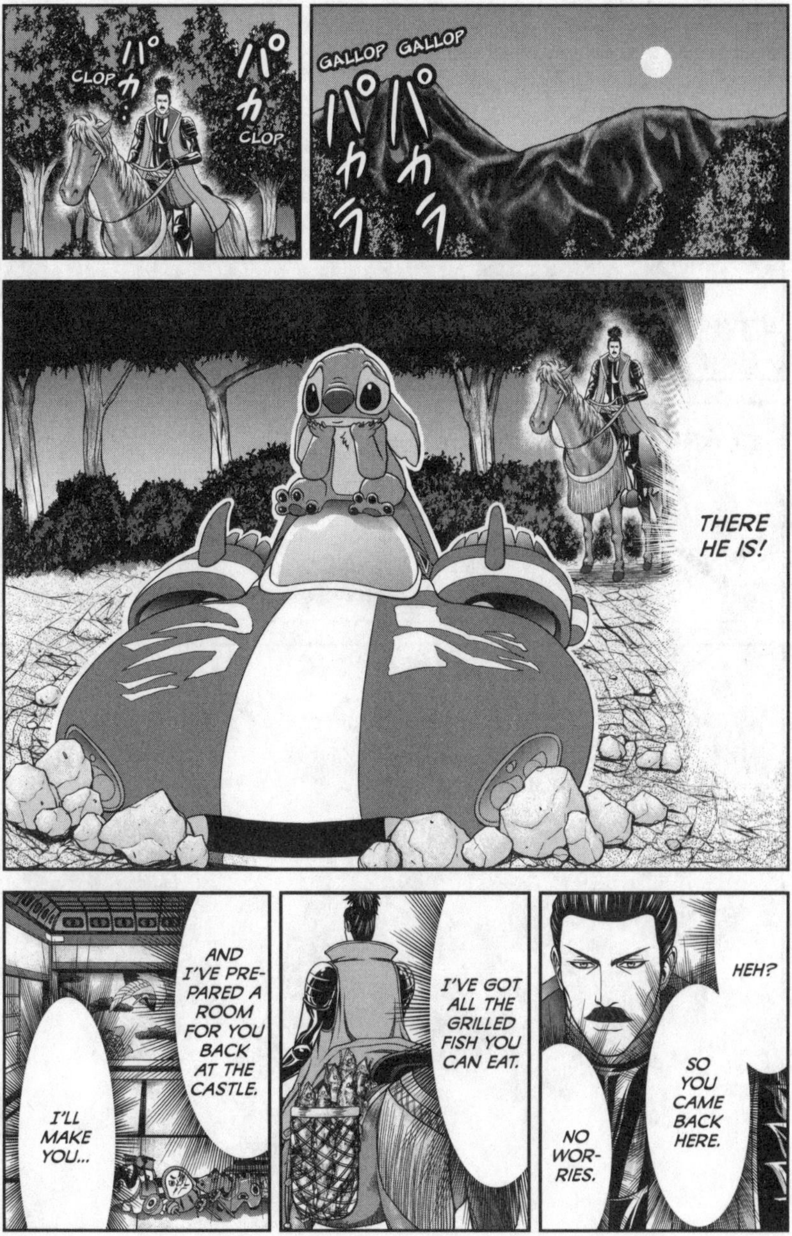
GALLOP GALLOP
パカラ
パカラ
パカ
CLOP
パカ
CLOP
THERE HE IS!
HEH?
SO YOU CAME BACK HERE.
NO WORRIES.
I'VE GOT ALL THE GRILLED FISH YOU CAN EAT.
AND I'VE PREPARED A ROOM FOR YOU BACK AT THE CASTLE.
I'LL MAKE YOU...

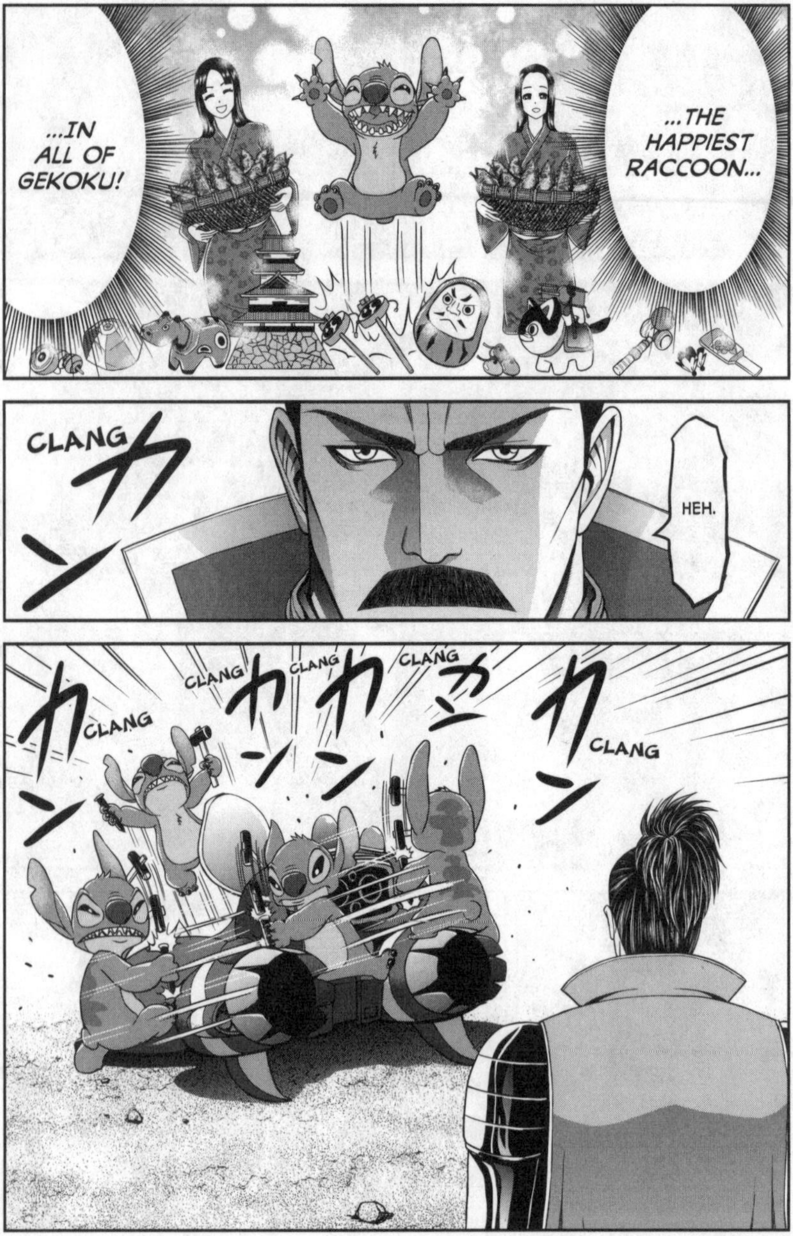
...THE HAPPIEST RACCOON...
...IN ALL OF GEKOKU!
HEH.
CLANG
CLANG
CLANG
CLANG
CLANG
CLANG

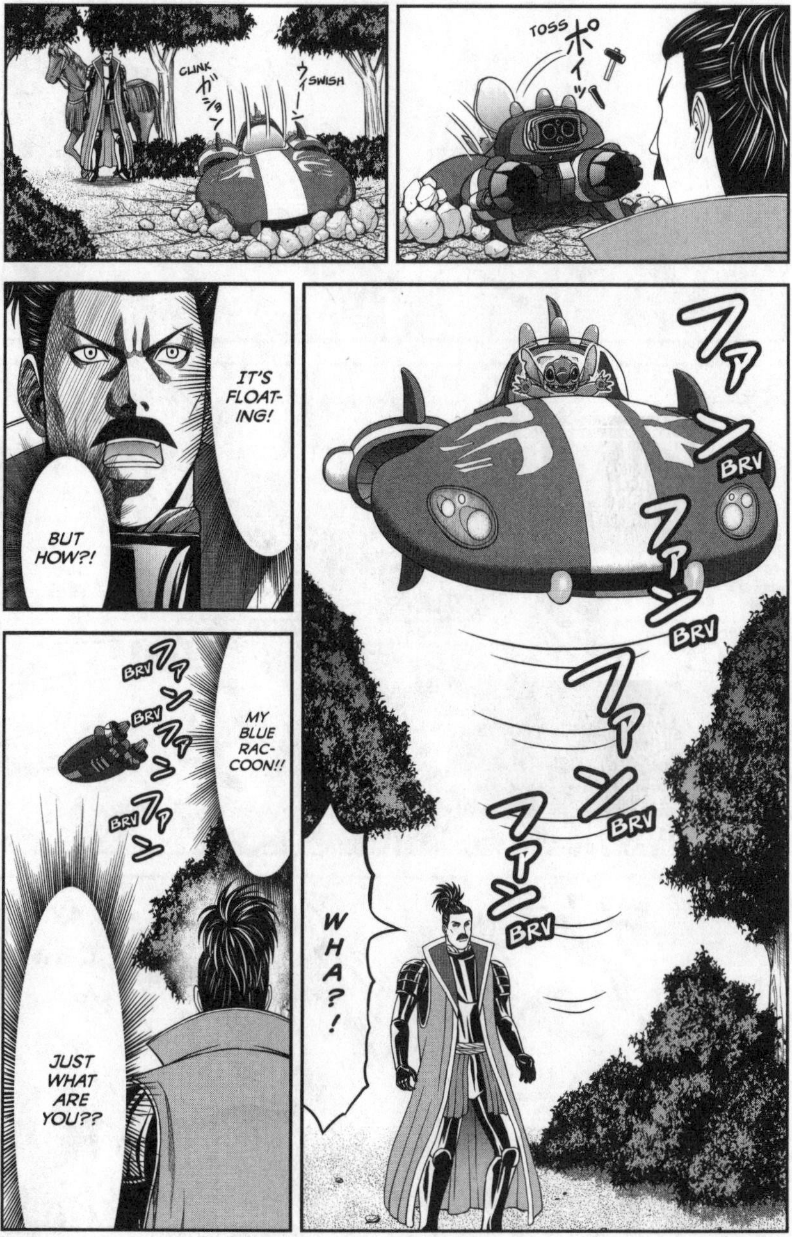
TOSS
ポイッ
CLUNK
ガション
ウィーン
SWISH
ファン
BRV
ファン
BRV
ファン
BRV
ファン
BRV
WHA?!
IT'S FLOATING!
BUT HOW?!
BRV
ファン
BRV
ファン
BRV
ファン
MY BLUE RACCOON!!
JUST WHAT ARE YOU??

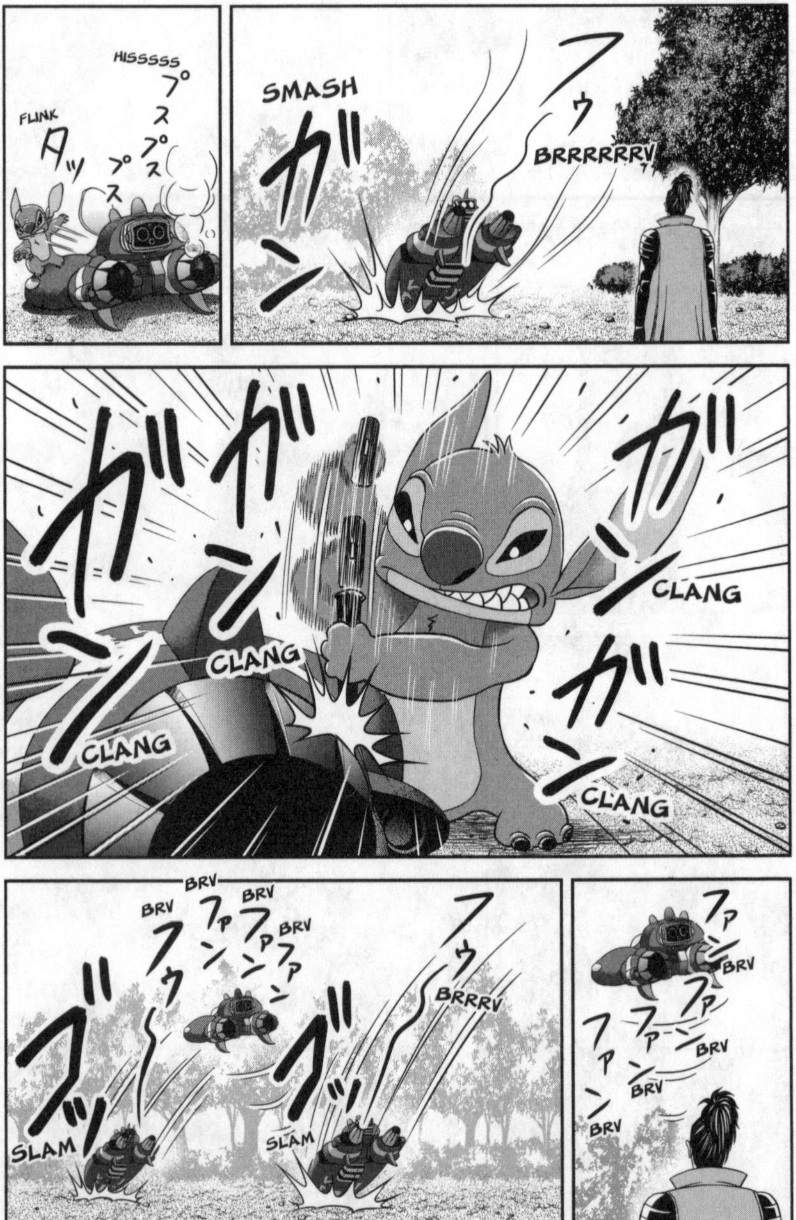
フゥ
BRRRRRRV
ガン
SMASH
HISSSSS
プスプスプス
FLINK
タッ
ガン
CLANG
ガン
CLANG
ガン
CLANG
ガン
CLANG
ファン
BRV
ファン
BRV
ファン
BRV
ファン
BRV
フゥ
BRRRV
ブッ
SLAM
ファン
BRV
ファン
BRV
ファン
BRV
ファン
BRV
フゥ
ブッ
SLAM

プス プス プス プス
HISS HISS HISS HISS

HOP ポッ

FLINK カッ

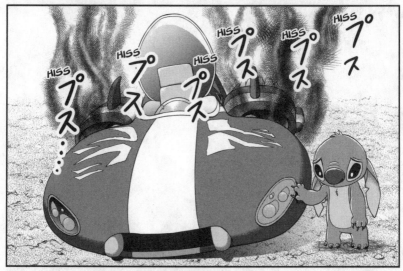

HISS プス...
HISS プス
HISS プス
HISS プス
HISS プス
HISS プス

SLUMP コロン

YOU POOR THING.

63

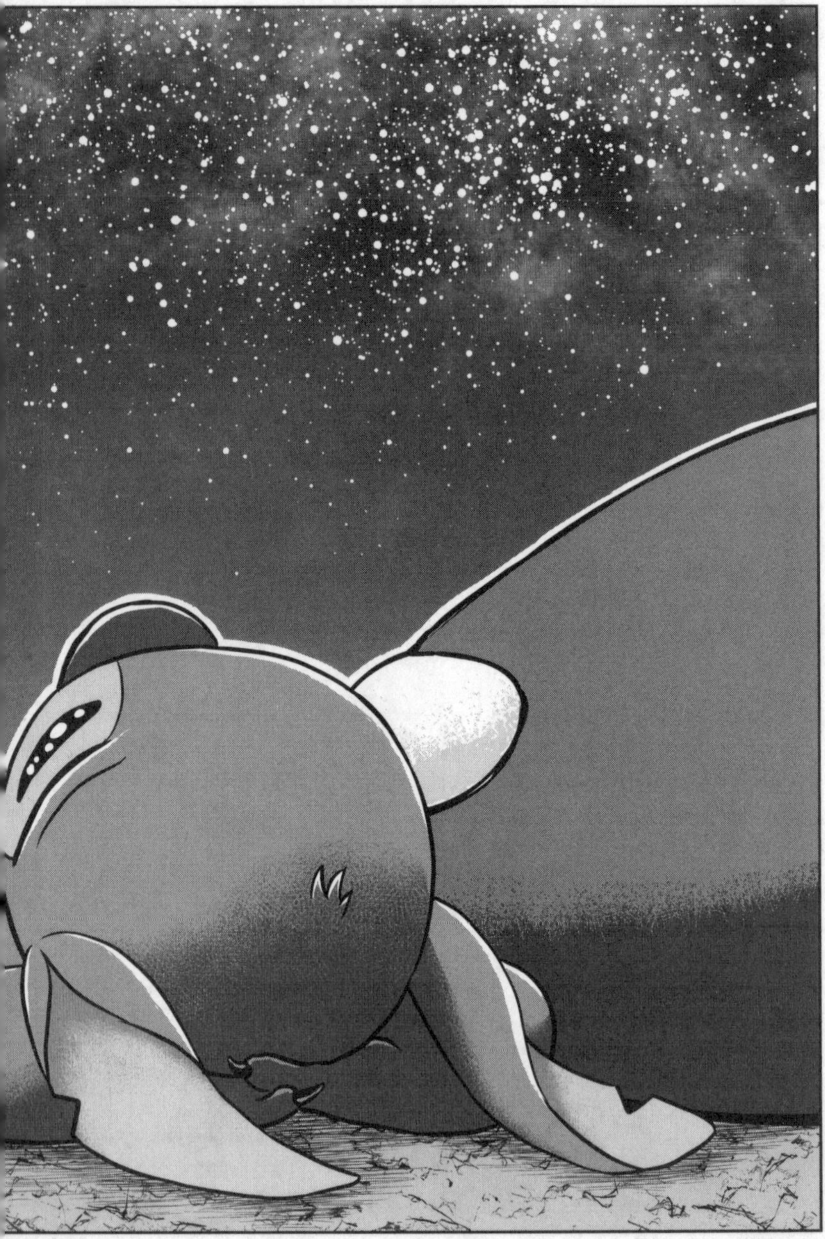

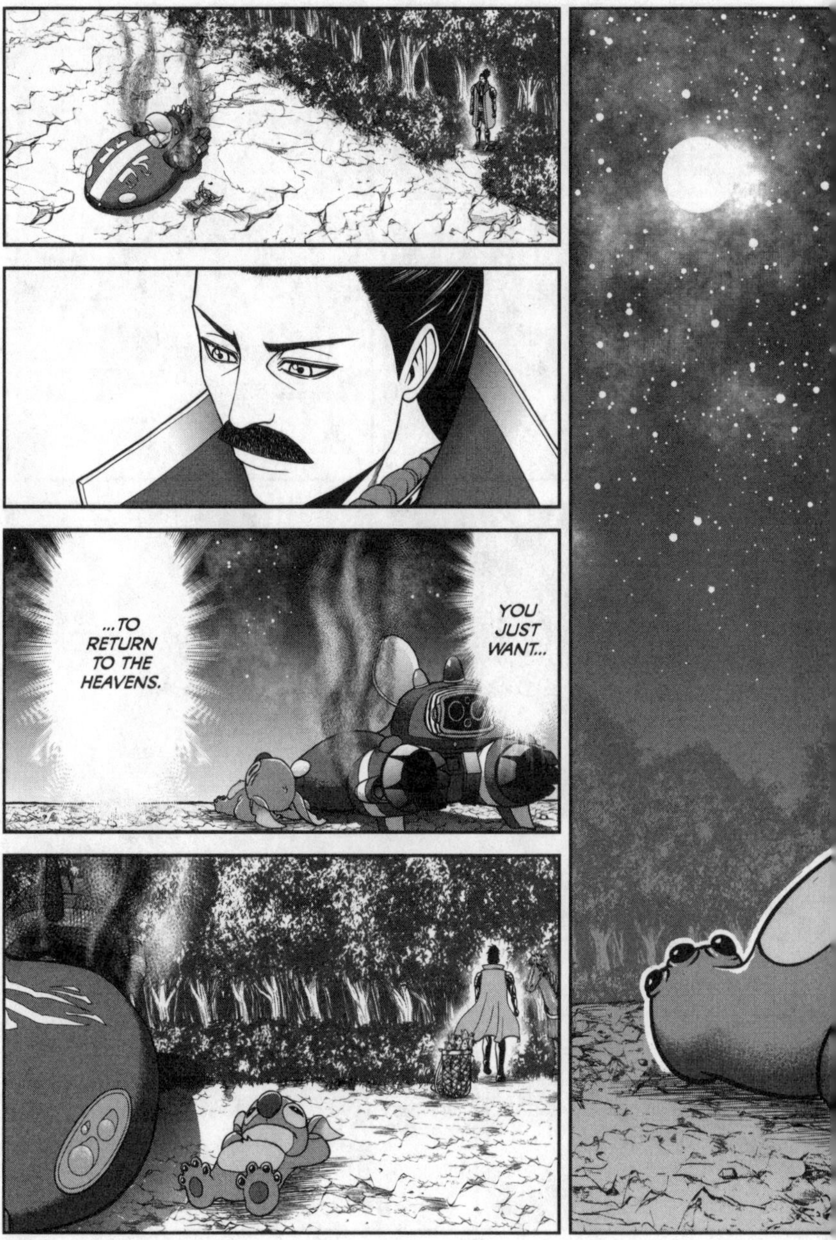
YOU JUST WANT...
...TO RETURN TO THE HEAVENS.

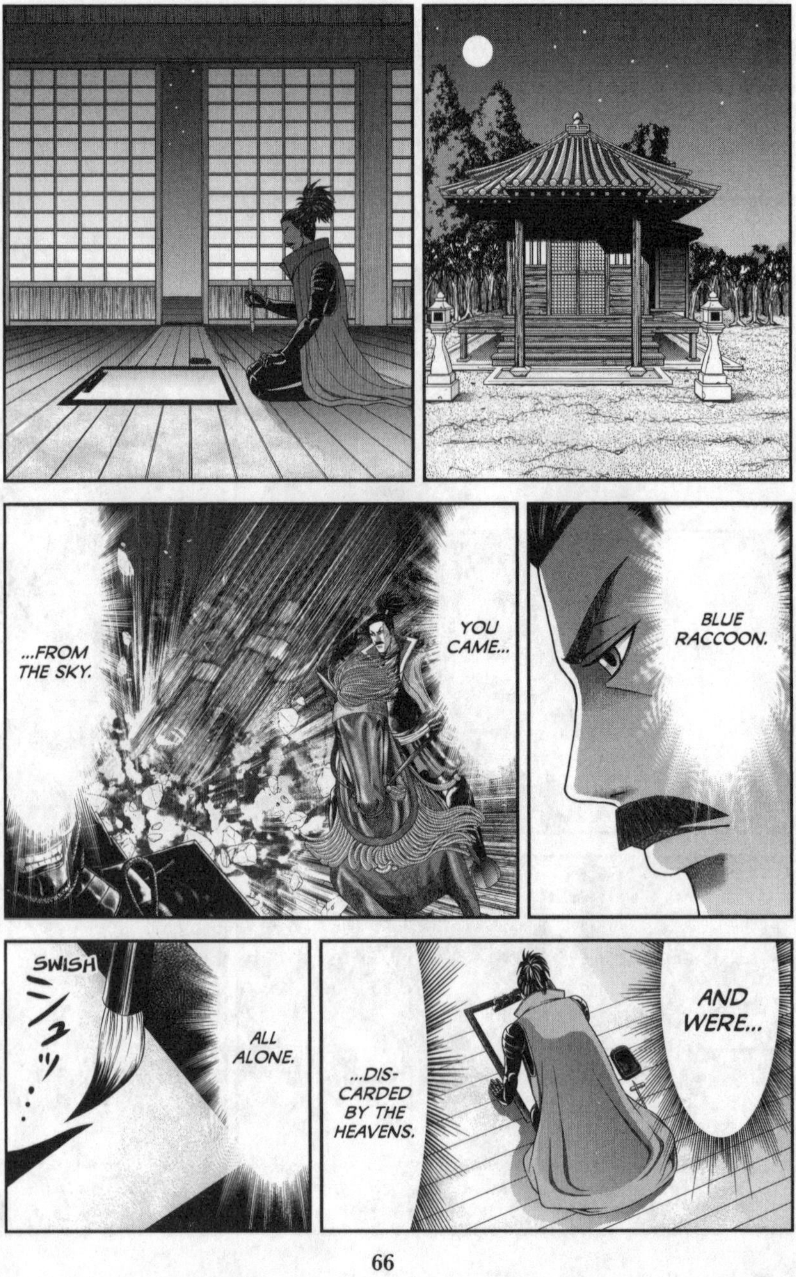
BLUE RACCOON.
YOU CAME...
...FROM THE SKY.
AND WERE...
...DIS-CARDED BY THE HEAVENS.
SWISH
ALL ALONE.

* THE KANJI HERE READS "DISCARDED ONE" (I.E., THE ONE WHO HAS BEEN DISCARDED) AND CAN ALSO BE READ AS "SUTE ICHI," OR AN APPROXIMATION OF "STITCH." ESSENTIALLY, MEISON IS USING WORDPLAY TO GIVE STITCH HIS NAME.

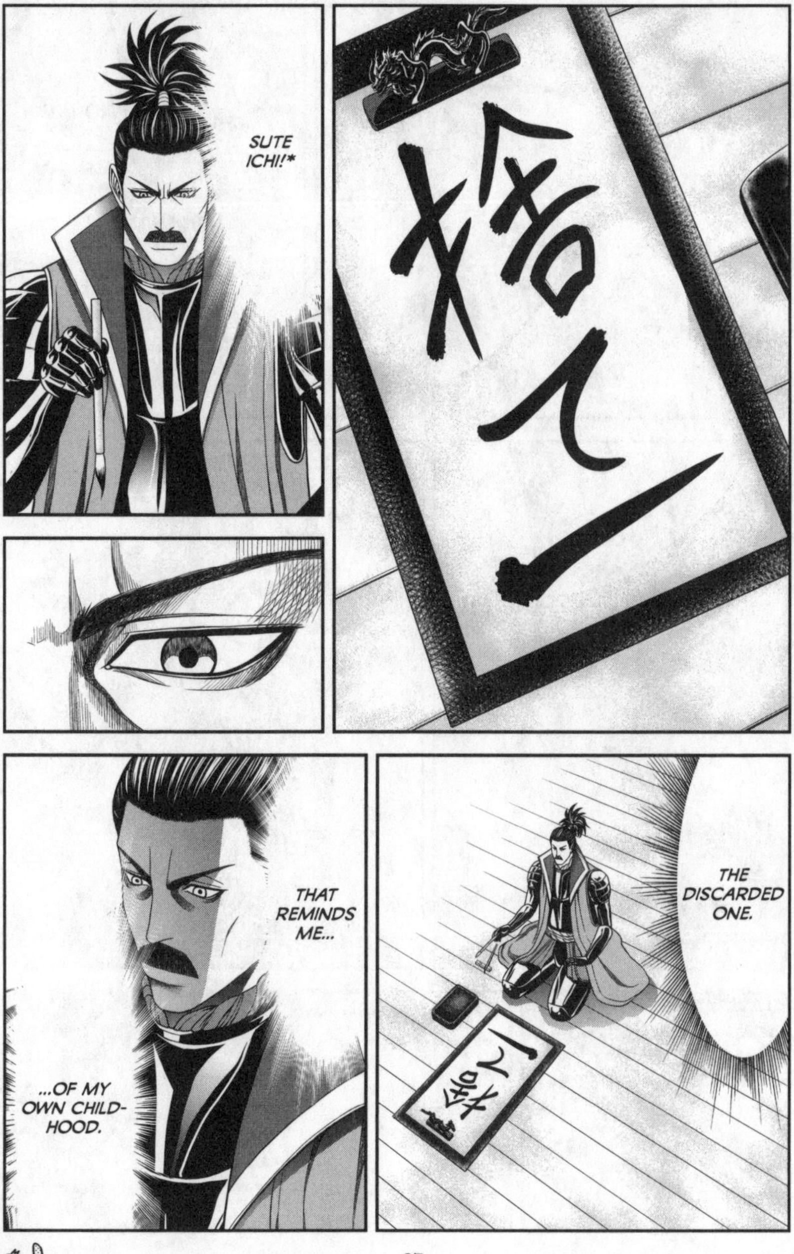
SUTE ICHI!*
THE DISCARDED ONE.
THAT REMINDS ME...
...OF MY OWN CHILD-HOOD.

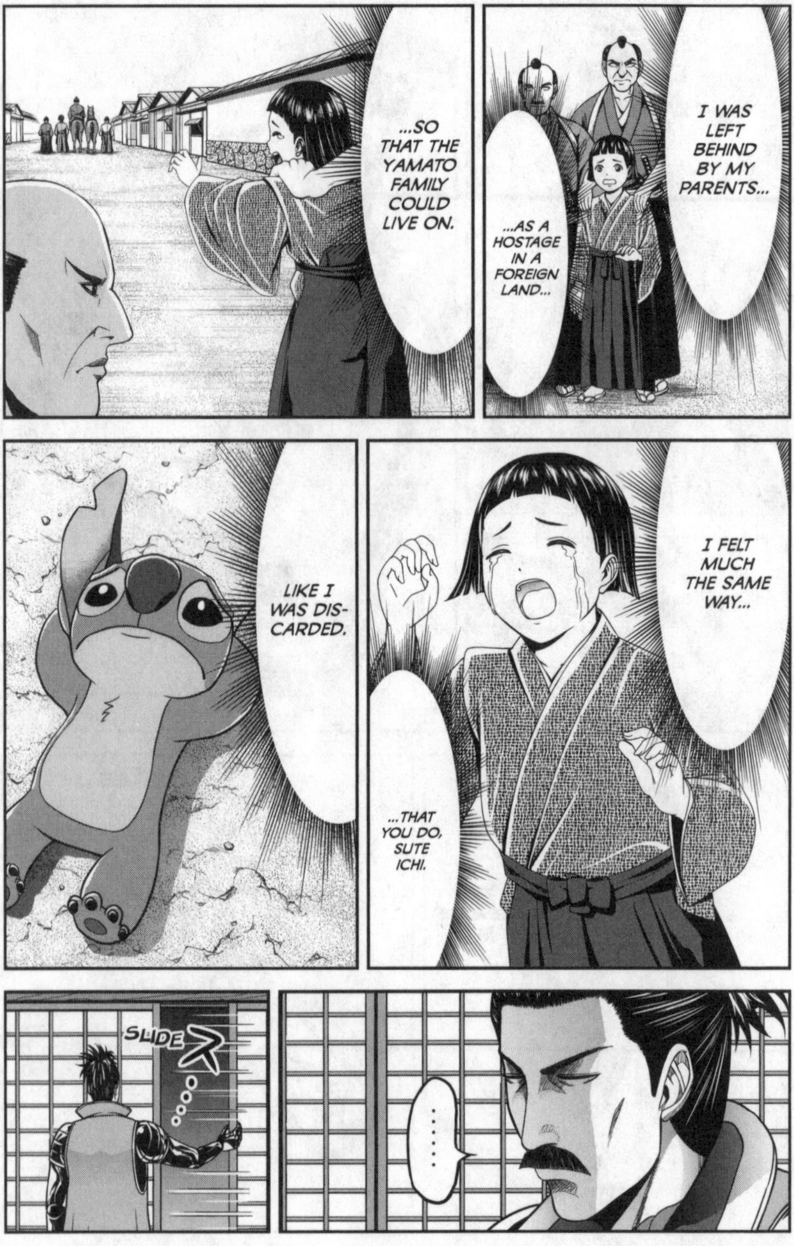
I WAS LEFT BEHIND BY MY PARENTS...
...AS A HOSTAGE IN A FOREIGN LAND...
...SO THAT THE YAMATO FAMILY COULD LIVE ON.
I FELT MUCH THE SAME WAY...
...THAT YOU DO, SUTE ICHI.
LIKE I WAS DIS-CARDED.
......
SLIDE

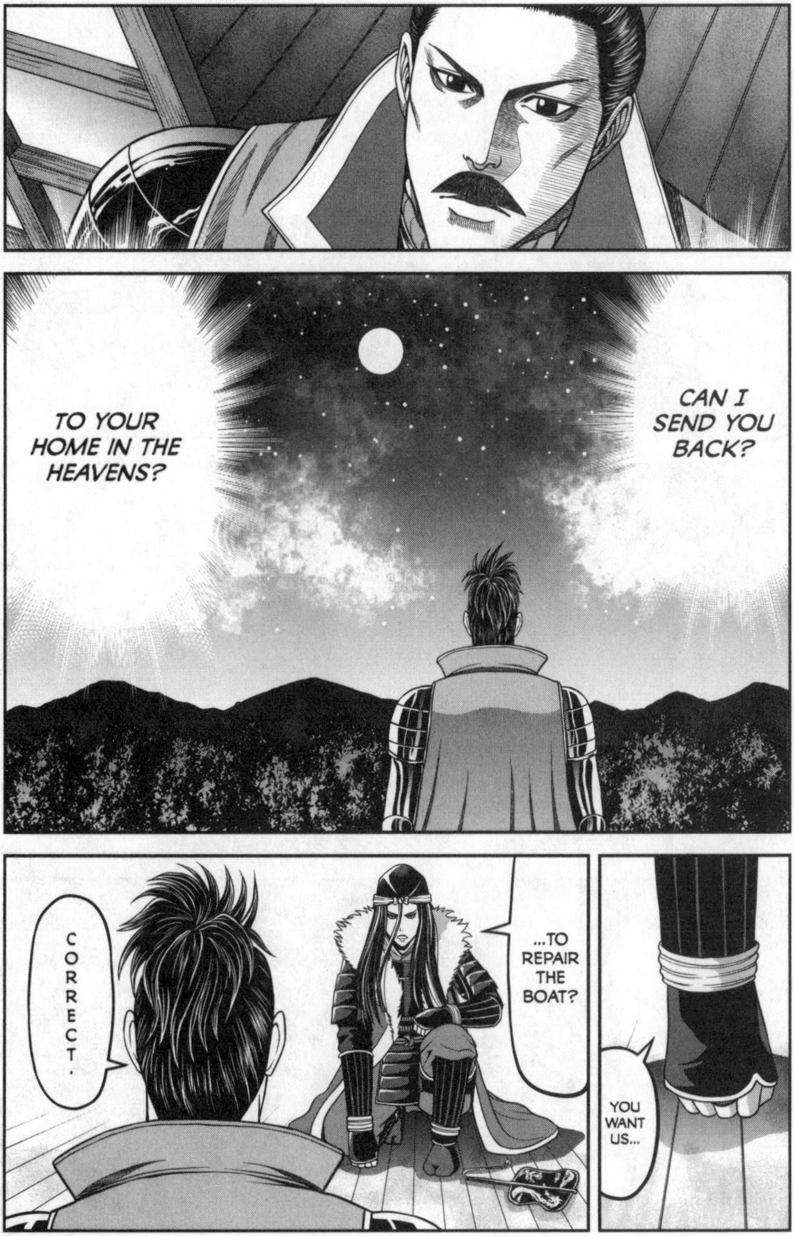
CAN I SEND YOU BACK?
TO YOUR HOME IN THE HEAVENS?
YOU WANT US...
...TO REPAIR THE BOAT?
CORRECT.

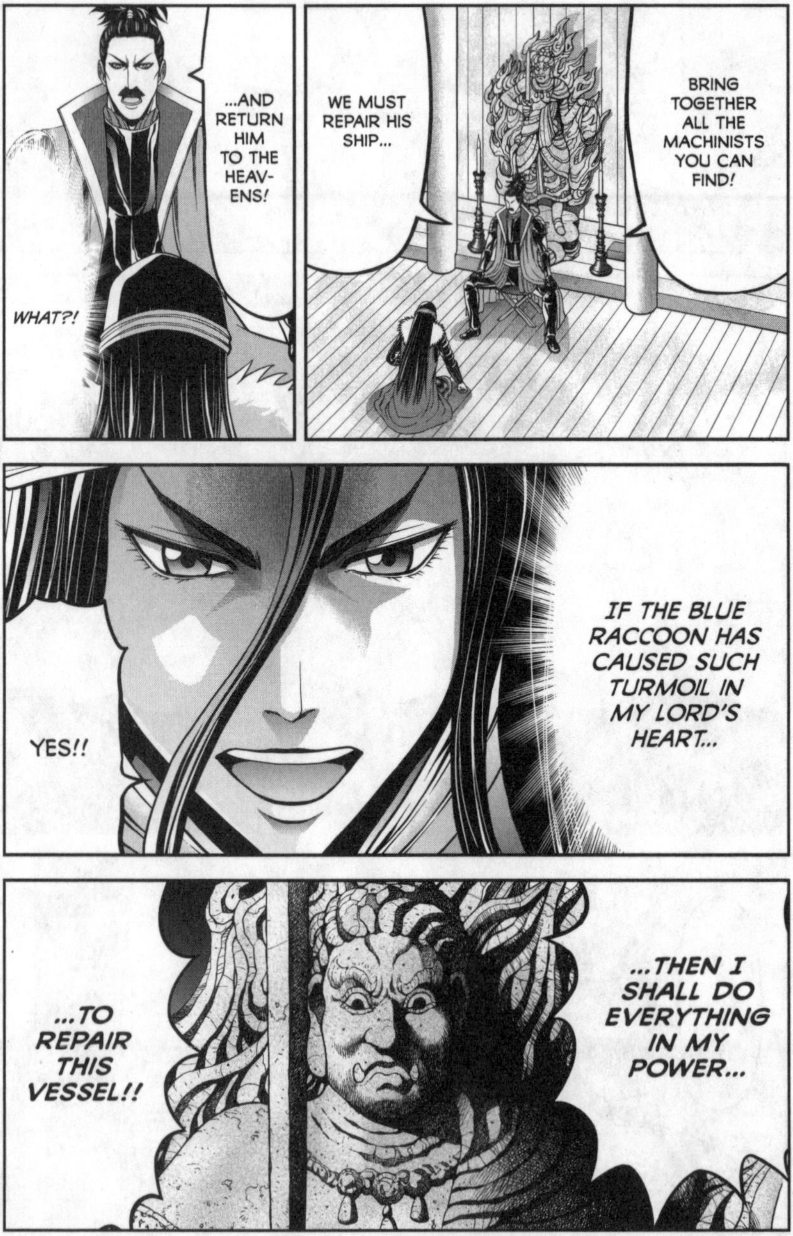
BRING TOGETHER ALL THE MACHINISTS YOU CAN FIND!
WE MUST REPAIR HIS SHIP...
...AND RETURN HIM TO THE HEAV-ENS!
WHAT?!
IF THE BLUE RACCOON HAS CAUSED SUCH TURMOIL IN MY LORD'S HEART...
YES!!
...THEN I SHALL DO EVERYTHING IN MY POWER...
...TO REPAIR THIS VESSEL!!

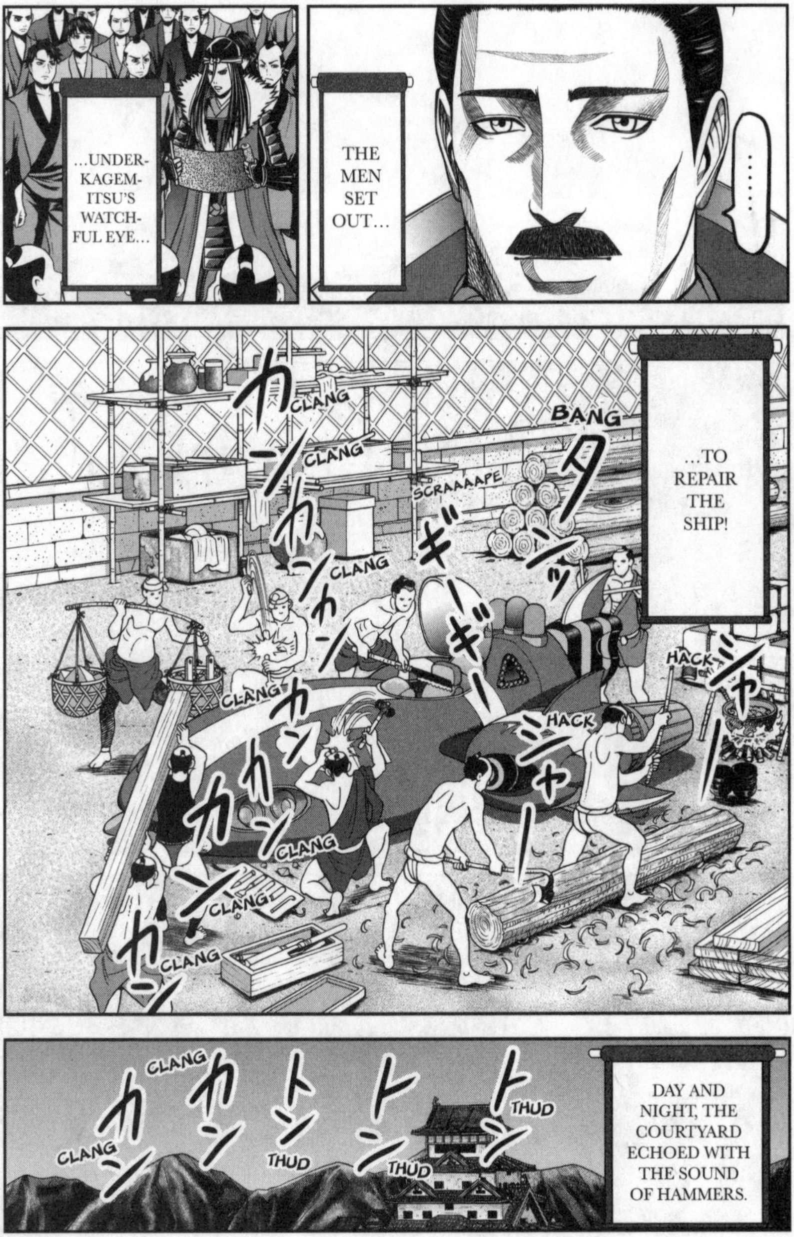
......
THE MEN SET OUT...
...UNDER-KAGEMITSU'S WATCHFUL EYE...
...TO REPAIR THE SHIP!
BANG
SCRAAAAPE
CLANG
CLANG
CLANG
HACK
HACK
CLANG
CLANG
CLANG
CLANG
DAY AND NIGHT, THE COURTYARD ECHOED WITH THE SOUND OF HAMMERS.
THUD
THUD
THUD
CLANG
CLANG

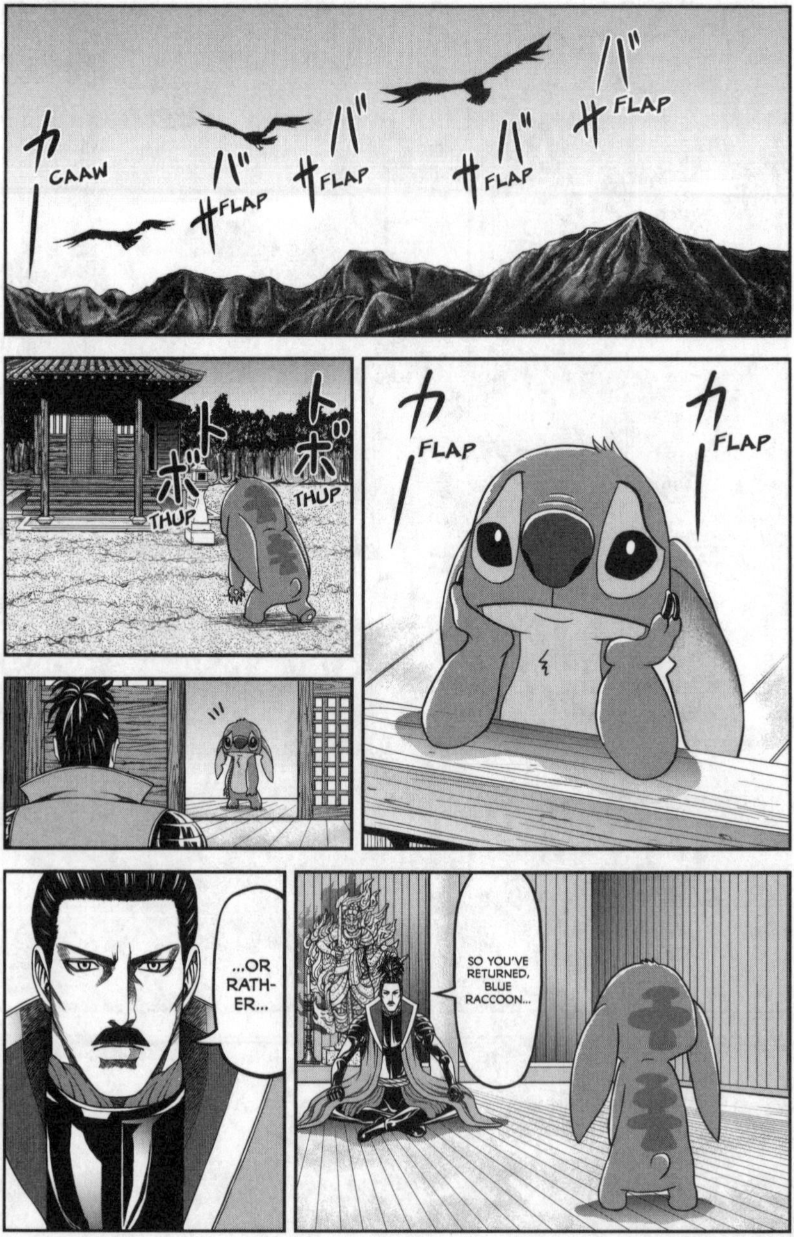

バサ FLAP
バサ FLAP
バサ FLAP
バサ FLAP
カー CAAW
カー FLAP
カー FLAP
トボ THUP
トボ THUP
SO YOU'VE RETURNED, BLUE RACCOON...
...OR RATHER...

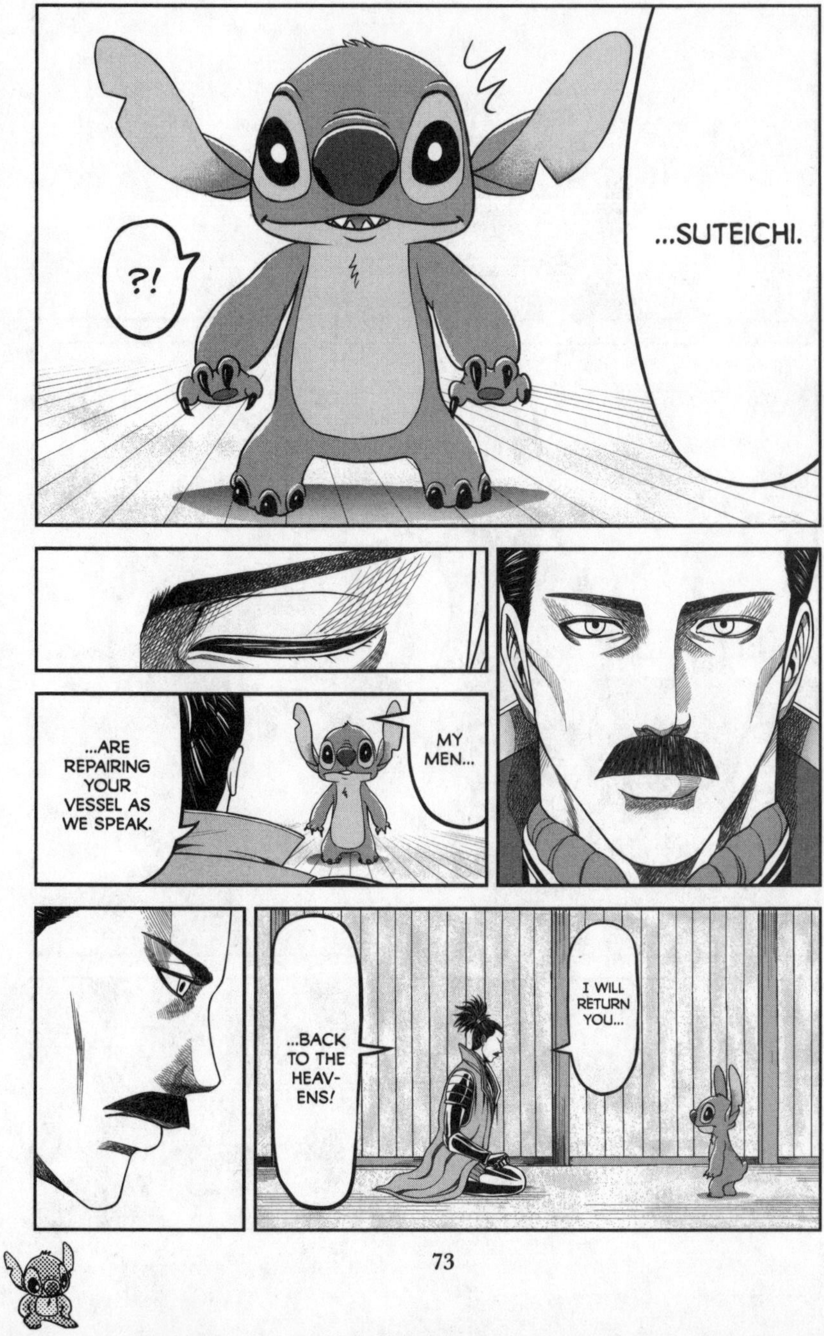
...SUTEICHI.
?!
MY MEN...
...ARE REPAIRING YOUR VESSEL AS WE SPEAK.
I WILL RETURN YOU...
...BACK TO THE HEAV- ENS!

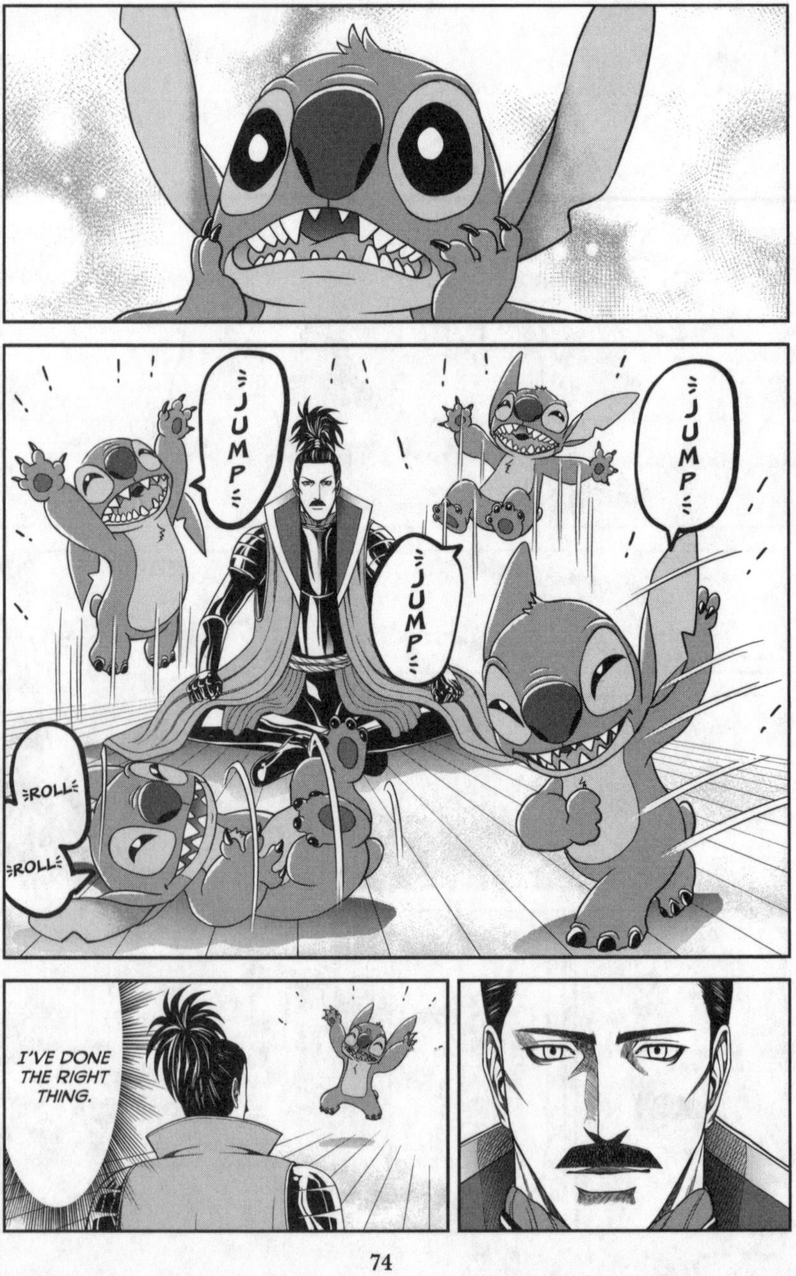
JUMP
JUMP
JUMP
ROLL
ROLL
I'VE DONE THE RIGHT THING.

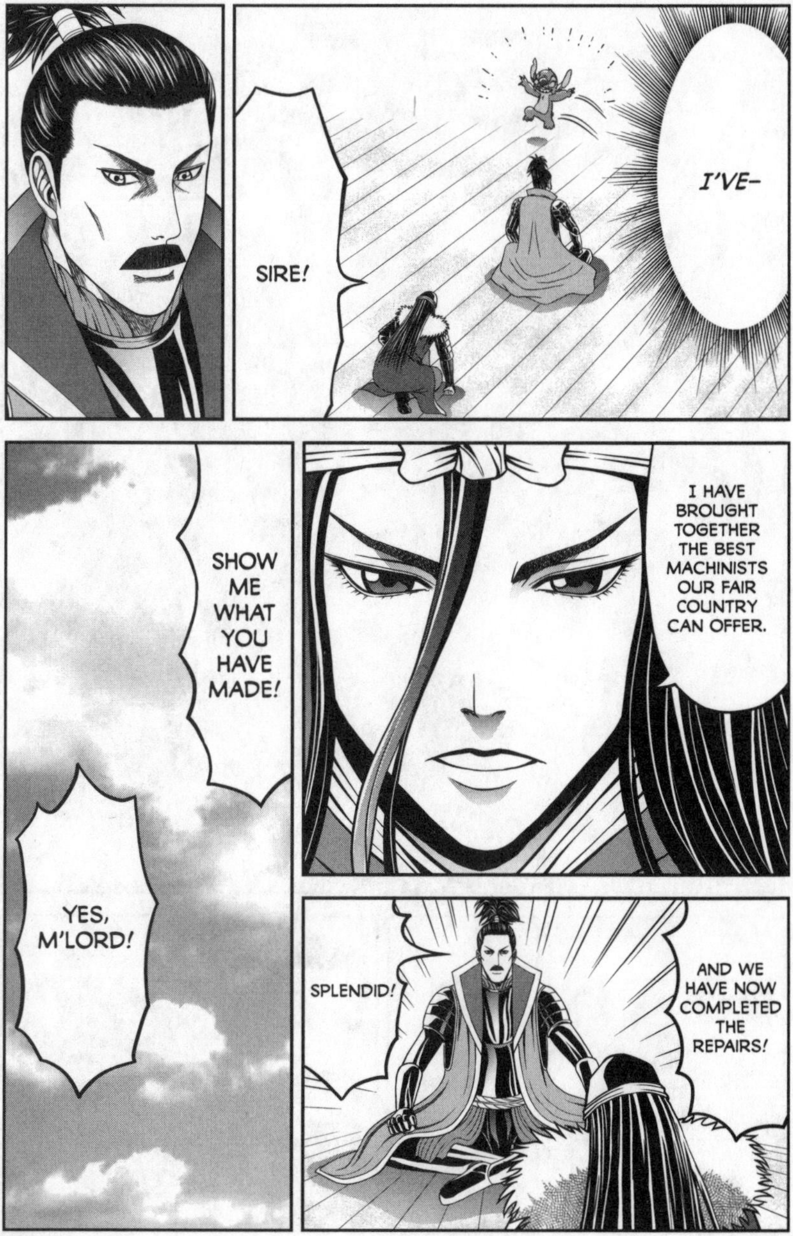
I'VE–
SIRE!
I HAVE BROUGHT TOGETHER THE BEST MACHINISTS OUR FAIR COUNTRY CAN OFFER.
AND WE HAVE NOW COMPLETED THE REPAIRS!
SPLENDID!
SHOW ME WHAT YOU HAVE MADE!
YES, M'LORD!

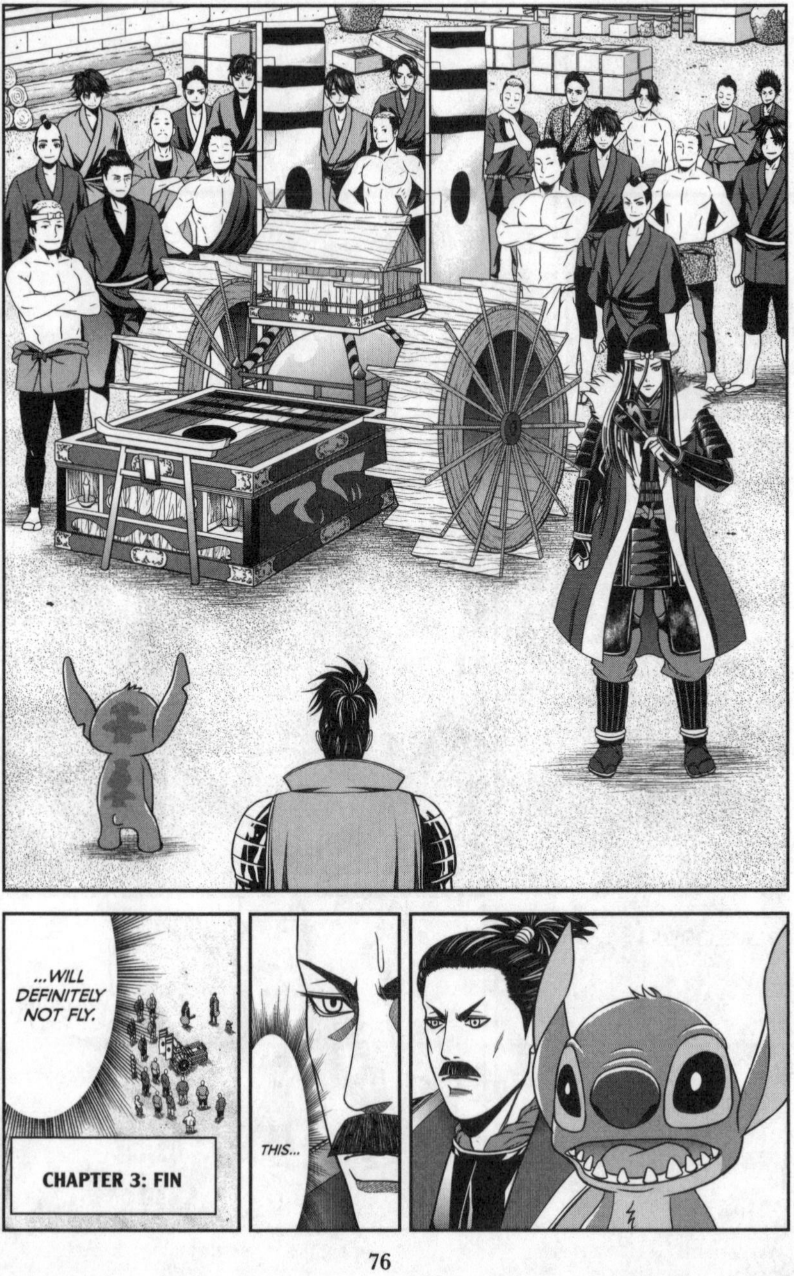
THIS...
...WILL DEFINITELY NOT FLY.
CHAPTER 3: FIN

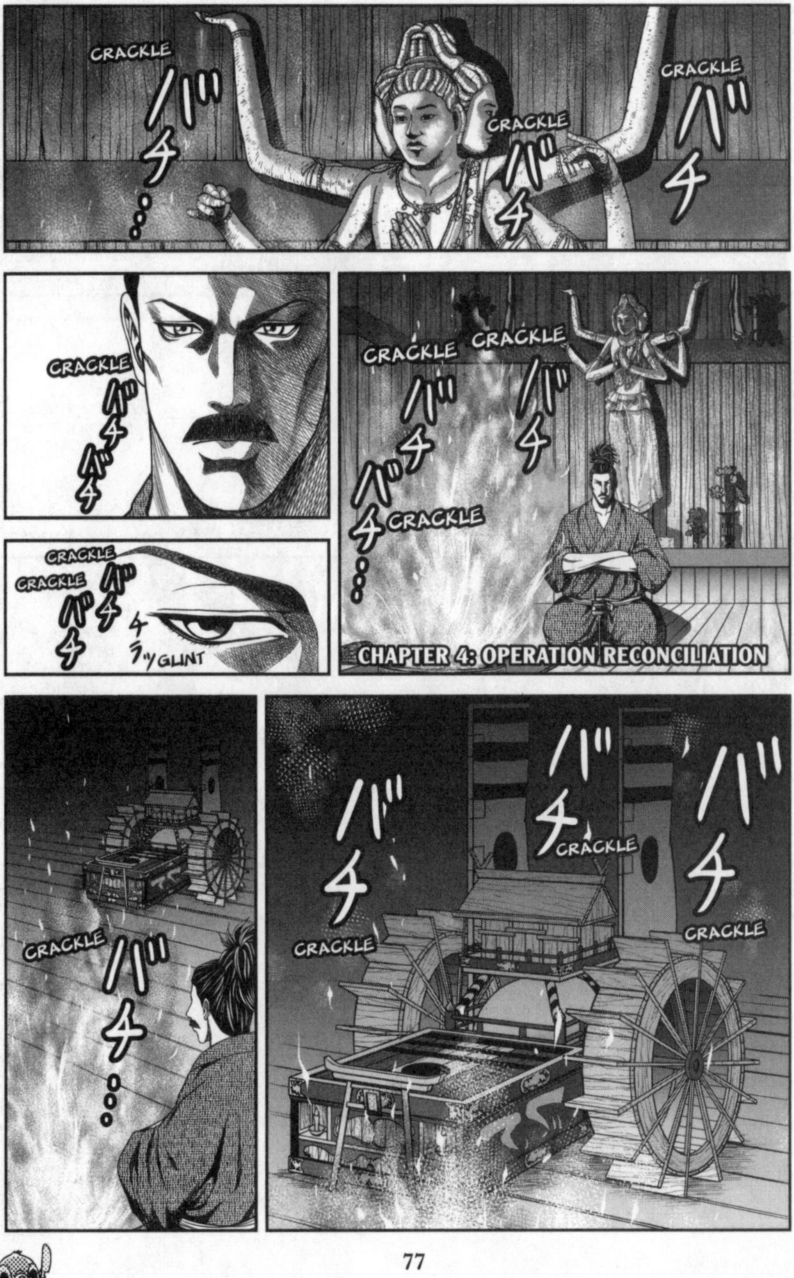
CRACKLE
バチ…
CRACKLE
バチ
CRACKLE
バチ
CRACKLE
CRACKLE
バチ
バチ
CRACKLE
バチ
バチ…
CRACKLE
CHAPTER 4: OPERATION RECONCILIATION
CRACKLE
バチ
バチ
CRACKLE
CRACKLE
バチ
バチ
チラッ GLINT
バチ
CRACKLE
バチ
CRACKLE
バチ
CRACKLE
CRACKLE
バチ…

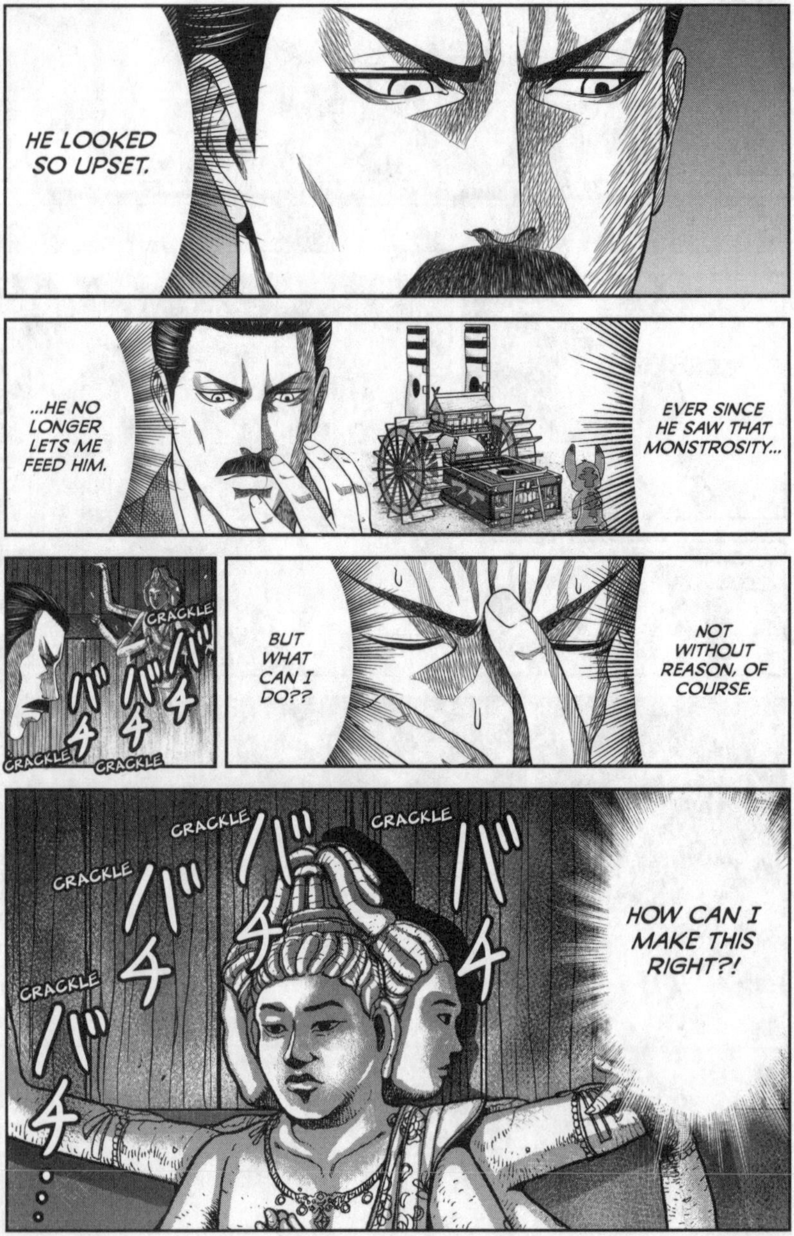
HE LOOKED SO UPSET.
EVER SINCE HE SAW THAT MONSTROSITY...
...HE NO LONGER LETS ME FEED HIM.
NOT WITHOUT REASON, OF COURSE.
BUT WHAT CAN I DO??
CRACKLE
バチ
バチ
バチ
CRACKLE
CRACKLE
CRACKLE
バチ
CRACKLE
バチ
CRACKLE
バチ
CRACKLE
バチ
HOW CAN I MAKE THIS RIGHT?!

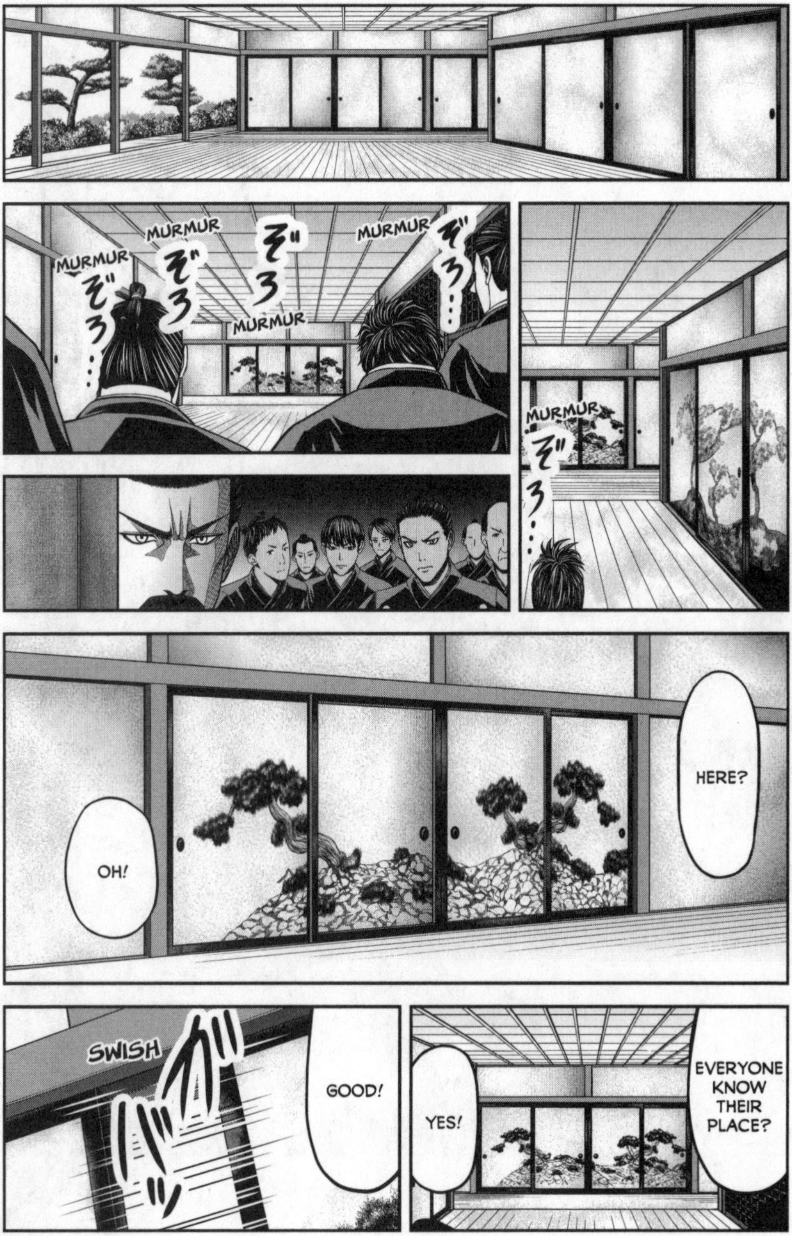
MURMUR
ぞろ…
ぞろ…
MURMUR
ぞろ
MURMUR
MURMUR
ぞろ
MURMUR
ぞろ…
HERE?
OH!
EVERYONE KNOW THEIR PLACE?
YES!
GOOD!
SWISH

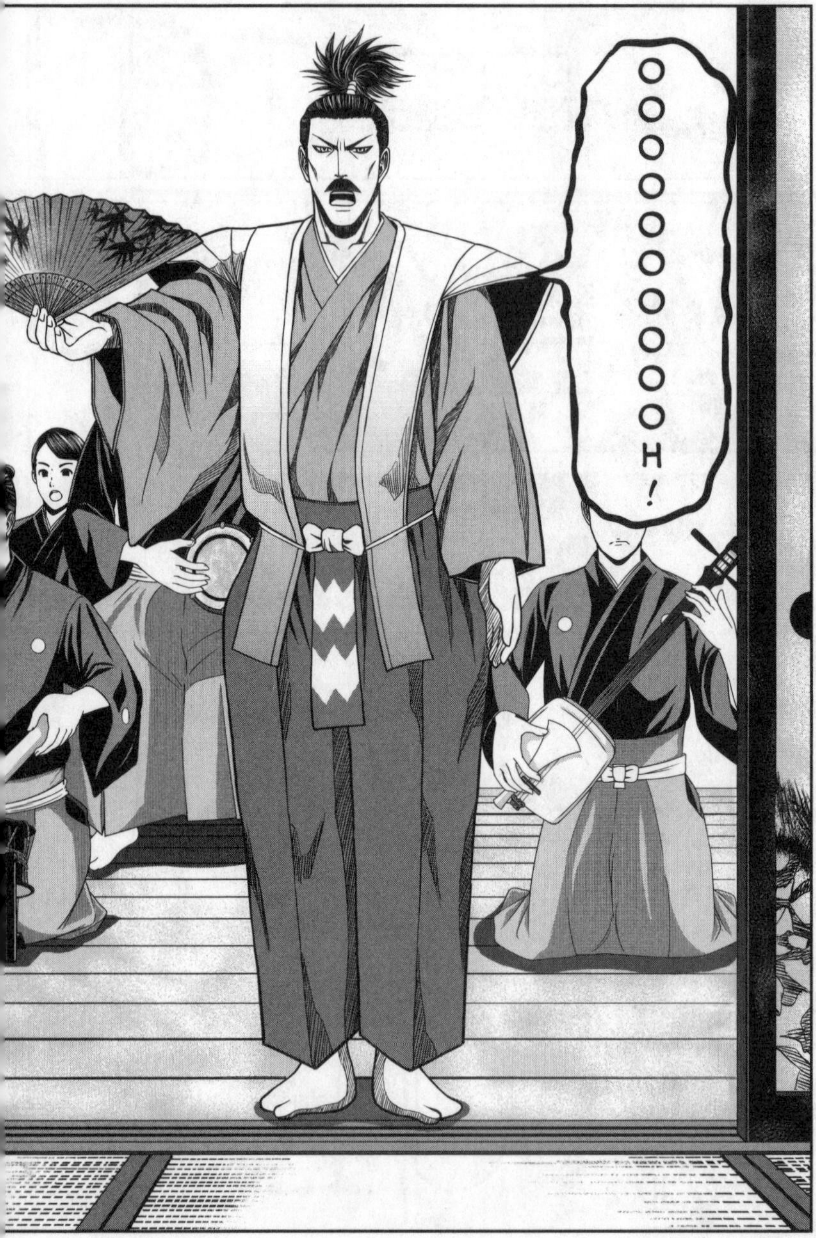
OOOOOOOOOOH!

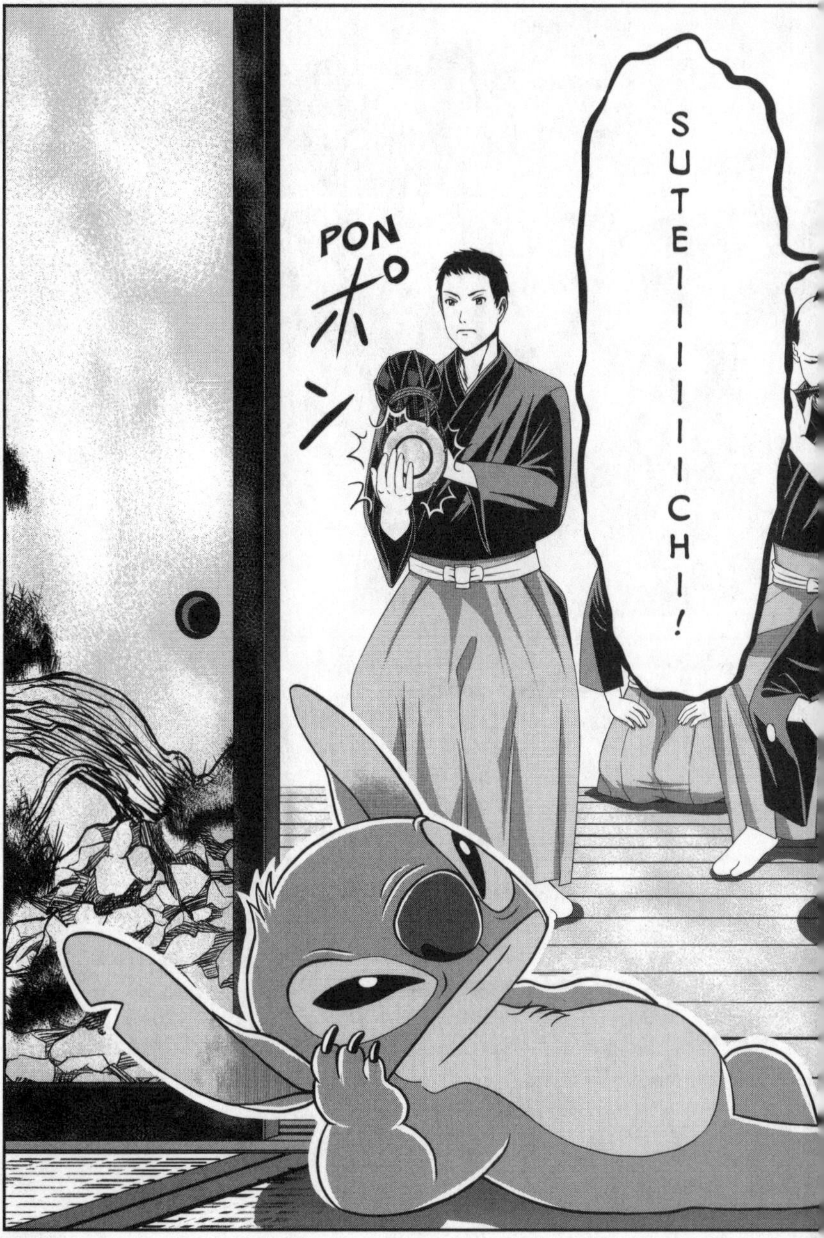
SUTE-------CHI!
PON
ポン

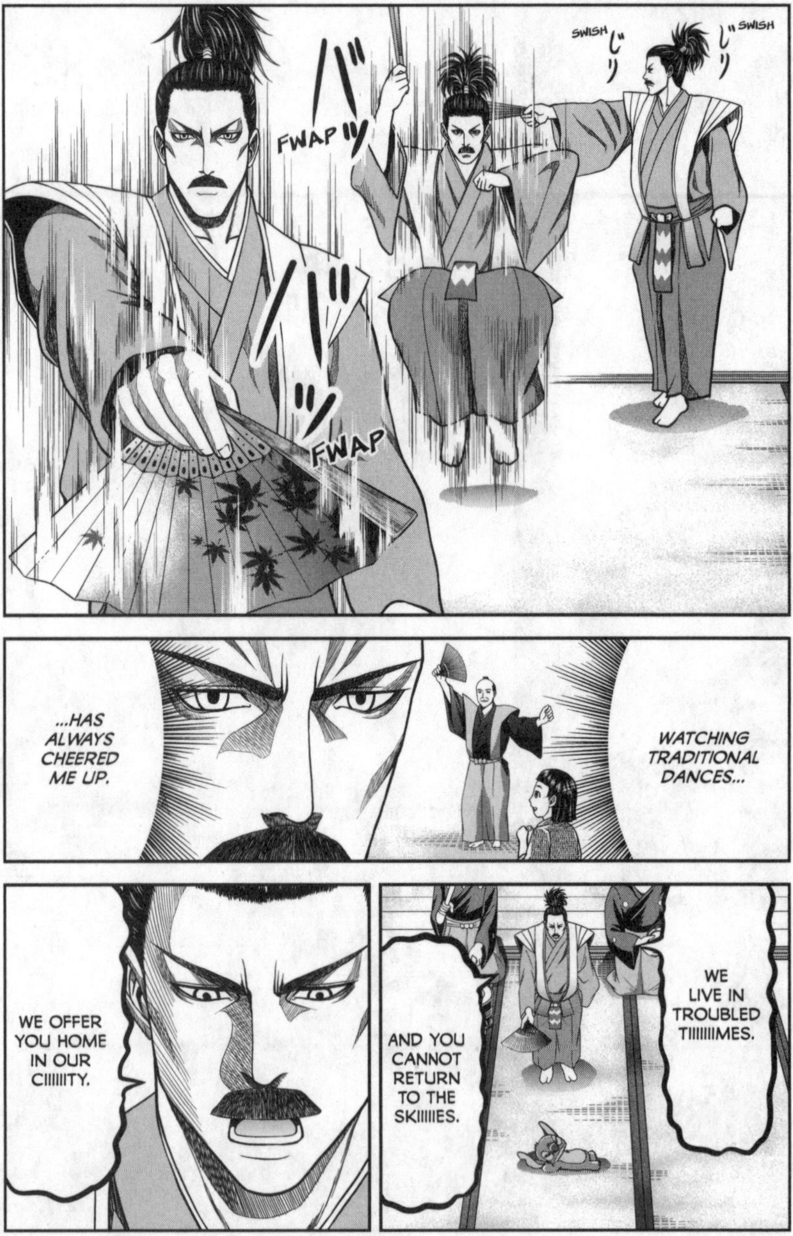
SWISH じり
SWISH じり
FWAP バ
FWAP
WATCHING TRADITIONAL DANCES...
...HAS ALWAYS CHEERED ME UP.
WE LIVE IN TROUBLED TIIIIIIIMES.
AND YOU CANNOT RETURN TO THE SKIIIIIIES.
WE OFFER YOU HOME IN OUR CIIIIIITY.

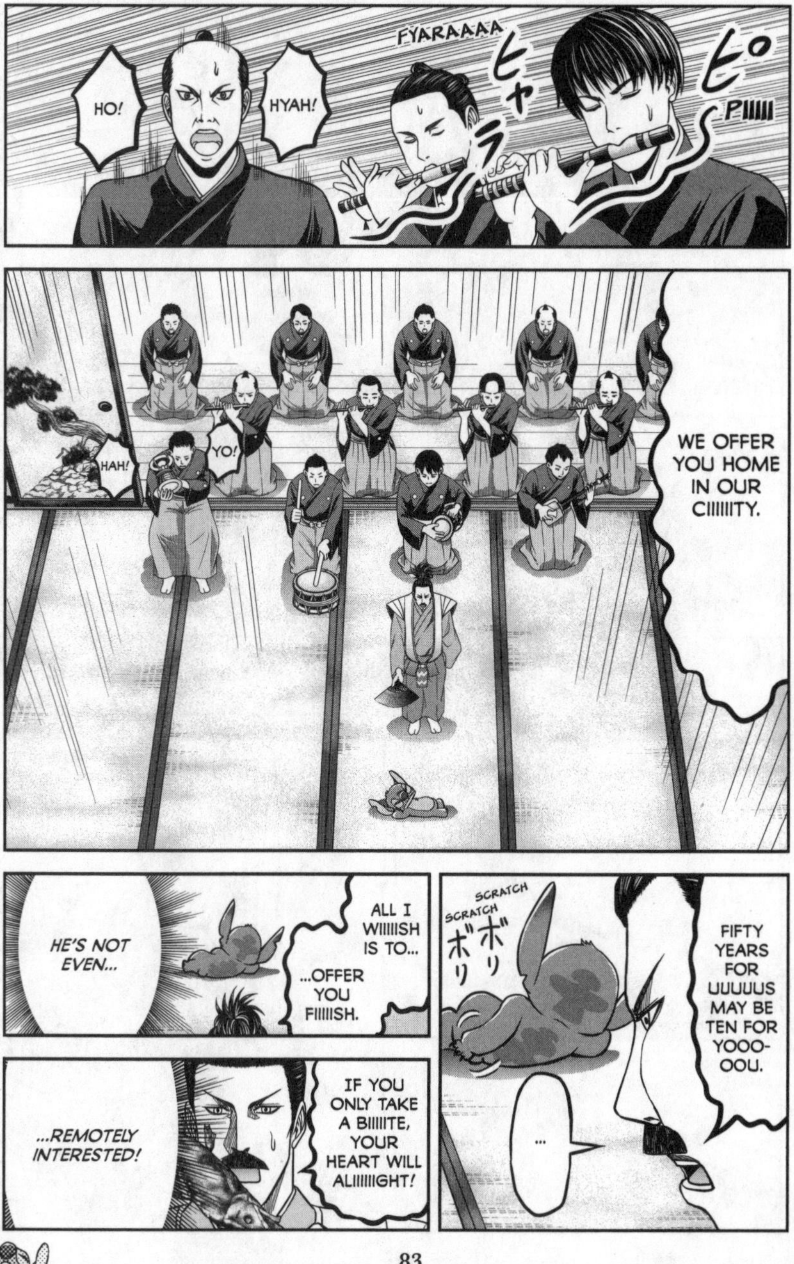
PIIIII
ピ
FYARAAAA
ヒャラ
HYAH!
HO!
WE OFFER YOU HOME IN OUR CIIIIITY.
YO!
HAH!
SCRATCH SCRATCH
ボリボリ
FIFTY YEARS FOR UUUUUS MAY BE TEN FOR YOOO-OOU.
...
ALL I WIIIISH IS TO...
...OFFER YOU FIIIISH.
HE'S NOT EVEN...
IF YOU ONLY TAKE A BIIIITE, YOUR HEART WILL ALIIIIGHT!
...REMOTELY INTERESTED!

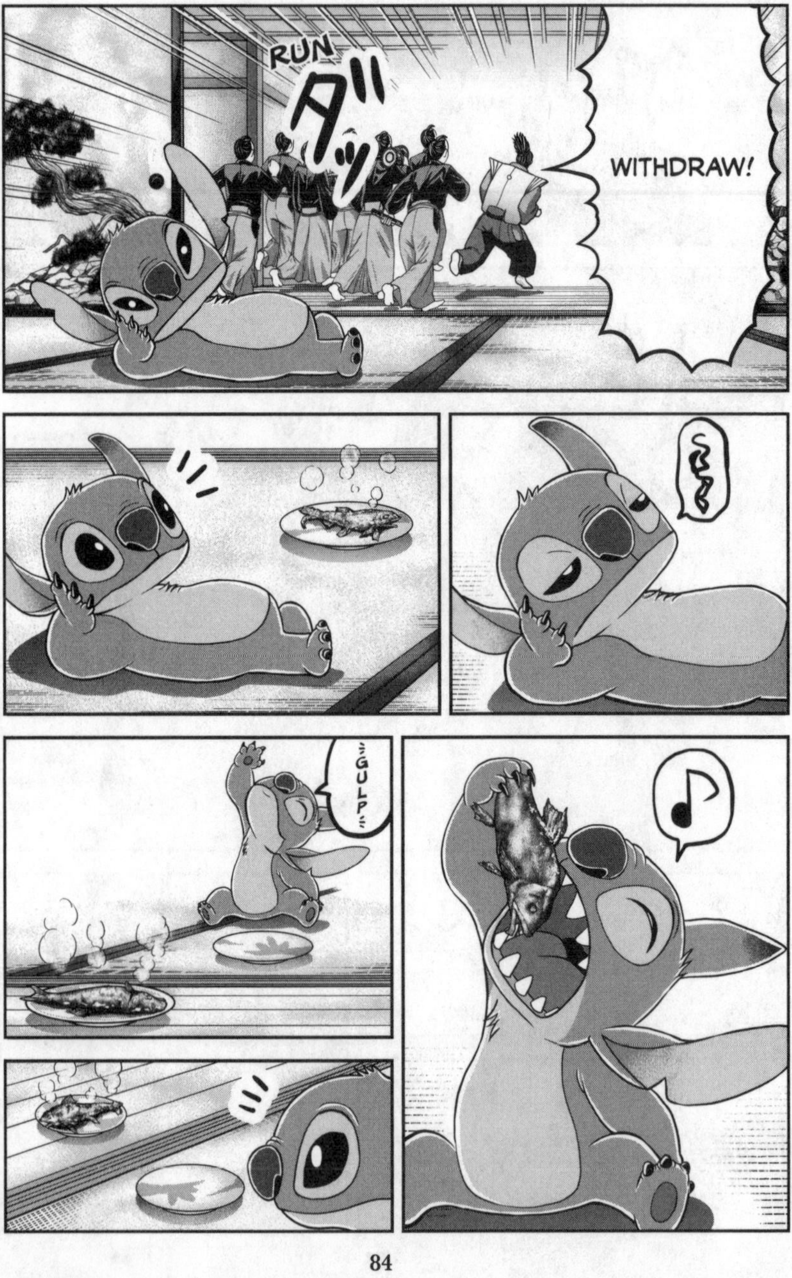
WITHDRAW!
RUN
ダッ
GULP
♪

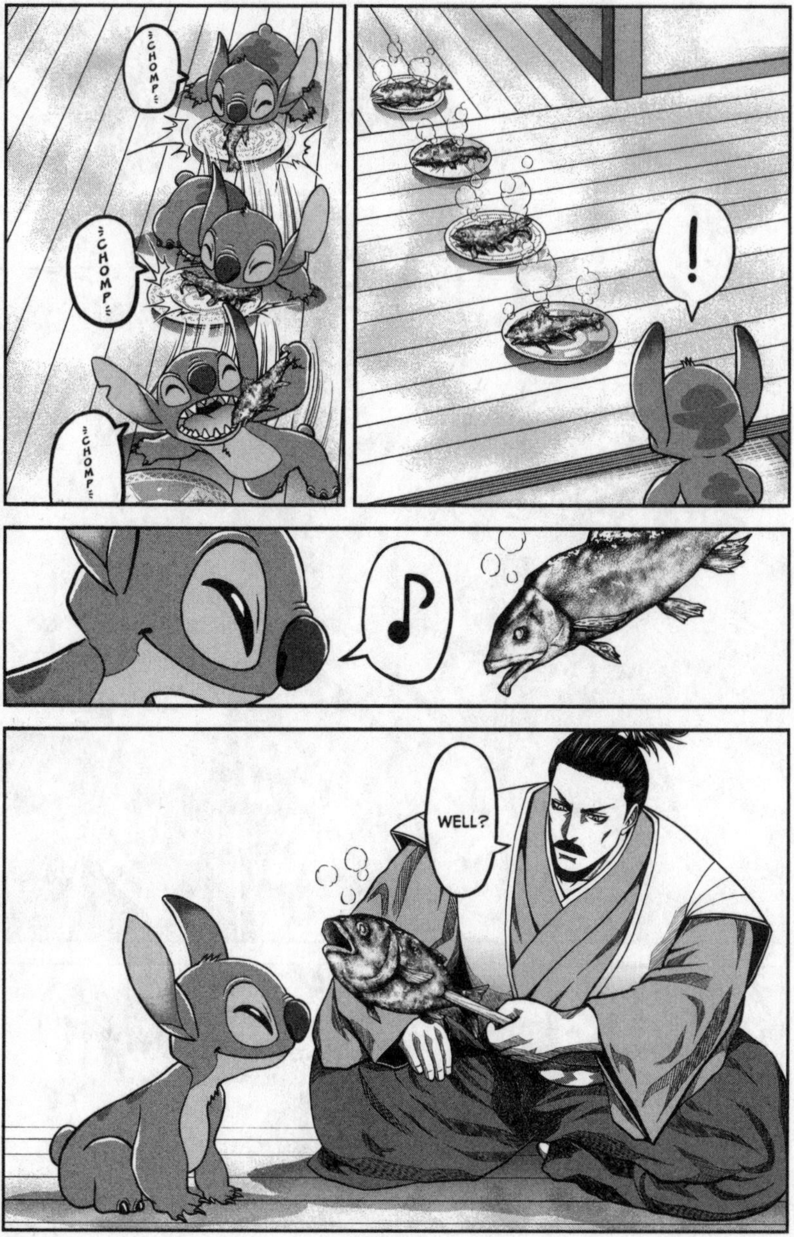
!
CHOMP
CHOMP
CHOMP
♪
WELL?

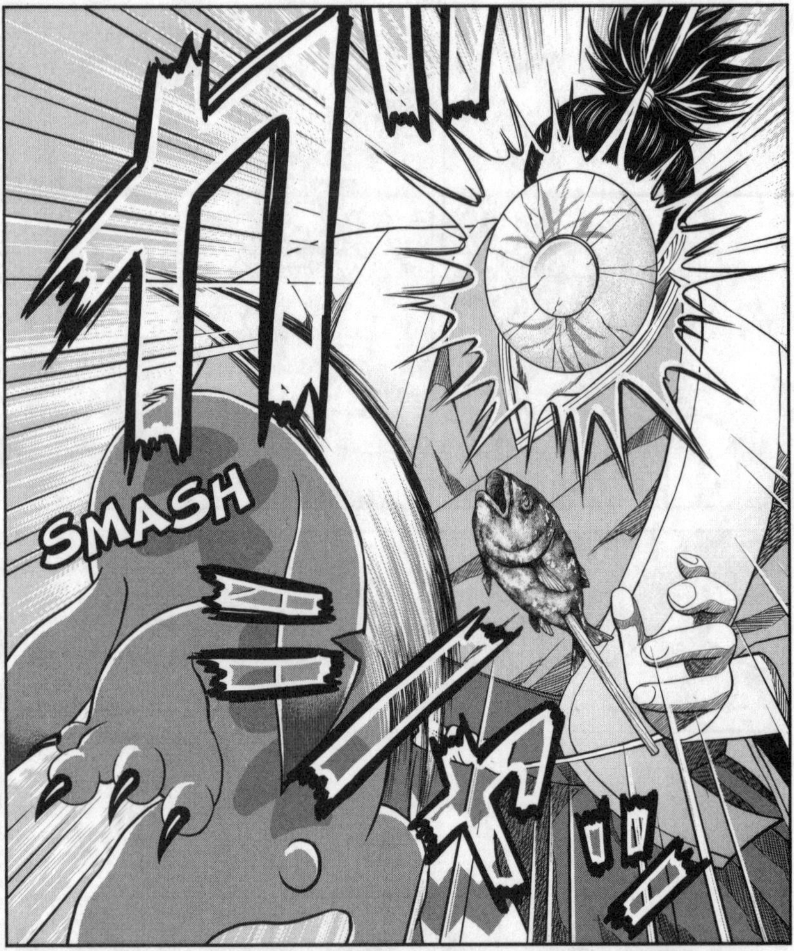
SMASH

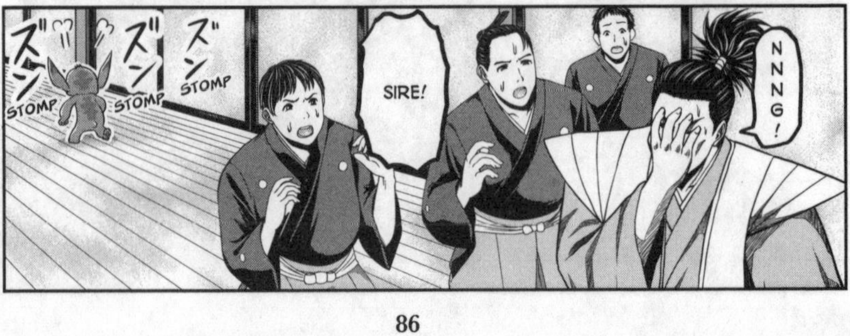
NNNG!
SIRE!
ズン
STOMP
ズン
STOMP
ズン
STOMP

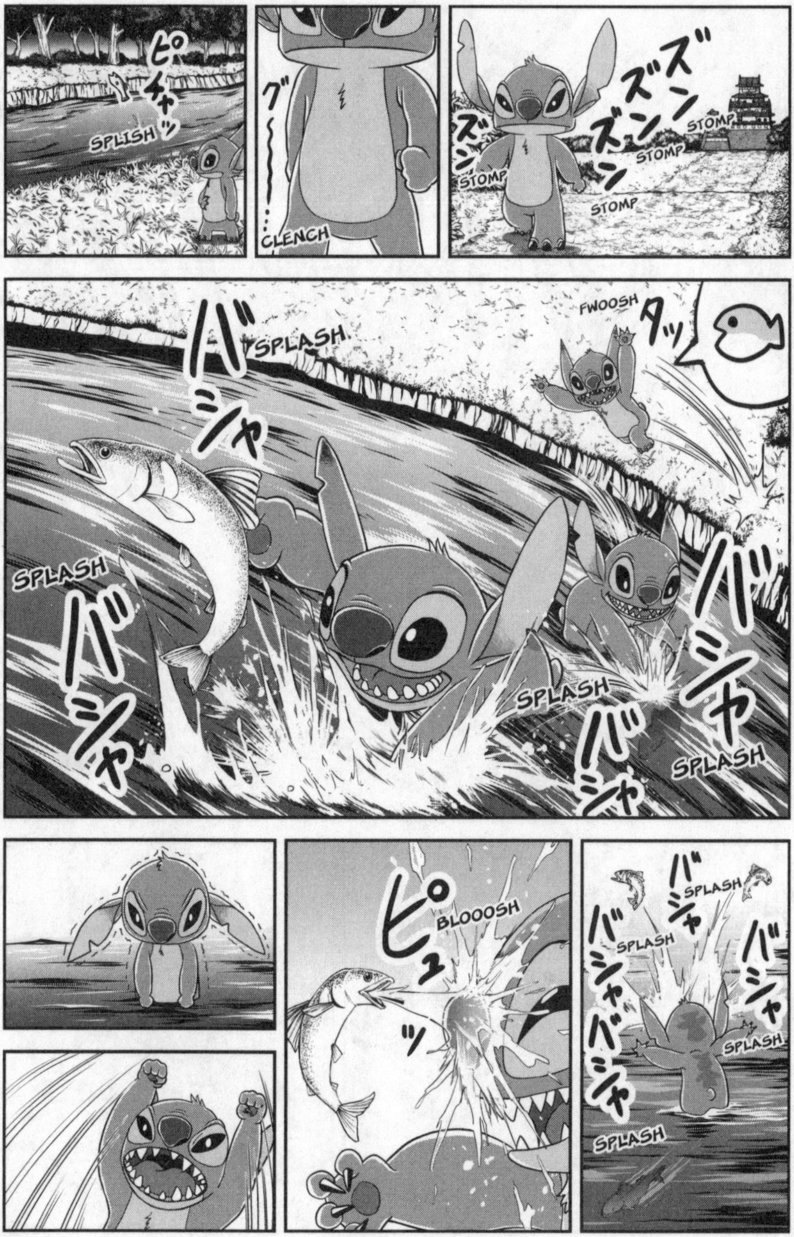
ズズン
ズズン
ズン
STOMP
STOMP
STOMP
STOMP
グ〜〜〜…
CLENCH
ピチャッ
SPLISH
タッ
FWOOSH
バシャ
SPLASH
バシャ
SPLASH
バシャ
SPLASH
バシャ
SPLASH
バシャ
SPLASH
バシャ
SPLASH
バシャバシャ
SPLASH
バシャ
SPLASH
SPLASH
ピュッ
BLOOOSH

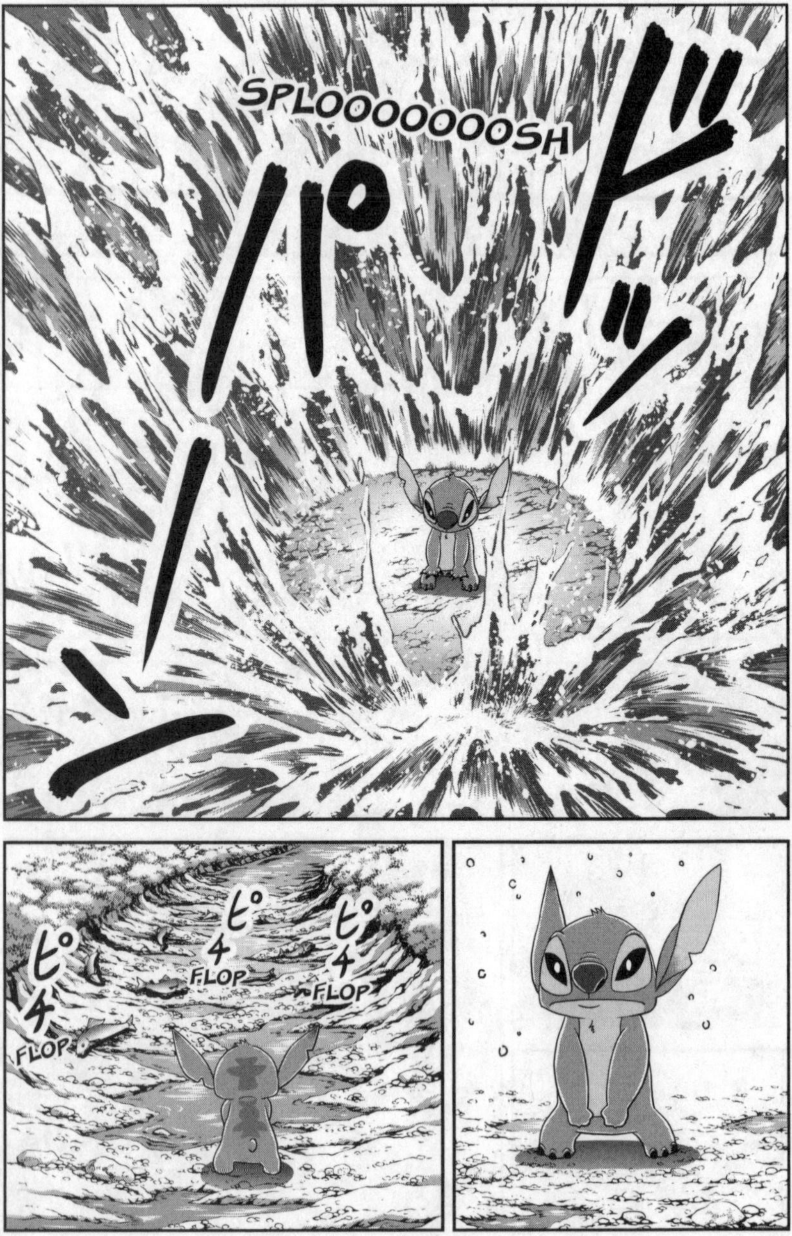
SPLOOOOOOOSH
ドッパーン
ピチ
FLOP
ピチ
FLOP
ピチ
FLOP

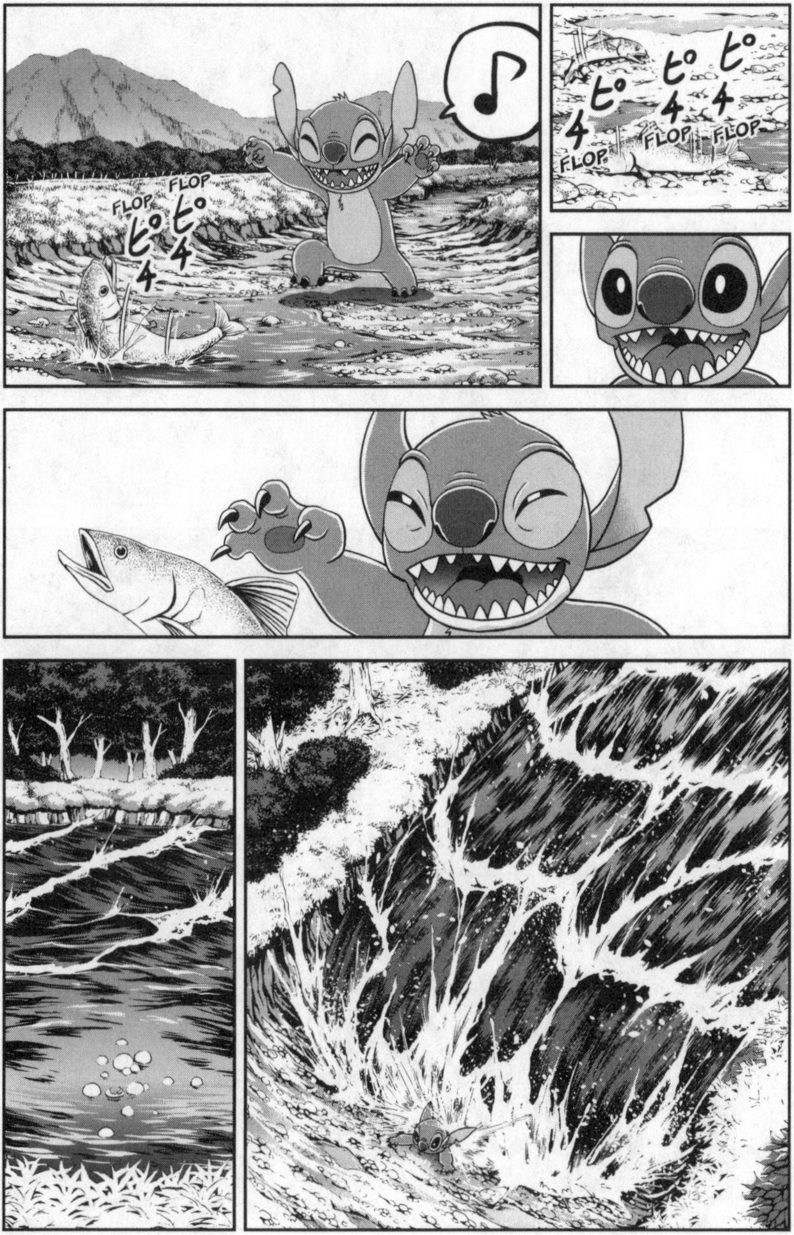
ピク ピク ピク
FLOP FLOP FLOP
♪
FLOP FLOP
ピク ピク

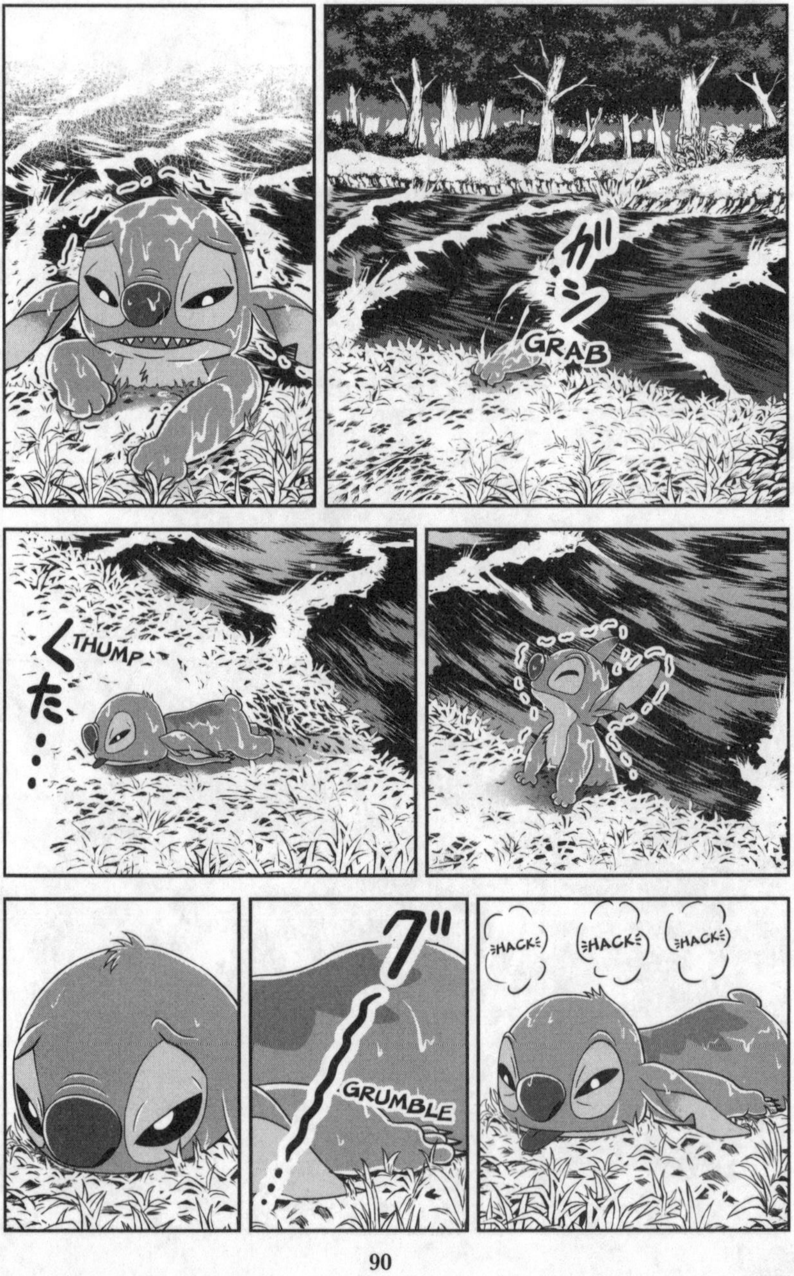
ガシン
GRAB
くた…
THUMP
HACK
HACK
HACK
グ
GRUMBLE

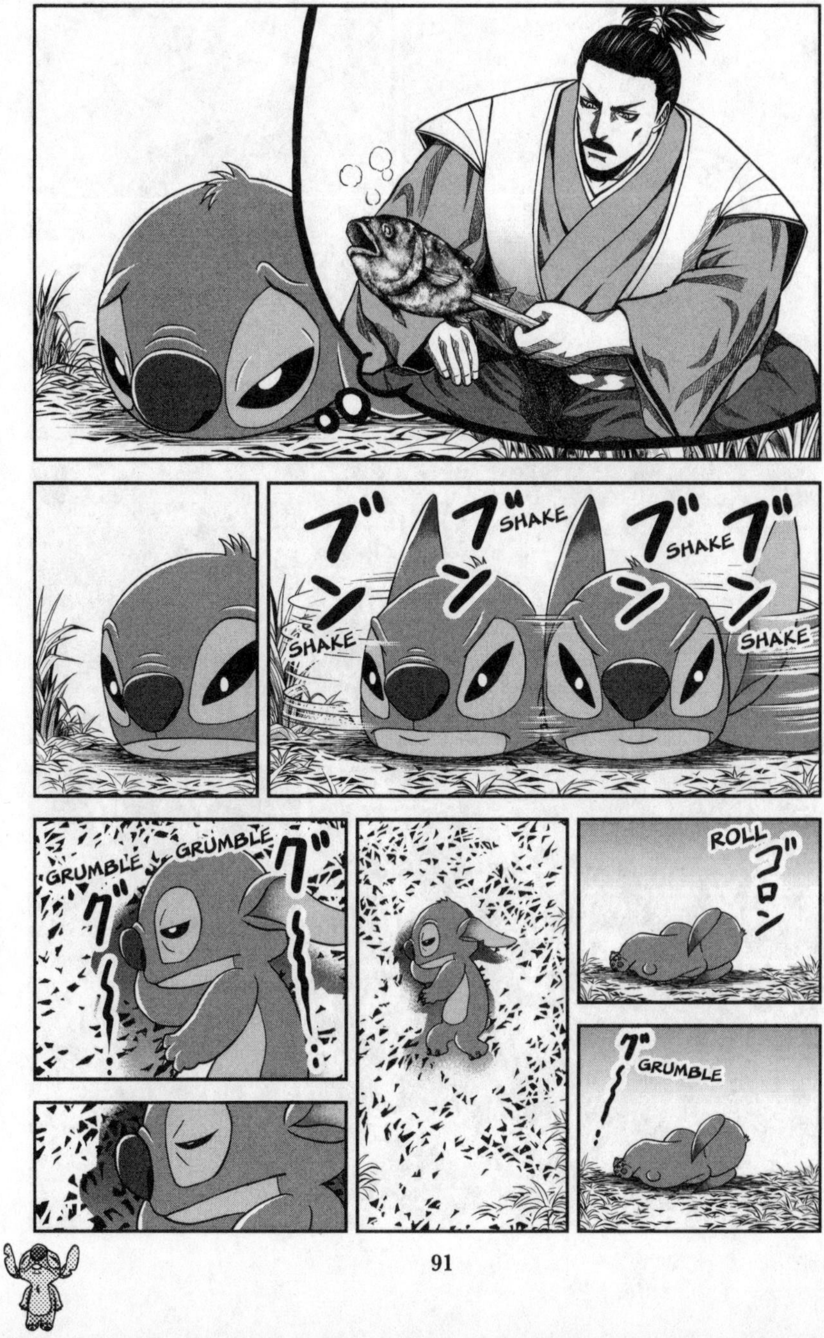

ブン
SHAKE
ブン
SHAKE
ブン
SHAKE
ブン
SHAKE
ROLL
ゴロン
グ
GRUMBLE
グー
GRUMBLE
グー
GRUMBLE

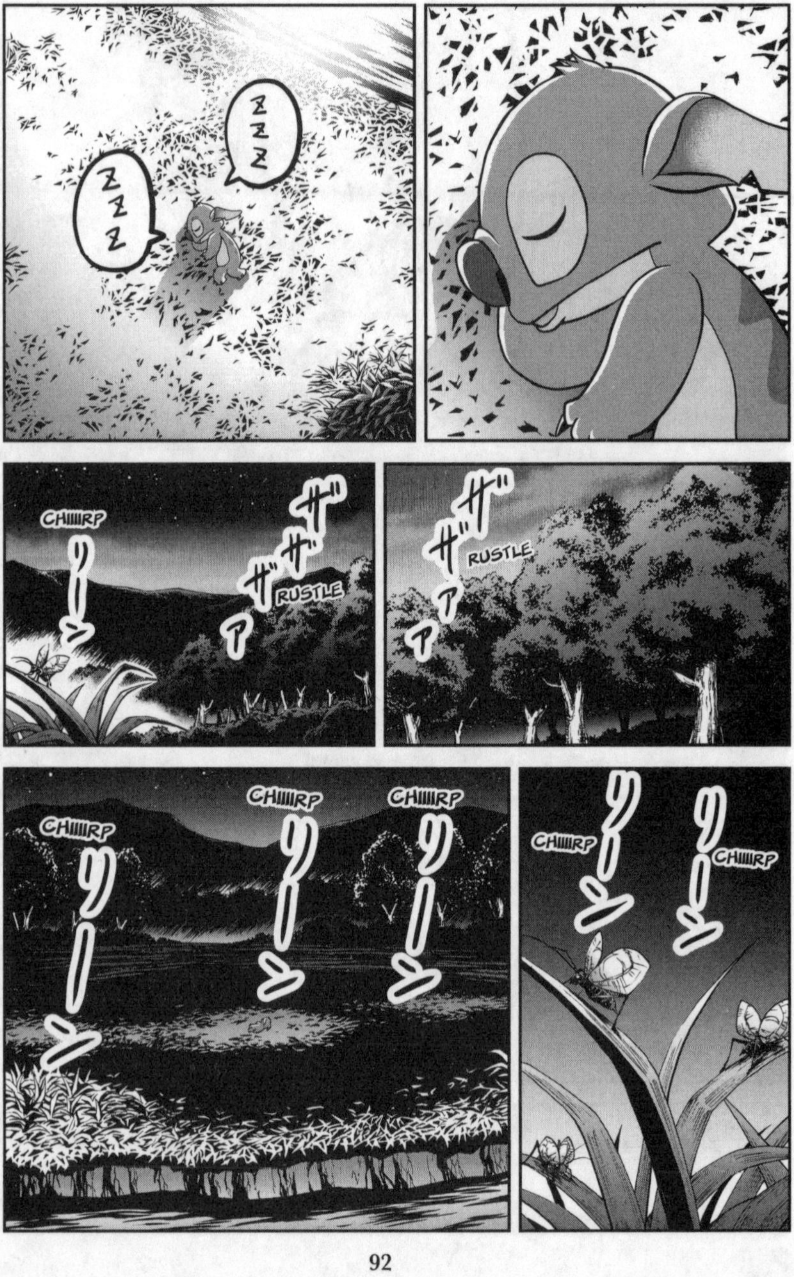
ZZZ
ZZZ
ザザア
RUSTLE
ザザア
RUSTLE
CHIIIIRP
リーン
リーン
CHIIIIRP
リーン
CHIIIIRP
CHIIIIRP
リーン
CHIIIIRP
リーン
CHIIIIRP
リーン

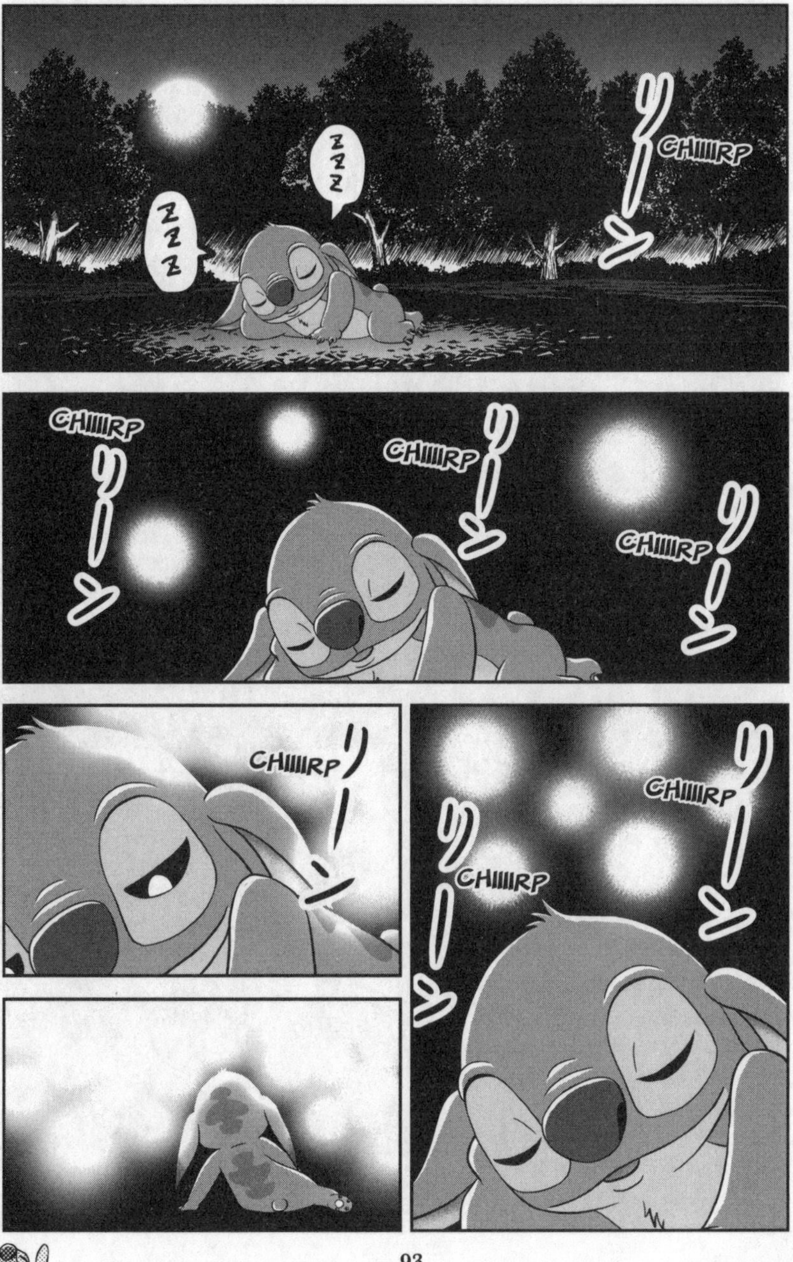
CHIIIIRP
ZZZ
ZZZ
CHIIIIRP
CHIIIIRP
CHIIIIRP
CHIIIIRP
CHIIIIRP
CHIIIIRP

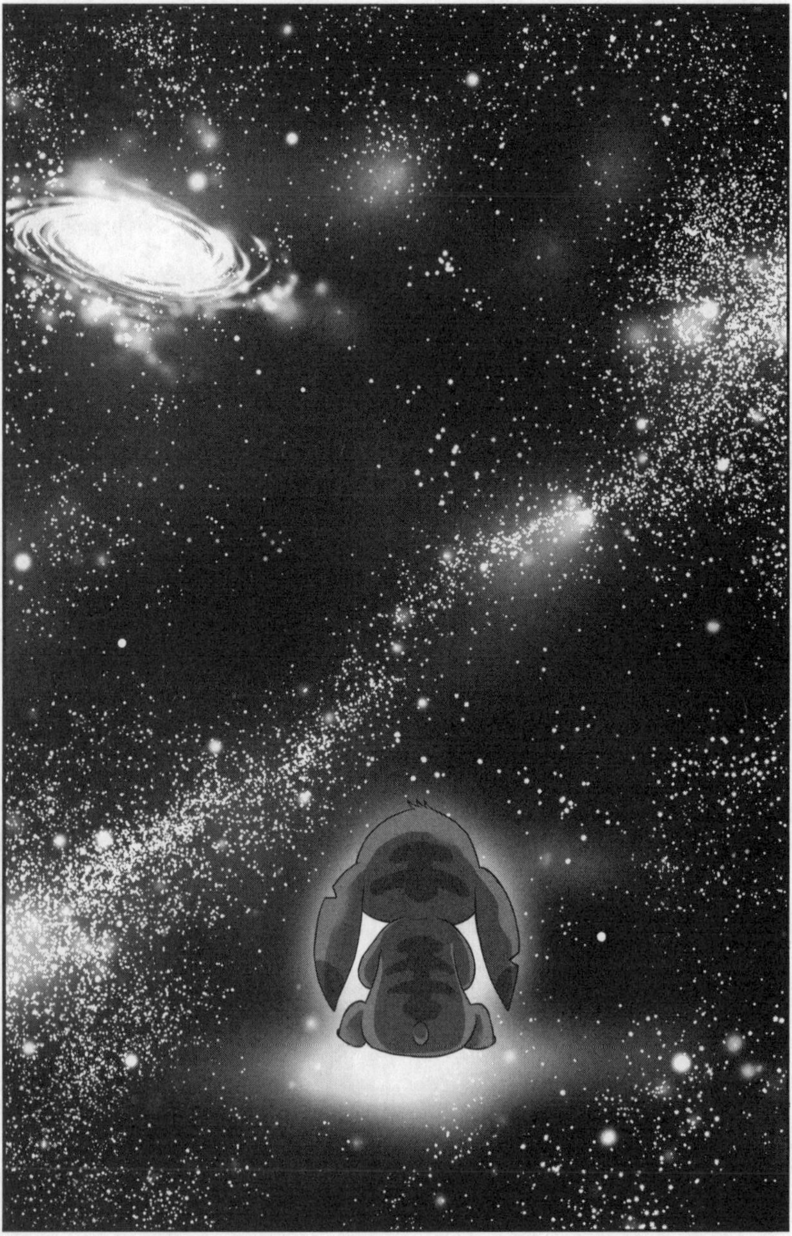

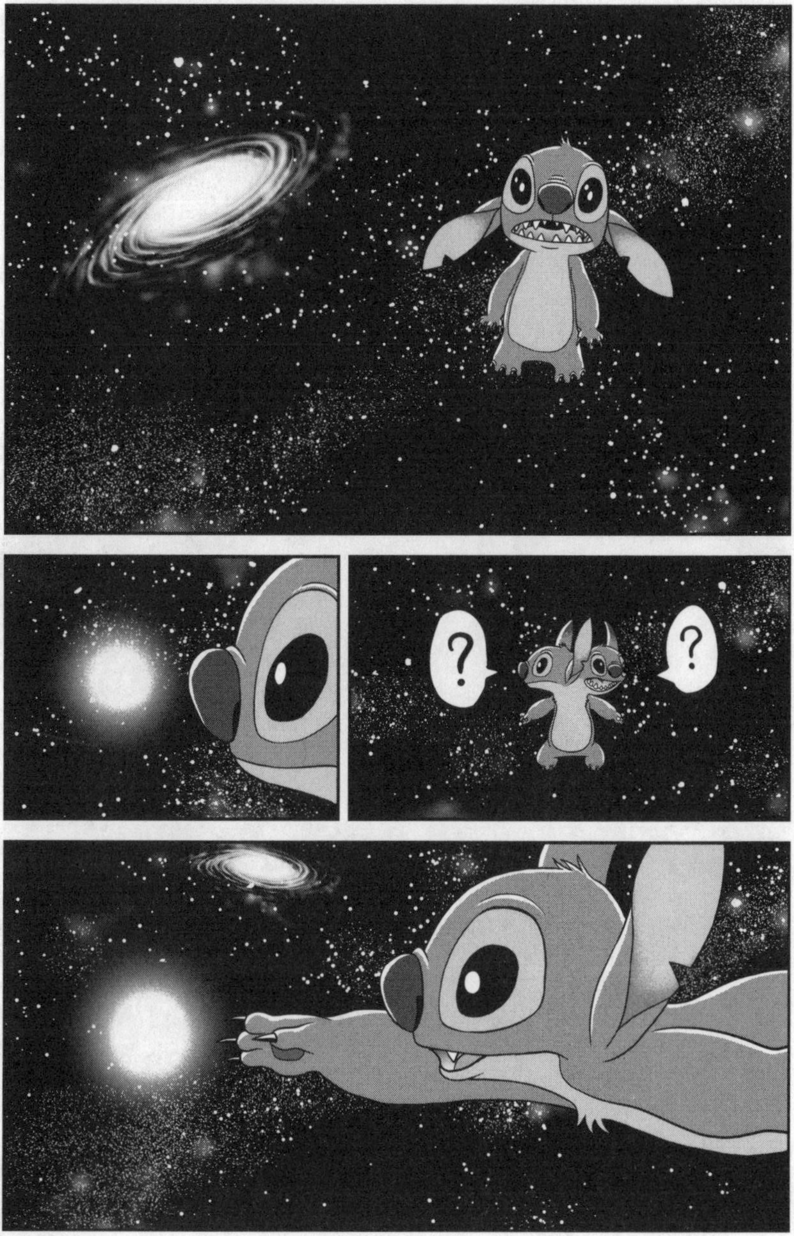
?
?

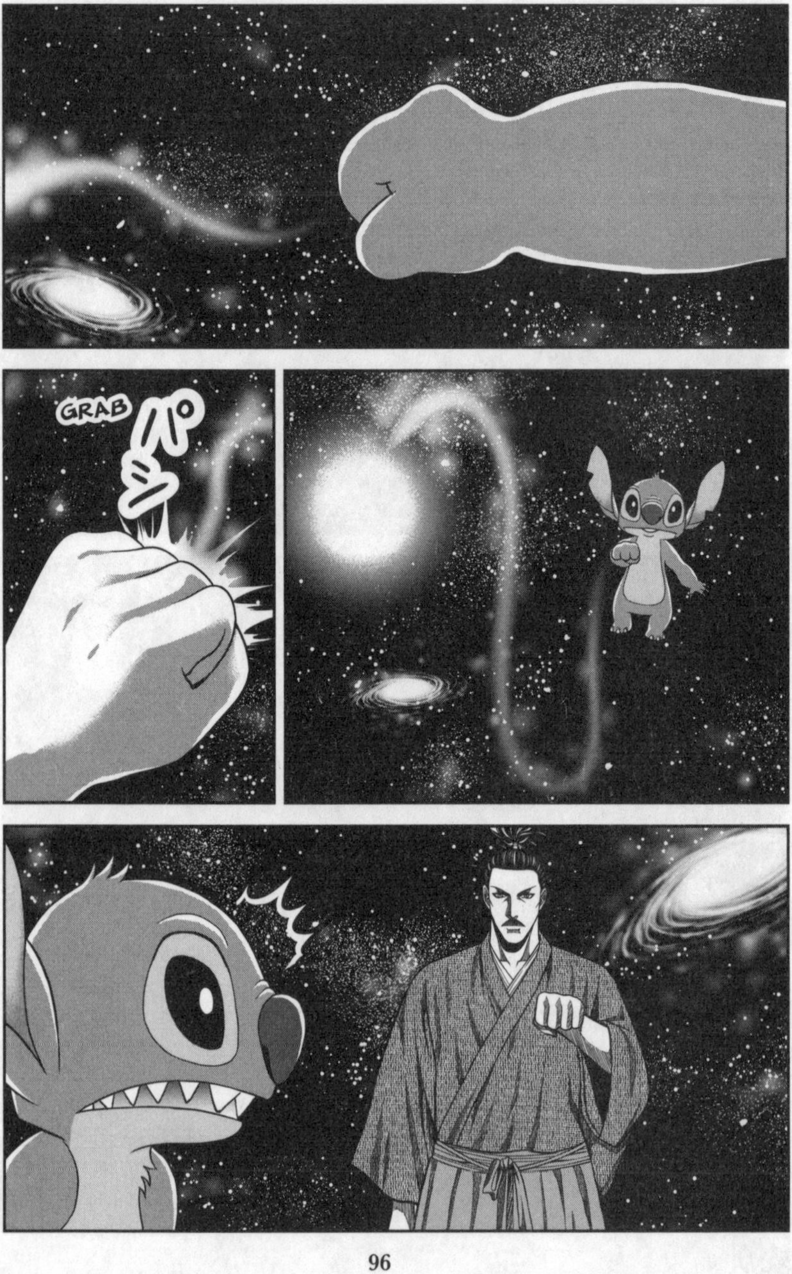
GRAB
パシ

CLENCH

NEVER SEEN ONE BEFORE?

IT'S A FIREFLY.

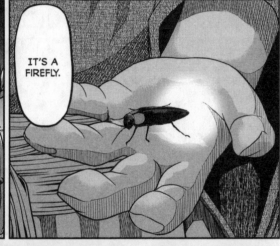

!

YOU'RE HUNGRY, NO?

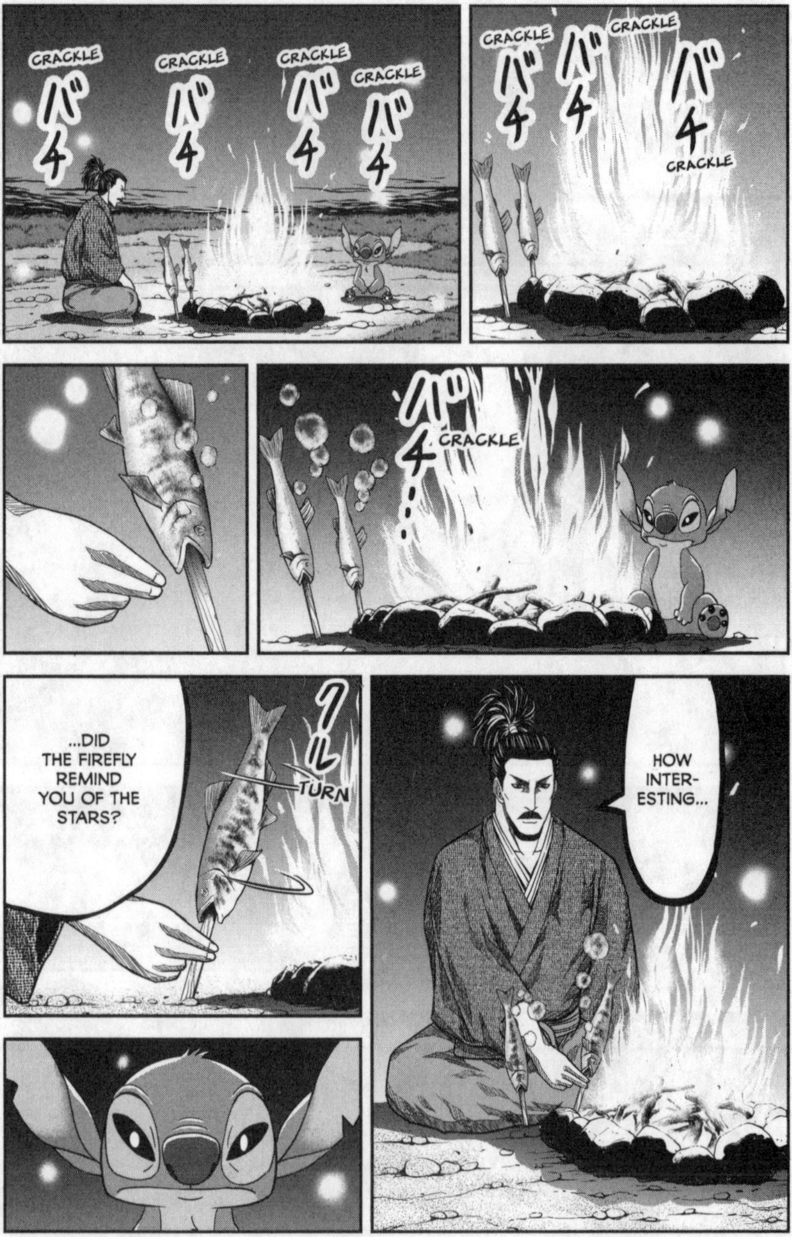
CRACKLE
バチ
CRACKLE
バチ
バチ
CRACKLE
CRACKLE
バチ
CRACKLE
バチ
CRACKLE
バチ
CRACKLE
バチ
バチ...
CRACKLE
HOW INTER-ESTING...
...DID THE FIREFLY REMIND YOU OF THE STARS?
クル
TURN

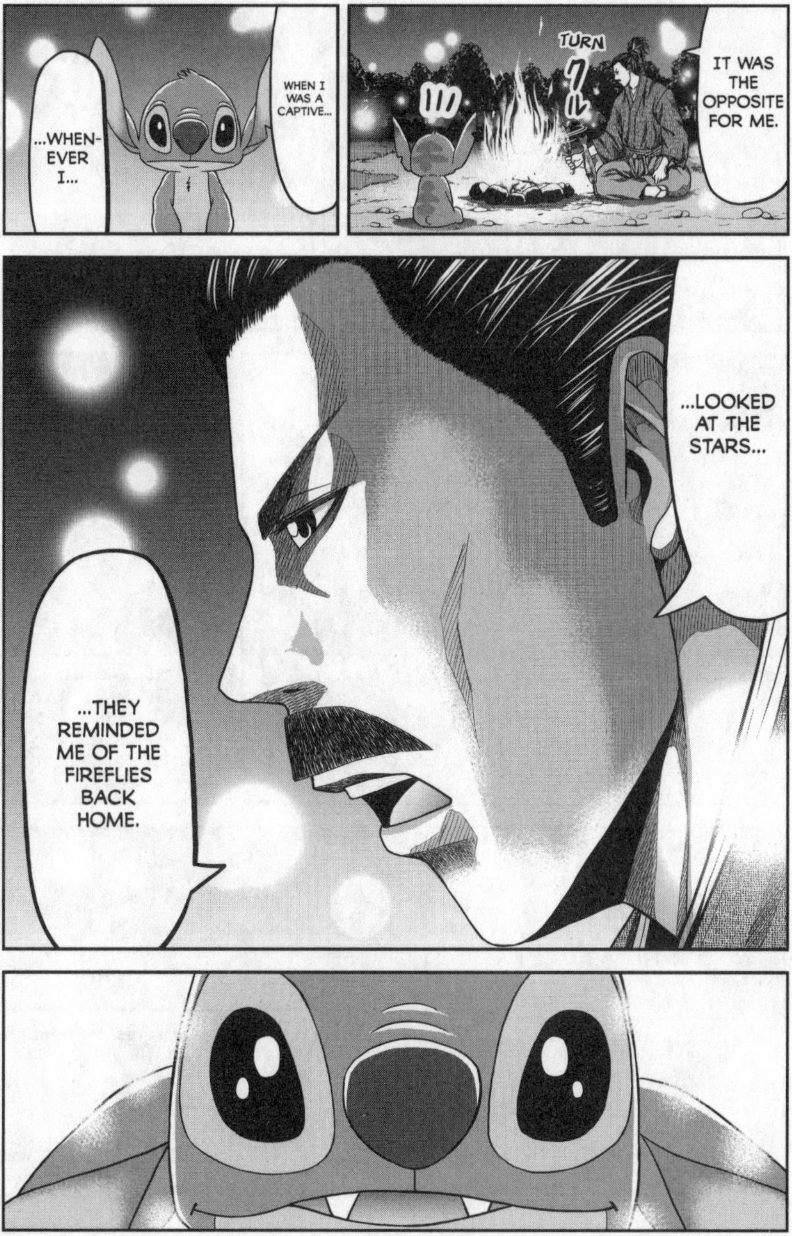
TURN
クル
IT WAS THE OPPOSITE FOR ME.
WHEN I WAS A CAPTIVE...
...WHEN-EVER I...
...LOOKED AT THE STARS...
...THEY REMINDED ME OF THE FIREFLIES BACK HOME.

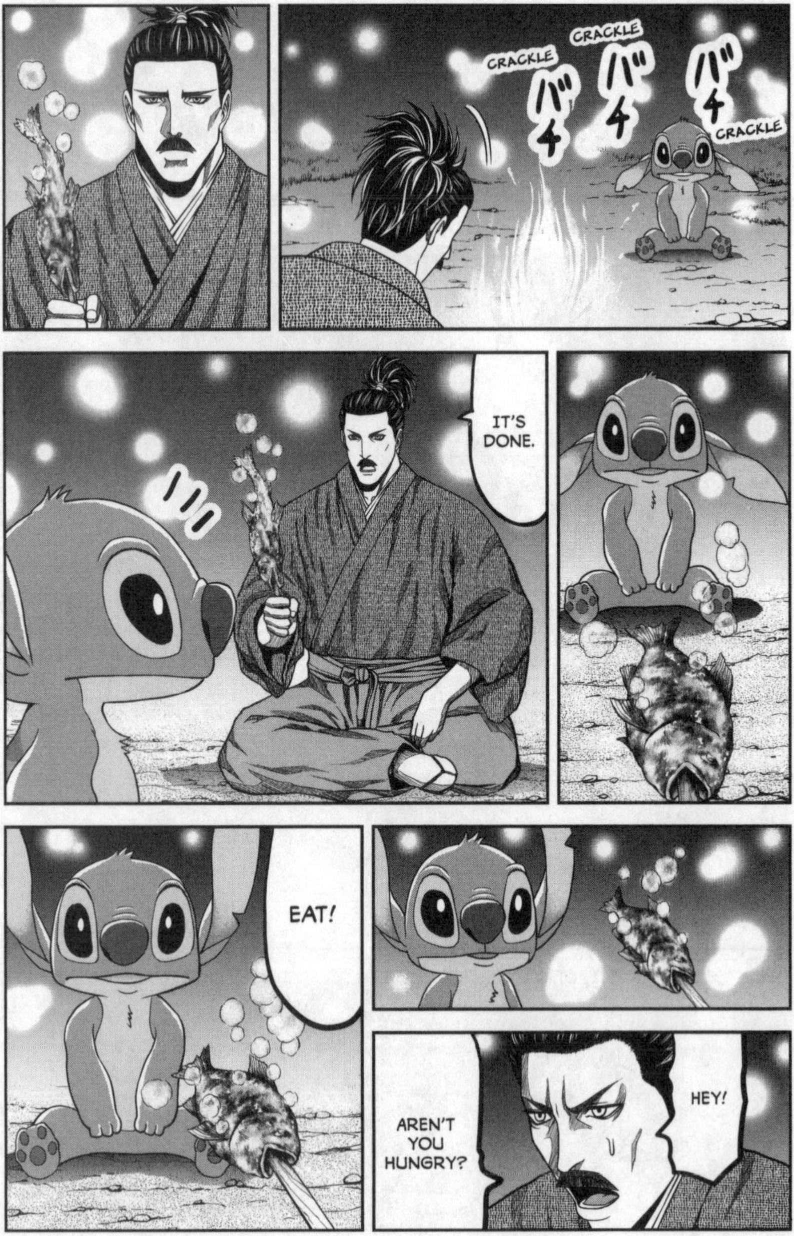
CRACKLE
バチ
CRACKLE
バチ
CRACKLE
バチ
IT'S DONE.
HEY!
AREN'T YOU HUNGRY?
EAT!

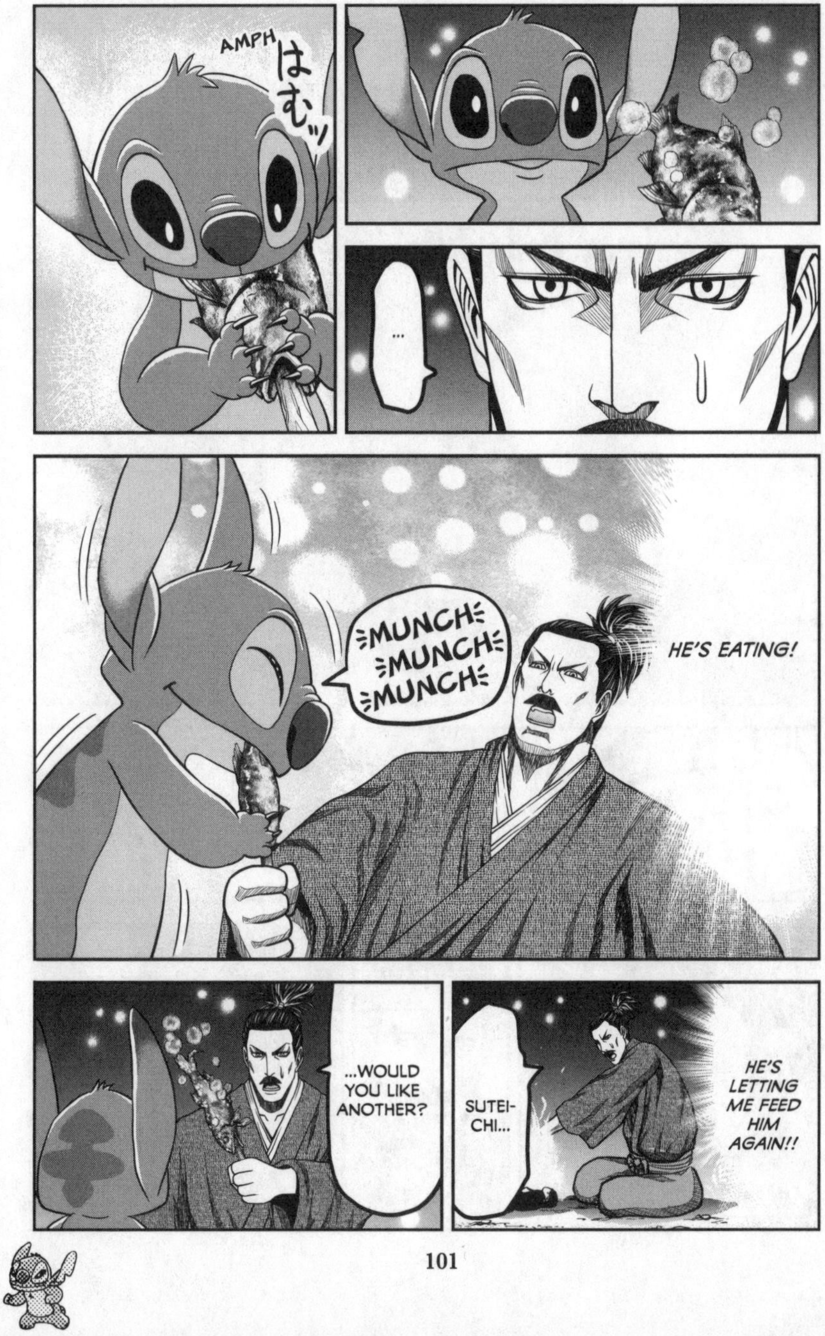
...
AMPH
はむッ
HE'S EATING!
MUNCH MUNCH MUNCH
HE'S LETTING ME FEED HIM AGAIN!!
SUTEI-CHI...
...WOULD YOU LIKE ANOTHER?

STITCH!!

D-DID HE...?

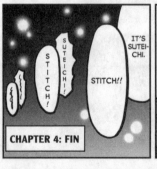

SUTEICHI!

STITCH!

STITCH!!

IT'S SUTEI-CHI.

CHAPTER 4: FIN

STITCH!

BUT YOUR NAME IS...

102

Disney

Stitch

STITCH & THE SAMURAI

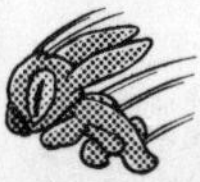

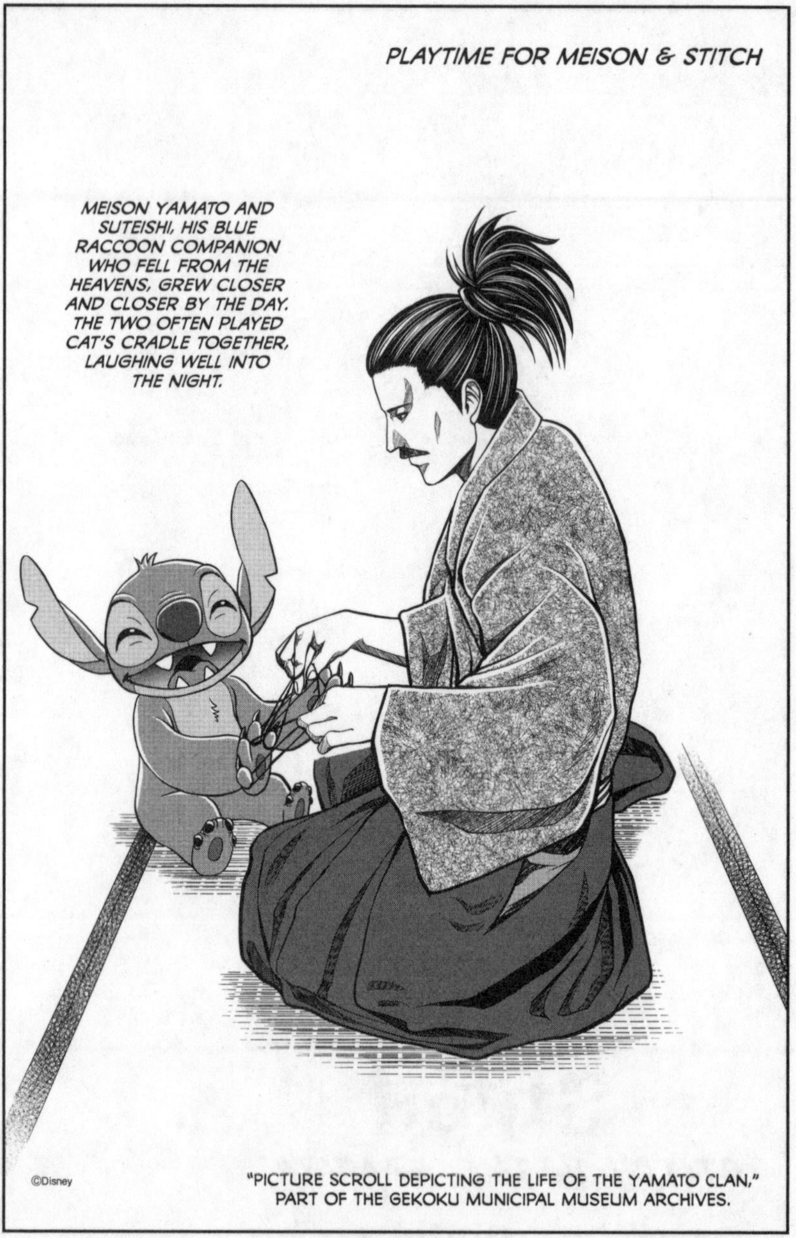
PLAYTIME FOR MEISON & STITCH
MEISON YAMATO AND SUTEISHI, HIS BLUE RACCOON COMPANION WHO FELL FROM THE HEAVENS, GREW CLOSER AND CLOSER BY THE DAY. THE TWO OFTEN PLAYED CAT'S CRADLE TOGETHER, LAUGHING WELL INTO THE NIGHT.
©Disney
"PICTURE SCROLL DEPICTING THE LIFE OF THE YAMATO CLAN," PART OF THE GEKOKU MUNICIPAL MUSEUM ARCHIVES.

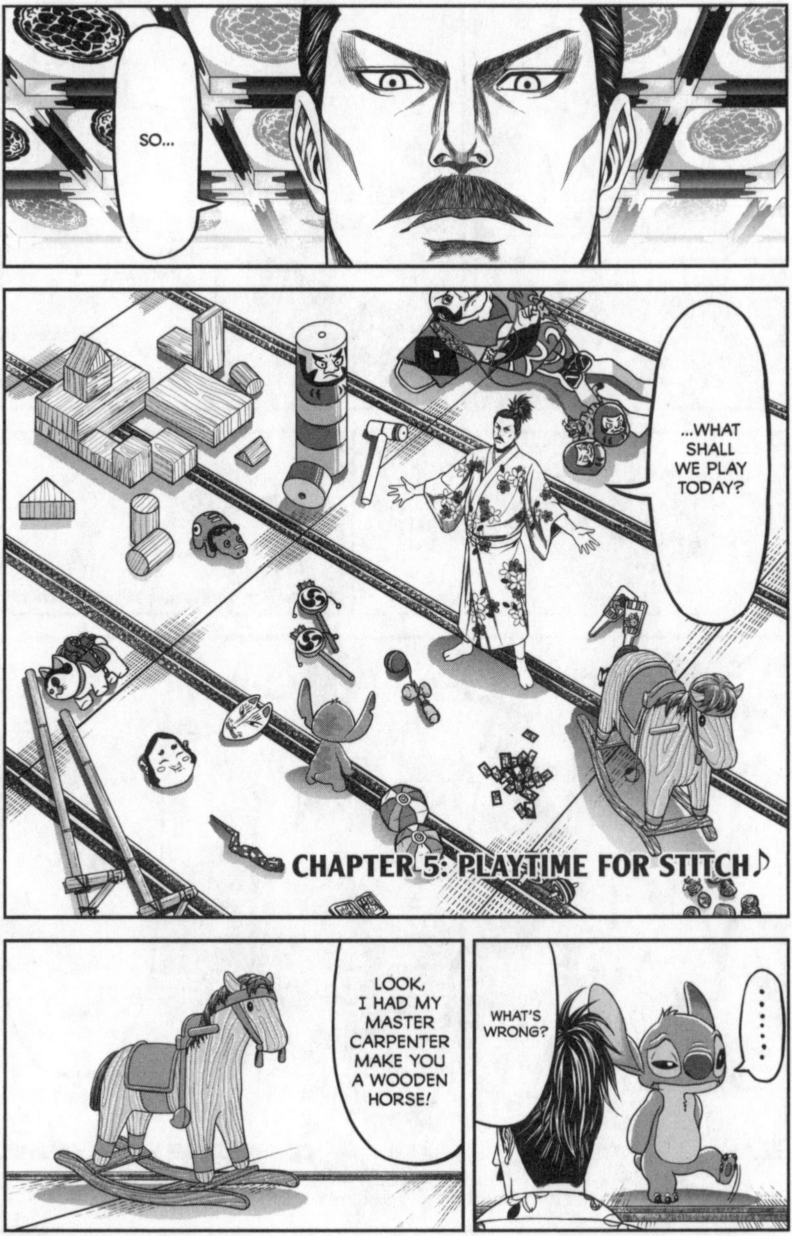
SO...
...WHAT SHALL WE PLAY TODAY?
CHAPTER 5: PLAYTIME FOR STITCH♪
......
WHAT'S WRONG?
LOOK, I HAD MY MASTER CARPENTER MAKE YOU A WOODEN HORSE!

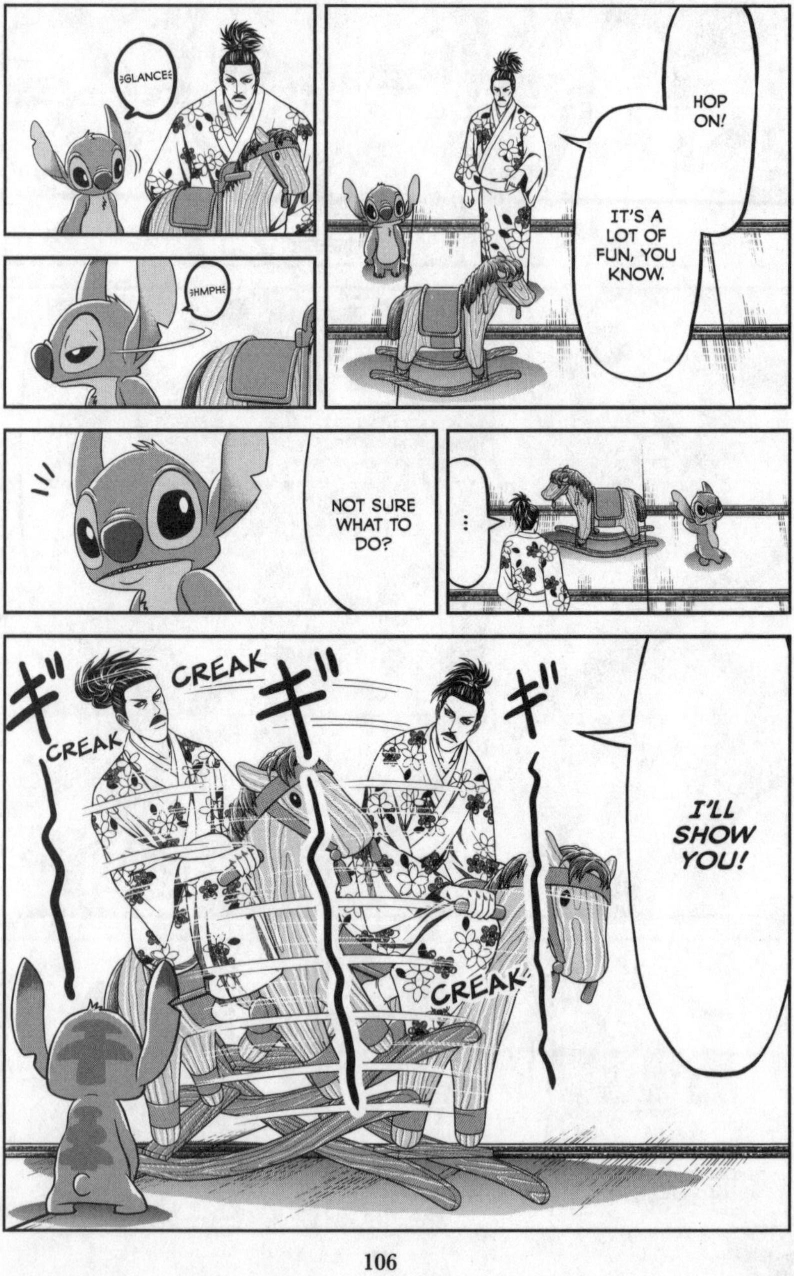
HOP ON!
IT'S A LOT OF FUN, YOU KNOW.
GLANCE
HMPH
...
NOT SURE WHAT TO DO?
I'LL SHOW YOU!
ギ
CREAK
ギ
CREAK
ギ
CREAK

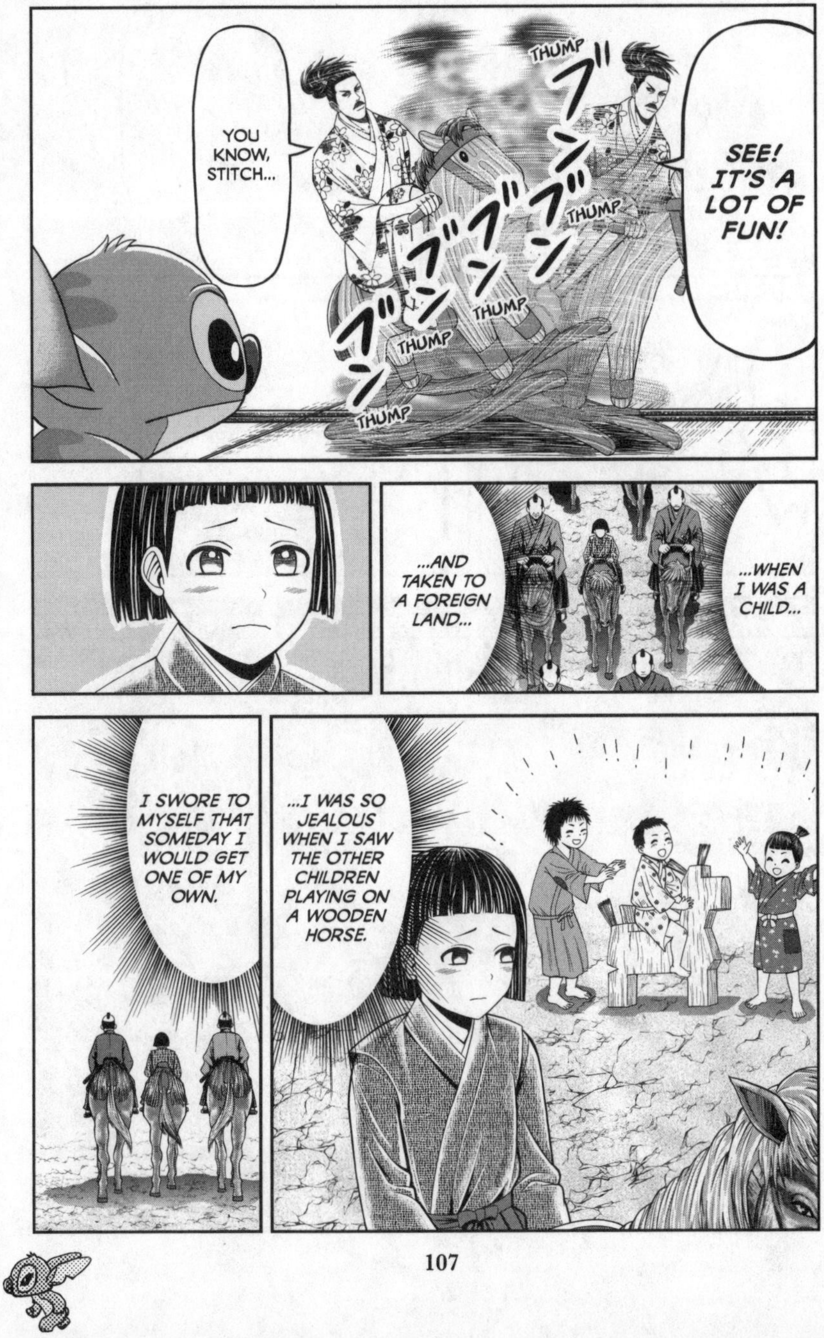
SEE! IT'S A LOT OF FUN!
THUMP
THUMP
THUMP
THUMP
THUMP
YOU KNOW, STITCH...
...WHEN I WAS A CHILD...
...AND TAKEN TO A FOREIGN LAND...
...I WAS SO JEALOUS WHEN I SAW THE OTHER CHILDREN PLAYING ON A WOODEN HORSE.
I SWORE TO MYSELF THAT SOMEDAY I WOULD GET ONE OF MY OWN.

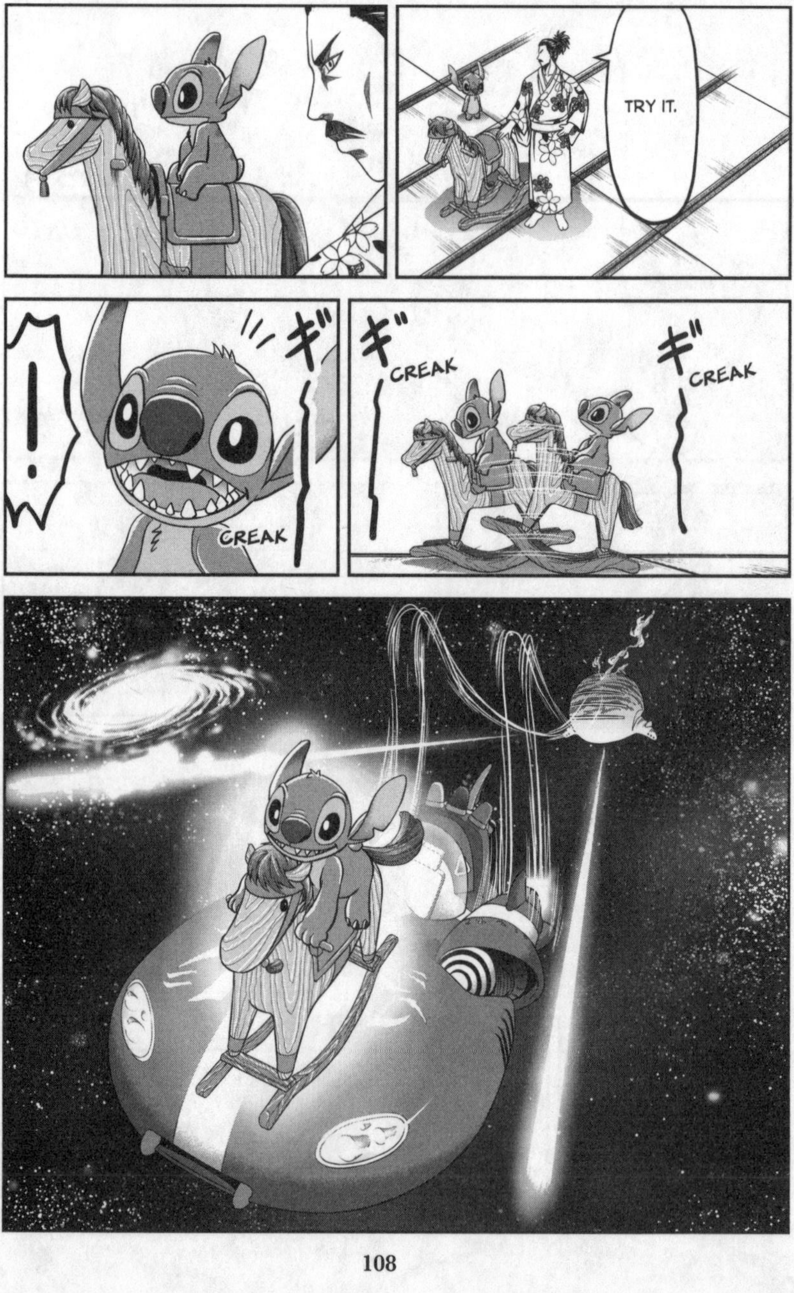
TRY IT.
ギ
CREAK
ギ
CREAK
!
ギ
CREAK

CREAK

CREAK

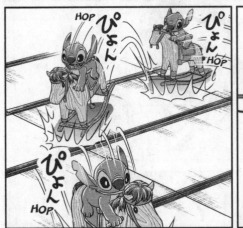

HOP

HOP

HOP

HAVING FUN?

IT'S GREAT, ISN'T IT??

109

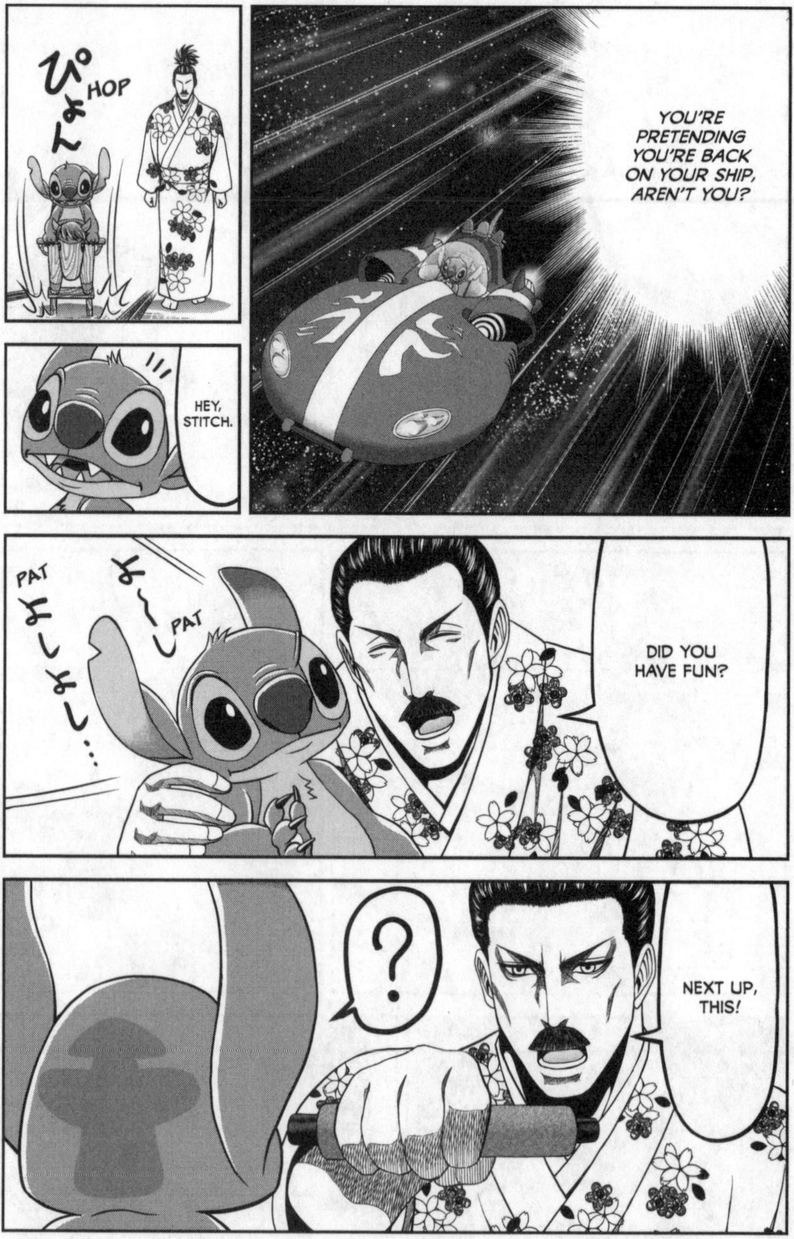

YOU'RE PRETENDING YOU'RE BACK ON YOUR SHIP, AREN'T YOU?
ぴょん HOP
HEY, STITCH.
DID YOU HAVE FUN?
よ〜し PAT
PAT よしよし…
NEXT UP, THIS!
?

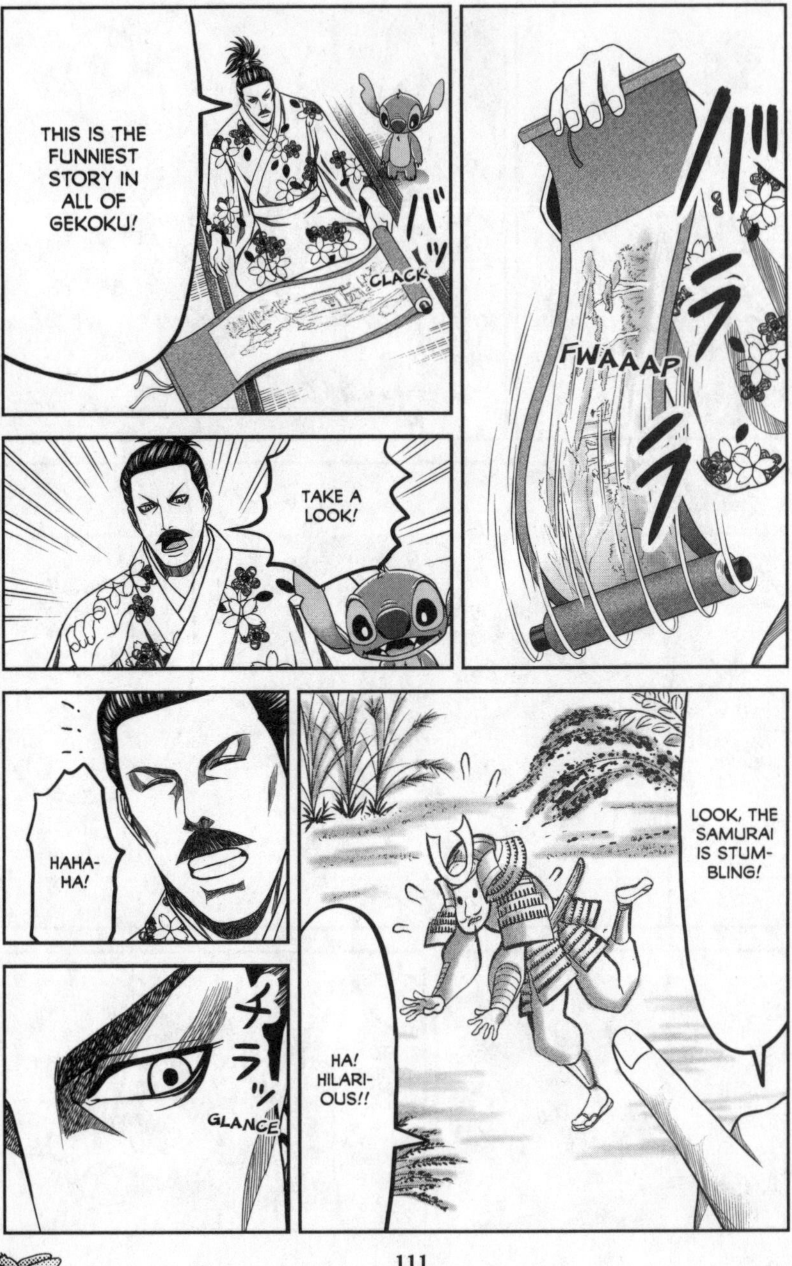
FWAAAP
THIS IS THE FUNNIEST STORY IN ALL OF GEKOKU!
CLACK
TAKE A LOOK!
LOOK, THE SAMURAI IS STUMBLING!
HA! HILARIOUS!!
HAHA-HA!
GLANCE

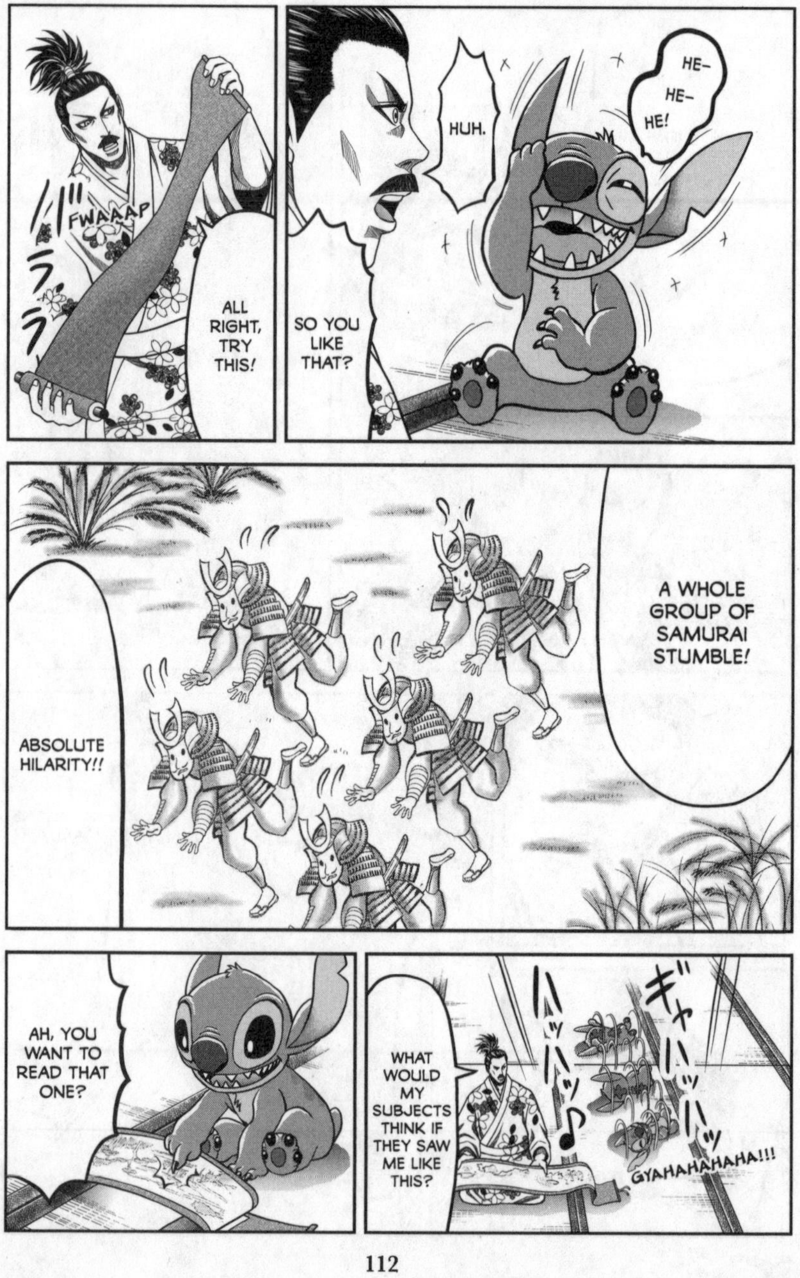
HE-
HE-
HE!
HUH.
SO YOU LIKE THAT?
ALL RIGHT, TRY THIS!
FWAAAP
A WHOLE GROUP OF SAMURAI STUMBLE!
ABSOLUTE HILARITY!!
GYAHAHAHAHA!!!
WHAT WOULD MY SUBJECTS THINK IF THEY SAW ME LIKE THIS?
AH, YOU WANT TO READ THAT ONE?

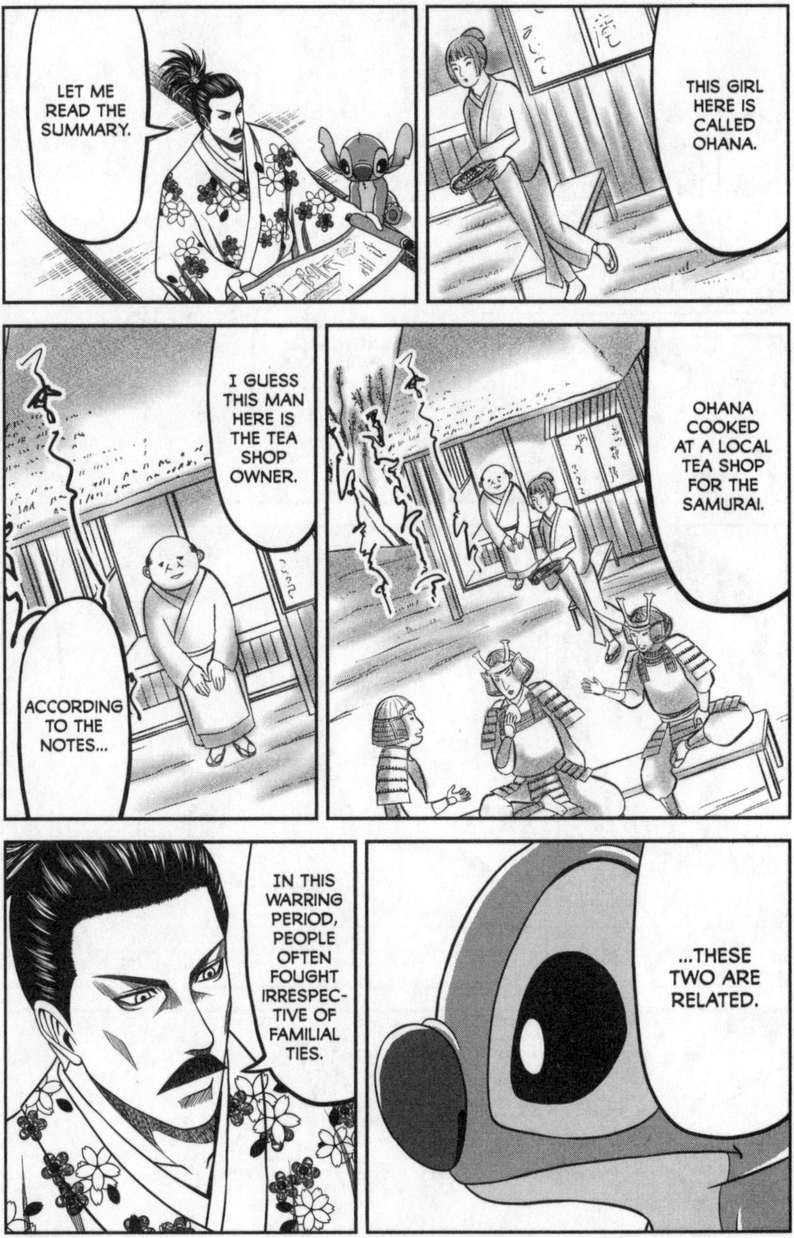
THIS GIRL HERE IS CALLED OHANA.
LET ME READ THE SUMMARY.
OHANA COOKED AT A LOCAL TEA SHOP FOR THE SAMURAI.
I GUESS THIS MAN HERE IS THE TEA SHOP OWNER.
ACCORDING TO THE NOTES...
...THESE TWO ARE RELATED.
IN THIS WARRING PERIOD, PEOPLE OFTEN FOUGHT IRRESPECTIVE OF FAMILIAL TIES.

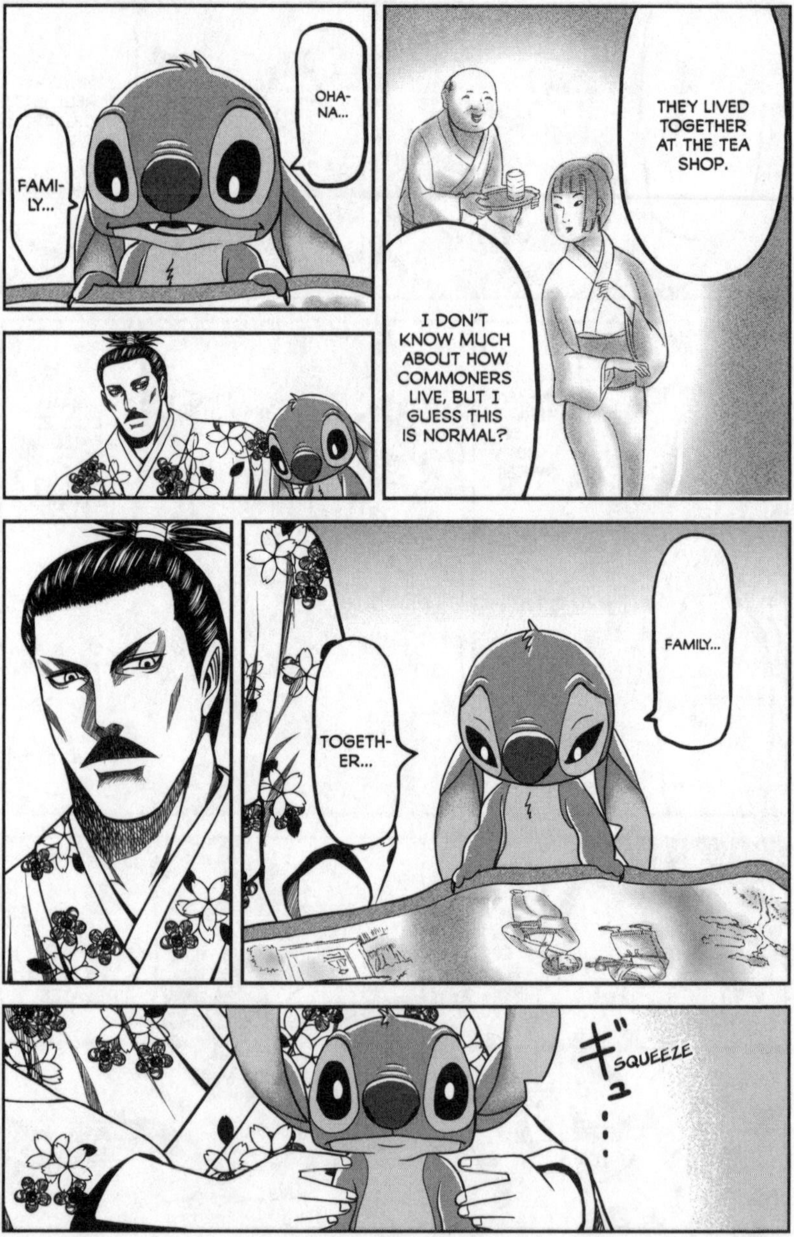
THEY LIVED TOGETHER AT THE TEA SHOP.
I DON'T KNOW MUCH ABOUT HOW COMMONERS LIVE, BUT I GUESS THIS IS NORMAL?
OHA-NA...
FAMI-LY...
FAMILY...
TOGETH-ER...
ギュ SQUEEZE
...

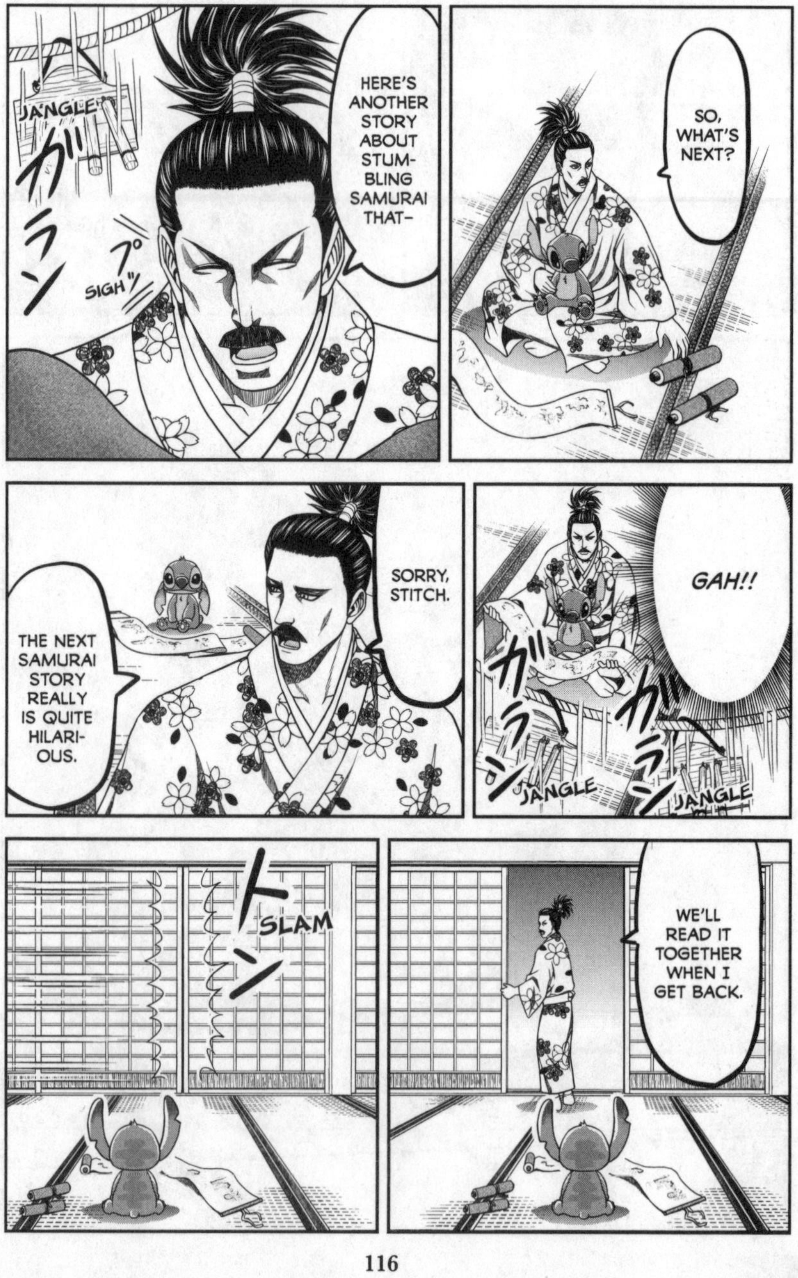
SO, WHAT'S NEXT?
HERE'S ANOTHER STORY ABOUT STUMBLING SAMURAI THAT–
JANGLE
SIGH
GAH!!
JANGLE
JANGLE
SORRY, STITCH.
THE NEXT SAMURAI STORY REALLY IS QUITE HILARIOUS.
WE'LL READ IT TOGETHER WHEN I GET BACK.
SLAM

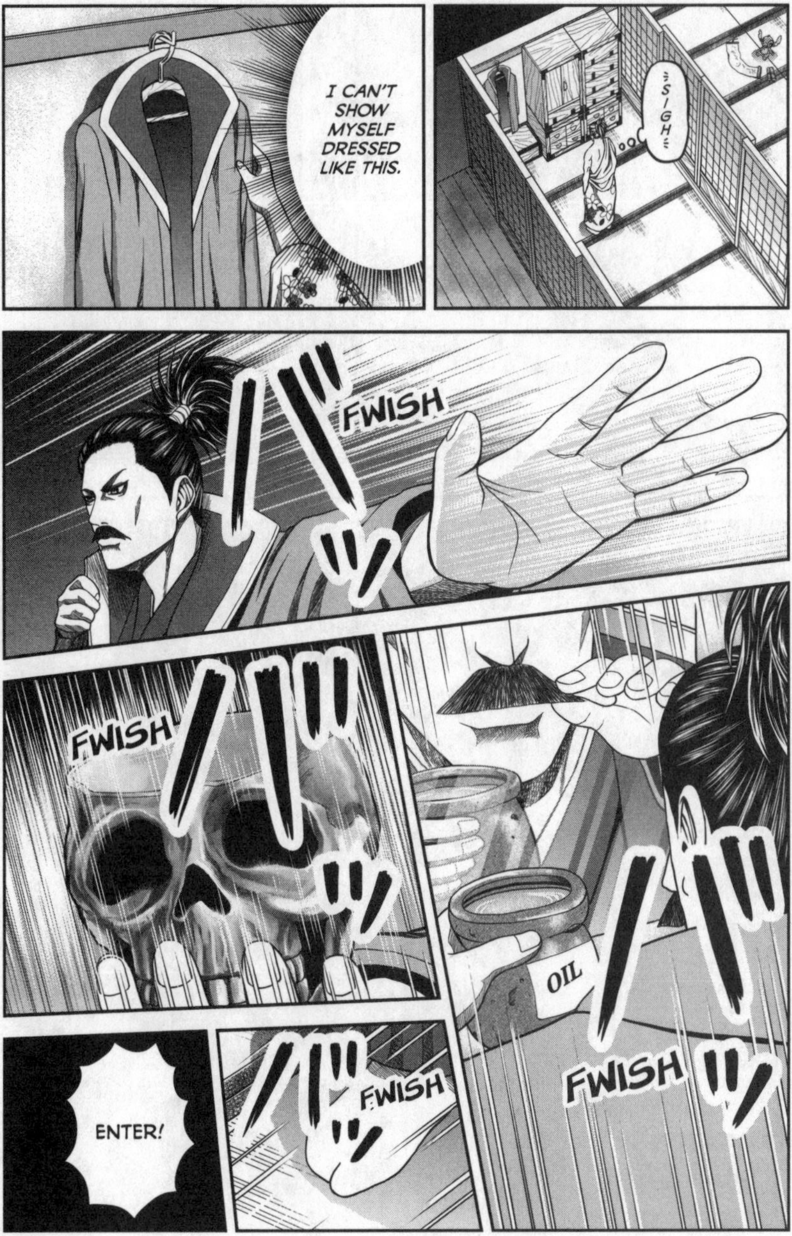
SIGH
I CAN'T SHOW MYSELF DRESSED LIKE THIS.
FWISH
OIL
FWISH
FWISH
FWISH
ENTER!

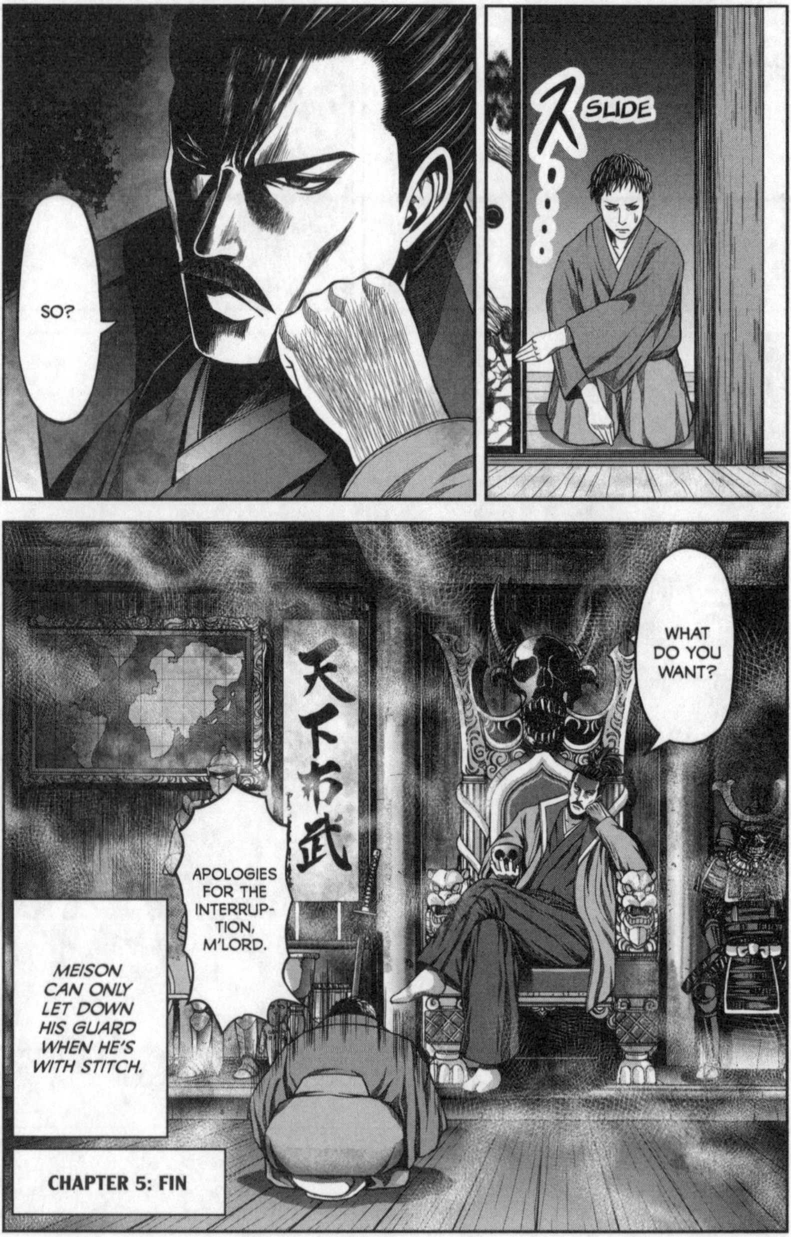
SLIDE
SO?
WHAT DO YOU WANT?
天下布武
APOLOGIES FOR THE INTERRUP-TION, M'LORD.
MEISON CAN ONLY LET DOWN HIS GUARD WHEN HE'S WITH STITCH.
CHAPTER 5: FIN

Disney
Stitch
STITCH & THE SAMURAI

PLAYTIME FOR MEISON & STITCH

ONE FALL DAY, MEISON YAMATO AND STITCH DECIDED TO PLAY A GAME WHERE THEY TOOK TURNS CARVING OUT SAND FROM A TOWER TO SEE WHO COULD KEEP THE STICK STANDING LONGEST. STITCH TOOK OUT A HUGE CLUMP IN ONE SWOOP, LEAVING MEISON STRUGGLING TO MAINTAIN A CALM DEMEANOR AS HE FRANTICALLY SEARCHED FOR A WAY TO RECOVER.

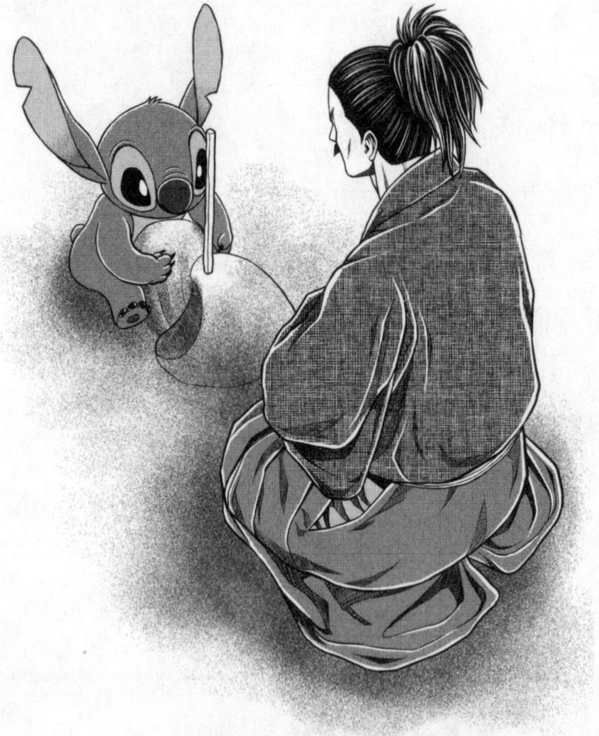

"PICTURE SCROLL DEPICTING THE LIFE OF THE YAMATO CLAN," PART OF THE GEKOKU MUNICIPAL MUSEUM ARCHIVES.

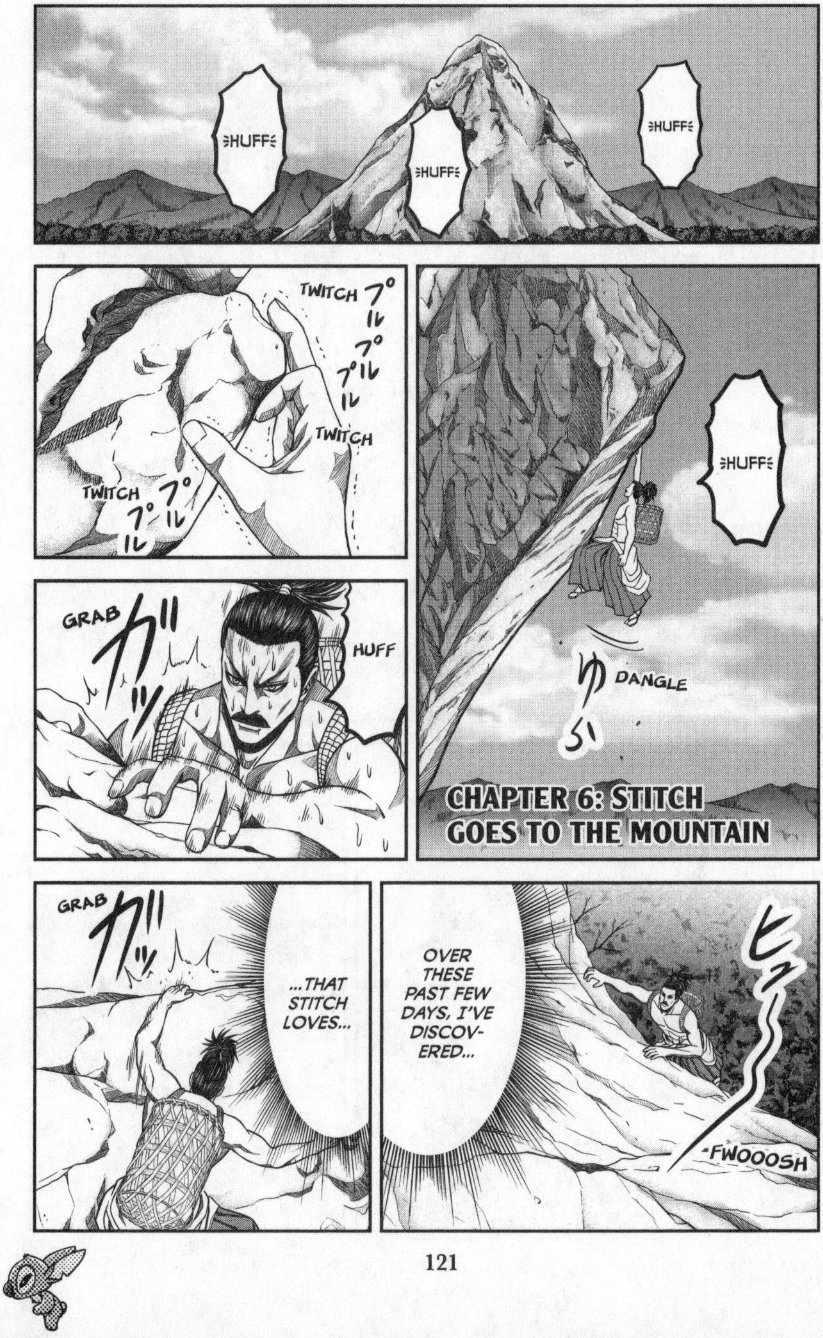
HUFF
HUFF
HUFF
HUFF
ゆら DANGLE
CHAPTER 6: STITCH GOES TO THE MOUNTAIN
TWITCH プルプルプル
TWITCH
TWITCH プルプル
GRAB ガッ
HUFF
ヒュー
FWOOOSH
OVER THESE PAST FEW DAYS, I'VE DISCOVERED...
...THAT STITCH LOVES...
GRAB ガッ

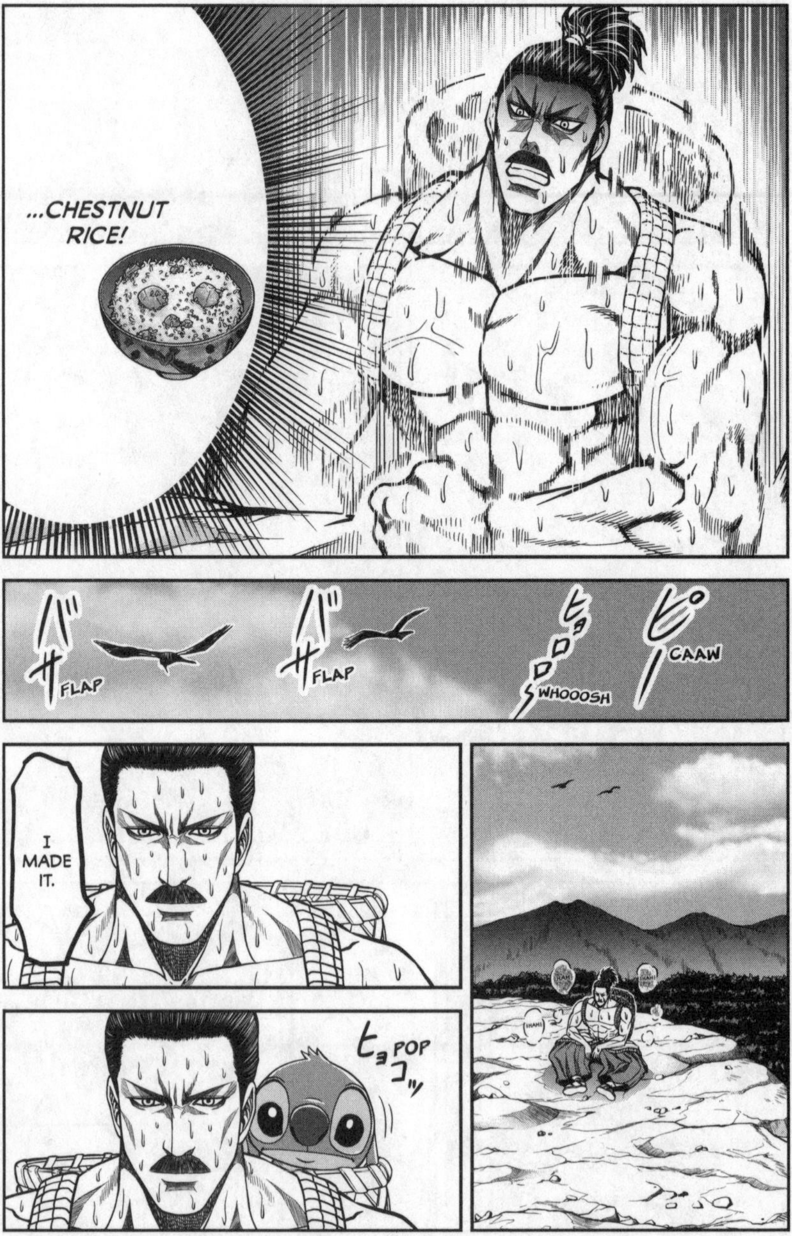
...CHESTNUT RICE!
ピ
CAAW
ヒョロロ
WHOOOSH
バサ
FLAP
バサ
FLAP
I MADE IT.
ヒョコッ
POP

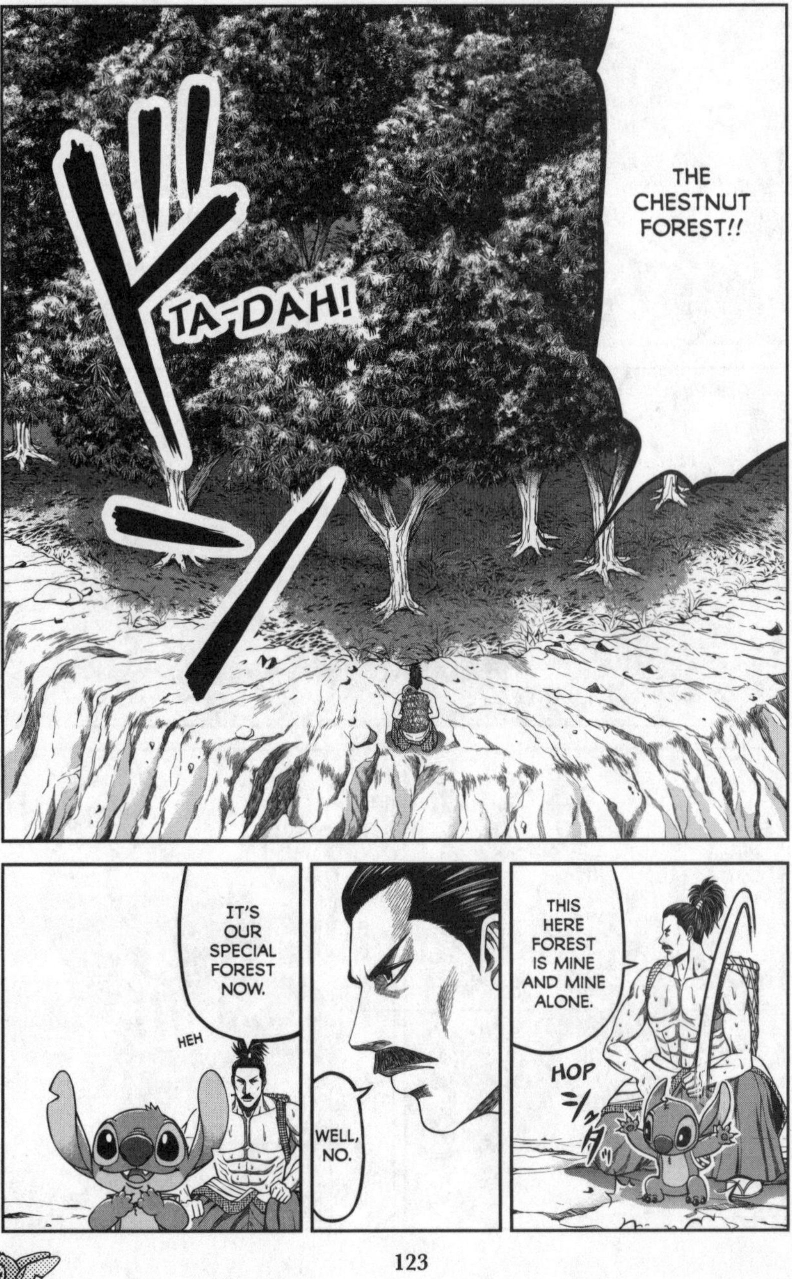
THE CHESTNUT FOREST!!
TA-DAH!
THIS HERE FOREST IS MINE AND MINE ALONE.
HOP
WELL, NO.
IT'S OUR SPECIAL FOREST NOW.
HEH

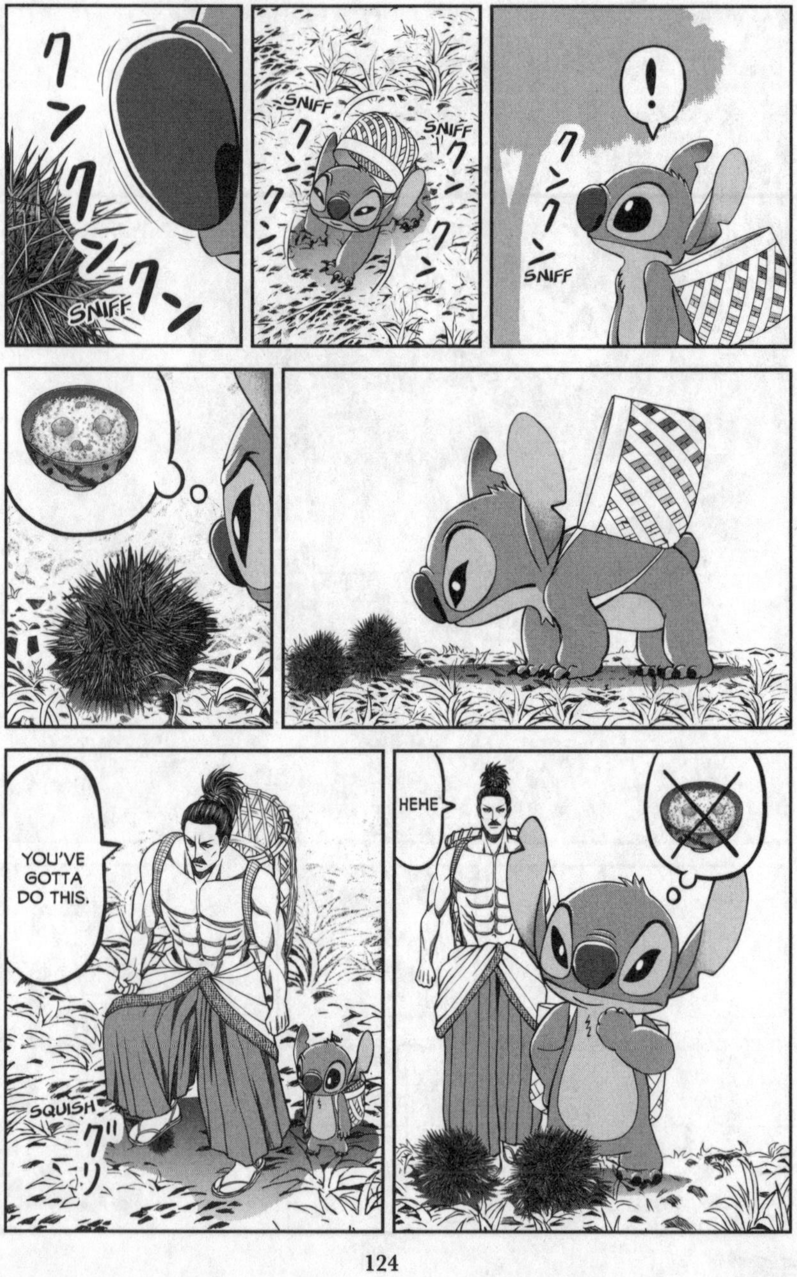
!
クンクン
SNIFF
SNIFF
クンクン
SNIFF
クンクン
クンクン
クンクン
SNIFF
HEHE
YOU'VE GOTTA DO THIS.
SQUISH
グリ

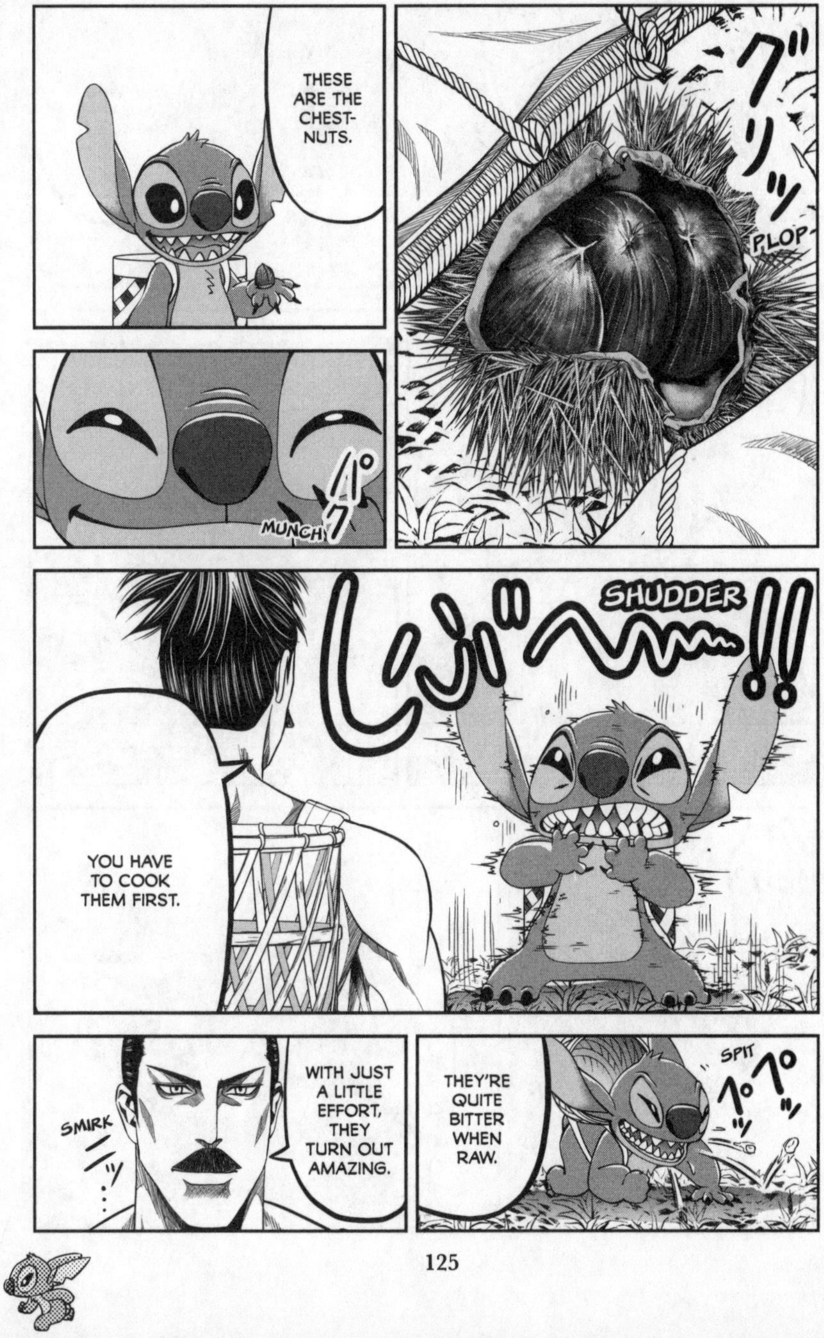
PLOP
THESE ARE THE CHEST-NUTS.
MUNCH
SHUDDER
YOU HAVE TO COOK THEM FIRST.
SPIT
THEY'RE QUITE BITTER WHEN RAW.
WITH JUST A LITTLE EFFORT, THEY TURN OUT AMAZING.
SMIRK

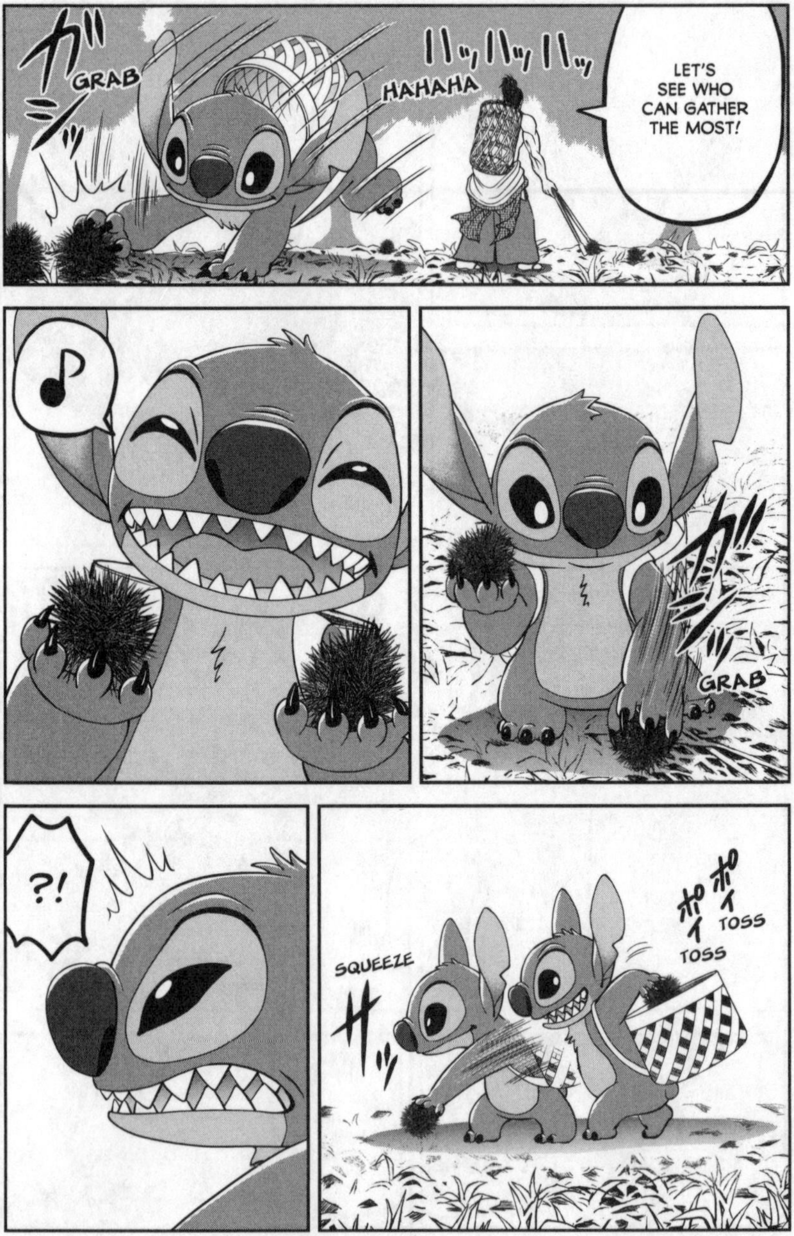
LET'S SEE WHO CAN GATHER THE MOST!
HAHAHA
GRAB
GRAB
♪
TOSS
TOSS
SQUEEZE
?!

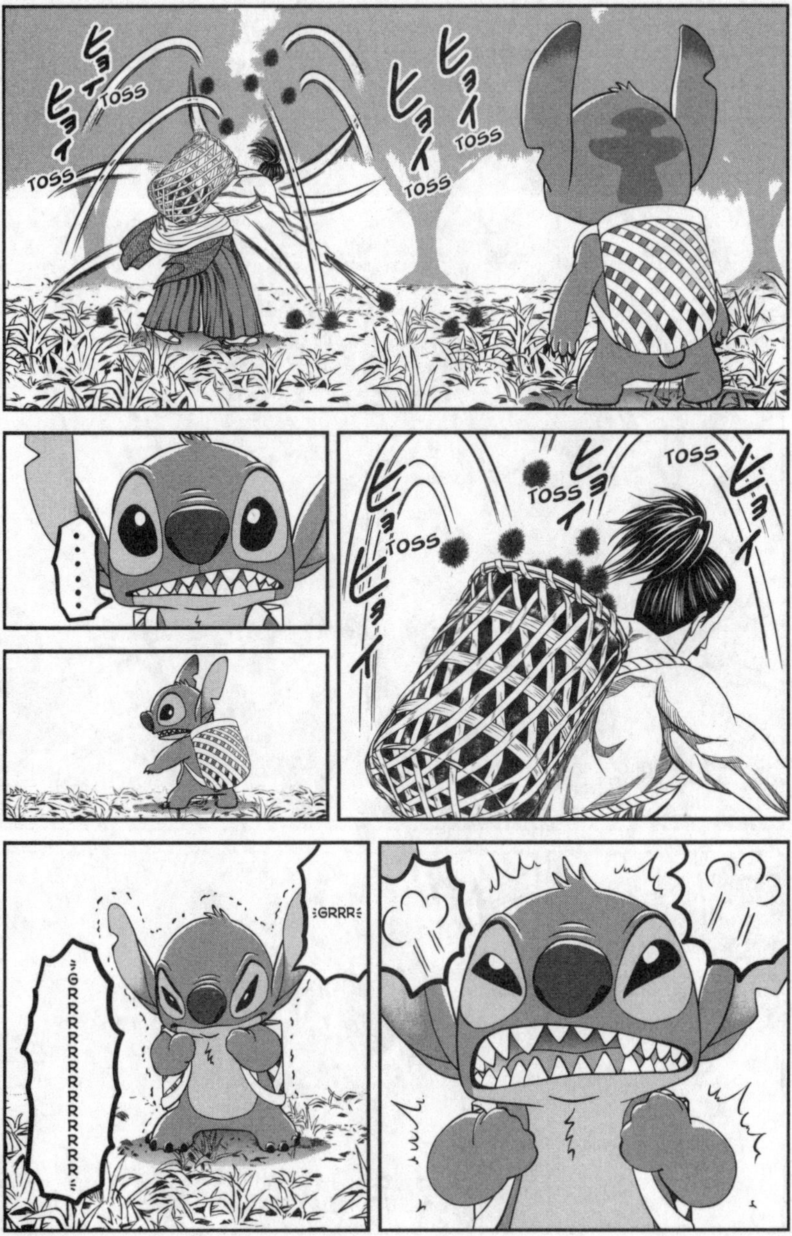
ヒョイ
TOSS
ヒョイ
TOSS
ヒョイ
TOSS
ヒョイ
TOSS
TOSS
ヒョイ
TOSS
ヒョイ
TOSS
ヒョイ
ヒョイ
......
GRRR
GRRRRRRRRRRRRRR

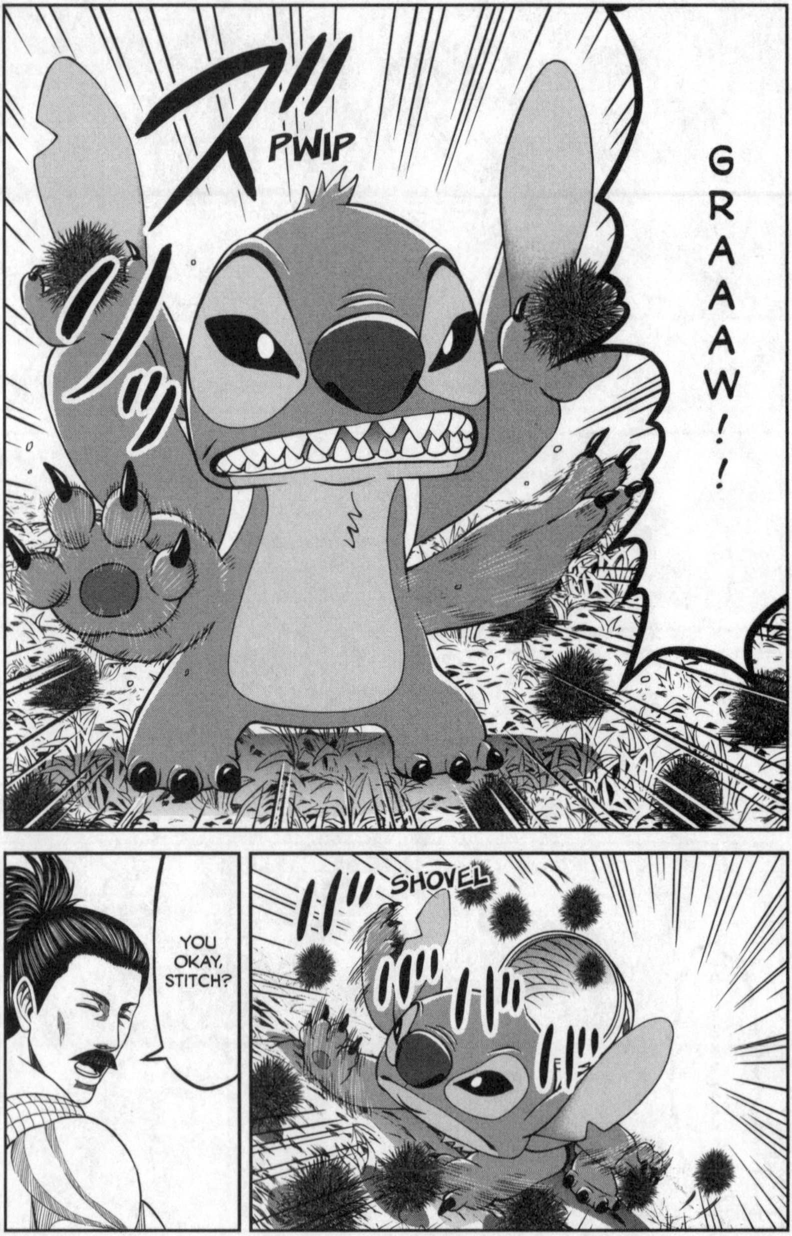
GRAAAW!!
PWIP
SHOVEL
YOU OKAY, STITCH?

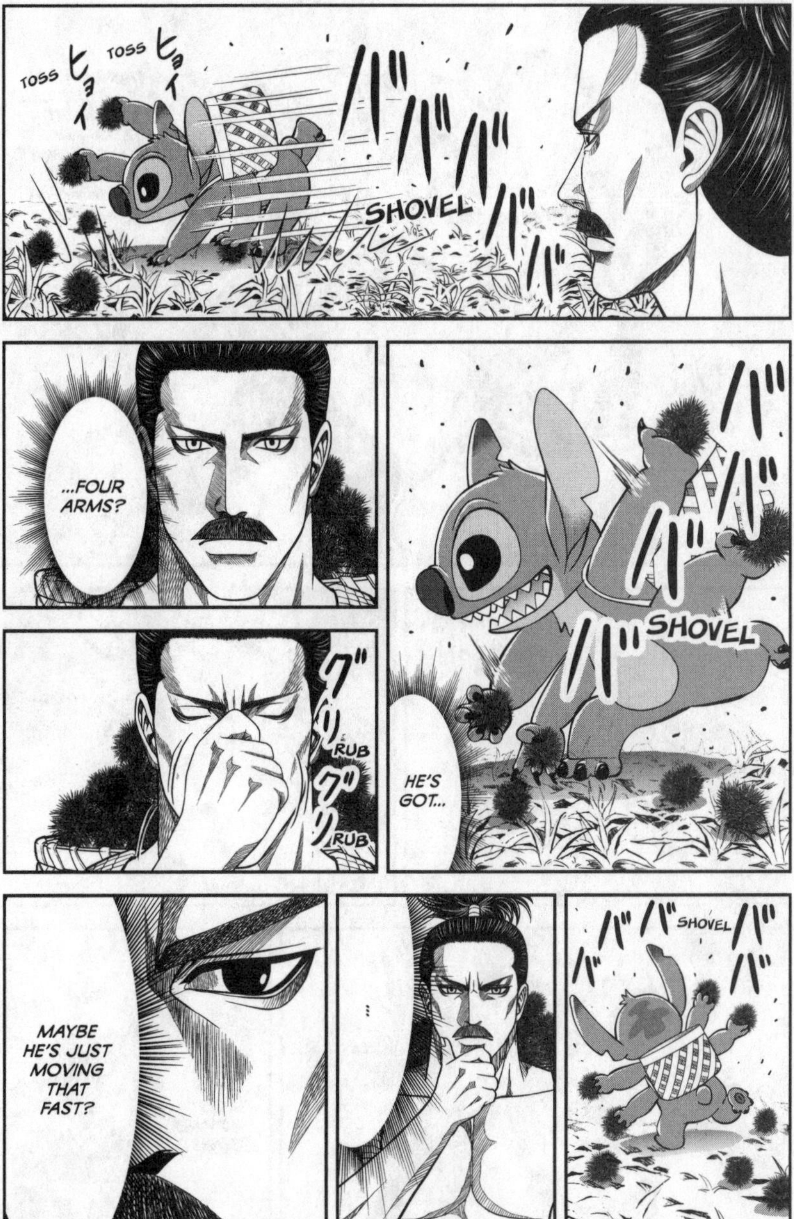
TOSS
ヒョイ
TOSS
ヒョイ
バババババ
SHOVEL
バババババ
SHOVEL
HE'S GOT...
...FOUR ARMS?
グリグリ
RUB
RUB
ババ
SHOVEL
ババ
...
MAYBE HE'S JUST MOVING THAT FAST?

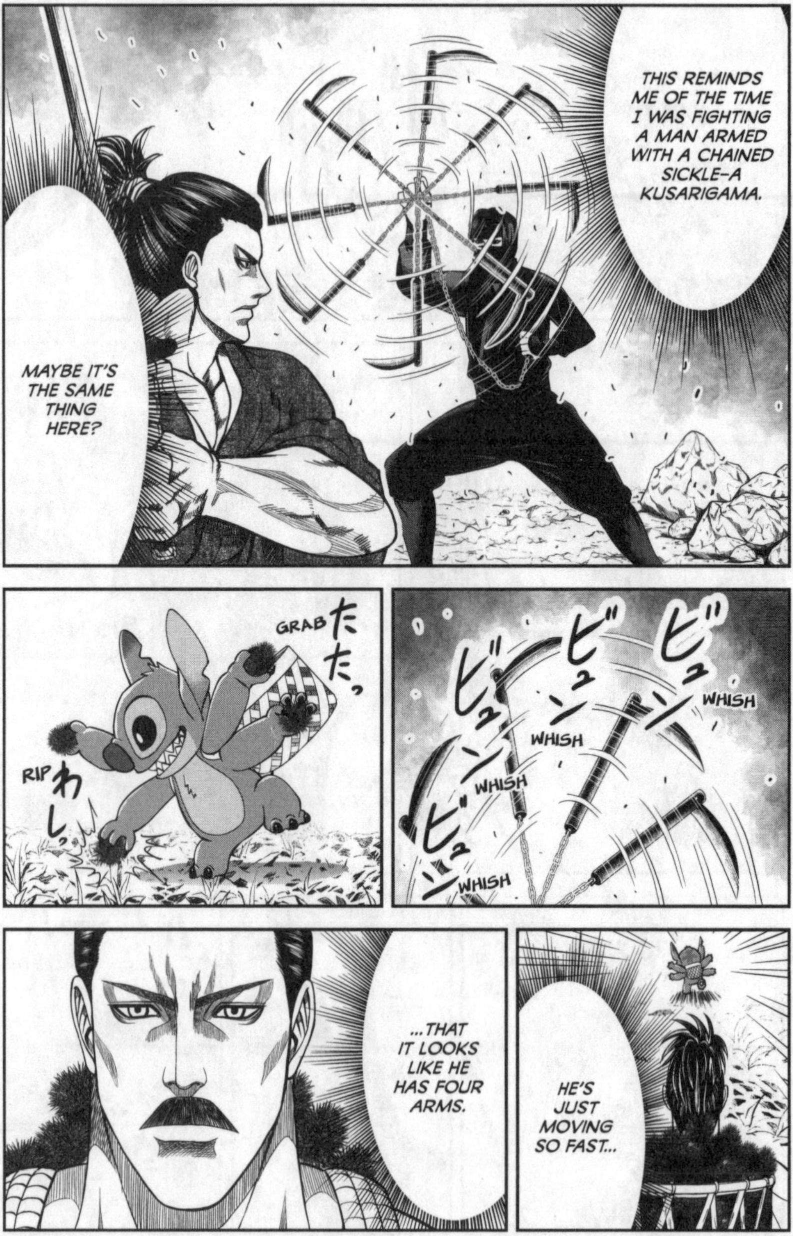
THIS REMINDS ME OF THE TIME I WAS FIGHTING A MAN ARMED WITH A CHAINED SICKLE–A KUSARIGAMA.
MAYBE IT'S THE SAME THING HERE?
ビュン
WHISH
ビュン
WHISH
ビュン
WHISH
ビュン
WHISH
たたっ
GRAB
わしっ
RIP
HE'S JUST MOVING SO FAST...
...THAT IT LOOKS LIKE HE HAS FOUR ARMS.

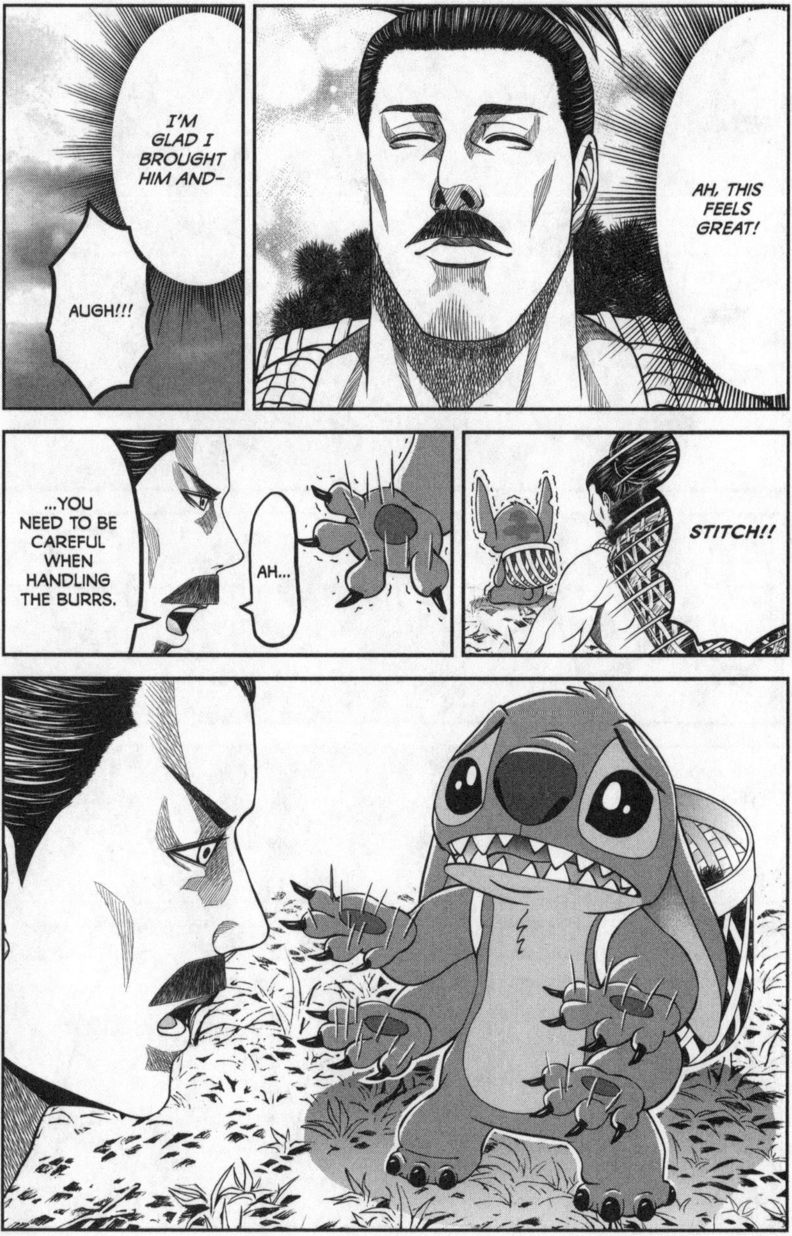
AH, THIS FEELS GREAT!
I'M GLAD I BROUGHT HIM AND-
AUGH!!!
STITCH!!
AH...
...YOU NEED TO BE CAREFUL WHEN HANDLING THE BURRS.

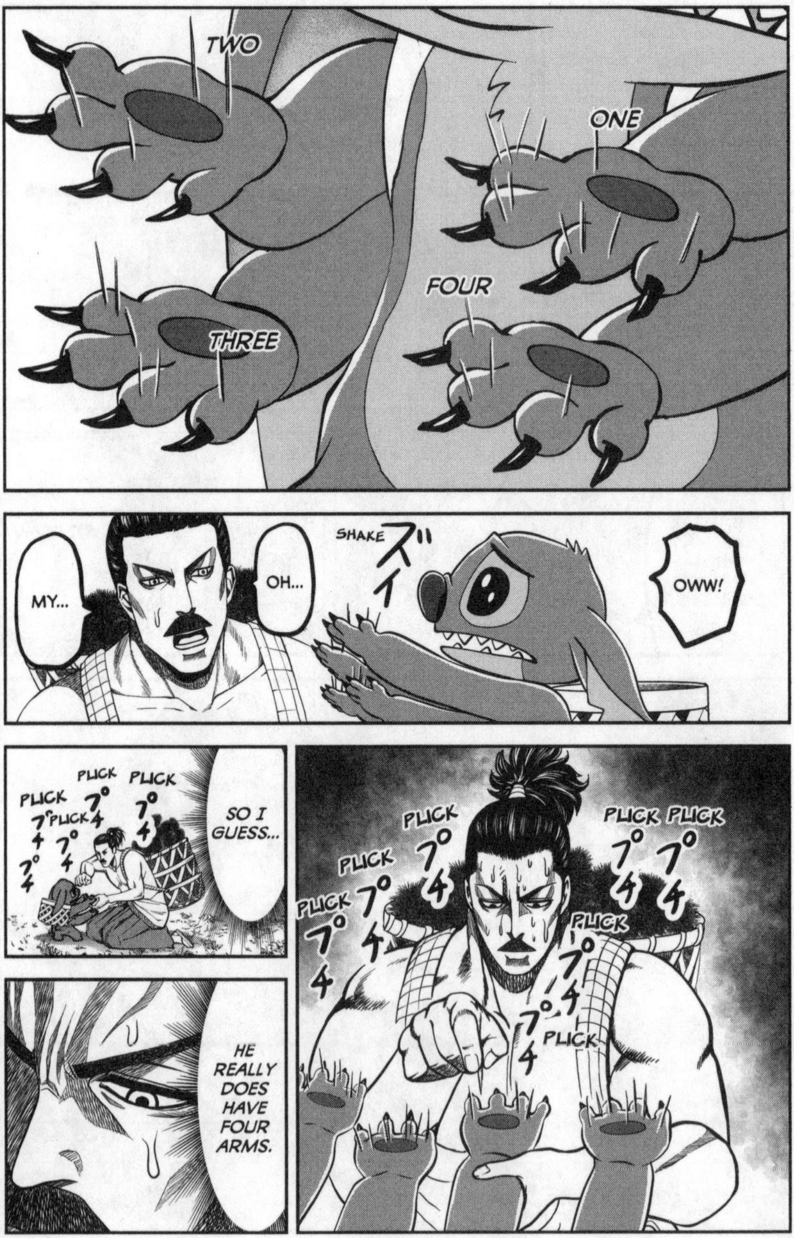
ONE
TWO
FOUR
THREE
OWW!
SHAKE ズイ
OH...
MY...
PLICK PLICK プチ プチ
PLICK プチ
PLICK プチ
PLICK プチ
PLICK プチ
PLICK プチ
PLICK プチ
SO I GUESS...
PLICK プチ
PLICK プチ
PLICK プチ
PLICK プチ
HE REALLY DOES HAVE FOUR ARMS.

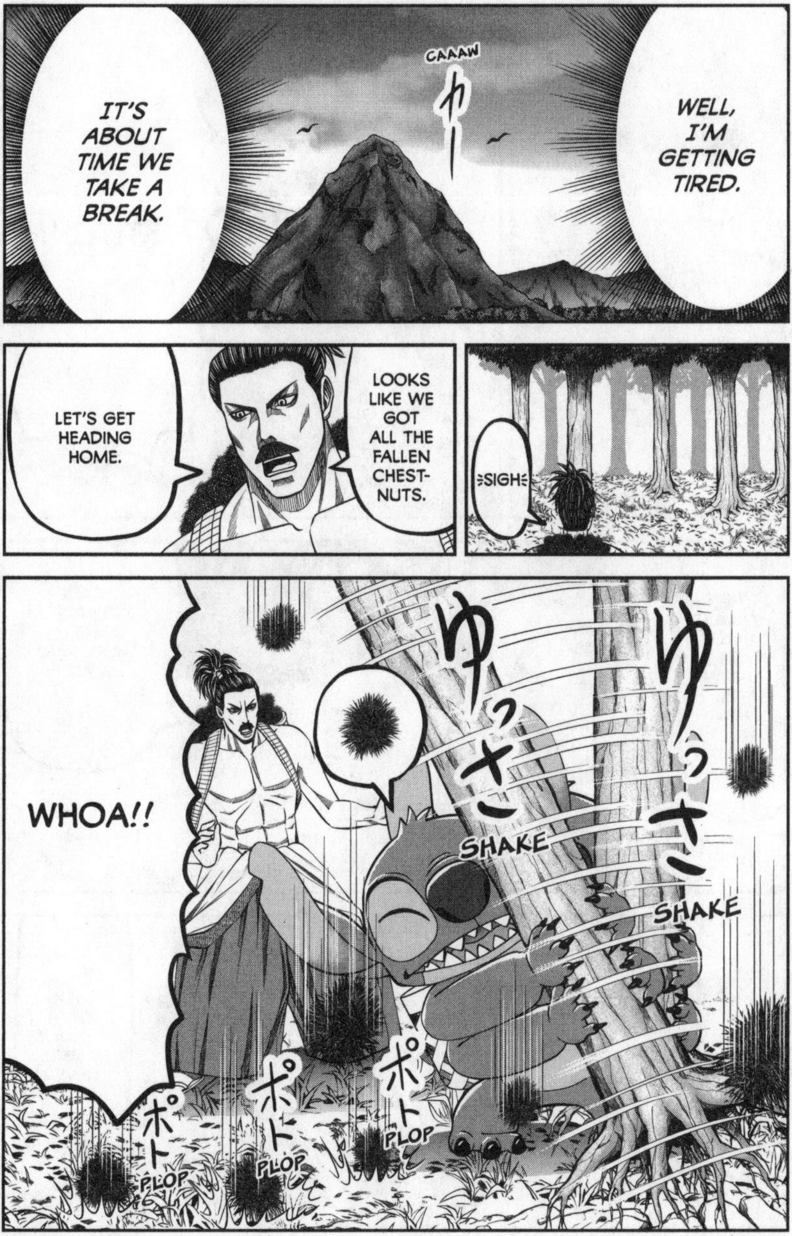
WELL, I'M GETTING TIRED.
CAAAW
カー
IT'S ABOUT TIME WE TAKE A BREAK.
SIGH
LOOKS LIKE WE GOT ALL THE FALLEN CHEST-NUTS.
LET'S GET HEADING HOME.
ゆっさ
SHAKE
ゆっさ
SHAKE
WHOA!!
ポト
PLOP
ポト
PLOP
ポト
PLOP

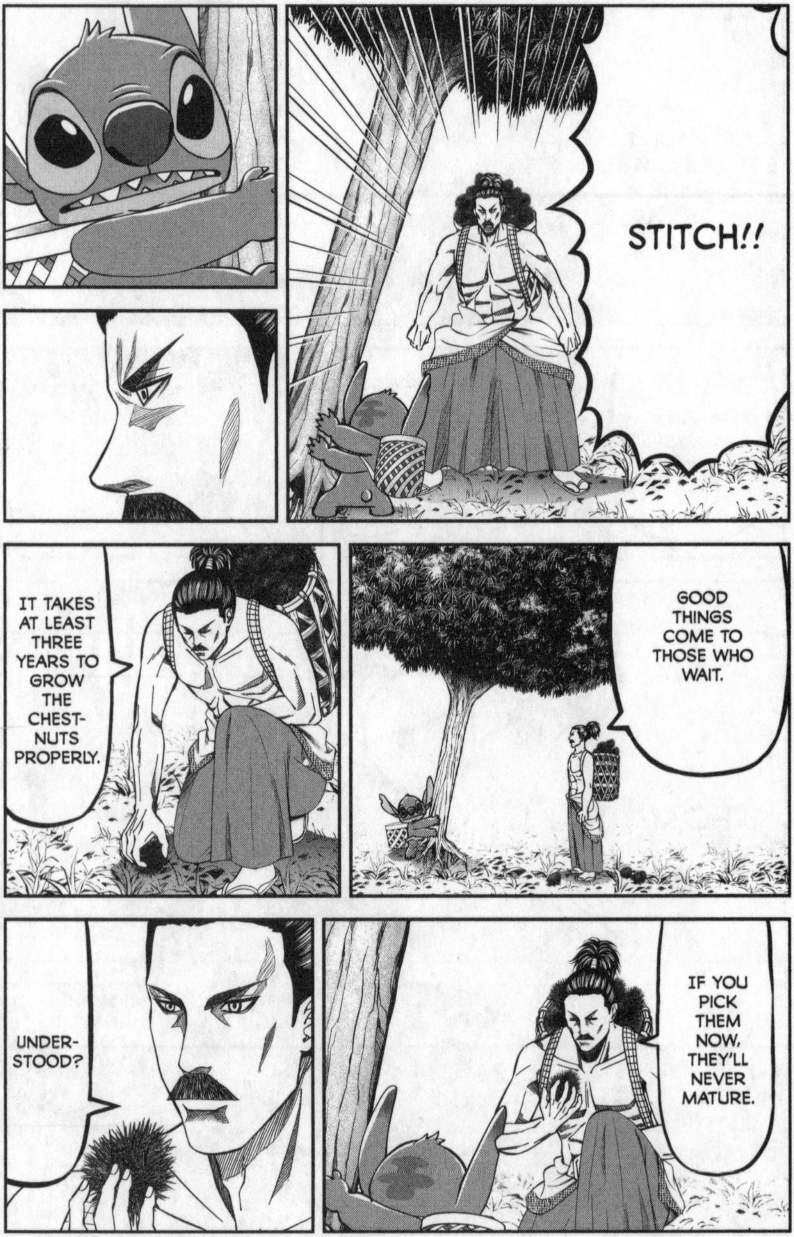
STITCH!!
GOOD THINGS COME TO THOSE WHO WAIT.
IT TAKES AT LEAST THREE YEARS TO GROW THE CHEST-NUTS PROPERLY.
IF YOU PICK THEM NOW, THEY'LL NEVER MATURE.
UNDER-STOOD?

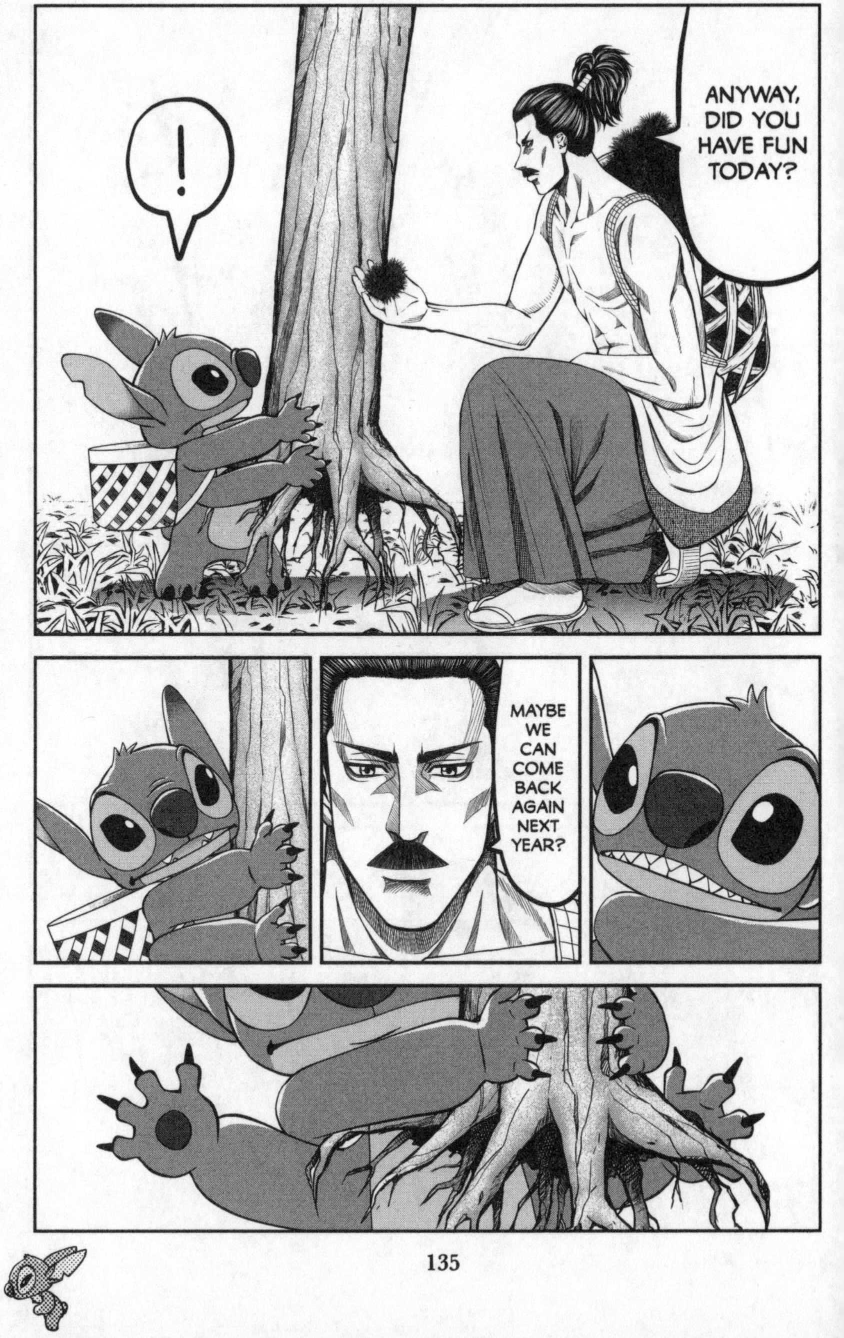
ANYWAY, DID YOU HAVE FUN TODAY?
!
MAYBE WE CAN COME BACK AGAIN NEXT YEAR?

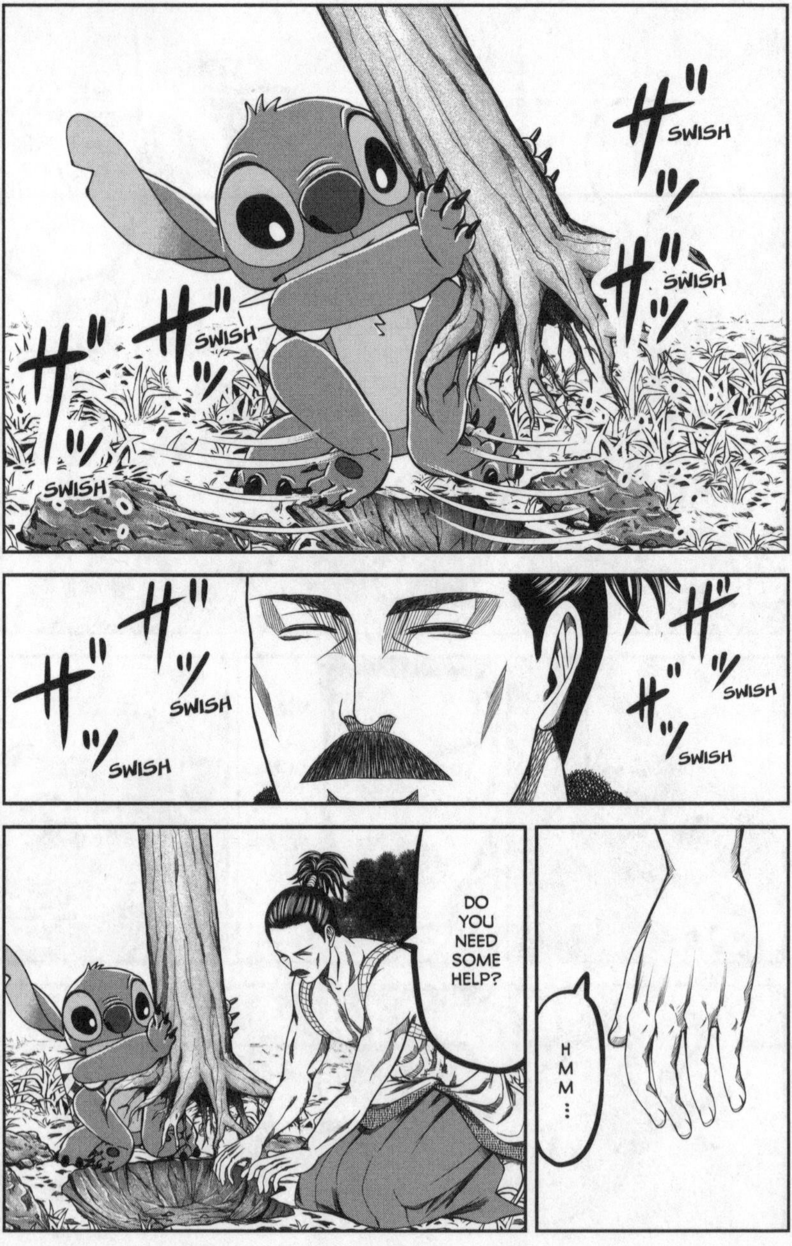
ザッ SWISH
ザッ SWISH
ザッ SWISH
ザッ SWISH
ザッ SWISH
ザッ SWISH
ザッ SWISH
ザッ SWISH
HMM...
DO YOU NEED SOME HELP?

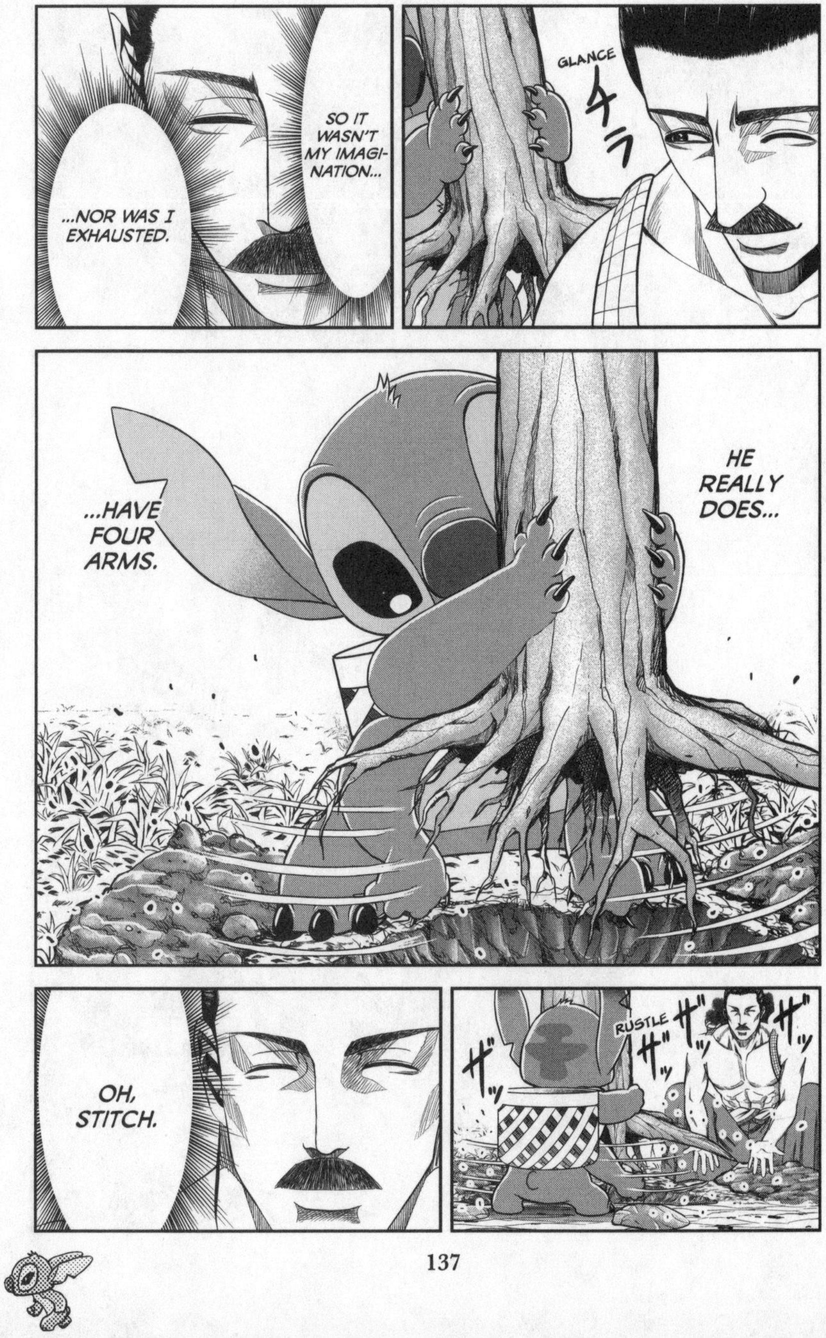
GLANCE
チラ
SO IT WASN'T MY IMAGINATION...
...NOR WAS I EXHAUSTED.
HE REALLY DOES...
...HAVE FOUR ARMS.
RUSTLE
ザッ ザッ ザッ ザッ
OH, STITCH.

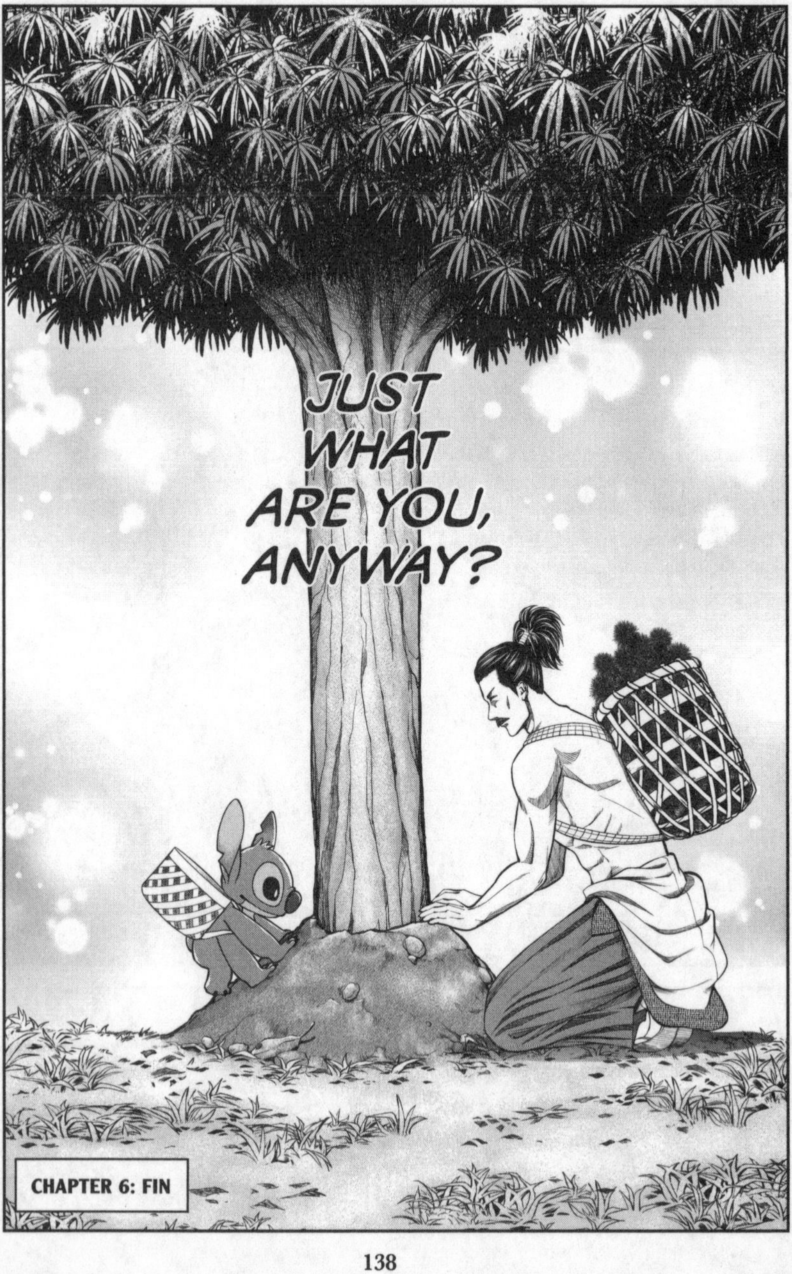
JUST WHAT ARE YOU, ANYWAY?
CHAPTER 6: FIN

Disney

Stitch

STITCH & THE SAMURAI

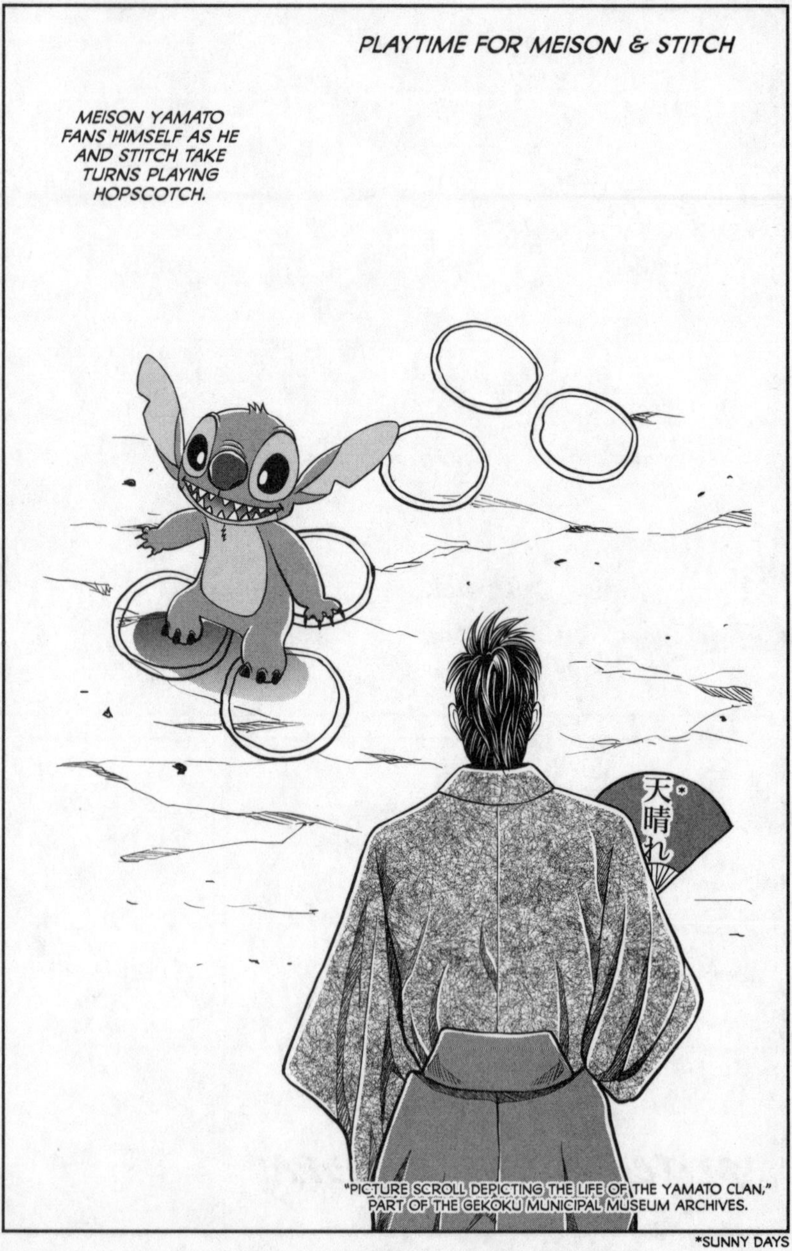
PLAYTIME FOR MEISON & STITCH
MEISON YAMATO FANS HIMSELF AS HE AND STITCH TAKE TURNS PLAYING HOPSCOTCH.
天*晴れ
"PICTURE SCROLL DEPICTING THE LIFE OF THE YAMATO CLAN," PART OF THE GEKOKU MUNICIPAL MUSEUM ARCHIVES.
*SUNNY DAYS

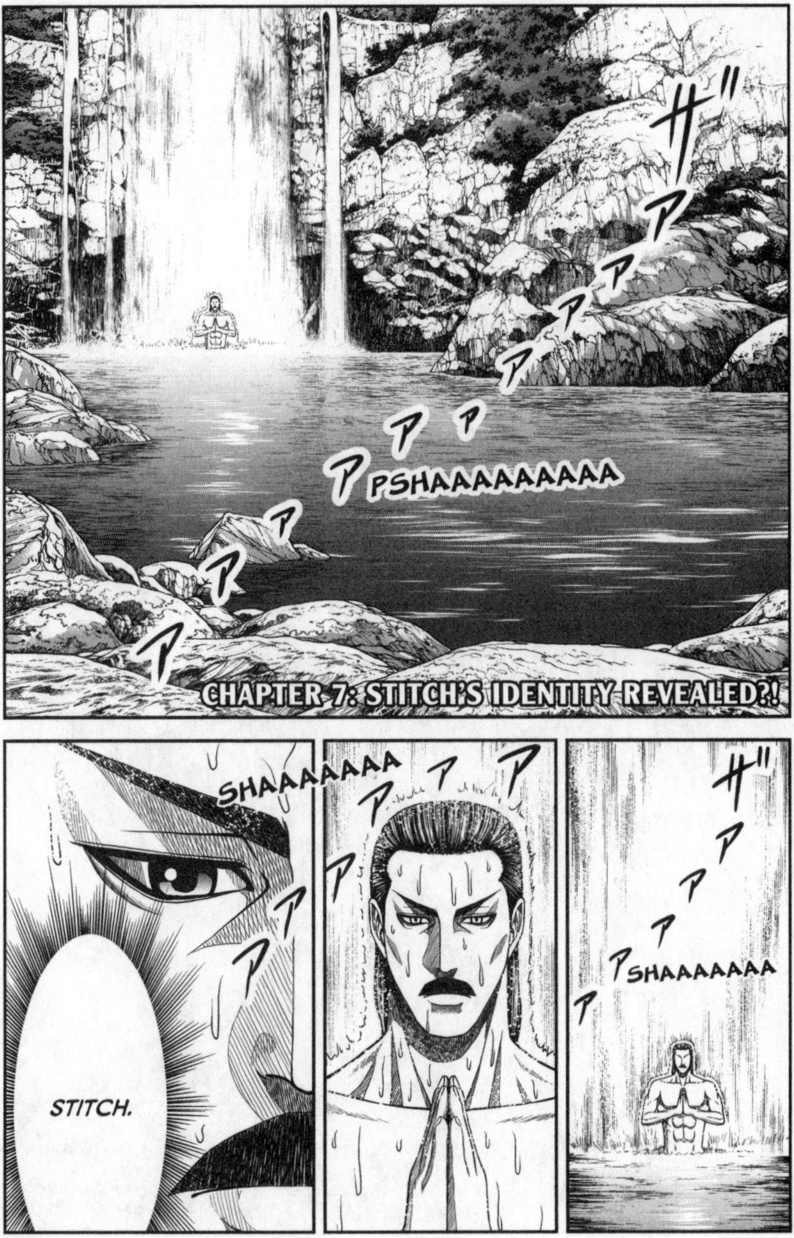
ザアアアアアアアアアア
PSHAAAAAAAAAA
CHAPTER 7: STITCH'S IDENTITY REVEALED?!
ザアアアアア
SHAAAAAAA
SHAAAAAAA
アアアアアアア
STITCH.

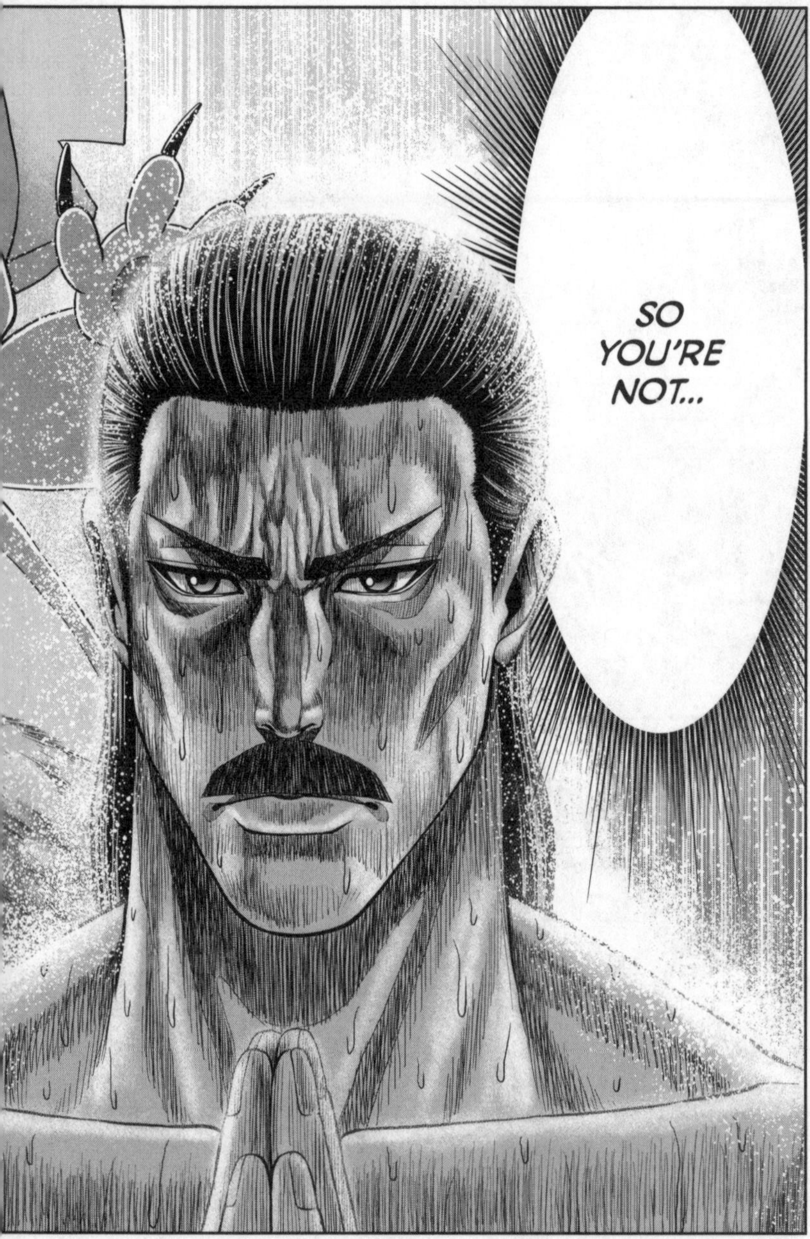
SO YOU'RE NOT...

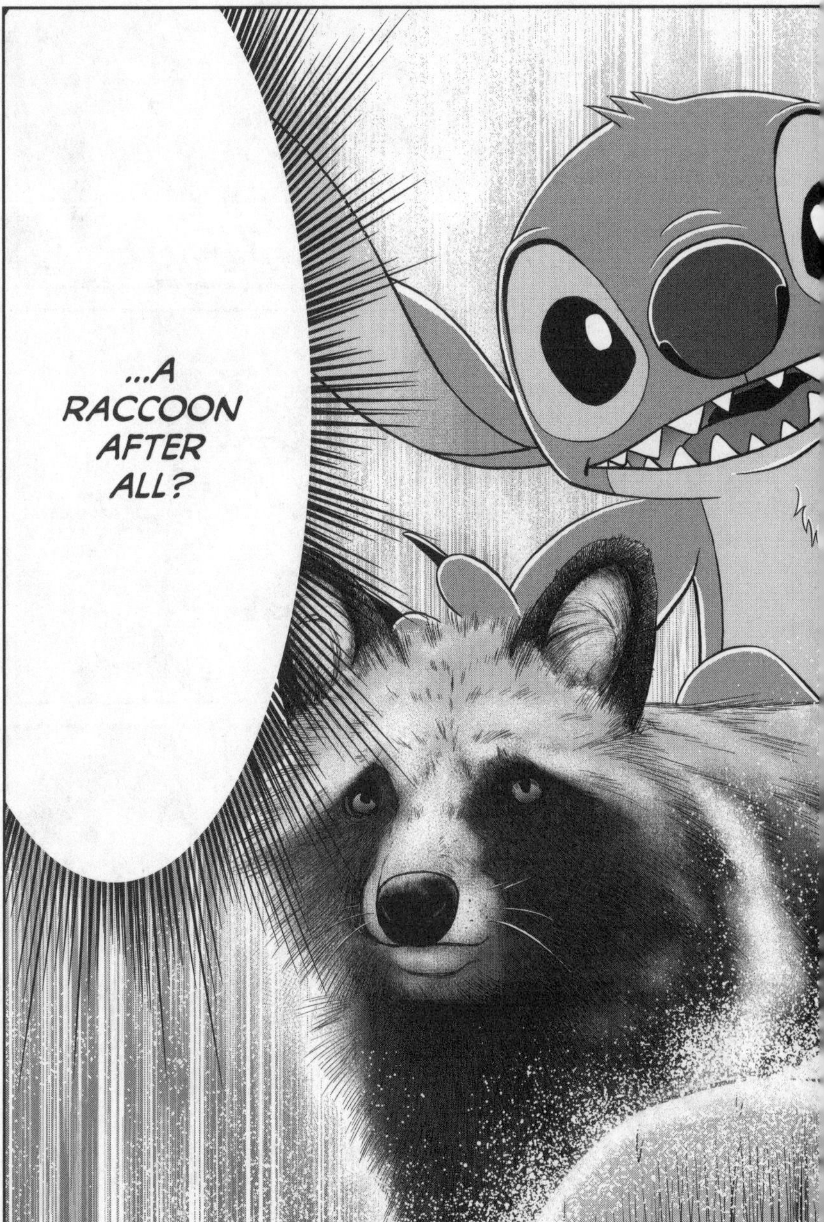
...A RACCOON AFTER ALL?

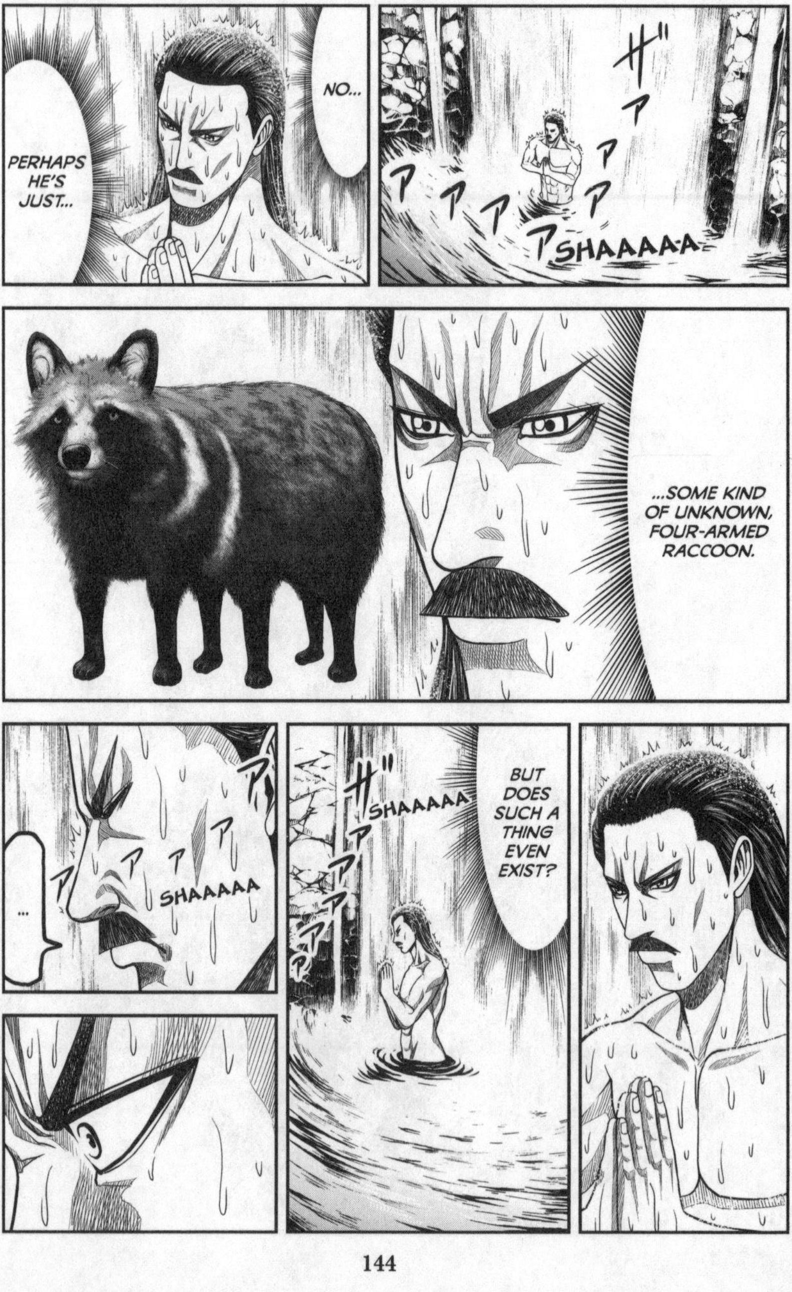
SHAAAA-A
NO...
PERHAPS HE'S JUST...
...SOME KIND OF UNKNOWN, FOUR-ARMED RACCOON.
SHAAAAA
BUT DOES SUCH A THING EVEN EXIST?
SHAAAAA
...

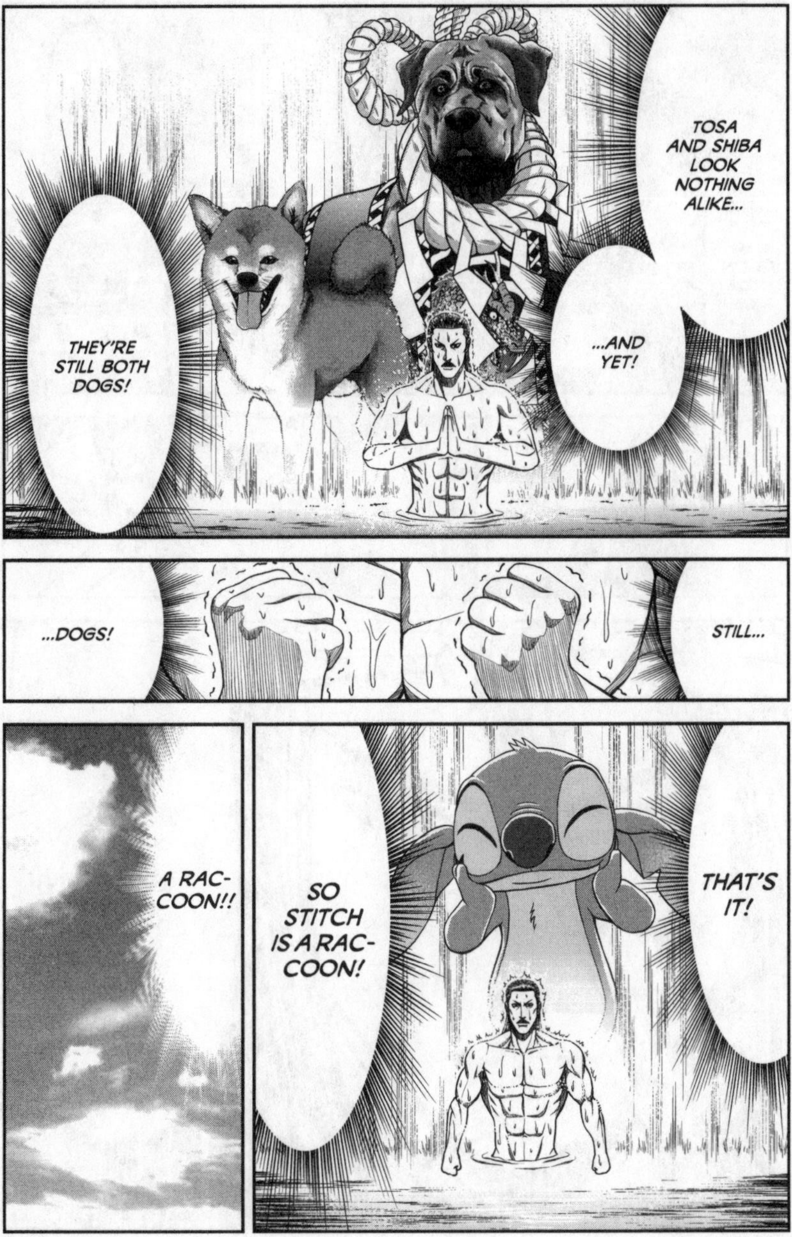
TOSA AND SHIBA LOOK NOTHING ALIKE...
...AND YET!
THEY'RE STILL BOTH DOGS!
STILL...
...DOGS!
THAT'S IT!
SO STITCH IS A RAC-COON!
A RAC-COON!!

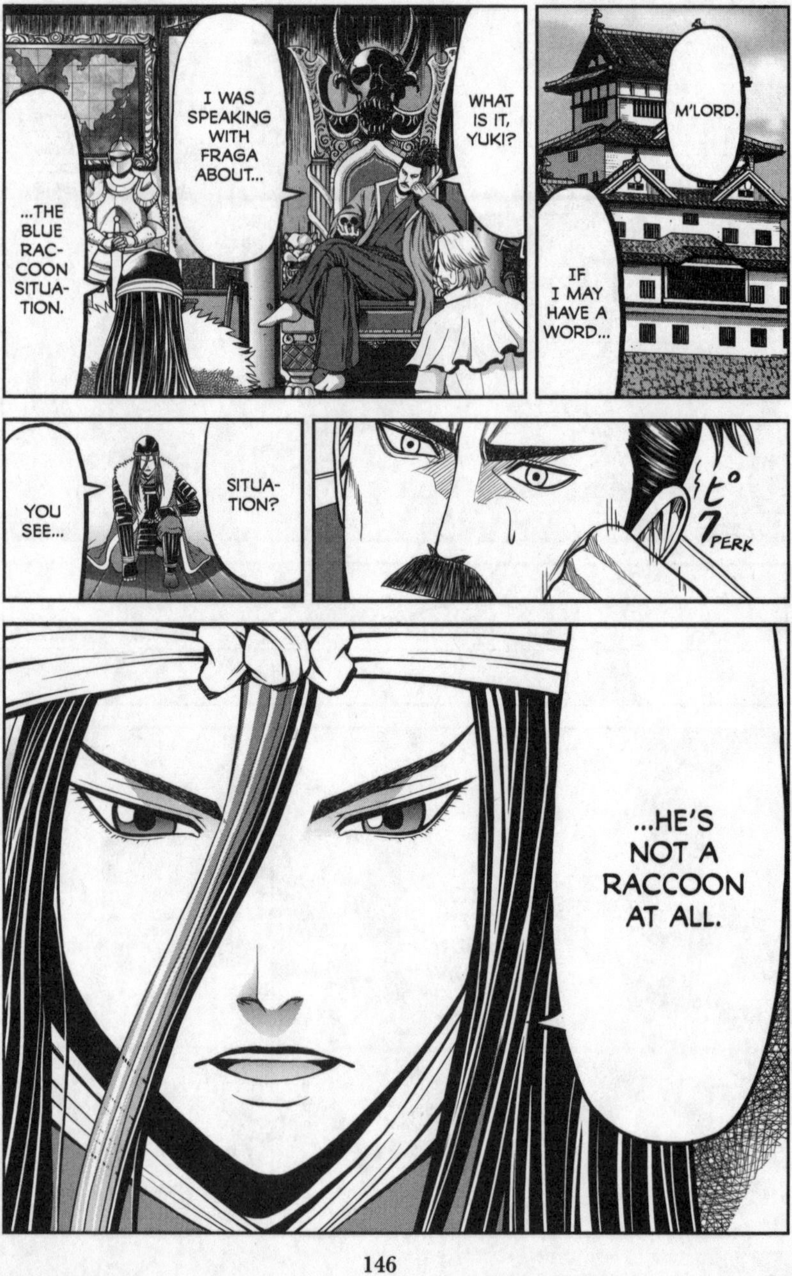
M'LORD.
IF I MAY HAVE A WORD...
WHAT IS IT, YUKI?
I WAS SPEAKING WITH FRAGA ABOUT...
...THE BLUE RACCOON SITUATION.
ピク
PERK
SITUATION?
YOU SEE...
...HE'S NOT A RACCOON AT ALL.

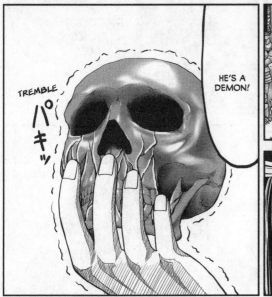

TREMBLE
パキッ

HE'S A
DEMON!

S-SO...

...WHAT
ARE
YOU
SAY-
ING?

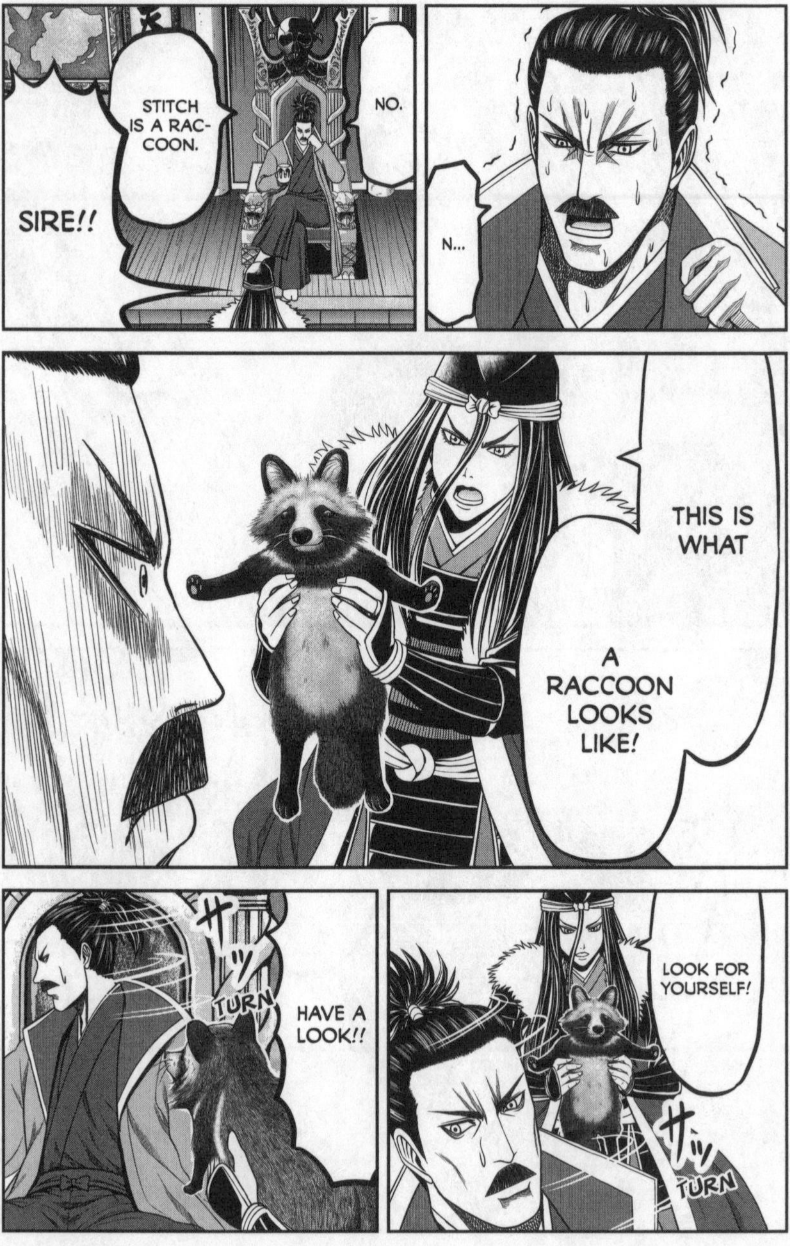
N...
NO.
STITCH IS A RAC-COON.
SIRE!!
THIS IS WHAT A RACCOON LOOKS LIKE!
LOOK FOR YOURSELF!
サッ
TURN
サッ
TURN
HAVE A LOOK!!

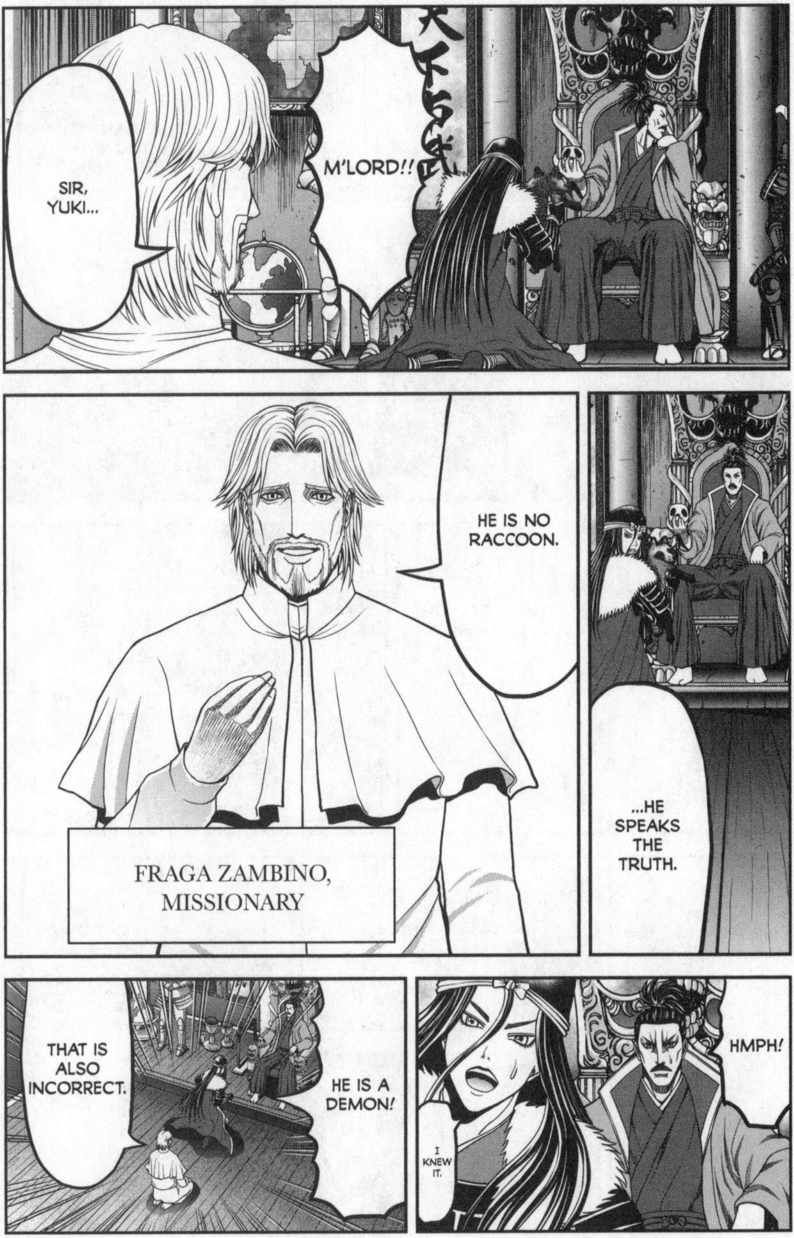
M'LORD!!
SIR, YUKI...
...HE SPEAKS THE TRUTH.
HE IS NO RACCOON.
FRAGA ZAMBINO, MISSIONARY
HMPH!
I KNEW IT.
HE IS A DEMON!
THAT IS ALSO INCORRECT.

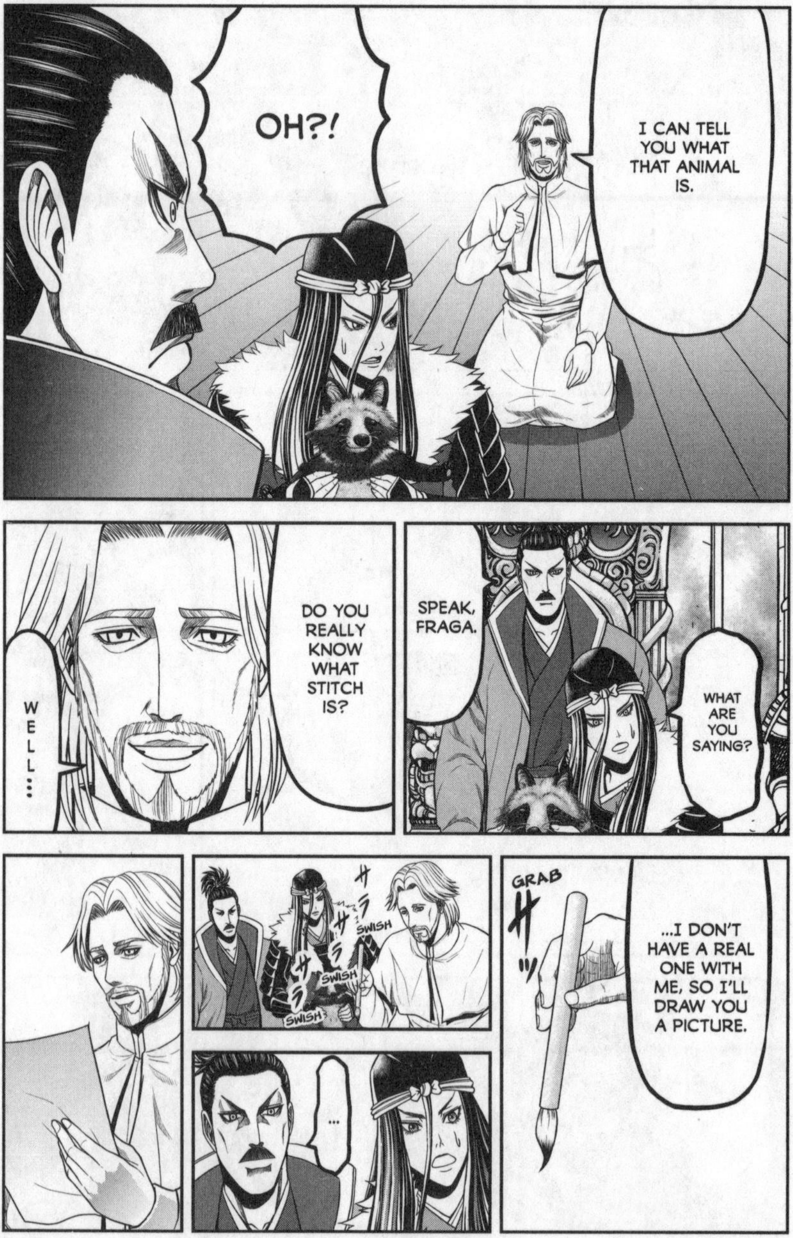
I CAN TELL YOU WHAT THAT ANIMAL IS.
OH?!
WHAT ARE YOU SAYING?
SPEAK, FRAGA.
DO YOU REALLY KNOW WHAT STITCH IS?
WELL...
GRAB
...I DON'T HAVE A REAL ONE WITH ME, SO I'LL DRAW YOU A PICTURE.
SWISH
SWISH
SWISH
...

IT'S AN ANIMAL FROM THE LANDS DOWN SOUTH.

A KOALA!

A PERFECT MATCH.

HAH?!

SMIRK

I SEE.

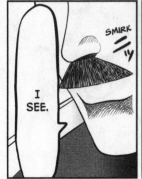

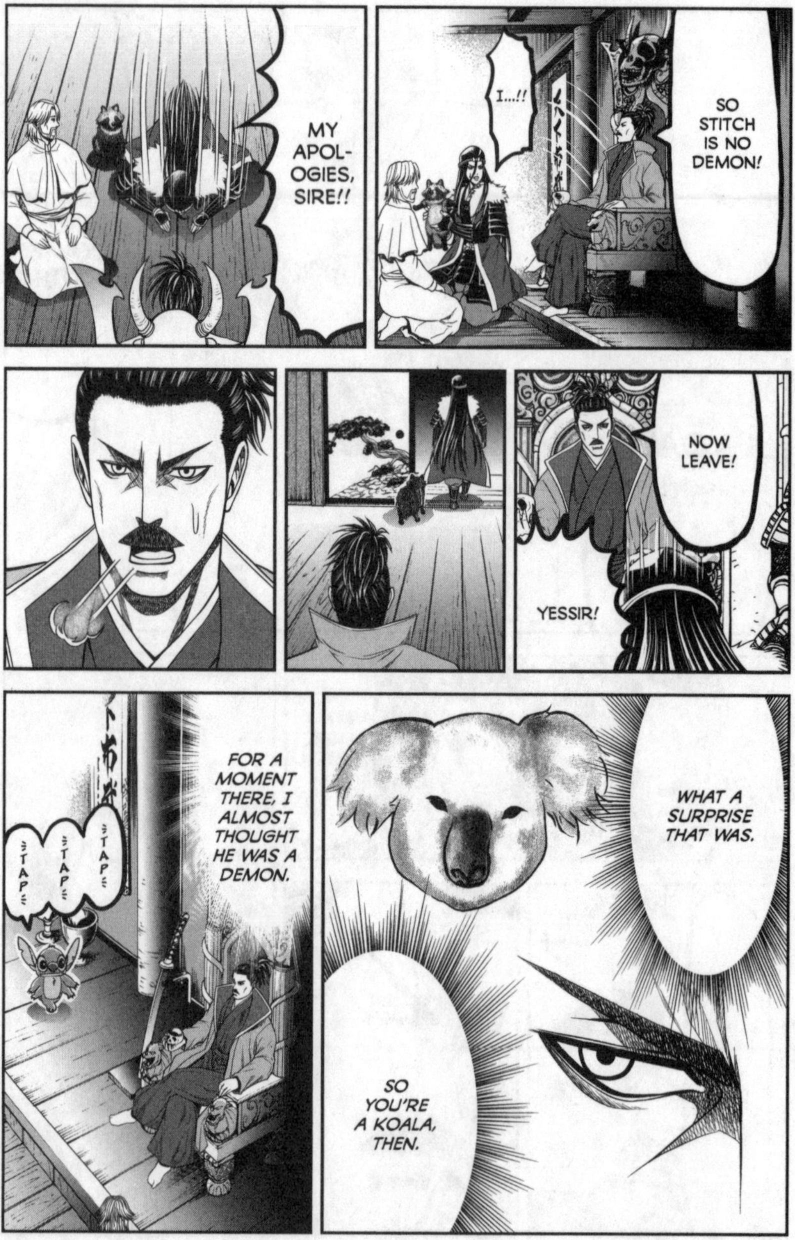
SO STITCH IS NO DEMON!
I...!!
MY APOLOGIES, SIRE!!
NOW LEAVE!
YESSIR!
WHAT A SURPRISE THAT WAS.
SO YOU'RE A KOALA, THEN.
FOR A MOMENT THERE, I ALMOST THOUGHT HE WAS A DEMON.
TAP TAP TAP

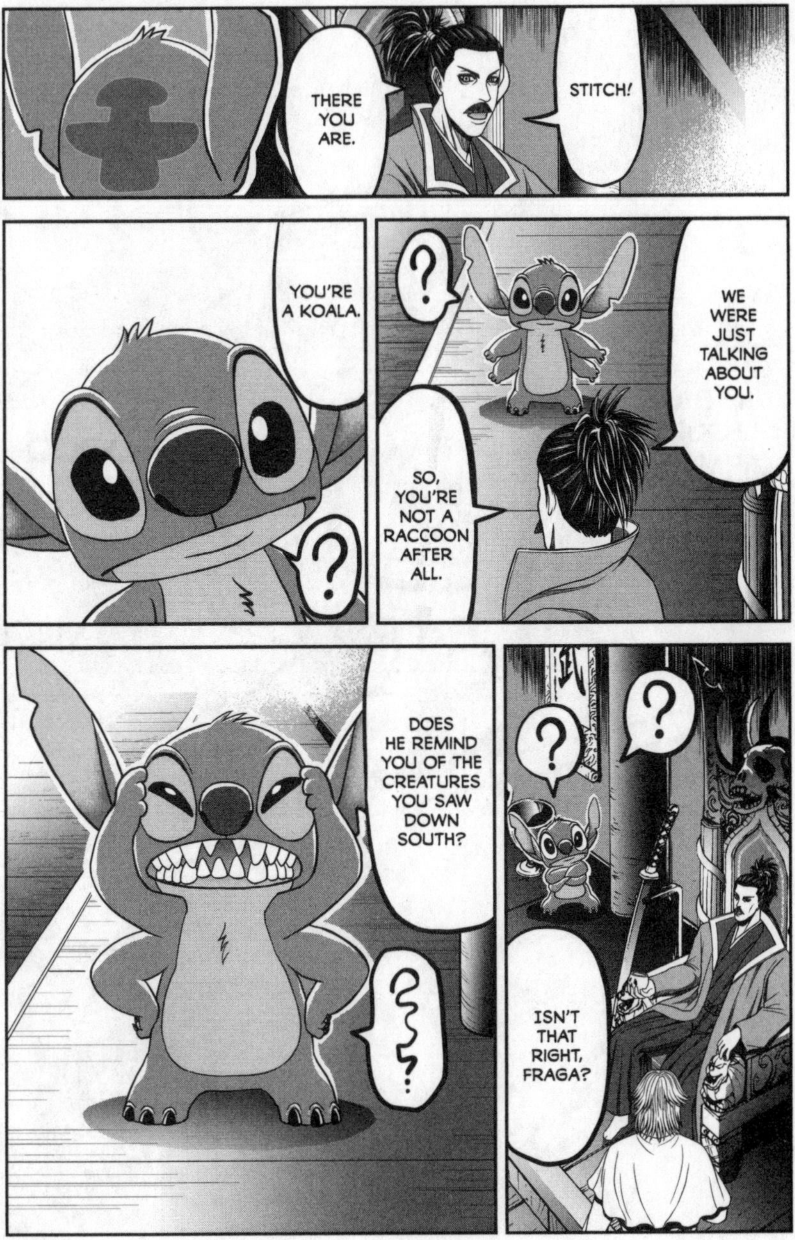
STITCH!
THERE YOU ARE.
WE WERE JUST TALKING ABOUT YOU.
?
SO, YOU'RE NOT A RACCOON AFTER ALL.
YOU'RE A KOALA.
?
?
?
ISN'T THAT RIGHT, FRAGA?
DOES HE REMIND YOU OF THE CREATURES YOU SAW DOWN SOUTH?
?

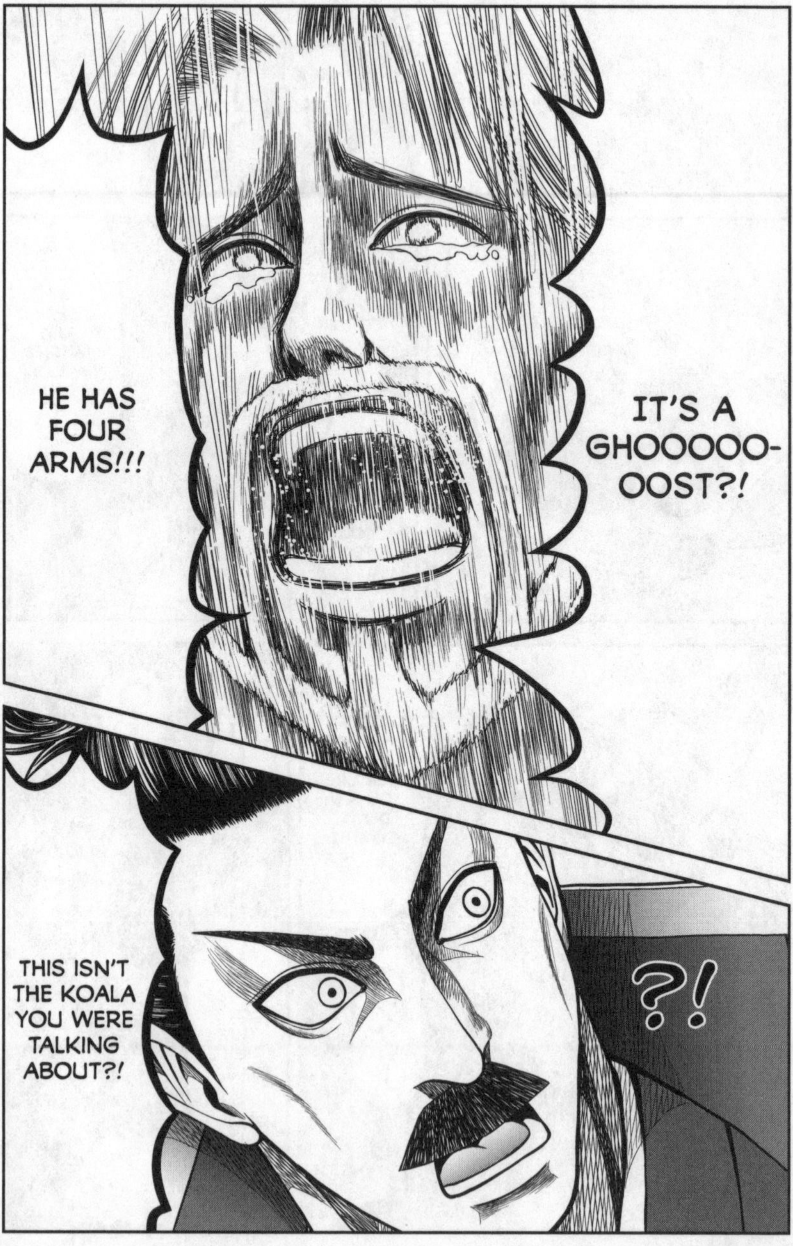
IT'S A GHOOOOO-OOST?!
HE HAS FOUR ARMS!!!
?!
THIS ISN'T THE KOALA YOU WERE TALKING ABOUT?!

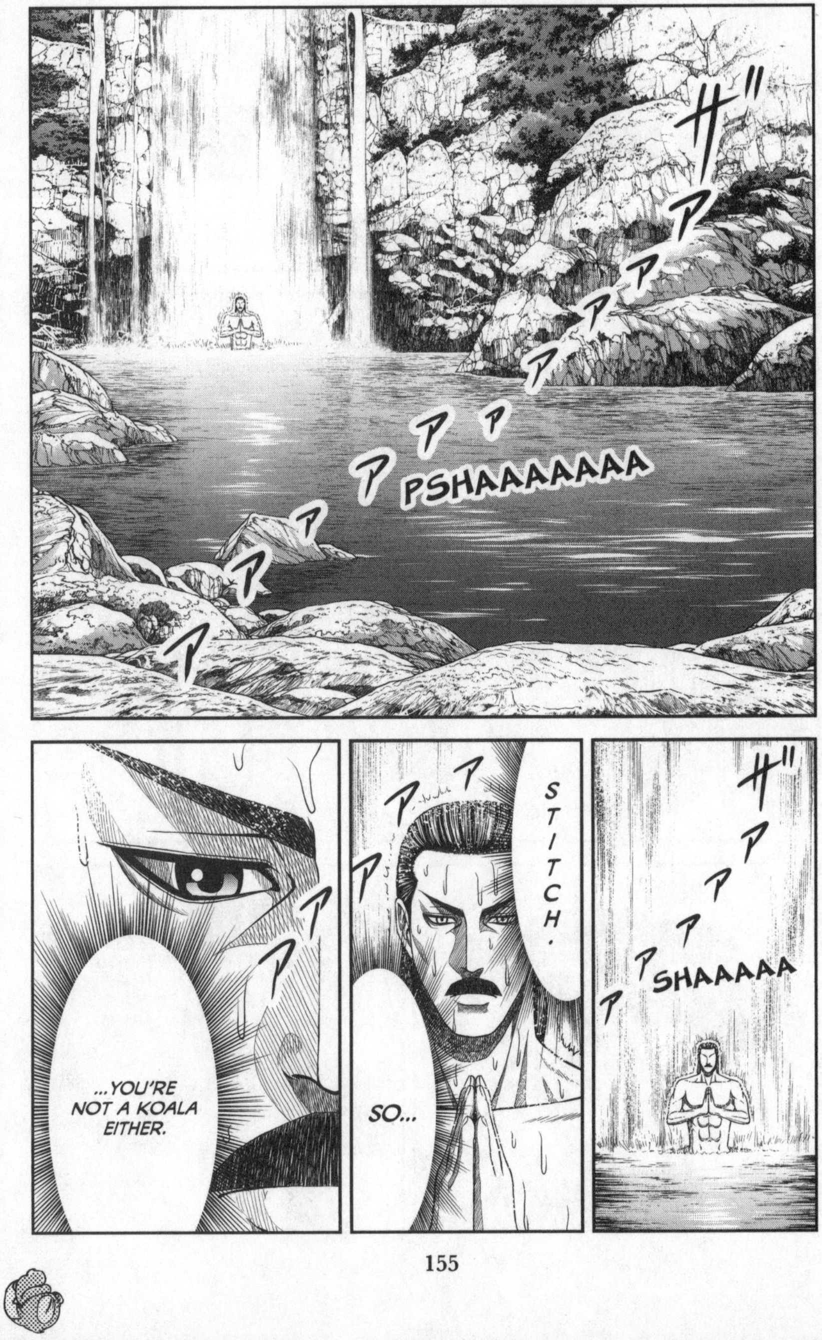
PSHAAAAAAA
SHAAAAA
STITCH.
SO...
...YOU'RE NOT A KOALA EITHER.

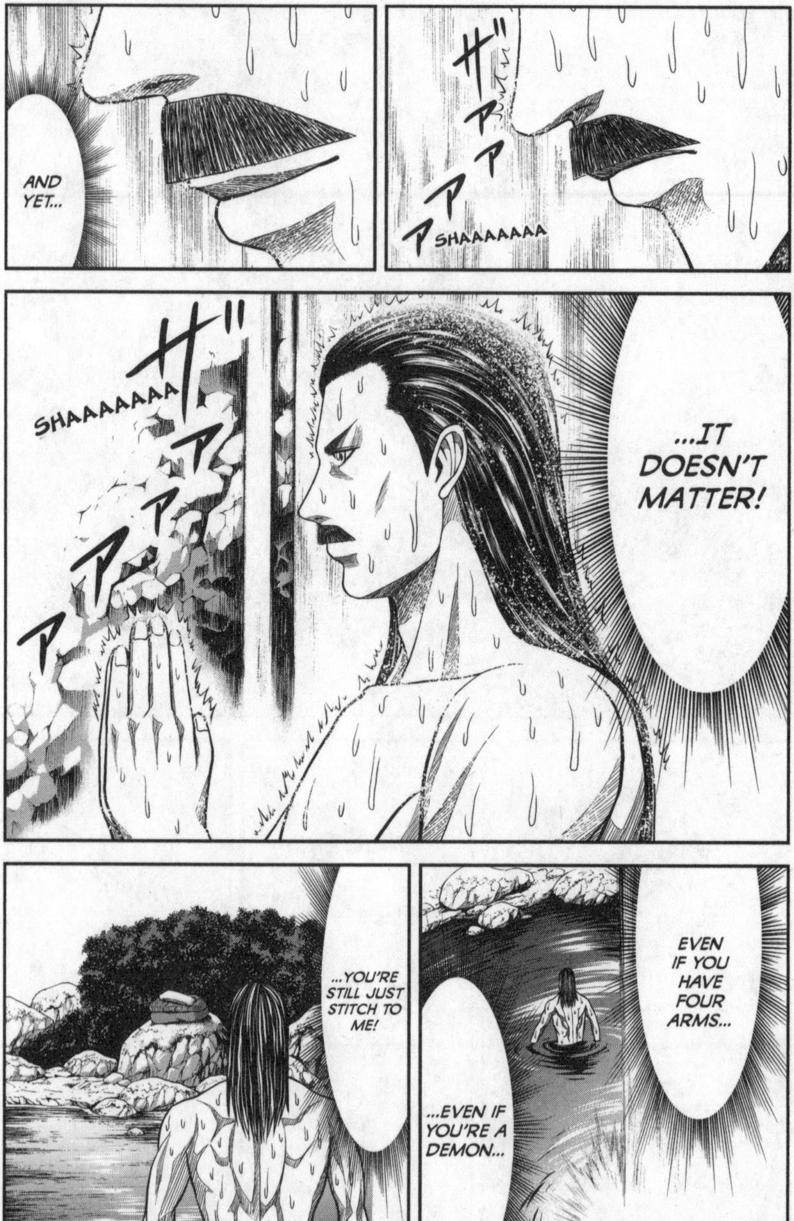

ザァァァァ
SHAAAAAAA
AND YET...
...IT DOESN'T MATTER!
ザァァァァ
SHAAAAAAA
EVEN IF YOU HAVE FOUR ARMS...
...EVEN IF YOU'RE A DEMON...
...YOU'RE STILL JUST STITCH TO ME!

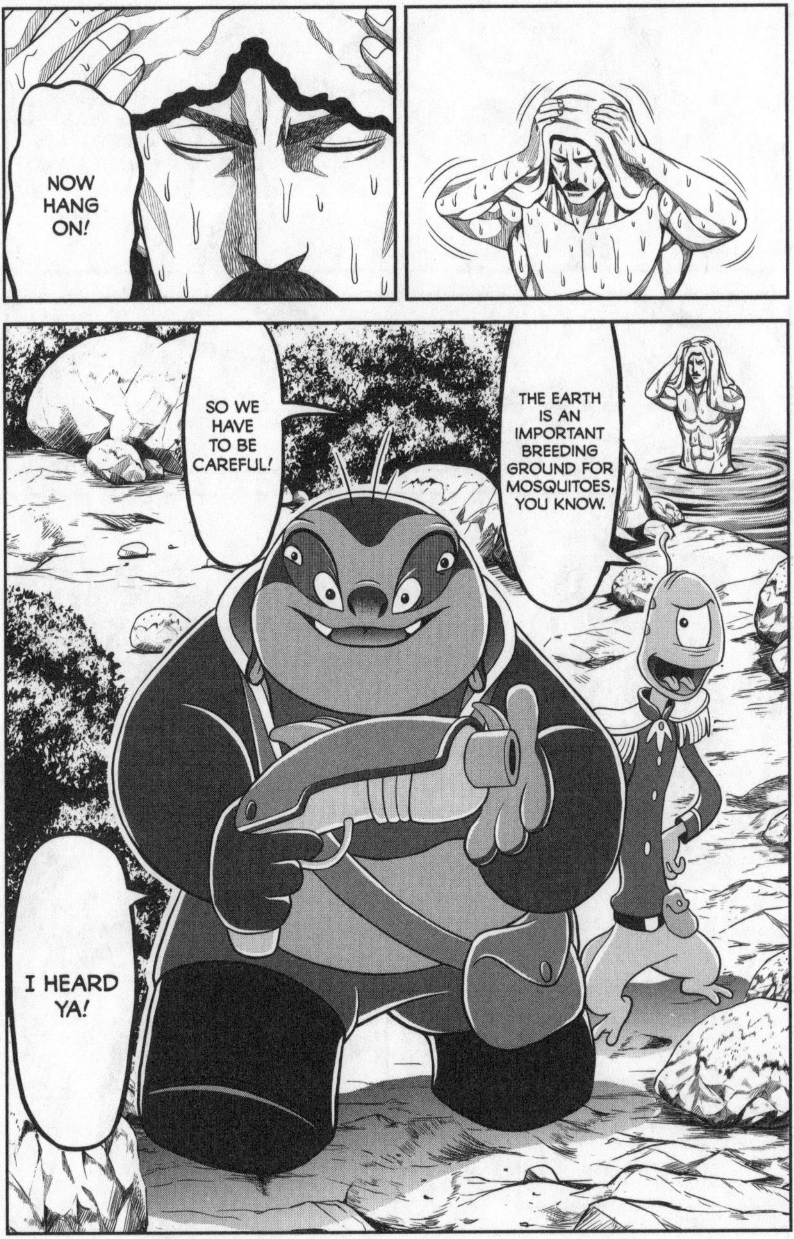
NOW HANG ON!
THE EARTH IS AN IMPORTANT BREEDING GROUND FOR MOSQUITOES, YOU KNOW.
SO WE HAVE TO BE CAREFUL!
I HEARD YA!

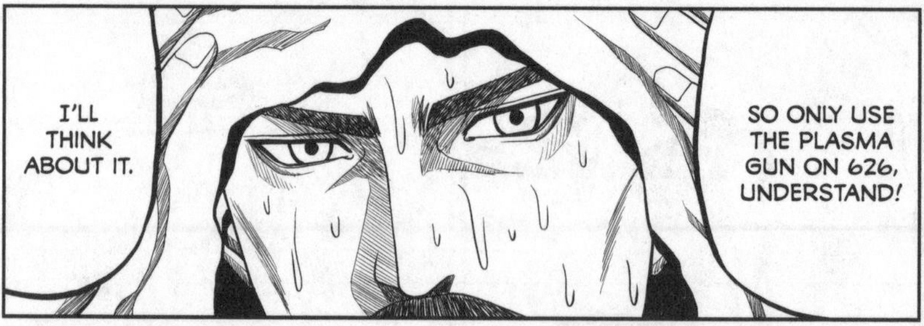
SO ONLY USE THE PLASMA GUN ON 626, UNDERSTAND!
I'LL THINK ABOUT IT.

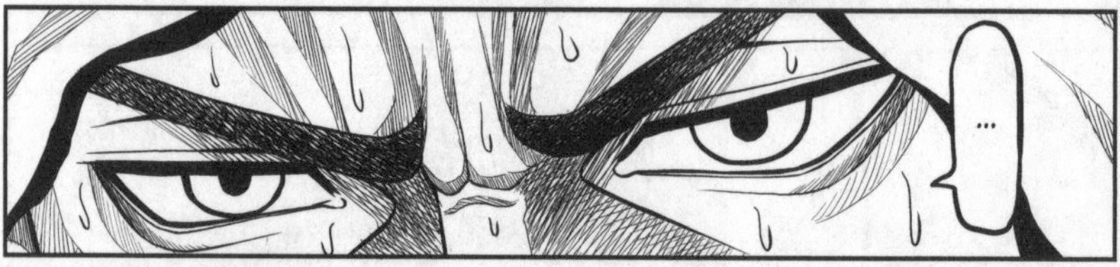
...

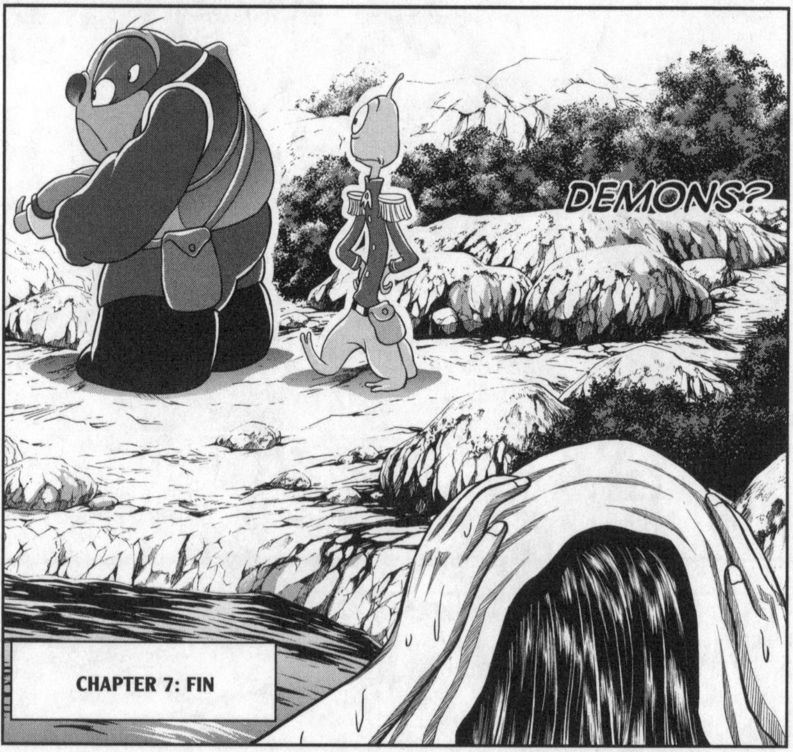
DEMONS?
CHAPTER 7: FIN

AFTERWORD

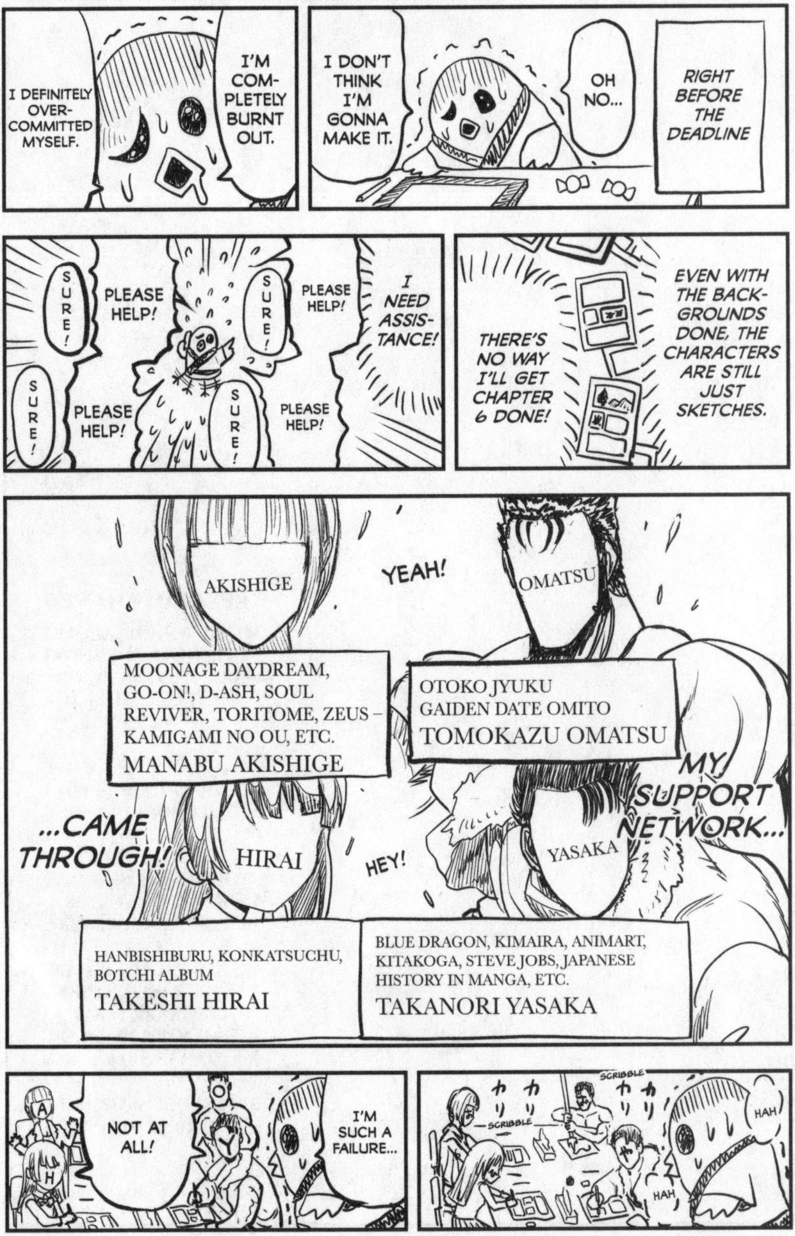
RIGHT BEFORE THE DEADLINE
OH NO...
I DON'T THINK I'M GONNA MAKE IT.
I'M COM-PLETELY BURNT OUT.
I DEFINITELY OVER-COMMITTED MYSELF.
EVEN WITH THE BACK-GROUNDS DONE, THE CHARACTERS ARE STILL JUST SKETCHES.
THERE'S NO WAY I'LL GET CHAPTER 6 DONE!
I NEED ASSIS-TANCE!
PLEASE HELP!
SURE!
PLEASE HELP!
SURE!
PLEASE HELP!
SURE!
PLEASE HELP!
SURE!
MY SUPPORT NETWORK...
OMATSU
YEAH!
AKISHIGE
OTOKO JYUKU GAIDEN DATE OMITO
TOMOKAZU OMATSU
MOONAGE DAYDREAM, GO-ON!, D-ASH, SOUL REVIVER, TORITOME, ZEUS – KAMIGAMI NO OU, ETC.
MANABU AKISHIGE
YASAKA
HEY!
HIRAI
...CAME THROUGH!
BLUE DRAGON, KIMAIRA, ANIMART, KITAKOGA, STEVE JOBS, JAPANESE HISTORY IN MANGA, ETC.
TAKANORI YASAKA
HANBISHIBURU, KONKATSUCHU, BOTCHI ALBUM
TAKESHI HIRAI
HAH
SCRIBBLE
SCRIBBLE
HAH
I'M SUCH A FAILURE...
NOT AT ALL!

SPECIAL THANKS

NOBORU ROKUDA, HIDEKI
MIYASHITA, TAKANORI
YASAKA, DAIJU YANAUCHI,
RYUUKI SATO, AIMI,
PAZUNAMI, PO

STAFF
SOUSHI ISHIKAWA, YUKI
TAKO, NORIHISA OIDE

HELP STAFF
TOKUYOSHI ISHIZAWA,
T.T, KATSUYA MORIOKA,
TAKURO KAMIMURA

SPECIAL HELP STAFF
TAKESHI HIRAI,
TOMOKAZU OMATSU,
MANABU AKISHIGE,
TAKANORI YASAKA

REFERENCE MATERIALS
HIDEKI MIYASHITA

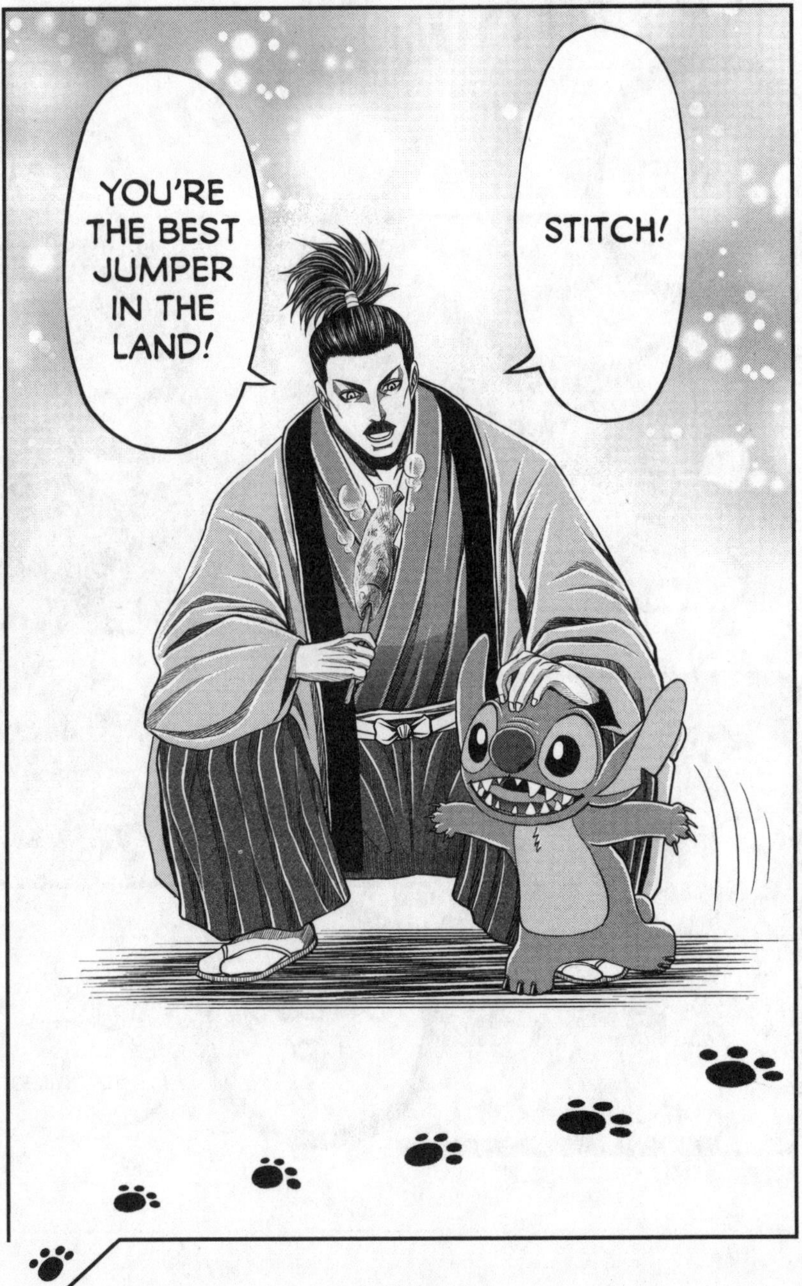
STITCH!
YOU'RE THE BEST JUMPER IN THE LAND!

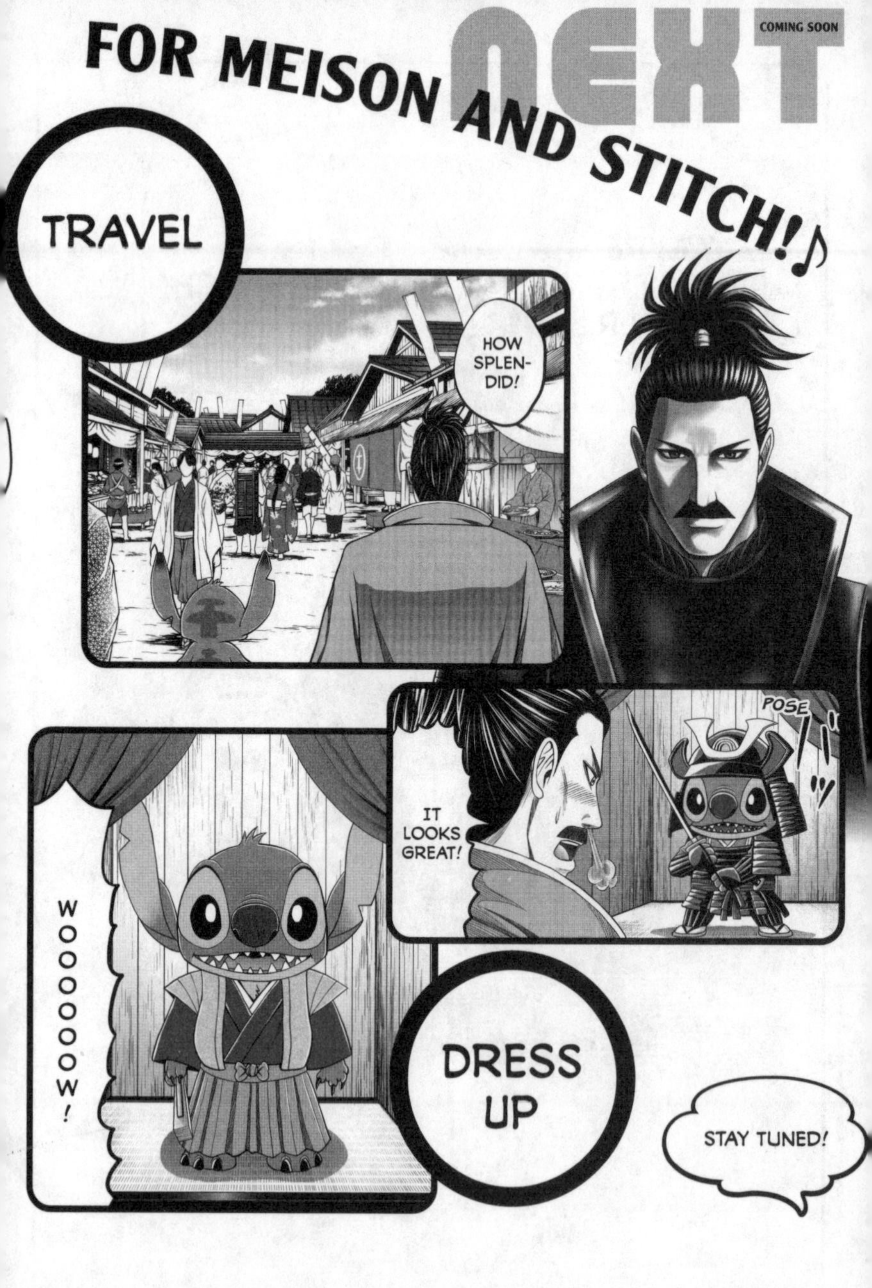
COMING SOON
NEXT
FOR MEISON AND STITCH!♪
TRAVEL
HOW SPLEN-DID!
POSE
IT LOOKS GREAT!
WOOOOOOOW!
DRESS UP
STAY TUNED!

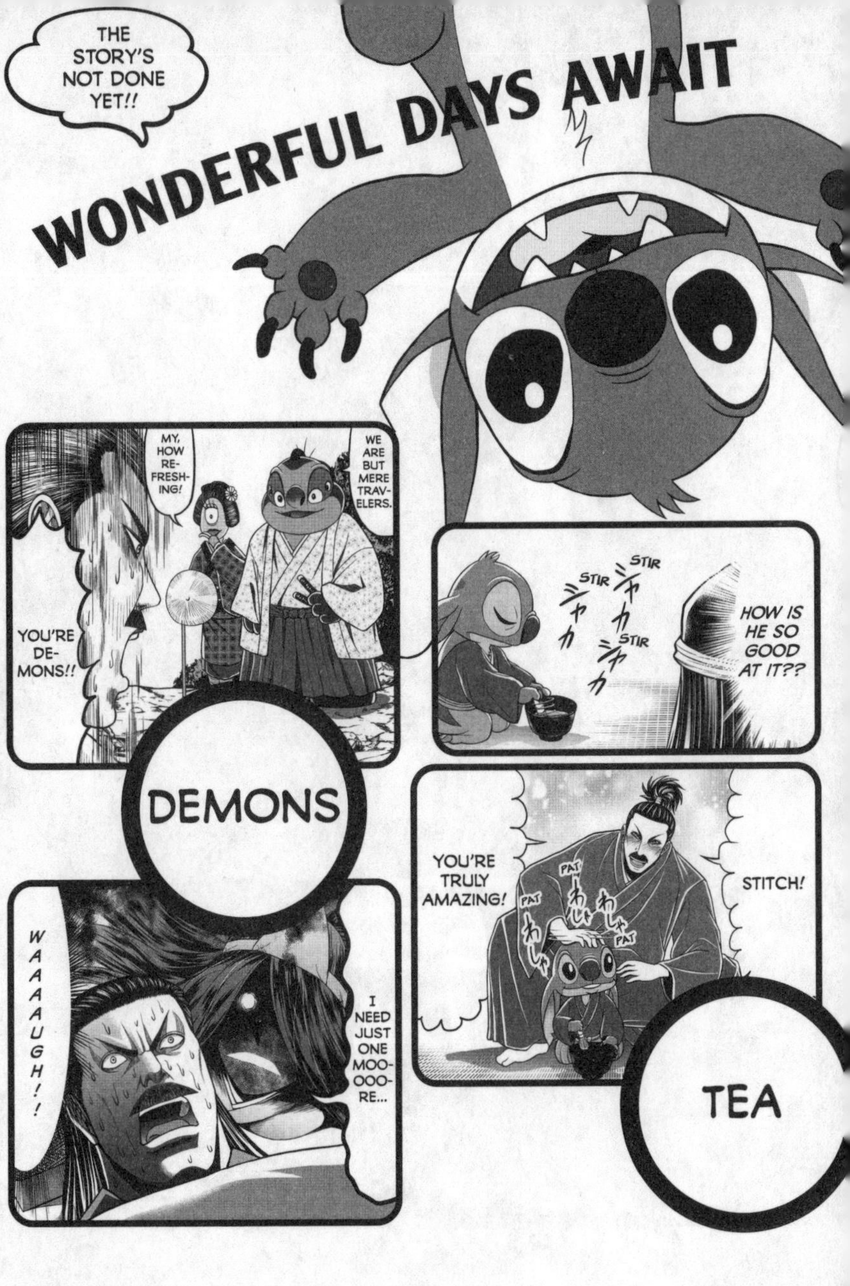
WONDERFUL DAYS AWAIT
THE STORY'S NOT DONE YET!!
STIR STIR STIR
HOW IS HE SO GOOD AT IT??
STITCH!
YOU'RE TRULY AMAZING!
PAT PAT PAT
TEA
WE ARE BUT MERE TRAV-ELERS.
MY, HOW RE-FRESH-ING!
YOU'RE DE-MONS!!
DEMONS
I NEED JUST ONE MOO-OOO-RE...
WAAAAAUGH!!

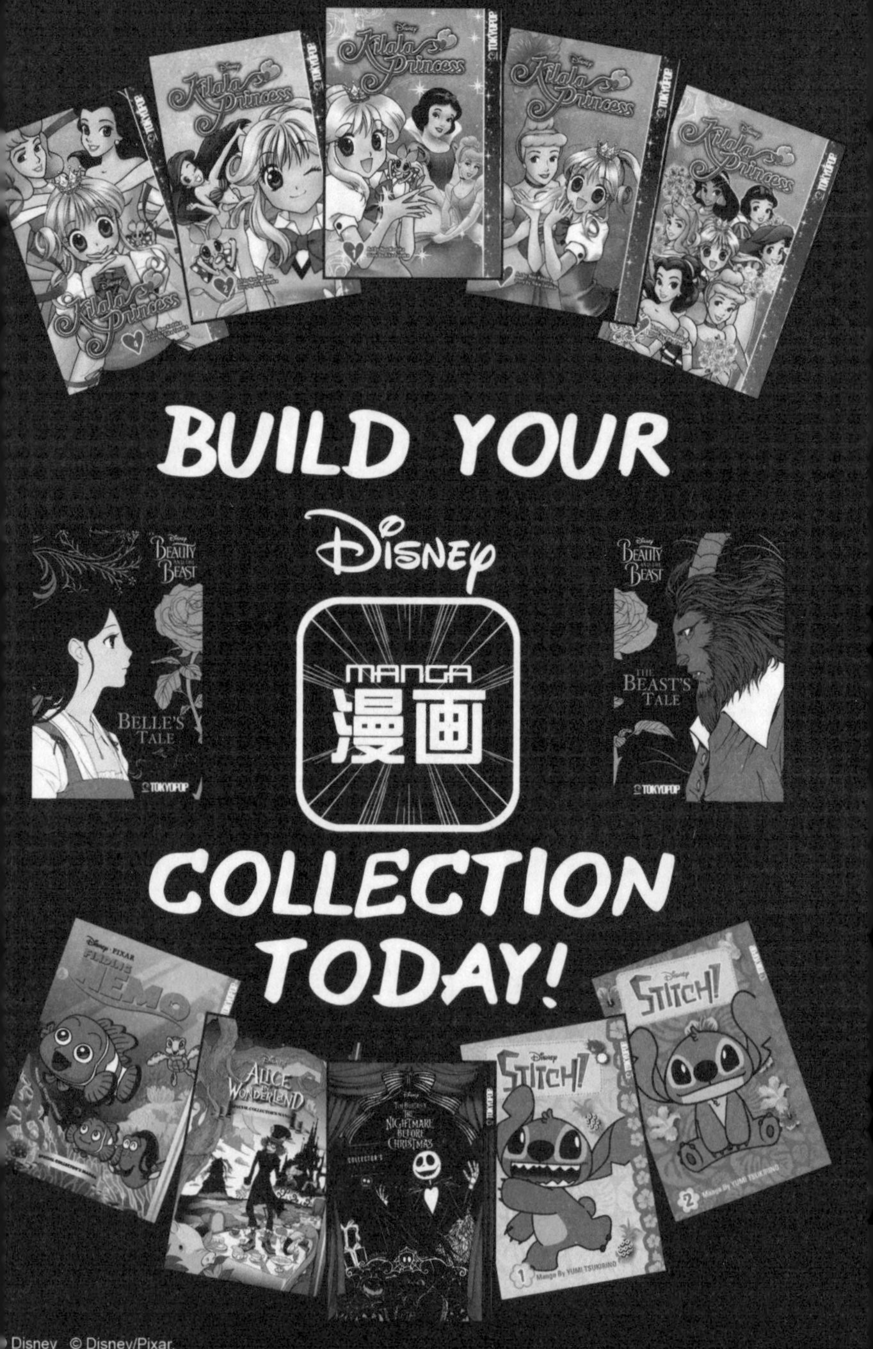
BUILD YOUR
Disney
MANGA
漫画
COLLECTION TODAY!

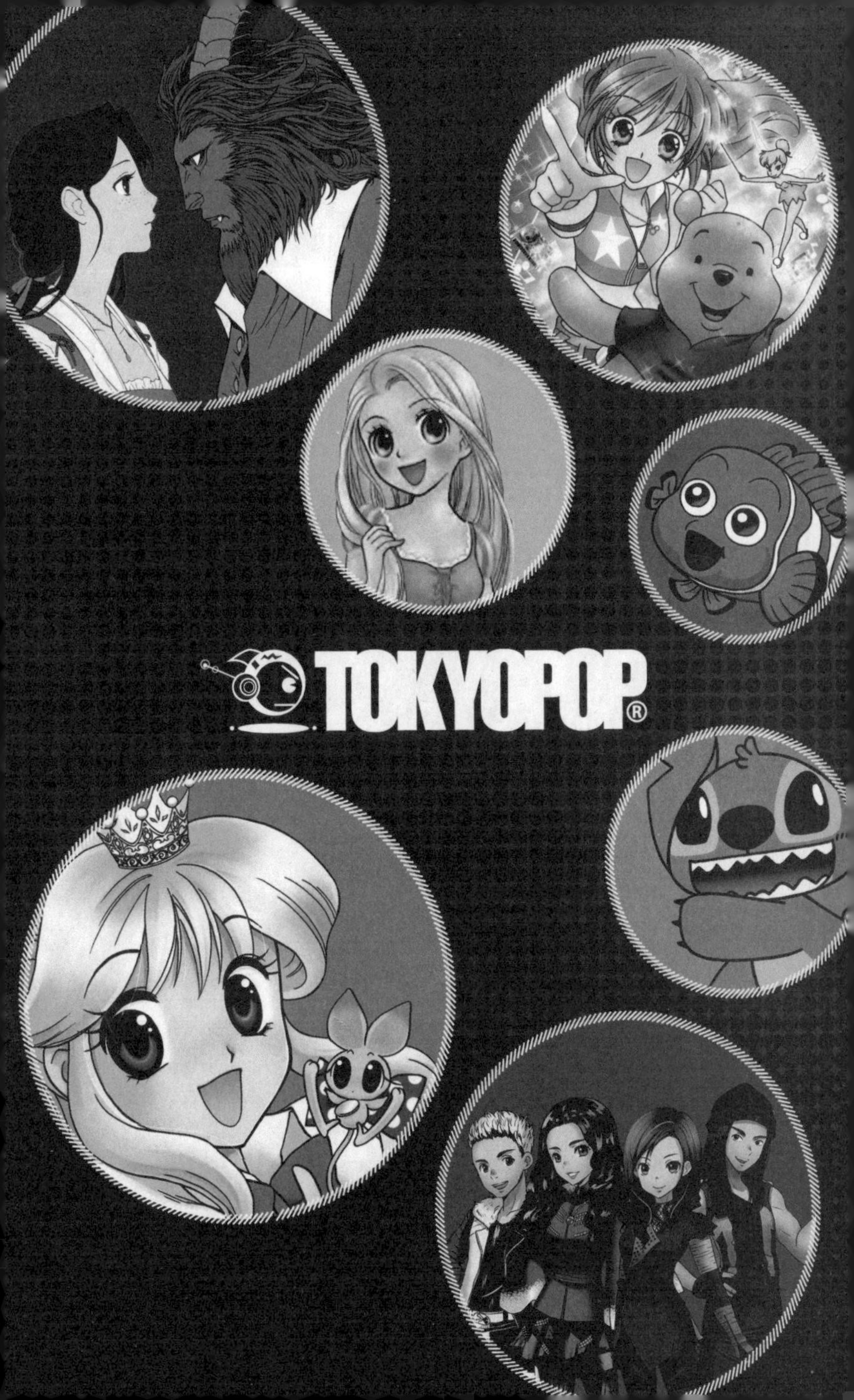
TOKYOPOP®

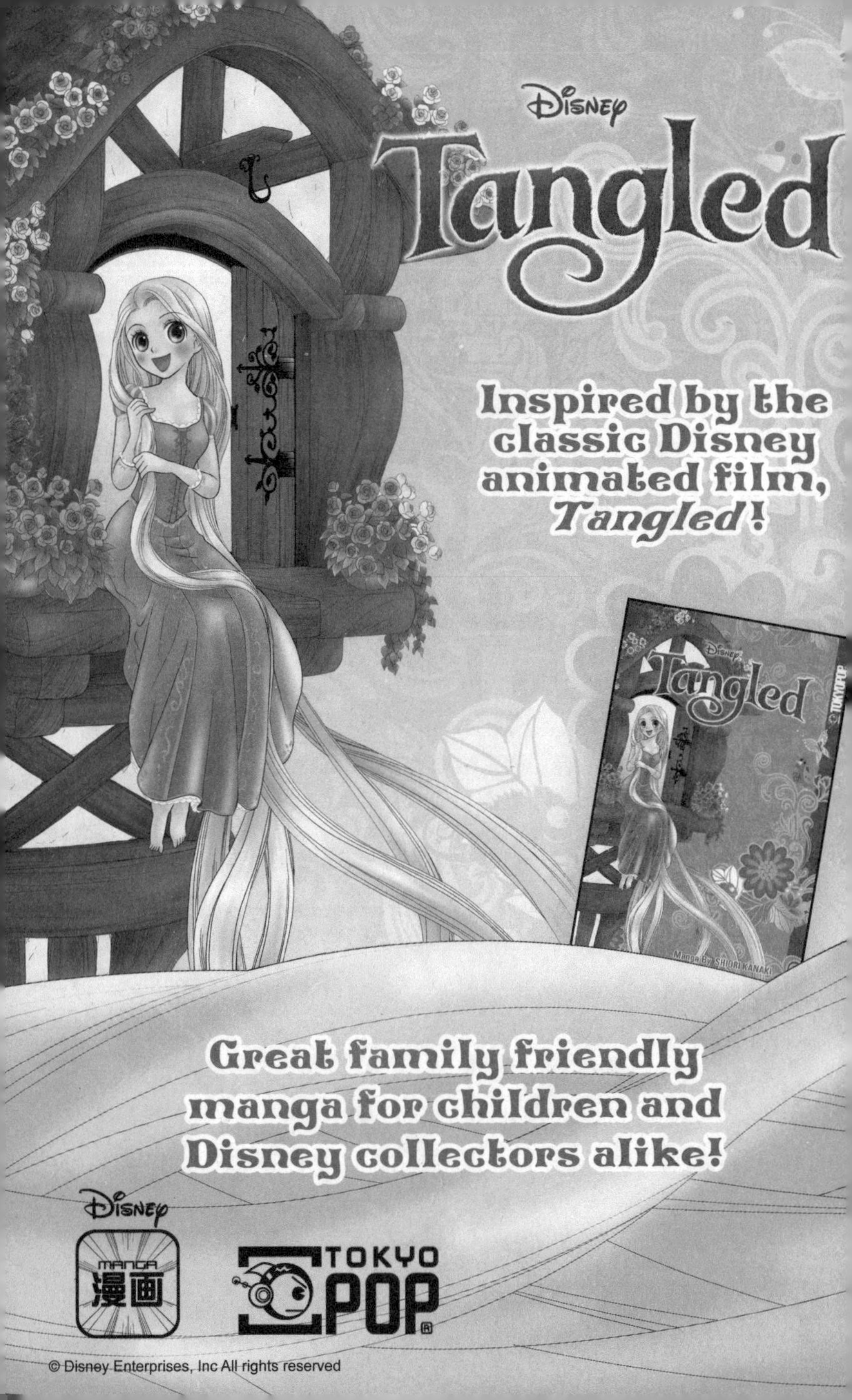
Disney
Tangled
Inspired by the classic Disney animated film, Tangled!
Disney
Tangled
TOKYOPOP
Manga By SHIORI KANAKI
Great family friendly manga for children and Disney collectors alike!
Disney
MANGA
漫画
TOKYO POP
© Disney Enterprises, Inc All rights reserved

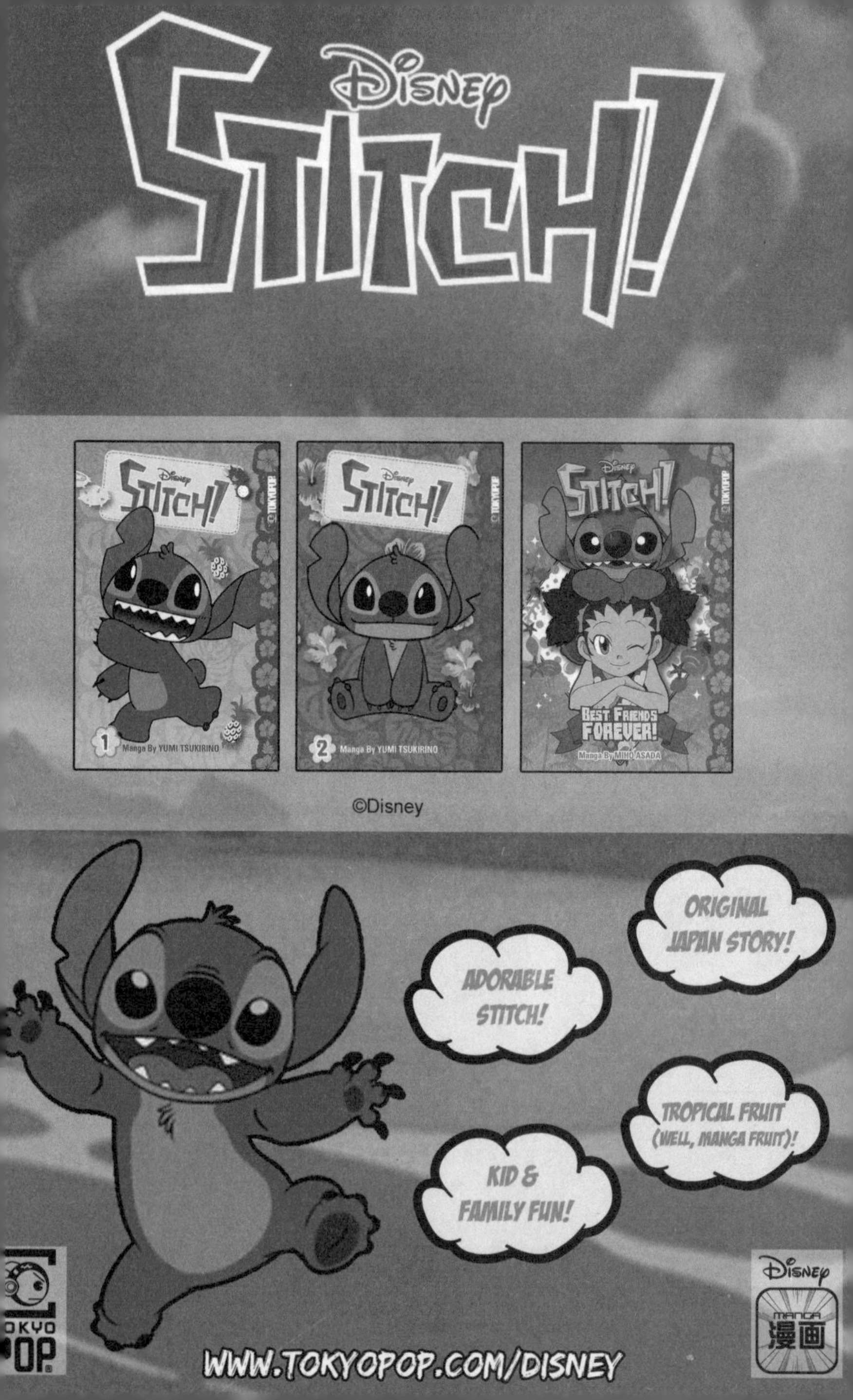
Disney
STITCH!
Disney STITCH!
1 Manga By YUMI TSUKIRINO
Disney STITCH!
2 Manga By YUMI TSUKIRINO
Disney STITCH!
BEST FRIENDS FOREVER!
Manga By MIHO ASADA
©Disney
ORIGINAL JAPAN STORY!
ADORABLE STITCH!
TROPICAL FRUIT (WELL, MANGA FRUIT)!
KID & FAMILY FUN!
TOKYOPOP
Disney MANGA 漫画
WWW.TOKYOPOP.COM/DISNEY

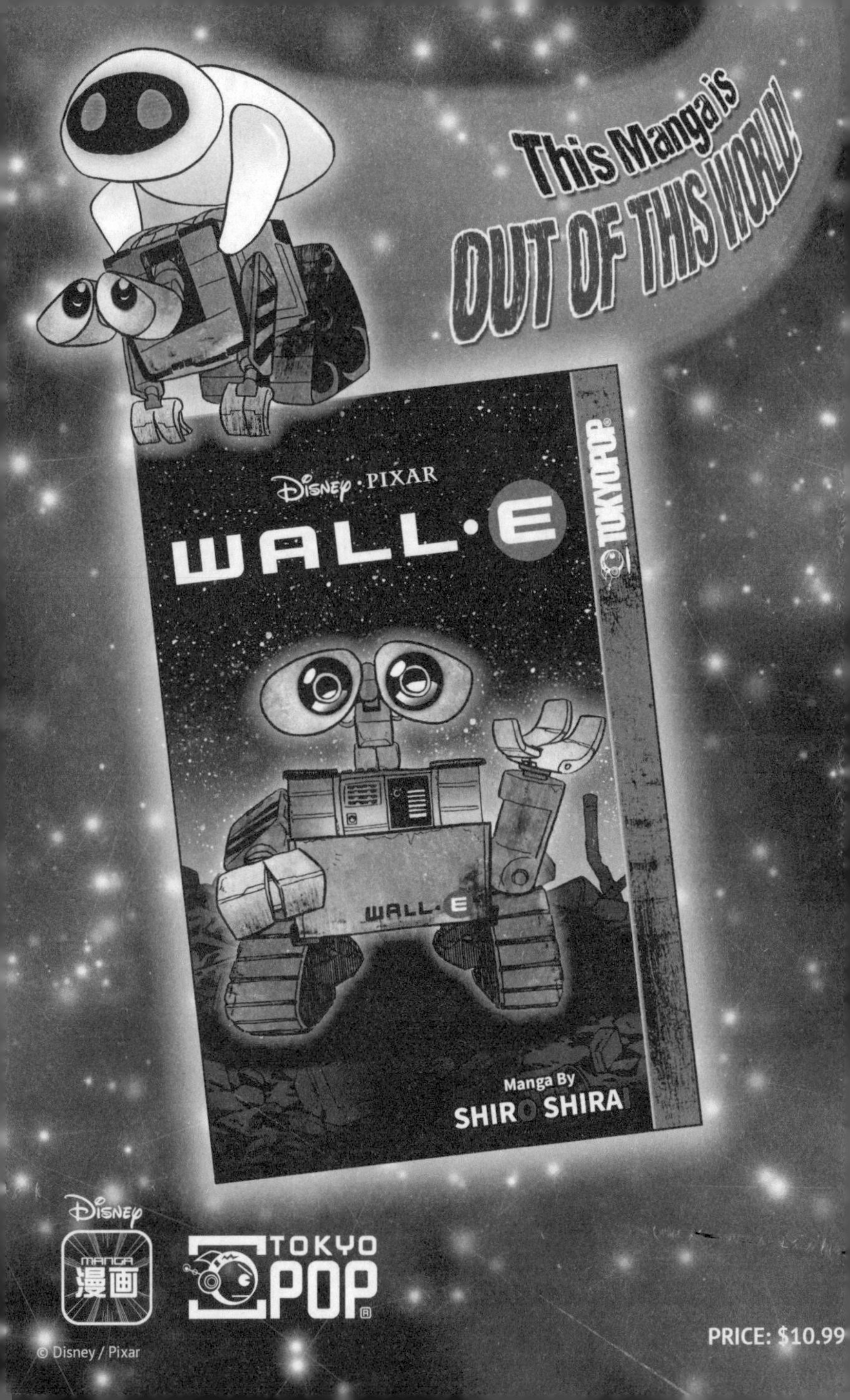
This Manga is
OUT OF THIS WORLD!
DISNEY · PIXAR
WALL·E
TOKYOPOP
Manga By
SHIRO SHIRAI
DISNEY
MANGA
漫画
TOKYO POP
PRICE: $10.99
© Disney / Pixar

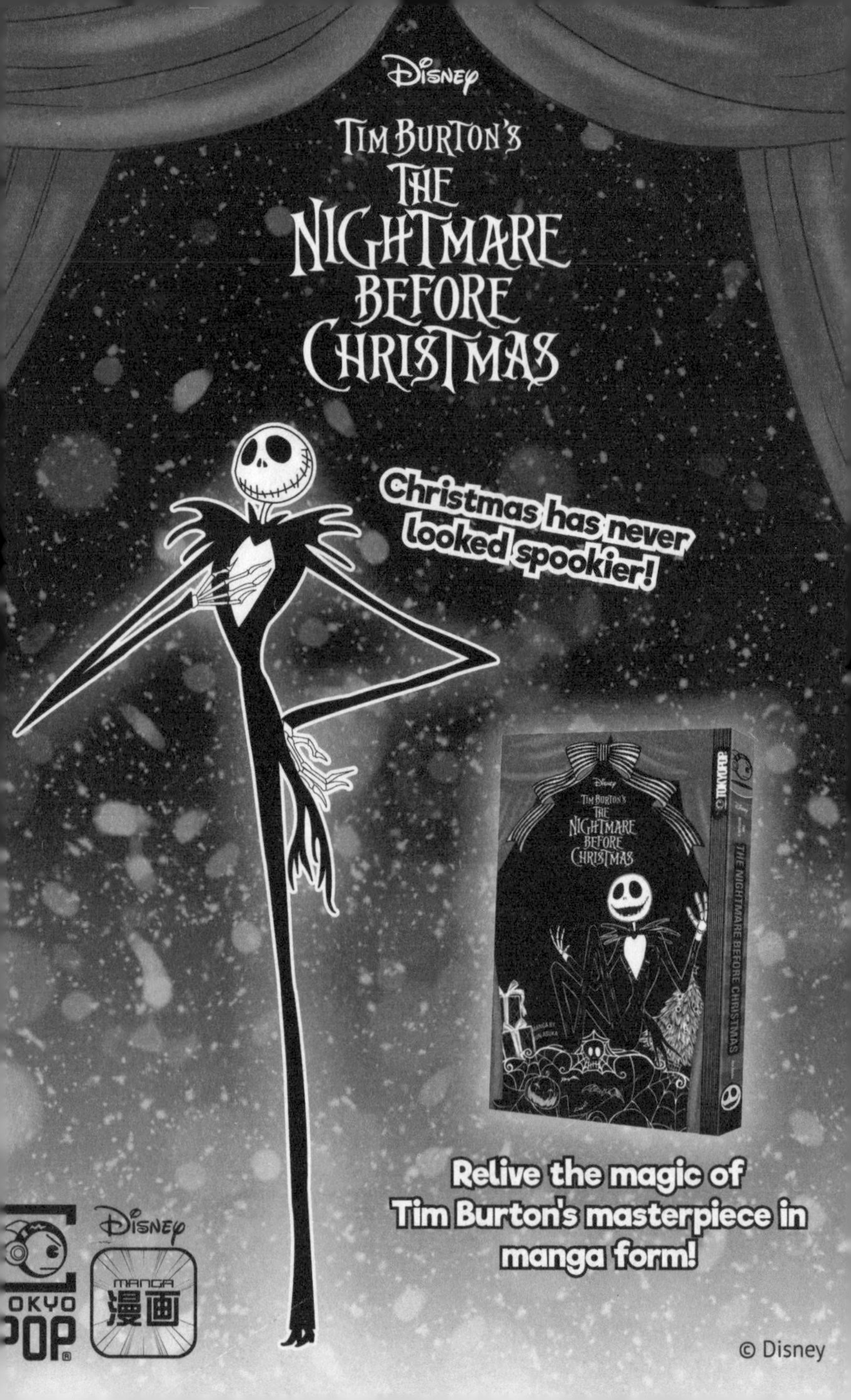
Disney
Tim Burton's
The Nightmare Before Christmas
Christmas has never looked spookier!
Relive the magic of
Tim Burton's masterpiece in
manga form!
Disney
MANGA
漫画
© Disney

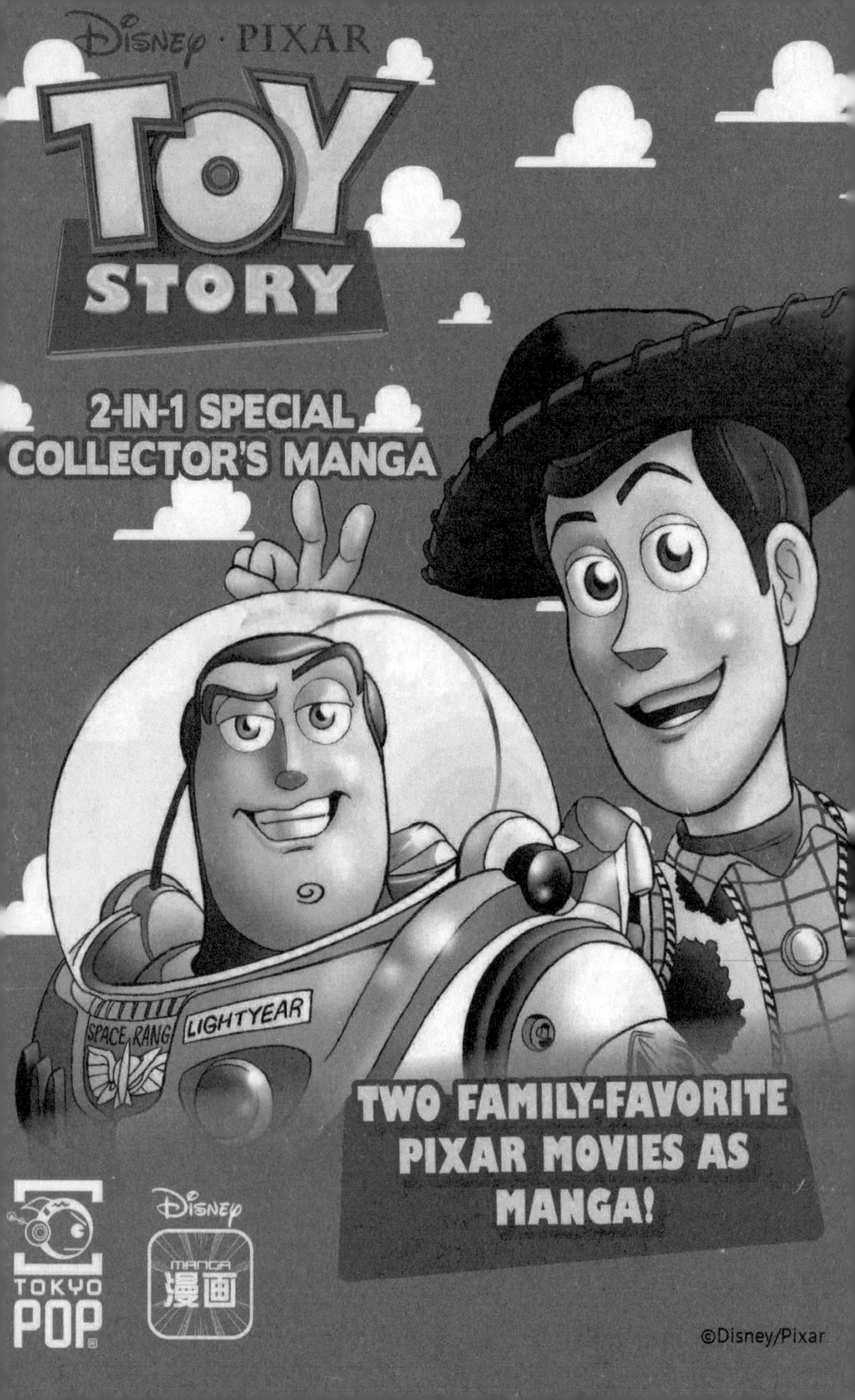
Disney · PIXAR
TOY STORY
2-IN-1 SPECIAL COLLECTOR'S MANGA
SPACE RANG
LIGHTYEAR
TWO FAMILY-FAVORITE PIXAR MOVIES AS MANGA!
TOKYO POP
Disney MANGA 漫画
©Disney/Pixar

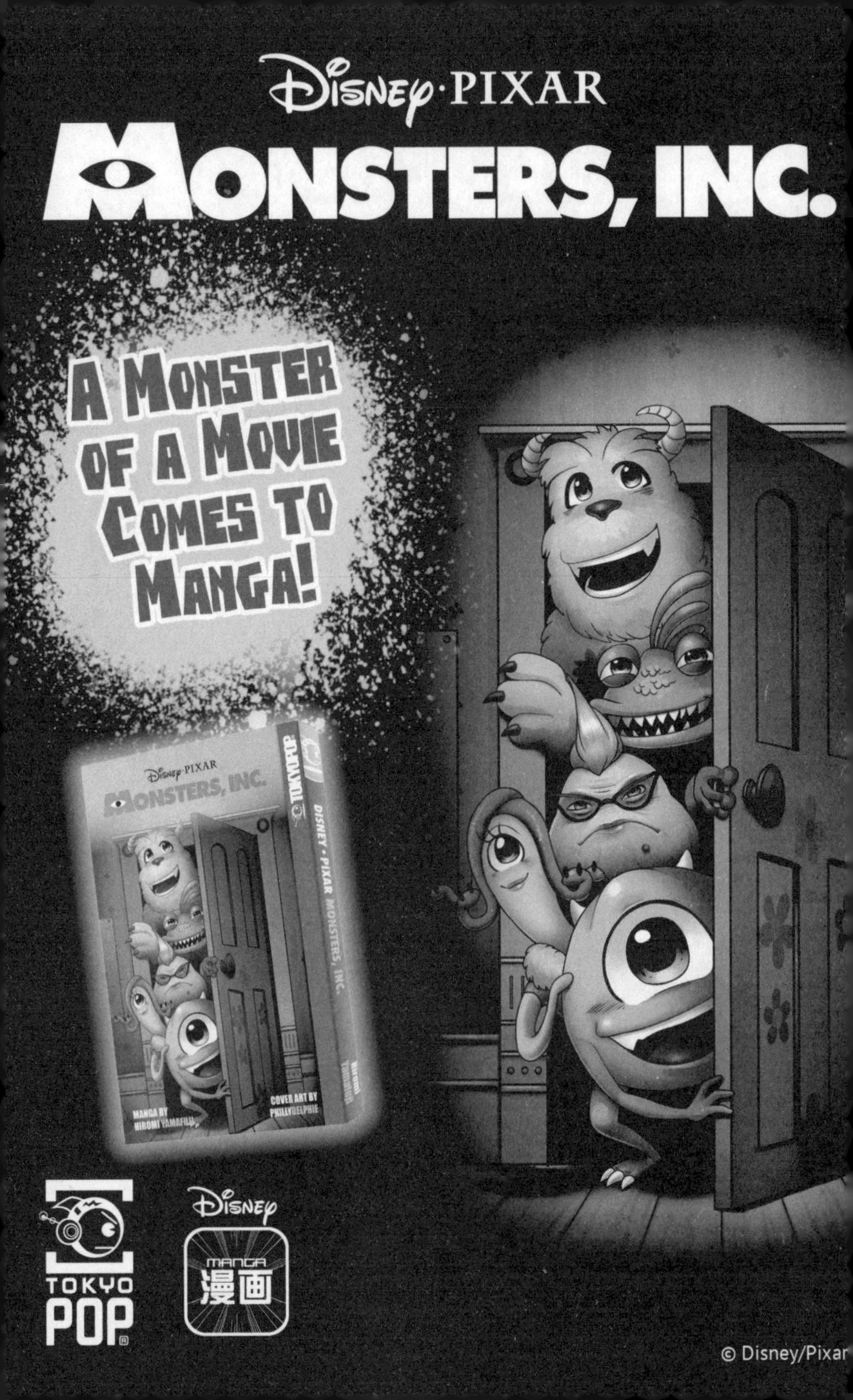
Disney·PIXAR
MONSTERS, INC.
A MONSTER OF A MOVIE COMES TO MANGA!
Disney·PIXAR
MONSTERS, INC.
TOKYOPOP
DISNEY · PIXAR MONSTERS, INC.
MANGA BY HIROMI YAMAFUJI
COVER ART BY PHILLYDELPHIE
TOKYO POP
Disney
MANGA
漫画
© Disney/Pixar

GRIMMS manga Tales

The Grimm's Tales reimagined in manga!

Beautiful art by the talented Kei Ishiyama!

Stories from Little Red Riding Hood to Hansel and Gretel!

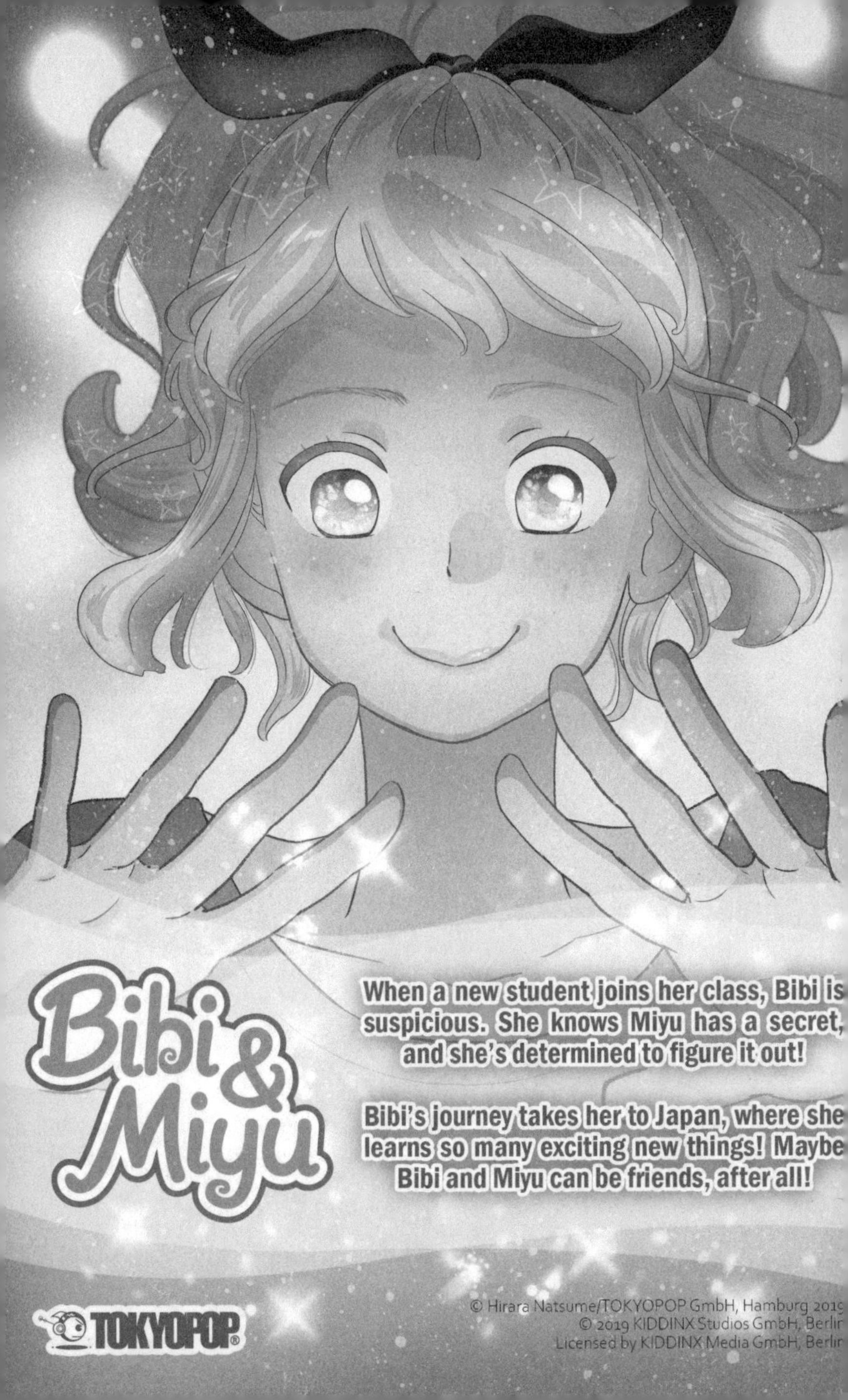
Bibi & Miyu
When a new student joins her class, Bibi is suspicious. She knows Miyu has a secret, and she's determined to figure it out!
Bibi's journey takes her to Japan, where she learns so many exciting new things! Maybe Bibi and Miyu can be friends, after all!
TOKYOPOP®
© Hirara Natsume/TOKYOPOP GmbH, Hamburg 2019
© 2019 KIDDINX Studios GmbH, Berlin
Licensed by KIDDINX Media GmbH, Berlin

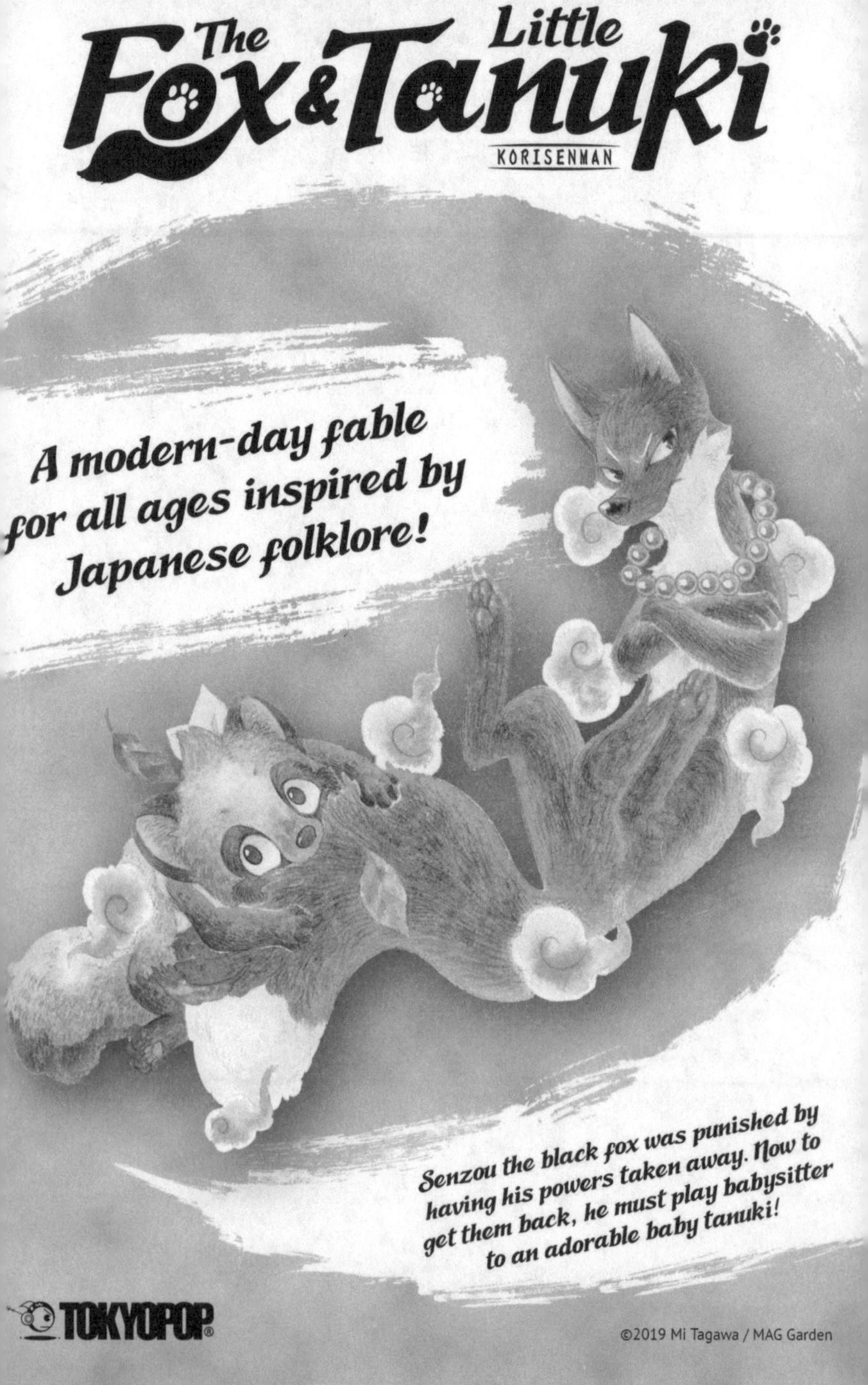
The Little Fox & Tanuki
KORISENMAN
A modern-day fable for all ages inspired by Japanese folklore!
Senzou the black fox was punished by having his powers taken away. Now to get them back, he must play babysitter to an adorable baby tanuki!
TOKYOPOP®
©2019 Mi Tagawa / MAG Garden

Disney Stitch and the Samurai, Volume 1
Art by Hiroto Wada

Editorial Associate - Janae Young
Marketing Associate - Kae Winters
Translator - Jason Muell
Copy Editor - Sean Doyle
Cover Colors - Sol DeLeo
Cover Designer - Sol DeLeo
Retouching and Lettering - Vibrraant Publishing Studio
Editor-in-Chief & Publisher - Stu Levy

A  Manga

TOKYOPOP and 🐾 are trademarks or registered trademarks of TOKYOPOP Inc.

TOKYOPOP Inc.
5200 W. Century Blvd. Suite 705
Los Angeles, 90045

E-mail: info@TOKYOPOP.com
Come visit us online at www.TOKYOPOP.com

f www.facebook.com/TOKYOPOP
🐦 www.twitter.com/TOKYOPOP
📌 www.pinterest.com/TOKYOPOP
📷 www.instagram.com/TOKYOPOP

ISBN: 978-1-4278-6739-1

First TOKYOPOP Printing: February 2021
10 9 8 7 6 5 4 3 2 1
Printed in CANADA

STOP

THIS IS THE BACK OF THE BOOK!

How do you read manga-style? It's simple! To learn,
just start in the top right panel and follow the numbers:

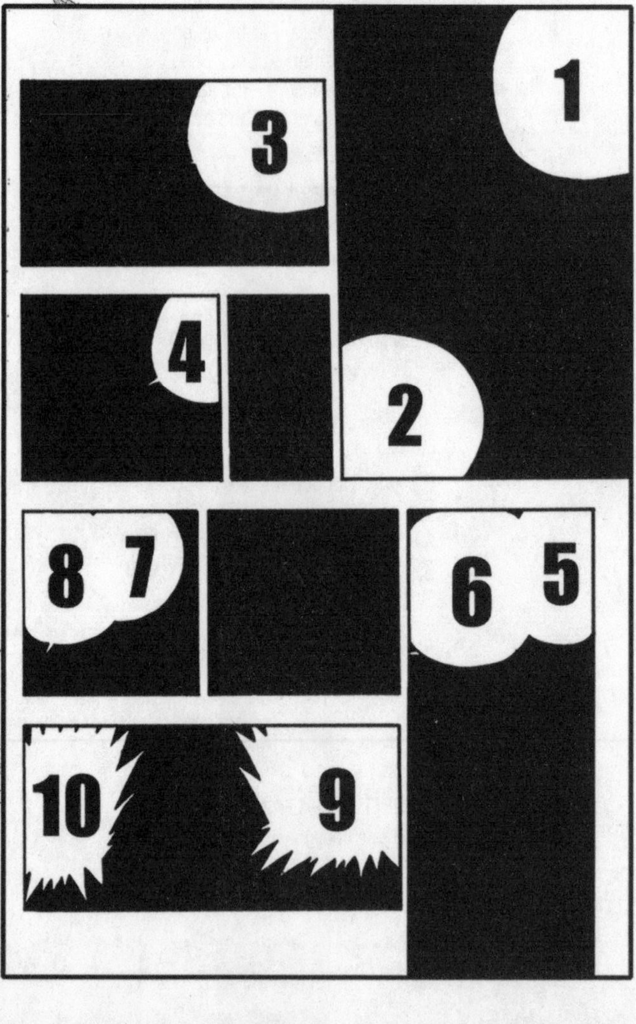
1
2
3
4
5
6
7
8
9
10

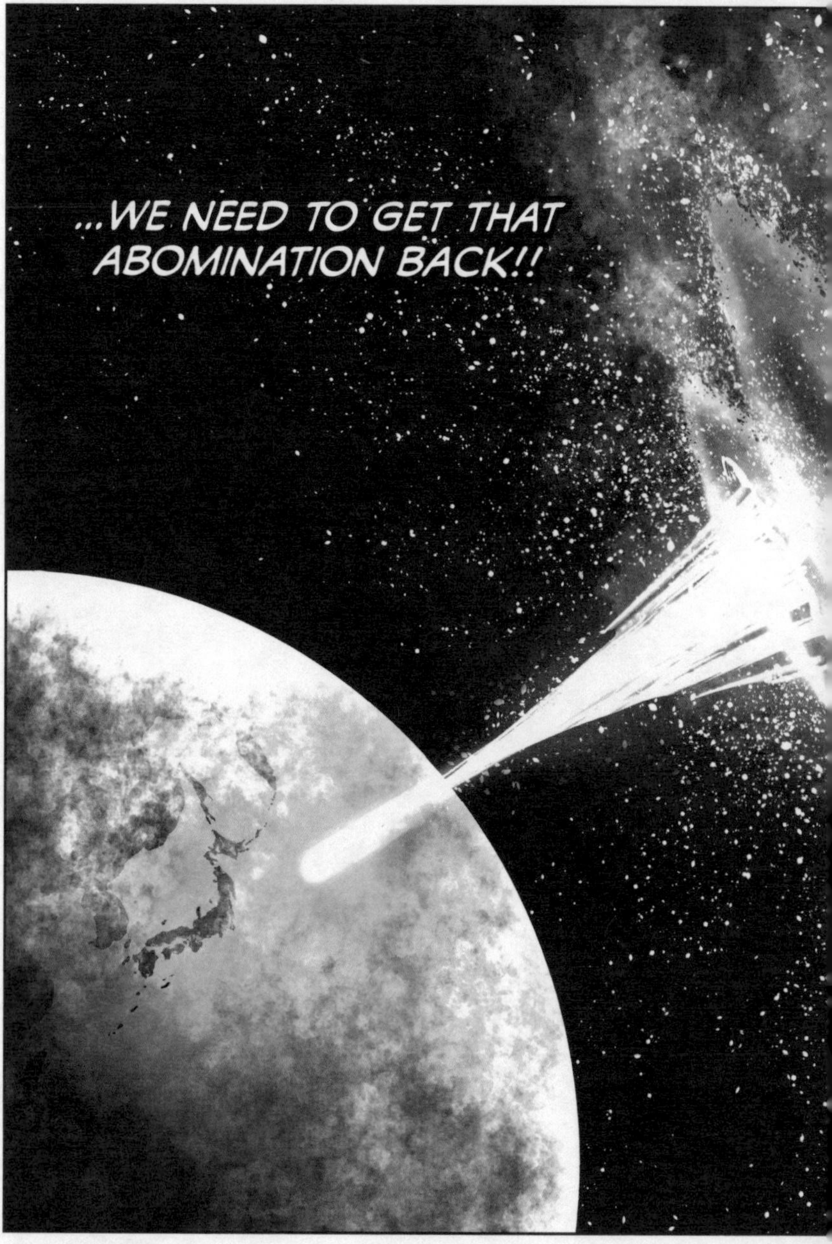
...WE NEED TO GET THAT ABOMINATION BACK!!

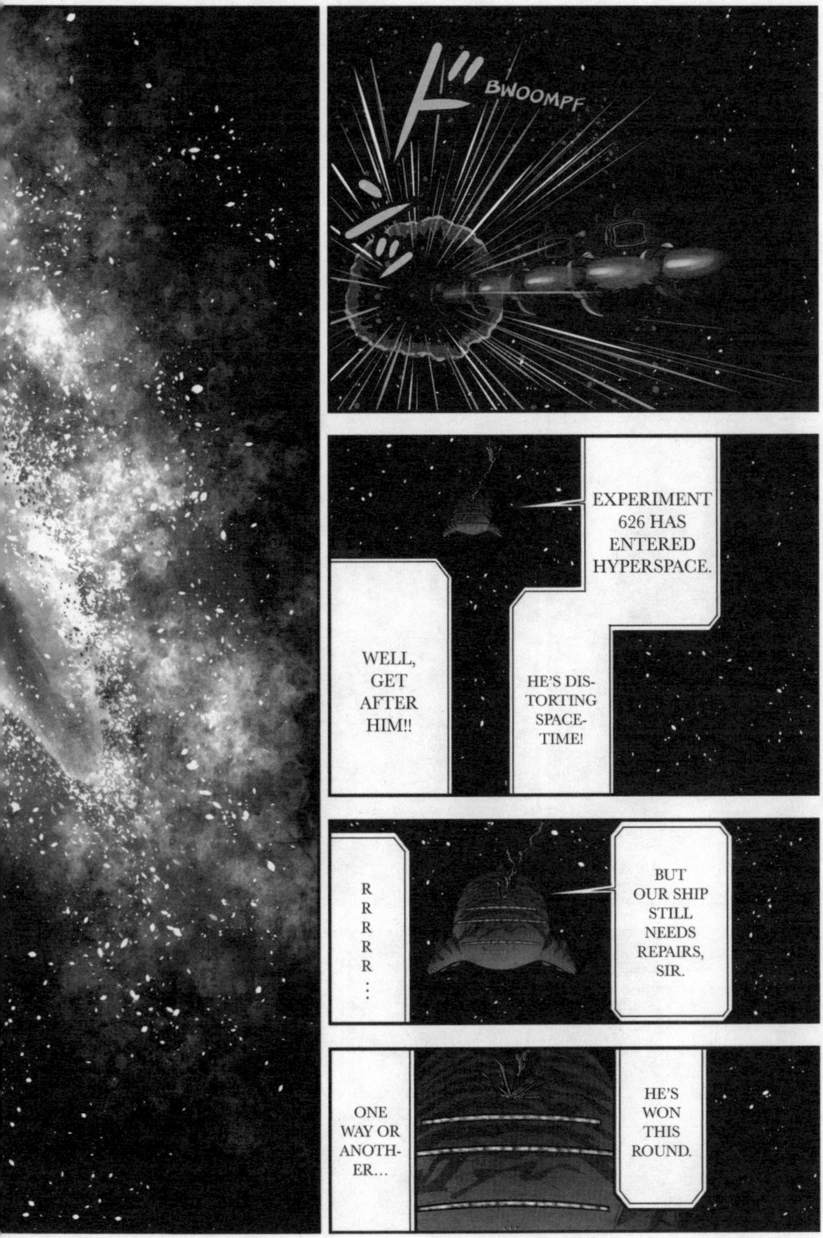
BWOOMPF
EXPERIMENT 626 HAS ENTERED HYPERSPACE.
HE'S DIS-TORTING SPACE-TIME!
WELL, GET AFTER HIM!!
BUT OUR SHIP STILL NEEDS REPAIRS, SIR.
RRRRR…
HE'S WON THIS ROUND.
ONE WAY OR ANOTH-ER…

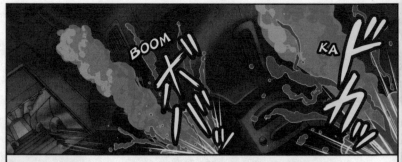

KA
BOOM
PUT SECTORS FOUR AND FIVE ON LOCK-DOWN!
EXPERI-MENT 626 IS TRYING TO ESCAPE AGAIN!
CRASH
DON'T LET 'IM GET AWAY!
IF YOU DO...
...THE WHOLE GALAXY WILL BE DOO-MED!
EXPER-IMENT 626 HAS LEFT THE SHIP!!
WHAT?!

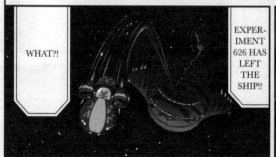